Almost Heaven

SUSAN X MEAGHER

Almost Heaven

© 2012 BY SUSAN X MEAGHER

ISBN (10) 09832758-6-6
ISBN (13) 978-0-9832758-6-2

THIS TRADE PAPERBACK ORIGINAL IS PUBLISHED BY BRISK PRESS, BRIELLE, NJ 08730

EDITED BY: LINDA LORENZO
COVER DESIGN AND LAYOUT BY: CAROLYN NORMAN

FIRST PRINTING: OCTOBER 2012

By Susan X Meagher

Novels

Arbor Vitae
All That Matters
Cherry Grove
Girl Meets Girl
The Lies That Bind
The Legacy
Doublecrossed
Smooth Sailing
How To Wrangle a Woman
Almost Heaven

Serial Novel
I Found My Heart In San Francisco

Awakenings: Book One
Beginnings: Book Two
Coalescence: Book Three
Disclosures: Book Four
Entwined: Book Five
Fidelity: Book Six
Getaway: Book Seven
Honesty: Book Eight
Intentions: Book Nine
Journeys: Book Ten
Karma: Book Eleven
Lifeline: Book Twelve
Monogamy: Book Thirteen

Anthologies

Undercover Tales
Outsiders

Dedication

To Carrie, my lawfully wedded wife.

CHAPTER ONE

IF SHE COULD'VE SUBTRACTED from her life all of the time she'd spent loitering around the Twined Creek Medical Clinic, Cody Keaton would've been a good year younger.

She'd never actually been inside any of the doctors' offices herself, but someone or other always needed to go. Given that she had one of the most reliable cars in her extended family, along with the fact that she had a hard time refusing a request, Cody found herself making the twenty-mile drive often enough to have the bumps in the road memorized.

It was a bitterly cold day, but she couldn't stand to be inside, especially today. The big waiting room was always jammed with people, but it was particularly crowded on Christmas eve. Strings of red and green garland hung from the acoustic tile ceiling, and an anemic plastic tree sat cockeyed on a wobbly table. Christmas was depressing enough for a lot of folks. Why did places have to remind everyone how nothing they had could compare to the stuff they saw on TV? Instead of the joy-filled folks finding a new luxury car in the driveway, this crowd sat on half-busted plastic chairs, trying not to catch the flu.

Despite the cold, Cody was warm enough. Her best winter coat was a hunter's orange model she'd won in a bet with Curly Reynolds, the biggest, and possibly meanest, and definitely stingiest guy in town. But it was both too garish and too large to wear when she wasn't actually hunting. Luckily, her cousin Devin had dumped all of his army gear on her steps when he came back from the war. Devin's digital desert field jacket was big too, but not so bad that people stared. One thing she had to say for the Army, they did a pretty good job of providing gear that would keep a soldier warm. Of course, staying warm in the Persian Gulf was pretty easy to do. Devin said the uniforms weren't nearly as good at keeping you cool.

Today's clinic passengers were another cousin's former girlfriend and their little boy. Amy was a nice girl, and seemed to be trying her best, but she didn't have the sense to come in out of the rain. She was only around nineteen, too old for high school, and too young for motherhood in Cody's estimation. But sixteen or seventeen was the prime age to get your life started on the road to nowhere, or so it seemed.

Amy was both shy and sluggish, and Cody knew she'd finish her appointment and bide her time in the waiting room for as long as she was left there. As expected, when Cody poked her head in, Amy and Adam were sitting there, mesmerized by the soundless TV hung in the corner of the room. Cody stood there for a moment, watching the pair. She knew she was the oddball, but she'd never understood the fascination people seemed to have for any show playing on any television at any time. At three, Adam couldn't have understood the context of a bunch of people sitting in a semi-circle arguing—silently. But he seemed as interested as his mother.

Cody entered fully and walked over to the pair. "Are you ready?"

"Not just yet. We got this…" Amy reached into her pocket and pulled out a slip of paper. "They said he needs it."

Cody took the paper and only realized, when she had it between her fingers, that she was holding two items. A rumpled slip was folded behind the fresh one. One prescription was for Adam, one for Amy's father. Kids got their prescriptions for free, but adults had a co-pay—even when they were on Medicaid. Amy's pale eyes didn't rise to meet Cody's. The girl was dirt poor, but at least she had some pride.

"I'll go get them filled. You can wait here."

Cody headed over to the adjacent pharmacy, wondering if Adam's trip to the doctor wasn't just a scheme Amy's father had cooked up to get someone else to pay for his prescription. She took a quick look. Blood pressure pills. No one liked taking them, so there was no chance she was being played. If it'd been for Viagra, she would've wadded the prescription up and tossed it in the trash, but you had to help a man out if he genuinely needed something and you could manage it.

She entered the tiny room that smelled like antiseptic and tuna sandwiches, handed over the prescriptions and waited—tensely. The young woman at the register took her sweet time, finally chewing on the end of her pen and mumbling, "Five dollars for this one." Luckily, after paying for gas, Cody still had seven dollars. Two dollars wouldn't take her far, but she had a tankful of gas and food in the freezer. She'd be fine.

"All right." Cody removed her wallet and carefully took out the bill and placed it on the counter. Then she headed for the door, always choosing to be outside when she had the option. Just as she crossed the threshold, a flash of green caught her eye and she stooped to pick it up. A dollar bill. Her heart thumped in her chest for a couple of beats. She never in her whole life had found an entire dollar. A dime here or there, maybe a quarter, but never a whole dollar. It was a tiny bit of money to get excited about, almost embarrassingly so, but she was thrilled to find it just lying there. Her elation lasted only a second. She hated to do it, but she had to turn around and go back to the girl at the register. "I found this outside," she said, holding up the bill by two corners.

Seeming as unconcerned as a human being could be, the girl shrugged. "So?"

"Somebody might come back for it."

Now the girl put down what ever electronic device had captured her attention and looked quizzically at Cody. "Nobody's coming back for that. It's yours."

"But they might. Maybe it only just happened a second ago."

"Nobody left a second ago. Hasn't been a soul in here for fifteen minutes. And if somebody gets fifteen minutes away from here, they ain't coming back."

"But they might."

The girl stuck her hand out. "Give it to me."

She hadn't counted on that. It wasn't the girl's money and, given her attitude, she probably wouldn't give it to the real owner if he returned. But Cody could hardly ask for it back at this point. It'd be a cold day in hell before she groveled for a dollar. She turned and started to walk away, but stopped when she heard the girl called out, "Hey."

"Yeah?"

She held something out, then put it on the counter. Cody walked back. Lying there was a ticket to the lottery game that West Virginia and a bunch of other states participated in. Cody had never bought a ticket, had never had a spare dollar to throw away on something that wasteful.

"Take it. It's your lucky day."

She was going to walk away. It wasn't her dollar, and that wasn't her ticket. But if she didn't take it, the girl was going to, and it was more Cody's than hers. She would've much rather have had the cash, but she carefully tucked the ticket into her wallet. It was silly, really, but it gave her a tiny jolt of excitement. It was probably a one in a billion chance, but hope was the thing with feathers, and she could let her imagination soar, even if just for a few moments.

Kaboom!

Got it! The dogs went wild. Stripes ran for the deer, while Blue's fear of guns made him take off in the opposite direction. They might not be the worst hunting dogs in the world, but they were close. If Cody didn't get to the deer in the next minute, Stripes would have already gnawed a piece out of it.

She hoofed across the sparsely forested spot, glad her too-large construction boots could get enough traction to let her run in the heavy snow. Panting as she ran, Cody decided that if Stripes did mangle the deer, the missing piece was gonna come out of Curly's half. That lazy miser might have been the only guy she knew who had a truck powerful enough to get traction on the icy, snow-clogged roads, but lending it to her didn't give him the right to demand half of her kill.

There was a chance she could get her own Jeep up and running in the next couple of weeks. But it was December the thirty-first, and the last day of antlerless deer season wasn't going to wait for her finances to improve. Since you could only take two deer in the season, she'd be darned if she'd let one go. Well, half a one. That Curly was a thief, pure and simple.

Luckily, Stripes was most attracted to the deer's tail, sparing the meat and hide. It took all of her strength to get his leash on and tie him to a tree, but his howling and braying would alert Blue to come on back, so his suffering was not in vain.

This was when Devin's military castoffs really came in handy. The field jacket and pants had well-placed pockets where she could store everything from her heavy rubber gloves to her knife. A lot of people made fun of her for wearing gloves, but she had no intention of having blood freeze her hands stiff. Besides, even though the deer in their area didn't have wasting illness, why ask for trouble? Granny always said being careful never killed anyone, and she was surely right about that.

Using the rope she carried bandoleer style, she quickly tied together the deer's rear hooves, then went about the backbreaking labor of hoisting the carcass over a tree limb. This was one of the few times she envied men. Having a lot more upper body strength would really come in handy on jobs like this. She sweated and strained and cursed to herself, but finally got the deer into position so she could properly field dress it. The work could be done with the animal on the ground, but her daddy had taught her that hanging it made everything cleaner and easier—except for getting the darned thing hung.

Being careful not to nick anything important, she worked away at the deer to the non-melodic accompaniment of both Stripes and Blue. Thinking about the time her cavalier uncle had punctured a bladder could still make her laugh. Being hit in the face with a stream of urine was a lot funnier to watch than it was to have happen to you. When she had the animal dressed, she untied it and gently lowered it to the ground. It was going to be a long walk back to Curly's truck, but the snow would protect the hide enough that she could drag it behind her. If she'd had to, she'd butcher the thing and take it out one half at a time. But the snow provided a benefit, as she struggled to remind herself while tromping through it. The frantic, lunging dogs were confused as usual, crossing in front of her and getting their leashes all tangled. How no one in the family had put them down was a question she'd frequently pondered on treks like this. A good hunting dog cost a fair bit, more than any of them had to spare. She'd never shoot a dog for being stupid, but these two would surely be the death of her.

—⁂—

After tagging it, checking in at the wildlife management station, and dropping her half of the deer off at her place, Cody took the truck and Curly's ill-gotten gains to his. Now that he feasted his eyes on the carcass, his orneriness abated for a few moments. "Want a drink?" he asked, gruff as usual. "Darned cold out."

"No, I'm fine." She offered a small wave, then tromped off down the long, rutted driveway to the road. All of a sudden, the uphill climb to her place seemed like a heck of a walk. Technically, it wasn't that far, and most days she walked ten times the distance, but she'd been up since five and had dragged a deer carcass an awfully long way. Even that wouldn't normally have tuckered her out, but the snow was substantial and continued to float down upon her head. It wouldn't take much to put a driver into a skid. Getting killed on the road didn't seem like a good way to end a very productive hunting day. Given that their house was a mile closer than hers, she decided to drop in on Uncle Shooter and Aunt Thelma.

After tying the dogs up outside, she opened the door and walked in. Her presence was vaguely acknowledged and, after walking out of her roomy boots and dropping her jacket onto a chair, she headed over to stretch out on the floor in front of the television.

The house wasn't large, but a good number of people were within the radius of the screen. Two of her adult cousins were home, along with a couple of little kids. The kids didn't belong to these particular cousins, but that didn't much matter.

Cody recognized the show on TV. Even though she didn't own one herself, everyone else in the family watched so much that she was able to speak knowledgeably about nearly every show the group found interesting.

The one on now was about country people living somewhere in Louisiana, and it was definitely a family favorite. Cody had to admit it was nice to see average people on television once in a while, instead of all the ones who looked like animated Barbie dolls.

Someone came out with a huge bag of tortilla chips, and a few squabbles ensued. Elijah had a bad temper for such a little cuss, but his mama spoiled him rotten. It'd be nice if Aunt Thelma could straighten him up, since he seemed to be there more than he was at home. Of course, she hadn't been able to do much with her own boy, but sometimes it was easier with grandbabies.

You couldn't actually fight with a four-year-old, so Cody only got a couple of handfuls of chips. That'd probably be all she was going to get for dinner. She was too tired to cook, and beggars can't be choosers. *Beggars can't be choicey*, she thought, rolling the expression around in her head, hearing her granny's voice. The phrase had more punch when she said it that way, but her mama had always required her to speak like city people. She said the only way to get a good job was to not sound like you were from the hollow. That hadn't worked out well, but her grammar was ready to go if needed.

After catching herself fall asleep a couple of times, she pried herself off the floor and went to put on her boots. In the kitchen, Aunt Thelma asked her, "What'd you think about the news?"

"What news?"

"You didn't hear?" Louder now, she shouted over the television, "Shooter? Didn't you tell Cody?"

"I didn't see Cody." He slowly pulled his focus from the TV, turned around and gave her a smile. "Hey, Cody."

Thelma scowled at her husband. "They sold the winning lottery ticket over in Twined Creek. Almost right here in town. And," she added dramatically, "It was the biggest jackpot *ever*."

Cody stared into the distance for a minute, frankly amazed that someone nearby had been graced with such a stroke of luck. "Some lucky devil is gonna have a nice New Year's Eve."

Thelma laughed. "Whoever won that money will *never* have another bad day."

—⁓—

Cody thought about the lottery winner on the way home. Aunt Thelma hadn't said exactly how much it was, but whatever the jackpot, whoever won it, needed it. There wasn't anybody within ten miles of Twined Creek who didn't need a hand up or had a hand out. She just hoped whoever won wouldn't do something stupid, like build a thirty room mansion with a place for a helicopter, and then not be able to afford fuel for the darned thing. They'd watched plenty of shows about people who won scads of money and piddled it away, and the bad decisions seemed to greatly outnumber the good ones. Actually, even though those shows were addictive, they'd always irked her a bit. It seemed like they went out of their way to find the most foolish people, and highlight their most outrageous foibles. They were invariably country folk, who were always fodder for poking fun at. That always had and always would rankle her. There had to be plenty of fools in big cities, but they seemed to get a pass.

She looked down at the dogs, now trotting companionably beside her, impersonating well-trained animals. "If I ever won money, I'd buy you two the biggest bones I could find." At the sound of her voice they both looked up attentively. "But I wouldn't bet your lives on it."

———

The dogs tried to convince her to let them come in, but they had a perfectly acceptable house and that's where they belonged. Once inside, Cody slowly got undressed. Her shoulders were so stiff she winced when she had to bend over to pick up her pants. As she folded her things, she mused that snow was easy on clothes. Her pants were soggy, but clean enough to get another day or two of wear out of them, saving a trip to the laundrymat.

So tired she felt a little sick to her stomach, Cody was just about to go down the hallway to her bed when she saw her wallet just sitting there on the kitchen counter. A smile settled on her face when she thought of her little secret. It was a silly exercise, but she carefully took the lottery ticket out, stood it up against the sugar canister and resolved to check the numbers in the morning. Well, *some*body had to win.

CHAPTER TWO

CODY DIDN'T SUBSCRIBE TO the newspaper, but her aunt's brother did. Rufus' place was roughly in the direction of a spot she liked to keep an eye on, about a mile and a half away. She took off early in the morning, just as the sun was cresting the mountain.

The dogs did not come along, since they caused more harm than good in most situations. It was hard getting her body to warm up this morning, but it was such a beautiful day, she shifted her focus to the lovely white blanket of snow, and observed how it stuck to the sides of trees, hid fences, and blurred the lines of a drive she was sure was right in front of her. This kind of snow made everything just a little off and let you feel like you were in a completely different place. Like going on a trip without having to leave town.

Since no one had yet been out to get the paper, Cody didn't have to walk all the way up to the house. Rufus' No Trespassing signs were covered with snow, making them illegible. That didn't matter, because they weren't intended for her. That didn't mean she wouldn't hear the distinctive sound of a shotgun being readied if she walked down his drive, but he'd never shoot at kin—on purpose.

The paper was stiff from the cold, and it took her a few seconds to open it to the right page. For a moment, she perused the numbers in a box in the corner—2, 3, 5, 31, 33, 40. Not a one of them lucky for her. Still, she took out the pencil stub she'd brought, found a piece of junk mail from the box and wrote them down. Then she folded the paper and put it back in the box. It would have been thoughtful to carry it up to Rufus' door, but she didn't want to have to skedaddle out of there if that shotgun got cocked.

The spot she'd been keeping an eye on was only about another half mile down the road. Given that it was private land, she wasn't even sure why she'd been in the area the first time she'd spotted it. She'd learned long ago that it wasn't worth the temptation to go traipsing around where she was prohibited from hunting. It was far too beguiling to have some lovely specimen cross her path and not be able to even take a shot. Since she wasn't armed, she didn't have to worry about her instincts getting the best of her today. She could just enjoy the place, dedicating only a tiny portion of her brain to remaining alert for the owner.

Licorice Creek wasn't far away, but Cody doubted it was the source of the beautiful brook set right out in a glade of shagbark hickory. Sometimes water had its own mind. It was ice cold, frozen along the edges, but it continued to bubble up, making the prettiest sound she'd ever heard.

Given that she loved shagbark hickory in the winter, this had to be her new favorite spot. A downed tree gave her a place to sit and reflect for a while, watching the clear, clean water bubbling from the earth, as though driven to leave the confines of the underground to sample the sweet life on top.

———

Cody'd spent far too much time playing, and not enough butchering. She wouldn't be punished for tarrying, however. It was cold enough that the deer carcass was as good as already in the freezer.

A few years back, she'd gone to great expense to put a concrete slab under the overhang of the shed her grandfather had built not far from the house. Now she could keep her meat freezer out there, provided she kept it locked up and protected from the elements.

After getting her butchering knives from the house, she unwrapped the tarp from the carcass. The dogs begged for just a bite or two, but the last thing Stripes needed was encouragement.

It took a very long time to remove all of the meat from the bones, put it into freezer bags, and label each piece, but it was worth it. She had enough for a lot of meals, with a couple of prime cuts she'd share with each of her uncles and aunts. Including the pieces she'd use to make jerky, she loaded all of it into the freezer and finally went inside to rest.

She was working her way through Dickens again, finding herself automatically going there in the winter. For some reason, Jane Austen and George Elliot made better summer companions. Her books were cast-offs from the library, but every word was in there even if the bindings had broken and people had doodled in the margins. After falling asleep while reading *The Pickwick Papers*, Cody woke, stiff and cranky. It was past time to eat. A big bowl of hot cereal sounded good. When she went to the cupboard to fetch the oats, the propped-up ticket caught her eye. She laughed at herself when she recalled she'd gone miles out of her way just to find the numbers, but hadn't yet bothered to check them.

The piece of junk mail had almost fallen from her pocket, but she wouldn't have noticed if it had. Her cousin Devin wasn't a particularly large man, but he was a good two or three sizes bigger than she was, and his pants were laughably large. Luckily, they had shock cords that let her snug them up around her waist and fold the legs under so she didn't trip on them. But they were loose enough that she might not have noticed if she'd had a live frog jumping around in the back pocket, much less a thin envelope sliding out.

She placed the envelope next to the ticket and started to scratch off the coating over each number with her thumbnail, saying, "Two…got it. Three…got that. Five…well I'll be a monkey's uncle. I got that too!" Cody briefly wondered if there was a prize for getting some of the numbers. Her heart started to race when she said the next number aloud. "Thirty-one." Damned if she didn't have that one too! At thirty-three she stopped speaking, letting her eyes race to the last number. Forty. She had five numbers out of five. There *had* to be a prize for that. There just had to be. Her hands shook like she'd stepped on a downed power line, but she managed to scrape the last number clean. It almost glowed, then it faded and sharpened in her vision. A big, fat forty. Clear as day.

Mind racing in all directions, she tried to concentrate and find the mistake. It was there, she just had to find it. Reading each number again and again, she couldn't change them, no matter how hard she tried. Each of those six numbers was on the card in her trembling hand. Time stood still, and she stared vacantly at the ticket. Everything seemed to sway and move, then she was jolted back to reality as warm liquid ran down her legs.

She'd pissed herself! Stopping the stream in action wasn't easy, but she managed to get to the bathroom in time to save having to scrub the entire place.

She sat there, unable to process what to do next. Putting on a fresh pair of pants and running to tell everyone she knew was her first instinct. But something held her back. After taking off her clothes, she got into the shower to clean up, then got dressed again and scrubbed the floor. Doing something with her hands helped settle her—a little. But she was numb. She'd heard people say that before, of course, but had never understood they weren't speaking metaphorically. Her body and her mind were shocked so badly she could hardly feel a thing.

Needing some form of companionship, she went outside and welcomed the dogs in, letting them roam all over after they stopped to smell the result of her shock. Maybe she needed some bleach for the floor.

———

Carrying a venison steak with her, Cody walked to her Uncle Cubby and Aunt Lurlene's house. The eldest of her mother's four siblings, Cubby had always been the de facto leader of the group. It seemed that whenever things went haywire, Cody naturally gravitated to his place. It was just after lunch and relatively quiet. Her cousin Jaden was there with a couple of his kids, one sitting on the kitchen floor, banging a wooden spoon on a pot. "I brought you a present," Cody said over the racket, laying the big steak on the counter. "Happy New Year."

Her aunt gave her a quick hug, murmuring, "Thank you." Given that physical affection wasn't the norm, Cody wondered if they were running low on food. The end of December was darned early to be low, but the dry summer had hurt everyone's garden. Truth was, even a productive parcel of land wouldn't cut it. They still needed some little bit of meat. Bringing that in was Uncle Cubby's job, a job that wasn't getting done. Stripes and Blue mutely testified to that as they stood wagging their scruffy tails at her trailer every morning. Despite their faults, Uncle Cubby took at least one of them along for companionship, if nothing else, when he went hunting.

She tried to shift her focus from the larder and go back to her situation. It was tricky, and she needed to play it by ear, partly because being careful was her style, but also because she had to be one hundred percent sure she wasn't making a fool of herself. Jaden had given his dad a fake lottery ticket a few years back, and they all still laughed about how Cubby had fallen for it and had cried about how he'd take care of all of them—after he got himself set. That wouldn't happen to her.

The newspaper never entered the house, but Cody knew the numbers would show up on the TV sooner or later. Having the ticket sold locally was huge news and would surely merit attention. She didn't have to wait long for the topic to be broached. "They said where the lottery ticket was sold," Cubby said. "Did you see?"

Cody walked over to sit next to him on the sofa. "No. Where?" Afraid he could hear her heartbeat, she leaned against the distant arm of the sofa and tried to look normal.

"The Clinic. Can you believe it?"

"No, I can't," she admitted slowly, a dull roar echoing in her ears. "I really can't."

"Yup. They sold the durned thing on Christmas Eve. It was all up in the news," he said gesturing with the remote.

"It was that *big* game," Lurlene added, wandering in from the kitchen. "The one they play once a week."

"I don't know much about the lottery," Cody admitted.

"You're too tight with your money," Jaden said. "You've gotta play to win."

Cody was going to snap off a response, but now wasn't the time. She didn't know where Jaden got his money, even though she had her guesses, but if he had enough to waste on the lottery, he ought to pay a little child support. Just because his former girlfriends hadn't gone to court to make him pay didn't mean he didn't owe the money.

"You'll find out all you need to know about the lottery as soon as the winner shows up," Lurlene said. "This is the biggest news we've had up here since…ever. The TV has been to the clinic already, but they're closed up on account of the holiday."

Cubby switched the channel, going to the public access station run out of Charleston. The picture was bad, as always, but across the bottom of the screen, numbers scrolled along, with Cody catching only the last one, the big, fat forty that had sealed the deal.

It was a crying shame to have to act so nonchalant with your kin. The vulture-like stare Jaden fixed on her made it clear that caution was mandatory. He wouldn't forcibly take the ticket, she didn't think, but he'd tell everyone in the county. She couldn't count the people who'd kill her for it without a flicker of remorse.

The message scrolled by again and her skin prickled with tension. A trickle of sweat rolled down her back, making it itch. She'd written the numbers on her arm, even though she hadn't needed to. They were locked in her memory, probably permanently—2, 3, 5, 31, 33, and 40. Sure enough, they rolled across the screen just like that. She had won. *She... had...won.*

Cody fell, or slipped to the floor, where the baby dove for her. He climbed onto her body, treating her as a big toy. "You all right?" Cubby asked. "You eaten?"

"I'm fine," Cody replied, her voice shaking. "Just tired...from hunting."

"When did you take the deer?"

"Yesterday. Last day."

"Oh, shoot! I was gonna get out there, but I didn't."

Lurlene gave him a scolding look. "He says it's too cold to hunt. Sorriest excuse I ever heard. If Cody can do it, so can you." She turned to Cody. "You didn't go by yourself, did you?"

"Yes, ma'am. I did." She'd never lie to an aunt. It wasn't right.

"You know you should go with someone, girl."

Cody didn't say the truth. That many of her cousins were poachers, and she wasn't about to have a thousand dollar fine following her around. The whole family had to chip in when Jaden got caught with an untagged raccoon...and who wanted to have to pay for an animal no one wanted to eat? But she didn't want to sass, so she said, "I'd love the company. I'll call next time I'm going out, but deer season's over now."

"I'll get out there soon as it warms up," Cubby said.

That was a lie. They only thing still in season was hare and rabbit and grouse, and Cubby didn't have the patience or the energy for any of them. Maybe he could get his blood fired up for spring turkey season, but Cody doubted it. She could only bag two, and she had a feeling she'd be sharing them with her less-motivated relatives.

Then it hit her again, like a fist to the chest. *She'd won.* "Hey, uhm, how does the person who won get their money?"

"I don't know," Cubby said. "They give them those great big checks someplace. Maybe Charleston?" He laughed hard. "Those folks always look so stupid, standing there holding that giant check like they've been hit in the head with a two-by-four."

"They don't look as dumb as you did when I gave you that fake ticket," Jaden said, laughing hard even though it had happened years ago.

"I wouldn't care how stupid I looked," Cubby said. "I'd be down there banging on that door today, wantin' my money. I'd kick up such a fuss they'd have to open the doors on New Year's Day."

That set off a heated discussion about how, when, and through what means a person would claim their winnings. None of the statements seemed backed up by facts. Cody tuned the voices out and made plans for how to claim her prize—without alerting the entire world.

CHAPTER THREE

MADDIE OSBORNE CAREFULLY LOOKED over both shoulders before opening the door to the bank. She thought the odds of being robbed were about as likely as finding a fine French restaurant in town, but her managers had assured her that even small towns in West Virginia could be targeted. Usually by local people high on drugs. Those were the folks Maddie worried about. Professional bank robbers were pretty much a thing of the past. Now it was amateurs, hopped up on something and prone to stupid violence.

Just before she put the key in the lock she looked to the right once again. It was early, just seven thirty, and the street was deserted but for the sole clunker parked a few doors down from where she stood. Not in the mood to play around, she slid the key in, opened the lock, and went inside. She had thirty seconds to turn the alarm off, and she'd gotten good enough to have fifteen seconds left. Small accomplishments led to large ones…or something like that.

Even though they didn't open until nine, she liked to be there well before anyone else. It set a good example and let her take care of anything she didn't want her employees to see. There actually weren't many instances where she needed privacy, but if she made coming in early a habit, no one would look askance if she had to do something momentous at the crack of dawn.

She was laughing at the thought of anything momentous happening, when she spied a figure standing across the street, assessing the bank. At least that looked like what the guy was doing. He definitely hadn't been there just a few moments earlier. He must have jumped out of that decrepit car and hustled over as soon as she'd come in.

Maddie went upstairs, to the break room, and looked out the small window where she wouldn't be noticed. Now that she looked carefully, it wasn't a guy, but a girl. She must've been in the Army, probably home for leave before being shipped somewhere dangerous.

Maddie had only been in the Greenbrier Valley region for a couple of months, but she'd been amazed at how many people were in the service. Of her seven employees, six of them had close relatives who were in one branch or another of the military.

Staring at the woman who was staring at her bank, Maddie decided she was pretty cute, especially if you liked butchy women—which she did. This particular specimen was at the limit of the butch scale for her, but the uniform had a way of making even an ultra feminine woman look a little tough.

The soldier was physically imposing, tall and thin and broad across the shoulders. Her dark, thick hair hung loose, but that's about all Maddie could discern from her distance. The woman leaned against a building, one booted foot casually placed on the wall behind her, just waiting. There was no way she was there to rob the place. She clearly wanted something though, since she hadn't taken her eyes off the front door.

Maddie went back downstairs, opened the door and waved. It was too cold to let anyone stand out there until nine o'clock.

The woman loped across the street, showing agility and grace when she moved. "Hi," she said, nodding her head in greeting. "I didn't know when you opened."

Maddie stood aside from the doorway and gestured for her to enter. "Not until nine, but you'll freeze if you stand out there that long." She looked at the horizontal stripe that said "Buchanan" over the breast pocket. Thrusting her hand out, she said, "Is it Private Buchanan?"

The woman took a quick glance down, then shook her head. "That's my cousin. I'm Keaton. Cody Keaton."

"I'm the new branch manager, Maddie Osborne," she said as they shook hands. "I can't offer much in the way of services because I don't have a cash drawer, but you're welcome to wait."

"I just have a question."

Maddie stood there, waiting for her to ask. When she didn't volunteer, Maddie prompted, "Ask away."

Cody looked uncertain, a radical difference from the cool, studied way she'd appeared on the street. "Let's say I was going to come into some money. What do I do with it?"

Interesting question. Maybe she could put it in a...I don't know...a bank? She reminded herself that patience was a virtue she had to work harder to possess. "I'm not sure I know exactly what you're asking. Do you want to know what you could do with money *other* than put it in the bank?"

Pursing her lips, Cody shook her head. "I'm not sure what I'm asking. I've got some money coming to me, and I need to keep it safe."

The precious minutes she had to herself were ticking away, but Maddie kept at it. "Your money is safe in your account. Is someone trying to..." She had no idea where that thought was going to end up. It must be the skittishness that Cody was displaying. That could be contagious.

"I don't have an account. Would it be safe in one?"

Boy, this one hadn't come down from the hills very often. Maybe never. "Yes, of course. Deposits are fully insured by the federal government for two hundred and fifty thousand dollars."

Cody blinked. "That's all?"

"Yes, that's all. Do you need to deposit more than that?"

That relatively open, quizzical expression shut down hard. "I don't know how this whole thing works. I've never had an account."

Maddie squinted her eyes, hoping a new perspective would let her get inside this frustrating woman's head and figure out what in the hell she was asking. "Well, if you wanted to open an account, we would take the check that you receive and deposit it."

"Who said it was a check?" she asked sharply.

Flustered, Maddie stammered, "I just assumed..."

"It probably is a check. A big one." She spread her hands wide apart, indicating...something.

"Okay. Well, as I said, we deposit it and you'd have access to your money by writing checks or using an ATM card to make withdrawals."

She looked very suspicious when she said, "So I give you my check and you keep it here. Then when I want a bit of it, I come and get it."

Smiling her best customer service smile, Maddie said, "Something like that, yes."

"But not exactly like that."

That seemed more like an accusation than a question, but Maddie tried to make herself more clear. "Banking is all done with entries on a computer system. We don't keep your actual check here, but we know how much you have and we can give you access to it at any time."

"So if I gave you a check for say…" It looked like she was thinking hard. "Two hundred and sixty thousand dollars, you'd make a note someplace that you owed me that money. But you'd only guarantee I'd get two hundred and fifty thousand back."

That was good enough. "Exactly." Now they were getting somewhere.

"And if I came back tomorrow, and said I wanted it all back, you'd give it to me. If you hadn't lost that extra ten thousand dollars by then."

Was she kidding? Given her intense gaze, probably not. "All of your money is safe. We only insure two hundred and fifty thousand, but no one has ever lost a cent at Appalachian States Bank." Her conscience nagged at her. This woman seemed very literal. "A lot of banks lost customer money during the depression. That's why the federal government stepped in to insure deposits. But we're very careful and all of your money would be safe here."

"So if I gave it to you today, I could come get it tomorrow."

"Of course. We'd have to make sure there were no outstanding checks written on the balance, but we'd write you a check for whatever your legal balance was."

"I'd want cash."

Okay. The woman must've been taking an introductory course on how to kite checks. Showing up at a bank well before they opened, then asking for instructions on exactly how to do that wasn't the smartest way to approach it, but they said criminals were generally not very bright. "We don't keep large sums of cash. We could get whatever we need, of course, but it might take a day."

The woman's shoulders slumped, making her look utterly defeated. She turned around to leave, but Maddie's determined side caught up with her charitable instincts and she fought to lure her back in. "If you have a good deal of money coming to you, it's not safe to keep it in cash."

Very suspiciously, Cody said, "It's safer to give you all of it and have you write a little note to somebody, then have you get somebody else to give you the actual money…days from now. *That* sounds safe?"

With as much confidence as she had, Maddie said, "Yes. That sounds very safe to me. It *is* very safe."

"No offense, but that's crazy. I'm gonna have to find another way."

Maddie's stubborn nature was not easily defeated. This woman was not gonna get out of that bank without a fight. "Come downstairs, and I'll show you the safest place in town."

The guard entered right when they were going down a set of stairs in the back of the building. "Oh, Ripley, can you keep an eye on things? We're going downstairs for a minute."

"Sure, Miz Osborne," he said, drawing out the words.

They walked downstairs and stood in front of an elaborate, gilded iron gate. Behind the gate was the safe deposit vault. The door, now closed, was about a foot and a half thick, and always impressed children visiting the bank on school trips. But even closed, it looked substantial. Cody eyed it suspiciously.

"If the only thing you care about is safety, you could put your money in our vault."

"How much of that is insured?"

"It's only insured by steel. You can keep anything you want in a safe deposit box. Since we don't know what you put in there, we can't insure it."

Cody nodded, looking a little more persuaded. "So I could put my check in there."

Doh! "Well, that's not a good idea. Checks have to be cashed or deposited. They get stale."

"Like bread?"

Maddie had never seen anyone look so amazingly confused about such a simple concept. "Kind of. Checks are generally valid for a year, so I wouldn't keep one here for long, but you could keep as much cash as you wanted." Making sure to give full disclosure, she added, "Your money wouldn't earn interest. If you put ten thousand dollars in, after ten years you'd still only have ten thousand dollars."

"I understand interest. How much do you pay?"

"It's very low right now, I'll admit. Only around one percent."

Shoving her hands into the slash pockets on her pixilated uniform jacket, Cody rocked back on her heels and said, "I'm supposed to give you all of my money and not know where you put it, so you can give me one percent interest?" Her raised eyebrow showed how silly an idea that seemed.

"Well, there are a lot of vehicles we have that can earn a higher rate of interest."

Cody's expressive eyebrows shot up. "Vehicles?"

Maddie wanted to slap her own face. "That's just a banking term. We have certificates of deposit and money market accounts and even investment accounts. We could definitely try to help you earn more interest."

Nodding slowly, Cody said, "I'm just trying to make sure I can keep what I get."

"When will you have the money?"

Once again Cody's expression turned to stone. "You don't have to worry about that." She bent over a little from the waist, making a strangely courtly bow. "Thank you very much for your time." Then she turned and climbed the stairs quickly. By the time Maddie had followed her up, she was gone.

———

One good thing about being from the hills. No one ever looked at you and thought you might have a little card in your pocket that made you a millionaire.

Cody sat high up above town in the car she'd borrowed, thinking about what to do. Looking down at the hustle and bustle of Greenville allowed her to relax and focus, something that was hard to do when she was surrounded by all of those people.

Looking only at the facts, she'd had the ticket for a week, and nothing bad had happened. But now that she knew it was a winner, it was like having something radioactive in her pocket. It gave off a heat that threatened to burn right through her pants.

She had to keep the darned thing safe until she could make some calls and figure out how to claim her prize. And, of course, she had to tell her family before taking any action. They'd be hurt beyond belief to know that she hadn't trusted them.

It didn't make logical sense, but she was terrified of even making a phone call with the ticket on her person. Like whoever she talked to could just zoom through the phone line and snatch it away. Clearly, she wasn't thinking straight, but knowing that didn't make it any easier to arrive at a decision.

In her heart, she knew the ticket would be safe if she hid it somewhere in the woods. She could climb nearly any tree, and she'd just have to shimmy up an innocuous one and stash it away. But what if someone saw her do it, or merely saw her footprints in the snow and decided to investigate? It was almost impossible to imagine that happening, but she could just see herself worried sick and pacing all night long.

No, she had to put it someplace safe. Now she just had to convince herself who she could trust. That was tough. The lady at the bank clearly thought she had all the answers, but trusting a complete stranger with goodness knew how much money seemed truly crazy.

She went through her options. She didn't know any ministers, but a lot of them seemed to like money more than Jesus. Politicians? *Please.* She might just as well slap it to her forehead and invite people to snatch it away. The sheriff? *Ha!* That guy was so crooked they'd have to screw his corpse into the ground. A few teachers had been kind and seemed honest, but she didn't know where any of them lived. No, the only people she trusted were family, and while only some of them would kill her for the money, all of them were blabbermouths. The only thing to do was put the ticket in that big safe and hope for the best. Making it clear she was talking about a whole lot of money had been ridiculously stupid, but now that she knew the rules a little bit she could probably be more stealthy. Her clammy hands gripped the steering wheel so tightly they ached. *Good luck with that.*

Maddie was sitting at her desk, talking to her manager on the phone when Cody ambled back into the branch. Catching her eye, Maddie pointed at the chair in front of her desk.

"I have a customer," she said into the receiver. "Can I call you back?" She hung up, then stood to close the glass door to her office. Now seated, she folded her hands on her desk, ready to catch whatever curveball her recalcitrant potential client threw at her. "It's nice to see you again. Can I call you Cody?"

"Sure. Uhm…I'd like one of those boxes for the safe. A little one." She held her hands up in a small square.

"Great. I can get you set right up. Our smallest box is thirty-five dollars a year."

"I don't need it for a year. Just…" She made a very thoughtful face. "Maybe a few days."

"Oh. Well, we only rent them by the year. Uhm…"

"I don't have…" Cody looked down, and shook her head quickly. "I can't pay today." She looked into Maddie's eyes. "But I need it. Right now."

Oh, boy. Urgency radiated from those puppy-dog eyes. What in the hell did she have to protect? Whatever it was, she was damned serious about it. *Shit.* She'd get her ass fired if she gave services away to every hard luck story in the county. But…damn, the poor woman looked like she was about to vomit. "Okay. I'll give you a box today and charge you for it next…week?"

"That'll work."

Maddie took out the forms, had Cody fill them out, then they walked down to the vault. With the door open it really did look impressive, and she could hear Cody suck in a breath when she saw it. "Here's your key. You have one and we have one. Both keys have to be used. If you lose yours, we have to drill the box open. You pay for that," she said clearly.

"What if you lose yours?"

That was a new one. No one had ever asked, but it was a logical question. "Then I guess we'd have to have you come in and watch the box be drilled open. That won't happen, though. We're very, very careful."

"How do I know you don't have a copy of my key?" Dark brown eyes bore into Maddie, making her step back to avoid their intensity.

She thought for a moment, then decided to be completely honest. "I guess you don't. All you have is my word, and since we don't know each other, that's probably not worth very much."

Her gaze softened and she blinked slowly. "Thank you. I hate to have people try to convince me of things I know are bull."

"We don't have copies of your key. People put jewelry, bearer bonds, gold coins, everything in their safe deposit boxes. If we stole from them, word would get around and we'd be out of business."

Showing a ghost of a smile, Cody said, "I don't know anybody who does business here. I only came because you're the only bank I know about. You could be as crooked as a dog's hind leg and I wouldn't have heard about it."

That was kinda charming. Refreshingly honest too. "Well, other people would have and we'd be gone. The mere fact that we've been here for eighty years must mean something."

"The government's been here almost two hundred and fifty years and they're deadly crooked."

That tiny smile was back, the one you would have missed if you hadn't been paying attention. "I don't think I'm going to convince you we're honest. You're just going to have to have a good experience with us." Maddie led the way into the vault, put her key into one of the twin locks and pointed at a matching spot. "Now put yours there." Cody did, and a little door opened, revealing a metal box that Maddie slid out. She placed it in Cody's hands. "You can go to the privacy room right there and put whatever you want inside. It's your box now."

Cody was visibly shaking, and Maddie led her to the room and urged her to sit down. "Stay as long as you like. No one can see you. I promise. Tell the guard when you're finished. He'll have the bank's key." Then she closed the door and went back upstairs, wondering if Cody would emerge before they closed.

Maddie's assistant manager walked alongside her as she went back to her office. "Got a minute?"

"Sure. Come on in."

Geneva sat down and took out a notepad. "Did you open a new account?"

"Oh, did you see her? Our new client seems about as calm as a cat on a hot tin roof." She laughed, thinking about the look on Cody's face when she saw the vault. "I don't think she's ever been inside a bank."

"That's not odd around here. I assume she's from the mountains?"

"I don't know. I just know she's poor."

"I couldn't tell that. She just looks like one more kid getting ready to be shipped out."

"Oh, she's not in the army, and she's no kid. I'd say she's around my age."

"Surprising. Maybe she looked young because her clothes are so big. It was like she was playing dress-up."

"I don't think she plays much. And if you'd talked to her you'd know she's poor. She's an attractive woman, but one of her front teeth is broken off. A woman would spend her last dime to fix something like that."

"Oh." Geneva put her hand over her mouth in sympathy. "I hope her husband didn't do it."

Maddie looked up and saw Cody exiting, still about the color of paste. "I don't know what's going on with her, but I think she has a tough life."

"Most people in the hills do. It's not likely she's the exception."

CHAPTER FOUR

SINCE CUBBY AND LURLENE HAD the biggest house, and Cubby was the de facto leader of the family, Cody got on the phone and called each branch of the family and told them to meet her there at eight o'clock. Cubby and Lurlene, Shooter and Thelma, her aunts Merry and Lily and each of their kids agreed, after a certain amount of expected curiosity.

To calm herself, Cody walked to one of her favorite spots. It wasn't anywhere near her aunt and uncle's home, but once she got there she decided that the stop had been worth the extra miles. It wasn't much, at least not to someone who didn't stop and take it in, but it was her sanctuary.

The foundation of a cabin lay in a small clearing in the heavy woods. A creek flowed weakly in the summer, but it was frozen over now. Still, she could imagine it, could hear it babbling, even through the thick blanket of snow.

If she had the knowledge, she'd do some digging and figure out how old the foundation was. Consisting of rocks and stones probably dug up right on the site, it was definitely hand laid. The place was small, likely just one room. A dozen yards behind was another, smaller foundation, and she reasoned that had been a kitchen. In her mind, the place was from the earliest days, when her part of West Virginia was settled by Europeans.

The cabin had been abandoned, and the ravages of time had left just the few rocks and stones she nudged with her boot. For all she knew, she was the first person since they left or died to discover it. She wasn't sure why it appealed to her, but it truly did. It was her own secret spot, where she could dream as well as look backward and try to imagine how people lived when every day was a struggle for survival—from disease, hunger, attacks from the natives. Every failed crop, every drought, every deluge, every invasion of harvest-destroying pests could have wiped them out.

Maybe it had. The whole family might have died on a single day, or maybe they'd been a success and had moved on to a bigger home. There was no way she'd ever know, but that mystery made it all the more interesting.

She sat on a fallen trees, this one looking like their unusually harsh winter had recently taken it. It was just a scrubby aspen, but it made a nice place to sit for a spell. Letting her mind wander for a good long while, Cody thought about the lottery and how her life would change forever in just a few minutes. She wasn't ready, but she probably never would be. Still, no one was making her take the money. She could tear the ticket up and never think about it again. That made her laugh, and the sound floated around the hollow and came back to her in a soft echo.

She told them quickly. That was the best way to get through things. Now around sixteen sets of eyes stared at her. Brett, one of her least favorite cousins, said, "That ain't funny, Cody. Makin' us drag our tails over here in the cold is just mean."

"I'm not kidding." She slowly moved her gaze across the packed room. "I won. I have to go to Charleston to pick up my check tomorrow, and anyone who wants to come is welcome."

"Oh, my sweet Lord!" her aunt Lily cried. "The girl is telling the truth!"

That vote of confidence set the whole group to squealing, and they caused such a ruckus that they were probably heard all the way up in Twined Creek. *Oh, my stars, this was gonna be a wild ride.*

Her cousin Mandy offered to give her a ride home. Carrying a paper bag filled with things she'd borrowed for the next day, Cody went out to the little sedan. Mandy's girls were chattering nonstop, talking about the money—a topic Cody was fairly sure would dominate conversation for at least a year. It wasn't a long trip, but Mandy kept staring at her, barely keeping her car on the narrow road. "How in the world are you going to spend all that money," Mandy finally said.

"Yeah, Cody," the girls said in unison. "How?"

"I don't expect to spend it all. I haven't really thought about the spending. I've been stuck on the claiming."

'Well, you'd best get to the spending part," Mandy said. "You've got money to burn!"

Cody lay in bed, unable to sleep. A few things kept poking at her, making her eyes blink wide open every time she started to relax.

One was when a few of her cousins kept asking when "we'd" get "our" money. That was worrisome. Not that she had any idea of shutting them out. She'd willingly, happily share with every single person who needed a thing. But it was her money, and she didn't appreciate someone else making assumptions. She'd never do that to any of them, and she wanted the same courtesy.

The other worry was about Devin. He'd always been closest to her, but he didn't even smile when she made her announcement. His personality had changed, probably forever, during his combat tour, and she could never guess how he'd react to things now. He probably had to go call his preacher and ask what he should think, since Pastor Jackson controlled just about every aspect of his life. Thinking about Devin just made her more antsy, so she put it aside, supposing she'd find out what was going on with him in the morning when they rode to Charleston together.

One thing was for sure. If she hadn't had the ticket locked up she would have gone right then and sat in front of the building until the lottery office opened. The waiting was awfully hard.

At nine a.m. Cody walked into the bank, nodded to Maddie on her way down to the vault, quickly got her strong box and took it into the little room. Once again her hands were shaking, but she took the magic ticket out of its cavernous home and put it into her wallet. After returning the empty box, she ran into Maddie, who was standing by the front door.

"Good morning," Maddie said.

"Hi." She wanted to tell her what she was doing, but it was still too hard. "I'll probably be back this afternoon or tomorrow morning. Then I can pay you for the box."

Maddie put a hand on her arm and in that moment Cody took a look a her. A real look. Dang, she was pretty! Had she been pretty yesterday?

Most likely. She could feel the blood rush to her cheeks, like it always did when a woman talked to her.

It was hard to believe she hadn't been nervous around her earlier. Probably because she'd been so nervous about everything else that she hadn't noticed. But Miss Osborne was the prettiest lady she'd seen in quite a while.

Hair the color of honey, worn short and styled some nice way that made it look neat but also…kinda carefree. Pale blue eyes that matched the stripe in her crisp shirt. And a smile that made Cody's ears heat up. She ached to let her eyes wander farther down, but Miss Osborne was looking right at her and she couldn't risk it.

"I have to run out to my car," Maddie said. "Can I walk you out?"

"Uhm, sure. I'm right there," she said, pointing.

"Right next to me."

Maddie opened the door and Cody tried not to trip on the single stair. They walked up to the passenger door of the car she'd borrowed, and Devin glared at their visitor. *Oh, no, he's giving her his evil eye.*

"My cousin," she said, cheeks flushing even more. "We're…late."

"Have a good day."

Maddie waved and opened her car door with one of those little beepers. That must've been nice in cold weather. Cody got back into her loaner and tried to settle her nerves. "I've got it," she told Devin tersely. "Let's get this over with."

―∾∾∾―

Maddie dashed back into the bank, rubbing her arms to warm them. "Wear your coat," Lynnette, the teller, called out.

"I usually do. I was just in a hurry."

"Most people run away from Montgomerys. You walked right out with one."

"Montgomery?"

"That girl you went outside with. She's a Montgomery."

"No, that's not her name. She's a…"

"Keaton. But she's really a Montgomery. They're rough, rough people."

Maddie swallowed, then said, "Her cousin *was* sitting in the passenger seat, holding a shotgun."

Lynnette nodded sagely. "They're from a little speck of a town a good hour from here. But everybody knows them. They're drug pushers."

Maddie's eyebrows shot up. "Drug pushers?"

"Yes, indeed. Her brother was killed a few years back cookin' up meth." She shook her head slowly. "If he'd been in town he would've blown up a whole street. Bad blood. All of 'em."

"She seems perfectly nice. Very mannerly." For some reason, she felt the need to defend Cody. Say what you would, that girl wasn't mean. Her mind wandered to how cute Cody had looked in civilian gear. She still wore the camouflage jacket, but it covered a blue sweater and a pair of women's slacks. Yes, the slacks were a little short, and the sweater was pilled. But why did everyone have to dress to impress? Cody might be from a troubled family, but that did *not* mean she was a bad person.

"They sell pills, they cook up meth and for all I know they still make moonshine."

That was uncalled for. It was clear Lynnette wasn't speaking of known facts. "I like her," Maddie said, narrowing her eyes.

"They don't have a pot to piss in, and they don't work. None of 'em," she added hotly. "That girl has never had the cash to buy a new pair of under-panties. Every stitch she had on had to be a hand-me-down or shoplifted."

"No matter what you've heard, I want all of you to be respectful of her. She's a client."

"Client," Lynnette muttered.

"She *is* our client," Maddie said clearly.

"How's she a client? I didn't get a deposit to open a new account."

"She opened a safe deposit box."

"A safe deposit box?" Lynnette eyes went wide. "What's she got in there?"

"I have no idea. It's *her* box."

"Let's see if you say that when there's a gunfight in here over a pound of meth or crank. The *only* thing she could be keeping in there is drugs."

Maddie moved closer to the barrier that separated the tellers from the clients. There were no customers at the moment, but she still wanted to be discrete. "Keep your thoughts about her, and all of our customers, to yourself, Lynnette. Cody Keaton is a valued client, and I want you to be as nice to her as you are to the mayor."

"The mayor," she grumbled, getting up from her stool to pour a glass of water. "That crook."

It was going to be a long day.

Maddie sat in her office, muttering to herself about Lynnette. She'd have to make it crystal clear that they weren't there to judge their clients, they were there to serve them.

Everyone at the branch had been there for years, and most of them seemed to resent Maddie to a greater or lesser degree. Because that made sense, it didn't bother her much. She certainly wouldn't have liked having a stranger come in and take over—especially if she thought she was competent to do the job herself. But Lynnette was the worst of the bunch. She didn't make many mistakes, but her customer service skills were atrocious, and Maddie wasn't about to stand for that. Lynnette would have to improve or she'd be out of a job. Every customer was precious—even the ones who were massive pains in the ass.

Damn that Lynnette for putting thoughts in her head! What if Cody was that nervous because she was hiding a stash of drugs in the vault? Why else did a woman need a grim-faced man holding a shotgun to accompany her when she came to make a withdrawal? *Damn it all to hell!*

Every member of the family, from Uncle Cubby to the new baby were gathered around her. They'd had to borrow six cars and use every one of their own to all make it, but they were there—and she was sick to her stomach.

The man from the lottery had been very nice, but it had taken a long time to get the forms all filled out and print her name on the giant check. Now she stood in the glare of some TV lights, holding the big check and waiting for the few reporters to ask a question.

"What will you do with all that money?" a woman called out.

"I just want to help my family," she said, having practiced that answer after the lottery man told her she'd have to talk to the press.

"What do you do for a living?" a man asked.

She hadn't counted on that. As usual, when embarrassed, she could feel blood rush to her ears, and they burned. "I…I…"

"Are you unemployed?" someone asked.

"I…suppose I am," she said quietly.

"When did you lose your job?" the same fellow asked.

The lights were really bright, and someone had stuck the baby in her arms. Her warm, squirming body made Cody even hotter and she was afraid she'd faint. But the question hung out there and she had to answer. "I suppose I've never had a job where I got a regular paycheck." My lord, that sounded stupid.

"Most people rush to quit their jobs when they win this kind of money," he said, in what she took to be a mocking tone. "You can just continue your life of leisure."

"What?" she demanded, shielding her eyes to be able to see him. "What did you say?"

"You said you didn't work…" he trailed off.

"I said no such thing," she snapped, hotly. "Who do you think puts food on my table? I work as hard as any man, woman or child in this state."

"I didn't mean…"

She was on a roll, and couldn't stop. "There's no jobs for honest, hard-working people where I'm from. There hasn't been a good job around here for thirty years!" Now she was really hot. Under the collar and everywhere else. "If companies didn't send our factory jobs overseas to jack up their profits, we'd…" she turned and scanned around her family. "All of us would be working."

"I didn't mean…"

"Yes, you did. We're not lazy," she growled. "We struggle for every dime. When the steel factory pulled out of Greenville, we lost five thousand jobs like that." She snapped her fingers loudly. "How many of those jobs have come back? A hundred? I bet not that many. We want to work, but we can't start our own companies!"

The nice man from the lottery came up alongside her and made a signal, shutting off the hot lights. "I'm sorry about that," he soothed. "I don't think he meant anything by that question."

"Yes, he did," Cody growled. "I've heard that stuff my whole life, and it never gets a darned bit easier."

It was going to be on the evening news, there was no way around that. And even though Greenville was about a million times bigger than Ramp, and people had more things to talk about, everyone in the big town would know about it.

It was around a hundred miles from Charleston to Greenville, and Cody decided to make the drive alone. Because everyone else went back to Ramp, she was able to spend the drive deciding how to talk to people about her win. It was going to come up constantly; she had to be prepared.

Cody was still nervous and very ill at ease when she returned to the bank. Already three thirty in the afternoon, she wasn't sure how late they were open, but when she cruised by slowly she could see activity behind the big window.

Not having far to walk, she left her coat in the car. While the sweater and pants she'd borrowed from her cousin weren't perfect, they were better than anything she owned. You certainly didn't need to look very good to go into a bank, but this was a big day and she wanted to look nice. Or at least not too bad.

As soon as she walked in the door, Maddie jumped up from her chair and walked over to her. "Hello, again," she said. For some reason, she looked a little agitated. Maybe she'd already heard.

"Hi. I can pay you now. Can we go in your office?"

"Uhm...sure." She led the way, sat at her big chair and stared.

This was really hard to do, but it would surely get easier with practice. Cody reached around and pulled an envelope out of her back pocket, then propped it up on Maddie's desk, holding on with both hands. "I've got a check here. I'd like to cash it and pay you back."

Maddie looked relieved when she smiled and said, "Oh, you can just give that to one of the tellers. They'll ask you for identification, and you'll be set."

Gravely, Cody said, "This is a big check."

Sticking her hand out, Maddie said, "May I see it?"

It was hard to take her hands off it, but Cody managed to remove the check from the envelope and slide it across the desk. Handing over the check, rather than talking about it had been a good idea. Cody could watch and see her reaction better than if they were talking. She wasn't disappointed. Maddie's blue eyes went from the check to her face and back again at least six times. It was when she tried to speak that was the most fun. "I…I…I…how…when…" She put her head down on her desk, and when she picked it up again she held the flats of her hands against her temples. "Jesus Fucking Christ!"

"I was surprised myself," Cody said, chuckling.

"Surprised? I would have had a fucking heart attack!" She clapped her hand over her mouth, eyes wide with alarm. "I'm so sorry! I just lost control for a minute."

Deciding to go ahead and be honest, Cody said, "I wet my pants. And the floor. Literally."

Maddie laughed at that, letting her head drop back and really getting into it. She was even prettier when she let herself go, and Cody's body started to twitch, just thinking about how cute she was. Cody needed her to keep laughing. "I should've been celebrating being a millionaire, but I was on my hands and knees, wiping up a puddle of pee."

That worked. She laughed so hard she coughed, then eventually settled down and wiped at her eyes with the back of her hand. "Best laugh I've had all week." It looked like she was trying to control herself, to act businesslike again. She snapped the check against the desk a couple of times and said, "You need to make some big decisions."

"What decisions? I want to cash it and keep the cash in my safe deposit box."

Maddie was shaking her head decisively while Cody was still finishing her sentence. "You can't do that. You just can't."

Why was she changing the rules? "You told me yesterday that you could get as much cash as I needed."

"Cody, there are so many things wrong with that idea that I barely know where to start. The first problem is that this would be a ridiculous amount of cash. Even if I could get this much, you'd use up every safe deposit box we have just to store it."

It was hard to believe that her cousin might've had a better idea. "Then I'll just take the cash and buy a safe. Someone said I could get one heavy enough that nobody would be able to take off with it."

Maddie's eyes popped wide open and her cheeks got pink really fast. "No, no, no. I *beg* you not to do that. Someone will come and torture you to get you to open the safe." She reached across the desk and grasped Cody's hand, squeezing it fiercely. "I don't think you've let this settle in yet. This kind of money will change your life in ways you can't imagine yet. *Please* take it slowly."

"What do you want me to do with it?" She'd had to listen to fifty different opinions last night about how Maddie would try to cheat her. She hoped to God that wasn't true.

"I can tell you what I'd do, but I have to be honest. I'm not a competent financial adviser. You really should hire a professional. You need an attorney and a good accountant, and you need them quickly."

This was when the ax would fall. She'd want to hook her up to somebody who would scam her out of the money and give Maddie a kickback. "I assume you know somebody."

"No, I really don't. I've only been in town for a couple of months, so I'm not as plugged in to the community as I might be. I've met some lawyers, of course, but I don't know if they're any good." She leaned a little closer and said quietly, "And I don't know if they're honest. I don't want to frighten you, but you've got to make sure the people you deal with are honest."

Her gut started to ache again. "How do I know that?"

Maddie shook her head, her eyes downcast. "I wish I knew. Sometimes you don't know how honest a person is until they have a chance to be dishonest. I don't want that to happen to you."

"So what do I do?" It was stupid to trust this woman, but she was the only port in this storm.

"Even though we can only insure your money for two hundred and fifty thousand dollars, the bank is in very good shape. I personally guarantee that you don't have anything to worry about if you open an account and deposit the check while you try to figure out what to do with it."

"I just can't do that. I need cash."

Maddie made that gesture again where she rubbed her head with her hands. It actually looked like she might grab a handful of that honey-colored hair and pull it out. "Do you need cash today? Do you want to go out and celebrate?"

"Celebrate how?"

"I have no idea. If it were me, I'd probably take everybody I knew out for a big party."

"That's...not something I considered. I just want to be able to rest, and I can't do that if all I have is a little piece of paper telling me you're gonna give me the money."

"Then we're at a bit of an impasse. The biggest bank in the world doesn't have this kind of money lying around." She held the check up and shook it back and forth. "You say you can't trust the bank, but you already believe this piece of paper is going to turn into a truckload of cash. So you've made that leap of logic. Depositing the check is just one more small step."

"I'm sorry, but I can't do that. I need to have something I can see."

Maddie grabbed her phone and said, "Let me make some calls." She started dialing, and told person after person that she needed a large sum of cash for a client. Cody wasn't sure what they were saying back, but, they must've been saying "no" because Maddie kept calling. Finally she made the last call and leaned back in her chair as she hung up. "If you'll deposit the check, I'll be able to have a million in cash by Friday."

"What about the rest?"

"We're going to have to do this one step at a time." She leaned over and gazed at Cody so earnestly that it wasn't possible to think she was lying. "News of this will be in the paper, right?"

"On TV," she said, feeling sick.

"Then you have to protect yourself. I think you should deposit the check now, and I'll give you all the cash I can spare." She looked up and bit her lip. "Everyone is gone, but I can get into the cash vault."

"That's really all you can do?"

"I swear to you, that's all I can do."

A half hour later, Cody sat by herself in the privacy room, counting out eight thousand dollars. It wasn't the first time she'd seen a lot of cash, but it was the first time it was hers. When she was done, she put seven thousand of it back in the box, pocketed fifty twenties and put the box back in its slot. She turned her key, Maddie turned the bank's, and Cody stood there, stunned. Maddie put a hand on her arm and said, "There's one more thing you really have to do."

They sat in Maddie's office, with Cody carefully looking over a standard form. "I don't need a will. I just don't."

Maddie's lips pursed and her eyes fluttered closed briefly. "Please don't take offense at what I'm going to say."

Cody's stomach tensed up as she waited.

"People have been murdered for far, far less money than this. If you make a will, and leave everything to…" Her eyes shifted around the room, like she was looking for something hidden. "Charity…no one will have a reason to kill you."

Now Cody's gut felt like it was filled with acid. She wouldn't admit it to a stranger, but at least two, maybe three cousins, wouldn't lose a heck of a lot of sleep after putting a bullet in her head. "But I'd have to tell everyone that I'd done that." The room felt like it was moving and she gripped the desk to center herself. "They'd know I didn't trust them."

"Yes, they'd know," Maddie said quietly. "But they'd also know you were playing it safe." She reached across the desk and gripped Cody's hand tightly. "That's a very, very important message to give to people."

Cody took the form and folded it, then tucked it into her pants pocket. "I'll think about it. Thanks." She nodded. "I appreciate that you're trying hard to look out for me."

"I really am," Maddie said, and Cody felt herself believing the word of a total stranger. They must've been right when they said there's a first time for everything.

They stood at the front door, with Cody wishing she could just lie down on the floor and rest for a while. The whole thing had made her both anxious and drained, and she looked at the big bars across the windows as a safe haven. She had nothing to say, and, even though it was tempting, she couldn't rely on Miss Osborne to make everything right. Managing a tight smile, she put her hand on the knob at the same time a hand pressed against her back and rubbed her soothingly. "It'll all work out," she heard before walking out into the cold wind, knowing the world would never look at her the same way again.

—///—

Miss Osborne had been right. Even though Cody had a million, make that many millions of new worries, she had to celebrate a little. It was just stupid not to. She made a few stops on the way home, and pulled into her uncle Cubby's drive by six o'clock. Aunt Lurlene poked her head out the door, waving gayly, and Cody knew she'd done the right thing. It looked like a load of troubles had been lifted from her aunt's care-worn shoulders, and Cody let herself feel some excitement instead of just anxiety and confusion. She opened her car door and called out, "We're having a party! Call everyone and tell them to come over and be hungry!"

—///—

An hour later, her aunts were still frying up steaks for the adults and hamburgers for the kids. A whole keg of beer was out on the front porch and the middle-school kids were having a ball repeatedly running out into the cold to fill everyone's glass. The front door opened so many times it would have been freezing but for the huge number of people crammed into the small house.

This was sweet, Cody thought as she watched everyone laughing and cutting up. The group was happier than they were at Christmas, and it felt great to be the one who could brighten their day like this. She let the feelings wash over her. No one would ever again have to try to make a can of chili serve four for dinner. No one would ever again have to beg everyone they knew to come up with the money to pay real estate taxes. No one would have to deny a child braces or put off getting a hearing aid or any of the hundreds of other things they as a family had been forced to forego. She was smiling like she was part stupid, and the cups of beer the kids kept foisting on her were helping reduce her IQ. But she couldn't put off the grim task she had to complete.

Cody stood up and raised her voice above the din. "The lady at the bank told me I had to take care of a few things and one of them is what would happen to the money in case I died."

The room became quiet enough to hear the spatter of beef fat in the cast iron skillet.

"I don't expect anything to happen, but just in case it does, I'm leaving everything to Uncle Cubby. He's the head of the family, and he'll make sure everyone is taken care of." She looked around the room, smiling tightly. "I've got to fill this form out and have two people witness my signature." She nodded at her most troubled and troublesome cousins, Brett and Ricky. "You two have good handwriting. My witnesses have to be people who won't get anything in case I die." She extended the form. "Sign right here, boys."

CHAPTER FIVE

THE NEXT DAY, CODY spent hours walking around the hollow. When she was outside she could open up her senses and let nature occupy her mind. The money, the fame, the questions her family seemed to have an endless supply of faded into a mildly annoying buzz that she could overpower without too much trouble. She had both dogs with her for a change, and she let them chase anything that moved. Giving them the freedom to do as they liked was strangely pleasurable. Barking and pouncing on everything their eyes or their imaginations encountered, they must've chased fifty squirrels up fifty trees. It was nice watching them cavort around the forest, with no one expecting anything from any of them, and Cody soaked up some of their joy. It took hours, but they were all tuckered out by the time they headed for home. There'd be two surprised pups when they got there. True to her word, when she was at the grocery store the day before she'd talked the man behind the meat counter into selling her the biggest, meatiest bones he had. The dogs were gonna think *they'd* won the lottery.

While she was still twenty yards away from her house, Cody's skin prickled and her hands tingled with alarm. There was trouble. There were fresh tire tracks on the drive, big ones, from a truck. A truck bigger than anyone in her family owned. Very cautiously, she approached the front door, and saw that it was ajar. She should have been more careful, but her temper got the best of her and she burst inside, ready to take on all comers.

Her tidy little trailer had been destroyed. Every book was on the floor, every pillow had been cut open, the cushions from her sofa were ripped apart, and her mattress had been slashed from North to South and East to West.

Her blood pounded furiously in her veins. If she caught the people who did this, she might kill them. She would go to jail, but that certainly wouldn't stop her. Once her temper got the best of her, she lost all control.

Wouldn't that beat all? Spending the rest of her days in prison, with millions of dollars sitting in the bank, mocking her. Cody sank onto the rocker by the door, trying, in vain, to get her anger under control. The whole world had changed in just a day. And that change was probably permanent.

—⁓—

She stayed with her mama's youngest sister, her aunt Merry that night since she had the longest couch and the fewest grandchildren likely to show up unannounced.

They sat up for hours talking about what had happened and what it meant. "Why would someone do it?" Cody asked for the tenth time.

"I'm telling you the truth, honey. Everyone who doesn't think they're gonna get some wants to take it from you."

She looked at her aunt, feeling like her guts were going to explode. "It's a rare day that I turn my back on someone who needs something I can spare." Her face hardened into stone. "But when you steal from me…it's on."

—⁓—

Cody spent the whole next day cleaning up everything she could possibly clean up. Because all of her food containers had been ripped apart, or the contents dumped out, the kitchen took a very long time to fix. At least they hadn't opened her cans and jars. Small comfort. At one point or another during the day everyone in the family had stopped by and helped to a greater or lesser extent, making her feel less alone—less violated.

The group had been as angry and outraged as she'd been, and that went a long way towards settling her down. Anger diluted quickly when it was shared.

She ruminated about the advice that had trickled in throughout the day, and for a change it had been unanimous. Everyone thought she should buy a real house, and outfit it with every kind of alarm and security camera available. But she wasn't going to do that. Her trailer was all she needed, and buying things just because you had the money was stupid. That's how people got in trouble. She would not be the kind of person who had it all and lost it all. There would be no TV show about her, crying as the sheriff dispossessed her from a big, gaudy house, with cars and boats being carted off to auction. No, she would spend what she needed to spend, and give what she needed to give. Everything else was security, and you could never have enough of that. That's why she was going to keep a gun with her more often. That was the type of security thieves understood.

———

Driving to Ramp, West Virginia, without asking for precise directions was not the brightest thing Maddie had ever done. Yes, her managers had made it clear that she was supposed to take an active interest in her clients and her community, but she knew this was taking it much further than that. But when she'd called to tell Cody her cash would be available tomorrow, and learned her house had been robbed—Well, she had to go check in on her.

Maddie wasn't usually the social-worker type, but Cody had struck a chord with her. It was hard to put a finger on her appeal. Maybe it was her naiveté. Actually, calling it naiveté was being generous. Cody knew nothing…nothing about managing money, and she'd had a load of it dumped into her lap. It was like putting a chimp in a spacecraft and expecting him to be able to figure out how to get to Mars. But it was clear Cody wasn't dumb; she just didn't understand money. Once she understood what to do and how to do it, Maddie was certain she'd be a good steward of her vast fortune. They just had to make sure she didn't get herself killed before she got there.

Maddie thought about the woman, picturing her when she'd revealed she'd won. She seemed happy, in a way, but strangely matter-of-fact. There was something admirable about that, in Maddie's view. She much preferred being around people who took things in stride and didn't freak out about the small things. Not that Cody's haul was small. It was ridiculously large, and Maddie could easily make herself shiver just thinking about the responsibility having it would entail.

She'd never been up in the mountains, even though she'd been in the area for a couple of months. People in Greenville acted like there was a virtual gate keeping "hill folks" up where they belonged. The further she got from Greenville, the more she thought they might have had a point. The hills themselves were rolling and filled with evergreens and sculptural trees, but humans had scarred the land, in places blowing entire tops of mountains off. And the garbage! People had heaped every kind of trash known to man onto their property. Abandoned cars, motorcycles with the front forks missing, ravines filled with household trash, a trampoline sitting in the front yard of a house, the front door so close you could have jumped right on—if one of the supporting legs hadn't been missing. These folks had stopped caring. There was no other explanation. They just couldn't or wouldn't go to the trouble of bringing their kids' toys into the house, preferring to let them be covered with mildew. What a depressing, hopeless way to live.

As she moved on, the houses grew further apart, then they stopped appearing completely. It seemed like there were homes—she saw wood smoke curling up into the sky occasionally—they were just tucked back, way back off the road. She looked at the GPS display on her dash. It showed the road she was on, and then...nothing. No roads branching off, no businesses, no schools. At the base of a long, winding hill a flat spot in the terrain revealed a gas station, and a small building next to it, but that was the full extent of obvious human habitation. She'd been driving for well over an hour. Ramp, ostensibly, was right around here. But Cody's address was more than elusive. Maddie's cell phone had zero signal, a situation that always made her anxious. She was as tied to her phone as she was to her dearest relatives, silly as that was to admit. Not being able to call for help was deeply unsettling.

The county road stretched out into the distance on the GPS, but the blip of a town it showed now was Delilah, and that was supposed to come after Ramp. She'd checked the map on her computer before she left, and had noted the colorful name. That meant she'd skipped right by Ramp. What had Lynnette said? That it was a squiggle in the road? That might have been giving it more credit than it deserved.

She was following tire tracks in the hard-packed snow, wondering if the state or the county ever got out there to plow. It sure didn't look like it. As she was ruminating about the lack of services in rural areas, she hit a depression and veered just far enough from the track to roll off the road and slowly drift into the ditch. Oh, this was a smart move. Fucking brilliant!

There hadn't been much snow in Virginia, where she'd learned to drive, but even Maddie knew that it wouldn't do a damned bit of good to try to force the car out by gunning the engine. That would only dig her in deeper.

She'd had the presence of mind to wear her heaviest boots, and her coat was quite warm. Hat and gloves were right on the seat. At least she was prepared for the weather. Now the question was where to go. It was about two, and that gave her a couple of hours before dark. Hell, if she hadn't found civilization by dark, the wolves would probably eat her. Were there wolves in West Virginia? Damned if she knew.

Running on the treadmill at the health club had her in shape to keep up a quick pace on her walk. She had no idea where she was going, but she was in a damned hurry to get there. She'd passed a couple of spots that might have led to houses, but the roads had been prominently marked with various threats of bodily harm to all trespassers. And she was being optimistic in calling them roads. They were more like paths barely wide enough for cars.

Something caught her eye up ahead. She eventually recognized it as a truck parked well off the road. Just as she got to it, two men in camouflage coats tromped out of the woods, each carrying a shotgun, or a rifle, or something you could kill someone with. She didn't know beans about guns, and wasn't in a curious mood at the moment. "Hello," she called out when they stopped dead and stared at her. "My car went off the road."

"Why're you here?" the bigger one asked. His words were relatively benign, but his affect wasn't. She could feel herself trembling, but fought to stay calm. Lots of people carried guns. They were probably hunters. But weren't hunters supposed to wear orange? Wasn't that some kind of rule?

"I'm looking for Cody Keaton," she managed. "Do you know her?"

"No," the smaller, yet meaner-looking man replied. Too quickly in Maddie's mind. "You'd best keep going, lady. You've got no business here."

"Well, actually I do." She wasn't going to act like a frightened child. People respected confidence. She hoped. "Cody's a client of mine. I manage the Appalachian States Bank branch in Greenville."

"Long way from here," the bigger man said, suspiciously.

"Yes, it is. And I'd love to get back to town. But I can't walk there and I can't push my own car. So I'd appreciate a ride or a push or something." She stood there, trying to look confident. "What'll it be?" she added, when they didn't respond quickly.

The smaller man pointed his gun at the truck. "Get in," he growled.

Great. Now she'd backed herself into a lovely corner. She had to get into a truck with two gun-toting strangers...on a road in the middle of nowhere...where her cell phone didn't work. Gee, maybe she could have made dumber decisions, but she doubted it.

The smaller guy got in, and the larger one opened the passenger door, signaling that she should get in next. Why not? It was undoubtedly best to be in the middle, with no chance of breaking away if they decided to kill, maim or dismember her.

They started off, with the big truck rumbling along the rutted road, chomping up snow with its massive tires. Small talk was mandatory. Her pounding heart would no doubt be audible in the tense silence. "Where are we headed?"

"You'll see," the chatty smaller man said, not uttering another sound. They'd only gone a few hundred yards when he turned abruptly and headed down what looked like no road at all. But after a few moments, Maddie could see tire tread patterns along the narrow drive. Then, in the clearing, was a trailer. It was old, definitely old, like from another era, but it looked neat and well-maintained. There wasn't one bit of trash lying about, no half-standing sheds and no ancient, overturned bathtubs, which was a relief. They pulled up to the front and Cody emerged, wearing a grey sweatshirt with "ARMY" stenciled across it, and a pair of blue sweatpants. Both were huge on her, and when she leaned over to look into the truck Maddie could see her bare chest through the neck of the garment.

Maddie hadn't known Cody had a sense of humor. But when she said, "Did your mail order bride come in, Stumpy?" Maddie almost choked.

"Found her on the road. Says she's from the bank."

"I might have met her before," she drawled, then gave Maddie a sly smile. "Following me?"

"No! Well...no, I'm not. I just came to see you. But my car got stuck not too far down the road and these gentlemen offered me a ride."

"We didn't offer," Stumpy said. "She almost took the keys from me."

"I'll see you home," Cody said and walked around to the passenger side.

"In what?" the larger man asked. "Your truck's still tore up, ain't it?"

"We'll manage. Thanks for helping," Cody said, nodding as the men backed up down the drive.

They stood there, watching them leave. "I guess I should have called first, but I...didn't. It was lucky for me those guys were out hunting."

Cody's expression was impassive. "They don't hunt."

"But they had guns..."

Shaking her head slowly, Cody said, "I don't know what they do, or where they do it, but they don't hunt." She raised an eyebrow, and her gaze grew more intense. "If it were me, I'd stay off their land. I wouldn't ask many questions, either. People around here like—no, *demand* their privacy."

Oh, fuck.

———

Cody stood there in front of the house, wondering why in the world she wasn't tongue-tied and nervous. She'd never had an unrelated woman in her house, not to mention a pretty one. But Miss Osborne was on her turf now, and that gave her access to most of her natural confidence.

She knew she was being a little dramatic with her warning, but she honestly didn't know what Stumpy and George were up to, and it was clear Miss Osborne didn't know how touchy local people could be.

"I'm so sorry for showing up without notice," Maddie said, dropping her head dramatically while grasping Cody's arm. "I should have told you I was coming."

She sure did have a habit of touching people. That was...different. "I think most folks around here are friendly enough, but I don't wander onto other people's land, and I've lived here my whole life. You'd best be careful, Miss Osborne." She'd forgotten her secret spot with the babbling brook was on private land, but that was a detail Miss Osborne didn't have to know about.

"I will. I definitely will. And you have to call me Maddie, okay?"

"If you're sure."

"I am."

Maddie's gaze went to the door and Cody snapped out of her fog to dash over and open it. "Come on in. It doesn't look too good for company, but..." She held the door when Maddie climbed the stairs and entered.

"Oh, Cody, this is so..." She actually looked like she might cry. Looking at it as an outsider would, Cody acknowledged it did look pretty bad. She'd had to put a sheet over the sofa, since the cushions were gone. The darned thing looked too sad without some kind of cover. Luckily, the thieves hadn't cut the frame apart, allowing a place for company to sit. They'd kicked her bookcases over, and, given they were old and cheap, they'd split apart at different spots. All of her books were stacked next to their former homes, awaiting stable shelves. Taking a look down the hall, you could see that her mattress was gone. She'd get a new one, and could afford it now, but still didn't have access to a truck. For now a sheet of bare plywood made it clear she had no decent place to sleep.

"Yeah, it was awfully upsetting. Not because of the stuff. I can replace everything. It was the invasion of privacy. That's a betrayal I can't abide."

"I've never been robbed, so I can only imagine how it must feel."

"Now imagine that someone you know did it." Just repeating that fact made her angry all over again. Only someone from the hollow would know where she lived.

"Horrible. Just horrible." She shook her head slowly. "Will you stay?"

"Where would I go? This is my home."

"Oh, of course. I just thought you might..."

"What?"

"Well, most people who come into a lot of money buy a big house. That's almost universal, I'd say."

"I wouldn't say it," Cody said, then walked over to the kitchen, asking, "How about some cocoa?"

———

Maddie hoped she hadn't upset Cody when she'd asked about moving. But who would want to stay in a small, old—no, ancient—trailer when you had millions of dollars? It boggled the mind.

Moving around the living space, Maddie noticed a large number of school photos taped or tacked onto the pine-paneled walls. Looking closely, she saw that some of them were decades old. "Are these your relatives?" she asked.

Cody came to stand by her. "Uh-huh. This is my mama and daddy when they were little." She pointed out two photos. "And this is them on their wedding day." A bigger, framed photo sat in a place of honor on a table by the sofa.

"They look happy," Maddie said.

"They were for the most part."

"Are they…alive?"

"No. Both passed on. Daddy when I was in fourth grade, Mama when I was about to finish my junior year."

"Of high school?"

"I didn't go to college."

Of course she didn't go to college! What a stupid question. Watch yourself, you idiot!

Cody walked over to the electric stove and stirred the pan of cocoa, then poured it into mugs and brought them back. "Here you go. It's hot, so be careful."

Maddie cooled it by blowing across the surface. "Is everyone else a brother or sister?" There were far too many people for that to be true, but she was interested and didn't take the time to frame the question properly.

"No. Just this one." She pointed at a photo of a boy about ten. "My brother, Keith. He's gone too."

Doh! Lynnette had said he'd been killed…in a meth lab explosion. It was probably best to keep her idle questions to herself. "He was a nice-looking boy."

"He was. He was seven years older than me," she said quietly, staring at his picture like he'd step out of it and be standing right next to them. "He was like a god to me when I was young."

That cold expression settled onto her face and Maddie wished she'd not started this walk down memory lane. Then Cody pointed at a faded photo of an older woman, and a smile came back to her face.

"This is my granny," she said with some pride. "She was the glue that held us all together."

"She's pretty. You look a little bit like her."

"I hope so, but I'd rather *be* like her. She was good people." Cody started to walk into the bedroom, and Maddie followed along. "Granny was a heck of a quilter." A quilt hanger sat under the small window. She removed a colorful quilt from it and spread it onto the platform of her bed. "If those fellas had hurt this quilt, I would have tracked them down and killed them."

She said that with such cold-blooded venom that Maddie felt a chill race down her spine.

But then Cody's voice softened and she added, "This was her place. After Daddy died and we couldn't make it in Greenville, we had to come home. I was glad, but Mama and Keith had to struggle with it."

How did you respond to that? Maddie tried to keep things upbeat. "I didn't know you'd lived in Greenville." *Of course you didn't, idiot!*

"Yeah. Born in Huntington, then moved to Greenville, then back here. I spent every summer here with Granny, so it felt like home already to me. But not Mama..." She trailed off, took the quilt and folded it carefully, then placed it back on the rack.

Maddie took that as her signal to head back to the living area. She chose the sofa to sit on, even though it was too low to sit upon with anything resembling grace. Next time she'd wear slacks. Skirts didn't lend themselves well to tromping through snow, pushing cars out of ditches, or sitting on sofa frames devoid of cushions.

Cody sat in the rocker by the window and sipped at her cocoa. She seemed perfectly at ease sitting quietly, but Maddie needed some chatter. "So...what are your plans for the money?"

"Don't have any. I just want to provide for my family."

"You can provide for every family in the county if you want to."

"No, thanks. Mine's big enough."

"Uhm, I hope this doesn't sound like I'm overstepping, but try to set some rules. I'd hate to see anyone take advantage of you."

Frowning, Cody said, "We're not like that. We do for each other. After Daddy died, and again after Mama went, everybody did whatever they could. They did without so we could have some. What's mine, is theirs. They just have to ask, and they can have it."

Oh, that sounded like a very, very bad idea, but it wasn't her place to push her point. "I…uhm…saw you on TV the other day. I know you don't have a full-time job, but you made it clear you work hard."

Cody started to laugh, and her hand snapped up to cover her mouth and hide that broken tooth. "I did make that clear, didn't I? He frosted me bad."

"He was an asshole," Maddie said, then slapped her mouth, mirroring Cody for entirely different reasons. "I'm so sorry," she added. "My mouth gets away from me. I'm really trying to stop using foul language, but…"

"You don't need to apologize to me. Given that he was, you're not even wrong factually." She chuckled, looking pleased. "It's hard to explain to folks from the city how a person can make do without much out in the hills. And…some of what we do isn't exactly legal…"

Damn! Was she going to confess to selling drugs? "Lots of things aren't exactly legal," Maddie said, although why that sentence had come out was beyond her.

"I pay my taxes, same as everyone else. The government has no right to tell me I can't take some moss. There's plenty of it, and I'm careful to never pick a spot clean."

Maddie nodded, then realized she had no idea what Cody was talking about. "Moss?"

"That's how I make money. I pick and sell moss when the weather's right. If I work hard enough, I can put away enough money to tide me over for the winter. Hunting helps, of course. That and my big garden let me get by fine." She got up and went to the kitchen, showing a cabinet full of Mason jars, lined up according to type. "Big year for beans and beets and asparagus and sweet potatoes. But my tomatoes didn't do diddly-squat. And planting corn is a complete waste of time. One of these years I'll learn my lesson and stop trying to grow tomatoes, but I dearly want to be able to make chow-chow."

"That's…remarkable. How do you…who buys moss?"

"A guy from over near you. He buys all I can pick and sells it to somebody…I don't know who."

"But *why* does anyone buy moss?"

"Oh. Florists, I think. They say there's good money in it. For someone. Then I trade and barter and fix things for people for a few dollars here or there. I'm handy," she added, looking down with apparent embarrassment. She probably didn't want to boast.

"That sounds like a lot of work. I can see why you said you work as hard as anyone."

"That was bragging," she admitted shyly. "But I work from can't see to can't see in the spring and summer. Twelve to fourteen hours in the woods, taking a little moss and walking farther on to make sure I don't make too big a mark." She stuck her chin out and added, "I know the forest is for all of us, and I'm taking things from federal or state land and that's a crime, but we've got to eat, and taking moss is better than selling drugs."

"A lot better. I wish there were more jobs around here. I see how people struggle."

With a scoff, Cody said, "You don't see much of it. People with bank accounts are doing fine."

She made having an account at Appalachian States Bank seem like having a numbered Swiss account. "What…how…don't you ever need to write a check? How do you pay your bills?"

"Fast Money in Twined Creek or the post office. One of us has to run up there almost every day to buy a postal money order."

Oh, that should have been obvious. Check cashing places like Fast Money prospered from charging high fees for cashing things like government checks, which were as good as cash. They were predators, taking no risk while fleecing people, but Maddie didn't think this was the day to lecture Cody about them. "That makes perfect sense. But you won't have to use them anymore. Your personal checks will be here in about a week. Then you can kiss Fast Money goodbye."

They hadn't known each other long, but Maddie knew the closed expression that greeted her meant that Cody wasn't at all sure she was going to maintain her checking account. She put her cocoa down and said, "We'd better get you on your way. It gets dark early up here."

Cody went into her bedroom, and when she came back she was wearing her normal Army uniform. She tugged at the field jacket and said,

"I wish my cousin had been sent somewhere cold. I'd really love to have one of those winter parkas. And snow pants."

Mattie reminded herself that it was going to take Cody a while to get comfortable with the fact that she could buy a chain of Army-Navy surplus stores. Probably a very long while.

They took off on their walk after Cody stopped at a small shed next to a very large cleared spot now covered in straw. That must've been the garden. She emerged with a shovel and a big rubber doormat. Holding up the mat, she said, "Good for traction."

They walked along the road, single file, because Cody said you never knew who was going to come roaring around a corner. That prohibited them from speaking much, but Maddie didn't mind. She almost never got out into the fresh air, and she had to admit the scenery was better than staring at the little TV on the treadmill at her gym.

"Sons of bitches," Cody muttered quietly when she caught sight of the car. Someone had thoughtfully moved it from the ditch, but they did it to remove the wheels and tires. The car perched precariously on a number of different sized rocks, looking like a strong breeze would send it tumbling back into the ditch. "Too lazy or too stupid to bother using concrete blocks." She shook her head, turned, and headed right back to her house, with Maddie struggling to keep up.

Cody spent a good fifteen minutes on the phone, calling person after person, demanding the return of Maddie's wheels. Finally, Maddie heard her say, "I'm sure you don't know where they are, Zeke, but let's say you have a guess. Maybe you could have that guess put those wheels back before I kick its ass." She was quiet for a minute, listening to the reply. "Yes, I did tell her that we don't like unexpected visitors. I didn't have to make too big a point of it, though. A couple of guys from back in the woods scared the puddin' out of her, keeping us all safe from lady bankers." She hung up and gazed at Maddie through half lidded eyes. "I'm really sorry about all of this. We act like that and then complain when people talk bad about us."

"Don't worry about it. I could call…somebody to come get me."

"No, your wheels will be there by the time we get back. I guarantee it."

Cody was a woman of her word. The wheels were stacked neatly, one next to the other, covering the entire road side of the car. Grumbling quiet curses, Cody got to work, using the jack and the tire iron like a pro. Maddie wouldn't say that Cody didn't break a sweat, but the sweat she broke was not as great as the one Maddie would have broken if she'd done the work herself. Actually, she'd have no idea how to change a tire. She'd probably be sitting in the dangerously tilting car, crying like a frightened child.

—⁓—

Cody was also right about how early darkness came. It wasn't even four o'clock, and the sun had disappeared behind the mountain. Now that the wind had picked up, Maddie was cold even with the heater on full blast. Cody warmed her hands on the air blowing from the vents. "This is nice," she said softly. "I don't think I've ever had a heater that worked."

Maddie tried to imagine what that would be like, but found she could barely summon it up. There was a world of difference between the way she and Cody lived. She silently worried if Cody would ever be able to be comfortable in her world...where you expected your car heater to work and complained bitterly when it didn't throw out just the right amount of warm air.

When they got to the turnoff for Cody's place, she instructed, "Just let me out here."

"I can take you all the way in."

"There's no need." She got out and walked around to the driver's-side window, which Maddie lowered. "Thanks very much for coming to check on me." As her mouth worked into a grin, her gloved hand covered it. "Now don't come again. I actually know a guy who hides animal traps around his place. I'd hate to see you have to gnaw your own foot off to escape."

—⁓—

Once again, Cody spent the night at her aunt Merry's house. She was going to have to hustle to borrow a truck to tote a new mattress home, but there was no way she'd ask Curly again. He'd want half of the mattress.

It was tough sleeping on the sofa. Cody's back ached bad, the pain waking her before dawn. Not wanting to make any noise, she got dressed and snuck out, headed for home. It was too early for most things to be awake, but years of experience and missed opportunities now compelled her to walk quietly and carefully no matter the time or season. You never knew when you'd see something doing something that brought a smile to your face. Since it was a habit, she naturally approached her own home with the same quiet regard. She'd obviously done a good job of being stealthy because about a dozen men attacking her garden with picks and shovels didn't hear her. Her instinct was to grab as many of them as she could and bang their stupid heads together. But then she realized they were actually doing a job she'd have to do in a few months. If these idiots wanted to turn her frozen garden over why not let them?

They were actually working as frantically as if someone was coming along after them with a whip. That made Cody laugh quietly. Some of those suckers hadn't worked that hard in ten years. She hoped they'd have a nice supply of blisters on their hands and aches in their backs when they were finished.

A couple of them leaned on their shovels, looking completely tuckered out. Given they'd turned over the entire garden, they'd probably been there most of the night. Just to make sure they had a friendly message from her, she snuck into the house, grabbed her shotgun, stood on her front steps and blasted it into the air. "I know every one of you sons-of-bitches, and I will *kill* you if you come again." As they scampered down the drive she laughed, holding her arm over her mouth to tamp down the sound. It wouldn't do to let them know she found the whole thing funny. Another shotgun blast made the slowest one, Butterbean Jerwin, grab his droopy jeans and run for all he was worth, which wasn't much.

She couldn't get hold of anyone at the newspaper until after eight a.m. Lazy fools. Finally, she was connected to someone who wrote for the county beat. "This is Cody Keaton," she explained. "The woman who won the big lottery. I have something I want to put in the paper."

"Uhm…I guess I could interview you. We don't let people just make statements."

"Fine. Interview me. Make your first question be what I'm doing with my money."

Okay," the man said slowly. "What are you planning on doing with the money?"

"I'm putting it all in the bank. By all, I mean all. I don't have any on my person, in my house, in my car, or in my yard. The only thing I'm *going* to have plenty of is shotgun shells, and I'm not afraid to use them. So, if people don't want to be picking buckshot out of their butts, they'd best stay away."

CHAPTER SIX

HAVING NOT SEEN AUNT Lily in a few days, Cody headed over there after her discussion with the reporter. Today seemed like a good day for some squirrel hunting while in her aunt's neighborhood. Squirrels had stored a hoard of acorns in the big oak trees that fall. If she sat quietly enough, long enough, it'd be like shooting fish in a barrel.

They sat at the kitchen table, quietly chatting over cups of coffee. She'd just finished telling her about that morning's interlopers when her cousin Bobby came out of the bathroom. He'd just heard the tail end, and his mother played the whole story out again, making it sound a little more colorful than it really had been.

"They'll come for us next," Bobby said. "It ain't safe here no more."

"It'll all die down soon," Cody said, not really believing that.

Bobby answered the ringing phone. "Yeah? No, I can't go all the way to Twined Creek!" He looked like he was going to throw the phone, and Cody hoped her poor aunt wouldn't have to once again pay the phone company come out to repair the wires. "If she needs to come home, you go get her."

"Who needs a ride?" Cody asked, wondering which car she could borrow.

"Melody," Bobby said, referring to his eldest child. "They want to send her home *again*. She's carrying on about something or other."

"I'll go," Cody said.

He looked like he'd argue, but put the receiver to his mouth again and said, "Cody's gonna go," then hung up. He looked at his cousin. "That child's always crying about somethin'. If she keeps missing days they'll keep her back. Then it's second grade all over again." He shrugged. "Hey, pick me up a six pack and a pack of Camels on the way back, will you?" His stormy expression turned into a smile and he amended his order. "You've got money. Make it a case and a carton."

———

She borrowed Bobby's car, which would probably get her there and back, and even though she knew it wasn't wise, she put her shotgun in the trunk. She would much rather have had it right on the seat, but she couldn't do that with a child in the car. Cody pulled up in front of the elementary school and parked in the crowded lot. She'd attended the same school after they'd moved from Greenville. Years later it still gave her the creeps. Things hadn't been great for her during those years. She could still feel the taunts of the other kids, singling her out for being new and poorer than most.

The principal's office was right where she'd remembered, but it seemed a lot smaller than it had when she was a girl. A pleasant-looking woman sat behind a high counter. Cody caught her attention by clearing her throat. "I'm here to pick up my cousin, Melody Montgomery."

"Oh, right. I'll tell the principal." She went into the office behind the counter and closed the door. A few minutes later, a woman emerged with Melody clinging to her skirt. The child's eyes were puffy and red and her cheeks were blotchy. She didn't even look up at Cody, which was a little surprising, since they were pretty good buddies.

The principal almost had to peel Melody's fingers from her skirt, then she gently pushed her towards Cody. "She had a tough time at recess. I think she might as well go home and start fresh tomorrow."

Cody reached out and took Melody's hand, but the child still didn't meet her eyes. The principal shrugged and said, "Congratulations on your good fortune. It must feel great."

"Uhm, it's good. Of course it's good," she said, knowing that was the right answer. "I'll see you."

They walked down the hall, with Melody sniffling and wiping her nose on her sleeve. "I think I have a tissue somewhere," Cody said, looking in her pockets. "You don't wanna get your coat all messy." As she said that she took a closer look at the child. Her coat was not only dirty and ill-fitting, it was torn all along one sleeve. Someone had used duct tape to mend it, calling attention to the rip like a neon sign. The little girl's running shoes were decent enough, but wholly inadequate to the snow and cold they'd been having. Cody was just about to ask if she didn't have boots when Melody let out a garbled cry.

Cody got down to her level and asked, "What happened, Little Bits?"

"Amber and Hayley said you must not love me if you let me go to school with a ugly coat. They said you've got more money than anybody, but you won't give me none." She threw her arms around Cody's neck and cried until she was gasping for breath.

That hit her like a kick to the gut. She gathered Melody up in her arms and carried her to the car, murmuring, "I love you more than anything in the world, Little Bits. Those girls don't know what they're talking about." They got in the car and Cody tried to sound upbeat. "We've got the whole day to ourselves. Let's go buy a few things."

An hour later, Melody had the spiffiest, pink, down parka available in Summit County. Her new pink jeans and pink turtleneck seemed like overkill to Cody, but Melody insisted pink was the only color anyone wore. Cody had insisted on navy blue boots, just so they'd look decent after jumping in the slush, and Melody seemed to agree they were cool. They were headed back to Ramp when Melody said, "Could I go back to school?"

"Really? You want to go today?"

"Yeah," she said, smiling brightly, showing a gap from the missing front tooth she'd lost the week before. "I wanna show everybody my new stuff." She gave Cody a look that bordered on idolatry. "I've never had a coat that was only mine."

Cody had to bite her cheek to keep from bursting into tears. It had been nearly twenty years, but she knew exactly what it felt like to be the one everyone picked on for being poor. It was a scar that would probably never heal, and she vowed to make sure none of her little cousins would ever again look like they got dressed courtesy of the rag bag.

The day had been so stressful, Cody figured she might as well go for broke. Her cash had arrived, and she was anxious to get her hands on it.

The concept of checks and savings accounts made sense in the abstract, but greenbacks were real.

She tried to settle her nerves while walking into the bank. There were quite a few customers milling about; nonetheless, Maddie quickly excused herself from a conversation she was having and came over. She wasn't smiling this time. "I have what we talked about in the vault. What would you like to do with it?"

"I want to put it in my safe deposit box."

Maddie's expression was grim, but she nodded. "You're going to need a bigger box."

―⁓―

Cody sat in the privacy room, gazing, open mouthed, at the cart Maddie had wheeled in. Banded stacks of hundred dollar bills filled six plastic cartons, almost to the brim.

She had no idea the money would take up this much space, and this was a relatively small piece of it. For no reason, she started counting it, feeling like Midas. Each pack had a hundred bills, and after counting a few dozen bundles of the individual bills, she satisfied herself with counting the packs. Then she arranged them in different patterns, piling them up as high as they could go without toppling over. She played with it for over an hour, relishing the deeply reassuring feeling of having cash in her hands.

Not generally a sentimental person, she spent a while daydreaming about how different things would have been if they'd had even a tiny fraction of this money when she was little. Some would argue the point, but she was certain her mama, daddy and brother would all be alive if they'd had any money at all. It was hard, really hard to enjoy it now since she didn't actually need it, or at least not much of it, but that was life. She had it, and even though it had come too late, it was there now.

She filled four of the bank's biggest boxes, then took the seven thousand dollars Maddie had given her the other day and put it in her pockets. Everyone was going to assume she had money on her. It probably didn't do any harm to carry some of it. Maybe that would satisfy whoever tried to take it from her.

―⁓―

Maddie looked up and saw Cody heading back across the lobby. Even from a distance you could see she was skittish. Maybe it was the money, or just being in the bank, whatever caused her nerves made her walk like she feared someone was behind her, about to catch up. Her head turned when she passed Maddie's office and she took a hard left when they made eye contact. Cody leaned against the door, clearly antsy. "Thanks for getting the money for me."

"My pleasure. It was kinda fun doing something a little different. Not many people ask for a million dollars in cash."

"I bet not." Cody walked in farther and closed the door. "Hey, I have a question. I want to get some things for my family. The kids could use new shoes and coats and things like that. How should I do it?"

Hmm…that question couldn't have been as simple as it sounded. "Do you mean…technically?"

"Yeah, I guess." With her lips pursed and eyes narrowed, she looked like a scholar figuring out a difficult problem.

"Why don't you give them five or ten thousand each and let them buy what they need?"

"Ten thousand?" She blanched. "I was thinking about a few hundred. I just bought a coat and jeans and boots for one of my cousins and everything was only fifty dollars."

Maddie had to laugh at that. Cody had obviously gone to the ramshackle place on the outskirts of town that specialized in deeply discounted merchandize. "Winter clothes?"

Cody nodded. "Yeah. Why does that matter?"

"It's the end of the season. Everything was probably half price or less." She gazed at Cody until she looked directly into her eyes. "You have to loosen up a little. They'll resent you if you don't. If those kids need shoes…"

"Yeah, they do," she admitted. "Some mean little cusses teased my cousin and said I didn't love her enough to buy her a decent coat." She punched her leg hard enough to make Maddie wince for her. "If it wasn't against the law to beat up a kid, I'd find those little monsters…"

Despite her venomous words, Maddie felt her heart go out to Cody. The poor woman was as lost as a little lamb. Maddie walked around to the front of her desk and perched on the edge of it. "Let's cut cashier's checks for your relatives. Then they can buy what they need."

"No, no," Cody complained. "They'll have to pay two percent to cash them. It's better if I give them cash."

"You have your checks now, don't you?"

"Yeah. I got them yesterday."

"Well, you can write a check anywhere. Take them out and buy them what they want. Then just write a check. We put fifty thousand in your checking account. Go crazy."

"I don't like to go crazy," she said, looking very worried. "I like to go slow."

"I understand. But don't hand out wads of cash. Someone will see them waving it around. You know that's not good."

"No, that's really not good. Did I tell you about the thieves I found digging up my garden?"

That made Maddie sick to her stomach. "Oh, Cody." She impulsively leaned over and hugged her, smelling woodsmoke on her jacket. "I'm so sorry."

"It's all right. I'll get this figured out."

"You could always open bank accounts for each of them. Then they'd have their own money and it would be safe."

She shook her head. "I don't think so. That's moving awfully fast."

"I know it's only been a few days…but your family might not see it that way."

"Yeah, they might not." She looked deflated when she got up, but she put on a small smile and nodded, then headed for the door. Maddie sat there for a while, wondering how long Cody's relatives would put up with her cautious nature. Not too long, she guessed. There would have to be a showdown.

—⁓—

When Cody got back to the hollow, she called every branch of the family and announced they were going shopping. Her announcement was greeted with such elation, she realized they'd been fully expecting the call. She should have gotten her butt into gear sooner, but it was hard to know what to do and when to do it.

As soon as the stores opened the next day she picked up all four of her aunts for their expedition. Her aunt Merry desperately needed a new refrigerator, so that was first on the list. Aunt Lily insisted she didn't need a thing, but she eventually allowed that a new stove and microwave wouldn't be unappreciated. Neither Lurlene nor Thelma would accept anything for herself, even though Cody knew her aunt Lurlene only had one burner on her stove that worked.

Then they went to the biggest store in town, the one that had mannequins and showed things nicely arranged, and bought clothes and shoes for each grandchild. The kids' moms could have done it, but Cody trusted her aunts more than her female cousins or her male cousins' current and former girlfriends. Her aunts had some sense. Even so, the checks she wrote staggered her. Buying each child two pairs of shoes and a pair of winter boots, along with jeans, shirts, underwear and jackets would have taken a working woman's entire salary for a month or two. How did people do it?

They headed home and were still unloading the goods when Uncle Shooter came out of his trailer and said, "How about the adults? We need some toys too."

He looked to be kidding, but she knew he wasn't. It was time to loosen up and let them go a bit wild. "Where do you want to go?"

"Outdoor Universe," he said without missing a beat. "We all want to go."

Cody had never been to the place, but several of her cousins had, and they regarded it with a kind of awe. "Tomorrow morning," she said. "We'll caravan."

They made a conscious decision to not take any children, which caused an amazing amount of wailing and moaning. But Cody, ten cousins and two uncles took off, childless, for Charleston in their caravan on a crisp, bright, cold morning.

The store was beyond imagining. They had everything from canoes, to sleeping bags, to all manner of firearms, to every kind of gear one could use when camping.

They'd been inside for scant minutes when the female cousins headed to the clothing section. Cody followed along, just to observe. She liked to get the lay of the land before she made any quick decisions. The girls took armloads full of stuff into a single large dressing room and started trying things on. Cody stood by the door, playing along while each piece was critiqued. But that got old fast, so she set out to find the men. She had an idea they'd be a good distance from the clothing section.

As she assumed, every man in the family was gathered in the hunting department. It seemed everyone wanted a weapon, and it made her nervous to see how many people wanted pistols rather than rifles. Yes, you could hunt with a pistol, but she worried they would use them against humans more than game.

One thing no one could get enough of was ammunition. They cleaned the shelves, filling up two large shopping carts, leaving nothing but BBs for the rest of the customers.

Devin surprised her by taking a hunting bow. He'd never been a bow hunter, but she supposed she could teach him. If he ever left home, that is. You couldn't bow hunt in the living room.

Surveying the men, Cody saw that Uncle Cubby didn't have a thing. "Don't you want a new shotgun?" she asked, sidling up alongside him.

"No, I'm fine." He had a happy smile plastered onto his face, and refused all enticements. "I can take care of myself," he insisted. "But it's nice you're being so generous with the kids."

"It's my pleasure," she said. "I'd love to get something for you too."

"No, thanks. My gun works fine. It's only my butt that needs a swift kick once in a while." He chuckled. "That's what Lurlene says."

She watched her cousins arguing about which caliber and style of weapon was best, while thinking about her uncle. She wouldn't admit it to anyone, but she was secretly pleased he was opting out of the buying frenzy. It was nice not to feel he thought she owed him anything. But she knew he'd take a gift. It'd be rude not to. She'd get to buying him something as soon as she could catch her breath.

When weapon shopping seemed to be petering out, Cody went in search of the girls. She was stopped dead in her tracks by a pair of boots. She almost laughed at how silly it was, but found herself regarding the boots with something akin to awe. They were sliced in half, sitting on an eye-level shelf, with all their wondrous qualities in stark display. She'd had boots before, of course, but had never owned new ones. There was always a pair at the resale shop that fit well enough and could last her a season or two. But they were usually construction boots, not really suited for trekking across hill and dale through snow, slush, ice.

But these…these miracles of technology…promised to keep your feet warm and dry come hell or high water. They also were significantly lighter and more flexible than any boot she'd ever worn, which made her mind do funny things…like think of herself bouncing along a trail, lifting off the ground as she sprang along after a day in the woods. She was being lured into buying something really, really expensive, but she was powerless. She had the money, plenty of money, and she had the desire. A desire she'd never let herself feel had overtaken her, and she had to have those darned boots. Waterproof, extra-insulated, fatigue-fighting, flexible, lightweight—all of the things she hadn't known she'd needed—she now needed badly.

Her skin itched and she scratched at her neck roughly, as though she could make the desire leave if she rubbed it away. The boots were a hundred and fifty dollars. A hundred and fifty dollars for a pair of shoes! She'd never paid that much for anything other than her car, and that had only been a thousand. Yet, here she was, working her way through the display, finding her size and trying them on before she could talk herself out of it. They felt like a little bit of heaven on her feet. As light as a pair of running shoes, but meant for a day of standing and walking and standing some more. *Heaven.* She tucked the box under her arm and went to find her cousins. It was time to leave before she started to run through the aisles, satisfying every other urge she'd never known she had.

No one else was ready to go, so Cody had to go along to the little cafeteria, where they nearly filled the place, laughing and joking like they were all slightly high. Then it was the time of reckoning. Cody was terrified they wouldn't let her write a check for such a huge amount. She stood in the checkout lane nervously chewing on the inside of her cheek. She'd be truly humiliated if they refused her. Frantic with worry, she didn't see Mandy come up and thrust something at her. Cody put her hands up defensively. "What's this?"

"Snow pants. I am sick to death of you tripping over those long-assed pants Devin gave you. You're not in the damn army, so get out of the uniform."

She itched to hand them back, but nodded her thanks and tossed them in the pile. No, she didn't need them, but that's not saying they wouldn't be nice. This was how it started. First a pair of boots, then pants, next would be the thirty-room house with the helicopter pad. She could just see the sheriff coming for her stuff when she'd blown through her whole fortune. But he'd have his hands full if he tried to take her new boots away. Her heart raced just thinking about having warm, dry feet at the end of a long day in the woods. The sheriff had better bring his dogs to repossess these suckers. He was gonna need 'em.

The next afternoon, Cody cocked her head as she walked out of her house. Booming, percussive sounds ripped through the still air. The sounds were close, but not so close as to be on her land. She took off down the road, winding up at her cousin Chase's place. As she got nearer, she saw that Bobby, Brett, Lucas, Jaden and Ricky had all joined him and were shooting at targets set up around the place. In the minute or two she stood there, they must have fired off fifty rounds. A barrel of monkeys couldn't have had a better time. Still, it was a ridiculous waste of money. Thankfully, a couple of them even wore the protective earmuffs she'd insisted they buy. If they didn't care about preserving their hearing that was their right. She just hated the thought of having to buy them all hearing aids.

A few days later, Cody sat at the counter at the diner on Main Street in Greenville. Her body ached, probably from the weight of the problems she'd had to face that morning.

When a hand landed on her back she swirled around, ready to fight.

"Oh! I'm sorry," Maddie said, still not removing her hand.

"That's okay. I'm just touchy. I always think somebody's going to rob me." She shook her head glumly. "Like they did this morning."

Maddie sat down at the empty stool next to her, concern pouring from her. "Oh, my God. What happened?"

"I don't mean literally. I had my car towed up here, but they know about the money and what they quoted to fix it is the same as robbery." She sighed deeply. "This is hard."

Looking very intent, Maddie sat there for a moment, then said, "Maybe I can help. I had my car tuned at a place here in town and they seemed honest. I'll call and arrange to have your car towed over there. Then you won't be associated with it."

Cody chewed on that for a while. "Do you really think that would work?"

"It might. And it would give you a number to compare. If my place costs less, that's good news. If they cost about the same, maybe your place was being honest with you. Either way, you're better off."

Cody put her hand over her mouth and laughed. "You forgot one outcome. Your place might cost more, then you'd be worried that they've been ripping *you* off."

—⁓—

Having Maddie look out for her cheered Cody up enough to give her the gumption to stay in Greenville for a spell and spend more of the money. It was like water running through her fingers; once you turned on the tap, it was darned hard to stop.

She didn't get back to the hollow until near dinnertime, but she headed to Uncle Cubby's anyway. They never minded being interrupted.

When she honked the horn, Cubby stuck his head out, cocking it quizzically. Opening the car door, she said, "I need a hand carrying a few things."

He walked out to the driveway and gasped when she got the trunk of her borrowed car open. Inside was a forty-five inch, flat-screen TV and one of those game consoles the man at the store said everyone had. "Are you shittin' me?" he said, his voice higher and louder than normal.

"No. I didn't have money to buy you a Christmas present. I'm taking care of that now."

He slapped her hard on the shoulder. "You don't need to do this, Cody. We're fine."

"I know, I know, but you've always got what seems like a dozen kids over here. I bought a bunch of games for them. That'll keep them out of your hair."

He gave her another rough cuff that felt like a tender hug. It felt so good to see his eyes dance like this, she would've cried if she wouldn't have been teased about it for the next twenty years.

CHAPTER SEVEN

IT TOOK OVER A WEEK, but Cody finally had her car back. She felt like a kid with a new toy, and the first thing she did was stop by the bank. The guard was going to think she was stalking Maddie, but he'd just have to deal with it. She entered, purposefully avoiding looking at the teller. That was a Goodwin girl, and they'd always been mean—especially to Keith. His high school years had been made miserable by the likes of those girls, and Cody would never forgive them. Once she'd made up her mind to cut you off, you were gone forever. If a Goodwin was on fire, she wouldn't spit to put it out.

Maddie was in her office and waved Cody in. She sat down and waited for her to finish her phone call. Maddie looked really nice today—well, she always looked nice, but today her sweater was bright red and it made her cheeks look extra pink. Idly wondering if she was married or had kids, Cody was snapped from her musings when Maddie said, "How's it going?"

"Oh! Good. Do you have a minute?"

"Sure. Any time."

"Get your coat. I have something to show you."

—⁓—

Maddie was swamped, but Cody seemed like the type to take offense if she didn't have time for her. They walked a few dozen yards down the block and Cody stood in front of a white Jeep. "All fixed," she said proudly. "I went a little crazy."

Maddie knew nothing about cars, but this one had been through the wars. Hard use had left it dented and dinged, and the paint had no luster at all. The dull white surface was clean, though, and bright red shocks showed around the wheels. "It looks great," she said with enthusiasm.

"As long as they had to put a rebuilt engine in I had the water pump and transmission and clutch replaced. New brakes and off-road tires, too. It's like a whole new car."

"That doesn't sound too crazy." A new Rolls Royce wouldn't have been crazy, but she wasn't going to say that.

"Oh. The crazy parts are here." She pointed at the shocks and a winch on the front. "I decided to get a winch, just in case, and to jack it up a little. That'll let me go deeper into the woods when I need to. I just wish they'd had the darned things in black. Red looks silly."

"I think it's cute," Maddie said. "It makes it distinctive. Did you have them fix the heater?"

Cody shook her head quickly. "No need for that. Winter doesn't last long, and besides, with the ragtop it's always freezing."

Interesting perspective. It's cold, so why not be colder? "I bet you're the first person to win the lottery and not buy a new car. Even the people who don't buy houses make sure to get a new car or two."

"Two?" Cody's eyes saucered. "Who'd need two cars?"

"Lots of people seem to. But I am surprised you didn't get a new Jeep. It had to cost a lot to do all of this."

"It did, but it cost less than my old place wanted to charge." She bowed briefly. "Thank you for that, by the way. I got the winch and the shocks and had all of the other work done for about the same price as my thieves."

"I'm glad." She grasped Cody's arm and gave it a quick squeeze. "If you're happier with your repairs than you would be with a new car, that's what's important."

"I'm not against buying new. But you can't have a car stay nice…not where I live. It's just transportation. The mountains take the shine off a new car in a matter of days." She giggled, managing to get her hand over her mouth just in time. "You should know that better than anyone."

"Yeah, I got that impression." It was damned cold out, but she didn't want to show what a wimp she was. Cody acted like it was a lovely spring day, and her coat was meant for a desert. "I haven't seen or heard from you for a couple of days. I was thinking about calling to make sure you weren't being held for ransom."

Chuckling, Cody said, "No, not technically. But it feels very strange to go into a store, point at something, and be able to take it home. My relatives are adjusting much easier than I am."

"Oh-oh. How easy is it for them?"

"I suppose most people wouldn't think they'd gone overboard, but I spent over twenty thousand dollars at the outdoor store, and it's still burning a hole in my stomach."

Maddie whistled. "That *is* a lot of money. Did they buy big things?"

"Only a couple of people. One cousin bought the most expensive rifle I believe anyone has ever made. Why he needs it, I don't know, since you have to stick dynamite under his butt to get him up in the morning to hunt."

"This is probably just the first flush of excitement. What have you bought for yourself?"

"My cousin forced me to buy a pair of snow pants, and I got sucked into buying ridiculously expensive hunting boots." She smiled like she was being stroked. "They're remarkable." She shook her head, probably forcing the image of her wonderful boots out. "Oh, and I got my mattress. I'm good."

Maddie laughed quietly. "Are you being serious? All you bought was a pair of snow pants and boots?"

"No, I said I bought a mattress. I found a nice one for two hundred. And it was silly to buy snow pants. I've never had a pair before, and their lack didn't make me suffer."

"I'm not sure if you'll ever get used to spending money, but I'm glad your cousin made you buy some warm pants. Take her with you more often."

"No, I'll have to figure this out for myself. I *would* like to…well, if you'd be interested…it wouldn't take too much…maybe tomorrow if you have time…"

"Cody, I have no idea what you're asking."

"Sorry. I'm not used to this. But I'd like to thank you for being so nice to me. Could I buy you lunch?"

"You certainly don't need to buy, but I'd love to have lunch with you. Tomorrow would be lovely."

They arranged to meet at the restaurant, with Maddie suggesting one o'clock, since she liked to be in the bank for the noon rush. That was a couple of hours past her usual lunch, but Cody didn't mind.

She'd gone from cousin to cousin, shopping for an outfit, finally deciding on a pair of jeans Melissa had bought during their spending spree. They were relatively close in size, but the pants hung on her hips. Thankfully, the light blue sweater she borrowed covered that up pretty well. Melissa had never minded lending her clothes before, but Cody sensed a little snappishness this time. Actually, she didn't have to be very perceptive to notice it. Melissa had said she should get her own damn clothes and stop being so cheap.

The restaurant they decided upon was one Cody had never eaten in. She assumed she'd been to restaurants when she was a little girl, and her family had some money to spend on luxuries, but she didn't have any memory of that. Just going to the diner for a cup of coffee the other day had been a new experience, but one she thought she should get used to. It didn't make you a better person to take meals at restaurants, but everyone had told her to live a little and she thought this was what they meant.

She stood by the front door reading the advertisements that littered the space. The colorful map showed the restaurant had four locations in West Virginia. That had to mean it was good. There wouldn't be any point in having a second one if the first didn't make people want more. She was trying to read the history of the place, but the type was small and set at an angle, making her twist around to see it clearly. When a hand tapped her on the shoulder, she jumped.

A familiar voice said, "I've got to stop doing that. I don't want to give my best customer a heart attack."

Just hearing Maddie's voice made her feel warm all over. "I've had lots worse scares. I guess I'm still jumpy. Are you hungry?" That was stupid. Of course she was hungry, it was one o'clock in the afternoon.

"I am. I come in pretty early, so I'm always starving by lunch."

The woman standing by a lectern made eye contact with Cody and when she nodded to show that they were ready, the woman started to walk away. When Maddie followed her, Cody followed Maddie, figuring she knew what to do.

They were seated at a booth in front of a window that looked out upon the state highway. "This is nice," Maddie said.

Cody didn't have any reason to dispute that, nor did she have anything to add. The woman who had brought them over handed them menus, then someone else came by and filled their water glasses. Maddie took the neatly folded brown napkin, shook it out and put it on her lap. Cody did the same.

Mirroring her to a tee, they ordered, then sat and waited for their food. Cody was trying to get over the concept of paying $6.95 for a hamburger, but she managed to hear Maddie say, "The other day you told me that you weren't born around here. But you have deep roots in the area, right?"

"Very deep. I've done a little digging, and I have pretty good evidence that the Montgomerys have been in America since the early 1700s."

"Wow. That's pretty early. Were they from England?"

"No, we're Scots-Irish."

A puzzled frown settled on her face. "I've heard people say that, but I'm not sure what it means."

"We were Scots who were persuaded to move to Ireland. Stayed there about a hundred years, never fitting in well, then a lot of us moved to America. It's a lot more complicated than that, but that's the short version."

"Sounds like you've done a lot of homework. Have you been into genealogy for a long time?"

"No, just since high school. I was mostly interested in my mom's kin. I guess I should get to work and figure out my dad's side."

"Where's he from?"

"At least three generations in Greenville, but that's all that I know about."

"Tell me how your parents got together. I love to hear romantic tales."

Cody chuckled at that, and took a drink of her water. "I don't know how much romance there was, but they met when they both worked at the steel plant. You've seen it if you've been out on the east side. They keep saying the government will do something with it, but nobody believes them."

"Yes, I've seen it. It closed a long time ago, didn't it?"

"Yep. They met here in Greenville, at the plant, and then moved to Huntington when my dad got a promotion. He was doing pretty well to hear tell, supervising people and all, but that fell through when they cut back, and they got sent back here."

"That must've been hard."

"I'd imagine. The plant hung on for a couple of years, bare bones, then closed down tight. If they'd closed a year or two earlier I probably wouldn't be here."

"What?" Maddie looked like she'd been pinched.

"My mama never said that directly, but she did say they'd planned on having more kids but decided not to after she lost her job. Since I was born right after she lost it, I got in just under the wire."

"I heard you talk about that on the TV clip I saw. I can't imagine what it would be like for a town this size to lose five thousand jobs."

"I'm sure it wasn't pretty. My dad was real handy, and knew how to build anything, so he did all right for a while just doing this or that. They had unemployment for a while, and some union benefits too. That's how they managed."

"But that didn't last," Maddie said.

Their lunch was delivered and Cody knew how to do this part all on her own. She liked a lot of condiments, and she used everything they provided. It was almost hard to get her mouth around the hamburger, as loaded as it was, but she managed to take a bite, then nodded in satisfaction. "That's darned good." She sat there for a moment, enjoying lunch, then realized that there was a question still unanswered.

"I think my parents could've been fine, but my dad was helping a friend fix a car and the jack broke. Killed him," she added when Maddie looked at her curiously.

Maddie had just taken a bite and she put her napkin over her mouth to say, "Oh, my God! That's horrible!"

"Yeah, it was. Without his income, my mama struggled. Daddy's parents lived in Greenville too, and my grandfather died not too long after my daddy did. Mama and Keith and I moved in with my grandma, but the house got sold out from under us when she died. We didn't have any other options, so we had to move in with my other Granny in Ramp."

Maddie's eyes were a little wide when she said, "Four of you lived where you live now?"

"Uh-huh. Mama and Granny in the bedroom, and Keith and me in the living room. I suppose it was a little tight, but I never minded."

Maddie looked thoughtful when she said, "You seem like a very adaptable person."

Cody started to laugh, barely remembering to cover her mouth first. "Do you get credit for being adaptable when you don't have any choice? But I enjoyed those years. I truly did."

"Because of your granny?"

"Yes, I dearly loved my granny, but I loved Ramp too. I loved everything about it, and to be honest, I still do."

"It's really important to love where you live. It's where you spend most of your time," Maddie said, laughing at her own joke.

"I don't love it just because I'm here. I love the setting, I love the seasons, I love the way the air smells in the morning. Most of the time I love the fog that we get in the summer, except that it hurts my tomato crop, and I love that I'm part of something. My people have been here for hundreds of years, and I have something deep in me that sees what they saw when they came. They chose this over any other place, and so do I."

When Maddie reached over and lightly grazed the back of her hand, goosebumps ran all up and down Cody's shoulders.

"That's beautiful, Cody. Really beautiful. You're very poetic."

"Oh, I don't think so. I read a lot of poetry, but I don't think I could write it."

"I saw all of those books in your house. You must be quite a reader."

"I do my share. I had a teacher in high school who really got me interested, and my mama loved to have me read to her." She thought of how that sounded and hastened to add, "She could read too, but she liked it when I read aloud."

"It sounds like a nice way to grow up."

There was something about the way she said that that made the reality of their life in Ramp hit her hard. "It was…for a while."

As soon as they were finished with their burgers, Maddie checked her watch. "I really need to get back. We were very busy today for some reason."

"Let me pay," Cody said. "I'd really like to."

Maddie looked like she was going to refuse, but then smiled and said, "Only if you let me buy next time."

Did that mean there was definitely going to *be* a next time? Or was that just an expression? Her mother had always said when someone told you you'd have to get together with them sometime, that meant "don't bother calling."

Cody picked up the plastic folder the check was in and started to go through her wallet. Something hit her and she swallowed hard at her own ignorance. "Hey, uhm…I leave extra money, right? For the waitress?"

Maddie looked puzzled, then a smile settled on that pretty mouth. "I usually leave around twenty percent."

Cody tried not to choke. Twenty percent? That seemed like an awful lot of money. She counted it out and placed it neatly on the table, then moved quickly to catch up with Maddie. There had to be someone else to check with on this tipping thing. Twenty percent was *crazy!*

They stood by their respective cars to say their goodbyes. "I talked about myself for a solid hour," Cody said. "You do make me go on." She laughed at herself, "I shouldn't blame you. I can be very chatty."

Maddie didn't think she was overly chatty at all. But the more time they spent together, the more Cody opened up. "I had a great time. We're gonna have to do this again."

"Say when," Cody said. "My schedule is flexible." She smiled when she said that, and Maddie realized she really was opening up. This time she didn't even cover her broken tooth.

When Maddie walked back into the bank, Lynnette, the head teller, signaled her over. Still wearing her coat, she walked over to the barrier that separated them. "Hi. What's up?"

"My sister's daughter-in-law works over at The Mountaineer. She said you were at lunch with that Montgomery girl."

Boy, small towns were a lot of fun. How did people ever have affairs? "Yes, I was. I'm going to have lunch with all of our big clients, so tell your sister's daughter-in-law to be on the lookout." That should do it. Maddie turned and started to walk to her office, but Lynnette made a loud *pssst* sound.

Steeling herself, Maddie walked back over to her. "Yes?"

"Just so's you know, people say she's a queer."

Maddie wasn't generally the type to flush, but she could feel her cheeks reddening. Her mentor had told her to keep her sexuality on the down low in Greenville, and she had, but now she thought that might have been a mistake. If people in the branch knew she was a lesbian, they'd at least have to keep such stupid comments to themselves. She took in and let out several slow breaths, then said, "Can you join me in my office for a moment? Geneva can watch the window."

By the time she got back to her office, she was a little calmer, but still plenty steamed. She took off her coat and hung it up, then sat down and waited for Lynnette.

"Have a seat," she said, amazed that the woman looked perfectly calm, clueless, really, that she was about to get chewed out. "I thought I made myself clear the other day, but I must not have." She leaned over and spoke slowly. "We aren't here to judge, categorize, belittle or gossip about our customers. You've got something in your craw about Ms. Keaton, but I don't care to know what it is. It's none of my business, just like her personal life is none of your business."

"It's more than her personal life that worries me. Everybody knows she's got all of that money in the safe. Someone will come in here and kill us all to get at it."

Maddie took in a slow breath. "One, that's not true. On either point. Two, what Ms. Keaton does with her money is none of your business. You're behind a security barrier. Feel free to duck in case of trouble."

"It's not right that I have to risk my life for the likes of her."

"You don't." Maddie pointed at the front door. "You're not being held here against you will."

The pointed words rolled right off Lynnette's back. "I'm only trying to help. You can't afford to be seen around with her. People will talk."

Leaning over so close she was almost lying atop her desk, Maddie tried again. "Listen to me. I don't *care* if people talk. I care that our customers are treated well. I care that the employees of this bank are dedicated to customer service. I care deeply about that, and you'd have a much better shot at keeping your job if you focused your energies on caring about those exact things." Her face hot and her heart beating hard, she sat up. "Unemployment is high, Lynnette, don't add yourself to the rolls."

"Why I never," she snapped. "I was working here when you were still in high school. You can't talk to me like that!"

"Yes, I can. I'm going to write up a summary of our conversation and ask you to sign it. I don't want there to be any chance that you've misunderstood me."

"I understand you fine." She got up and went to the door, standing there for a minute before she said, "Everyone knows you haven't had a date since you've been here. I guarantee no decent man will want you if you're seen with the likes of her."

"My personal life is also on the list of things that you need not concern yourself with."

"Fine. But don't come crying to me when you're home alone every Saturday night."

Maddie gave her a very unenthusiastic smile. "I promise I won't." As Lynnette walked back to the teller area, Maddie quietly growled, "Miserable asshole. Thick headed idiot. Homophobic jerk." She realized she was speaking aloud and got up to close the door because she wasn't at all sure she was finished with her list of names for her least favorite employee. Her vow to limit her cursing was also suspended for the day. "Fuck-stick!"

She sat there, steaming, letting her anger flow through her for longer than was wise. Clearly, she was being overly protective of Cody. In fact, Lynnette was probably right. Cody had never said one word about an intimate life, and there hadn't been pictures of past or current lovers or anything of the sort in her trailer. Maybe it was hard to meet people in such a small town. But no matter what her sexual orientation, people would be trying to hook up with her. Maddie just hoped she didn't have to worry about that too. It was almost a full time job urging her to spend a little money. Urging her to give up more personal assets was outside the realm of her duties as a banker.

CHAPTER EIGHT

ONCE A MONTH, MADDIE had to drive to Huntington to meet with her managers and the heads of retail banking. The bank operated over a hundred branches in West Virginia, Kentucky, North Carolina and Ohio, and all of the branch managers had to make an appearance.

She didn't relish the drive, or the meetings, since they usually lasted all day and could be deadly dull. But her former boss and now friend, Avery Jones, was always there to relieve the tedium.

Maddie walked into the big auditorium-style meeting room at eight forty-five, searching for Avery and the seat she knew he'd be saving for her. She smiled when she caught sight of him, then dashed to grab the seat before anyone beat her to it.

Avery kissed her on the cheek. "Sit right down and tell me more about your big celebrity client!"

Avery was gay, gay, gay, in every way. He was one of those guys who had convinced himself he was flying under the radar. Radar couldn't get that high. At various times in their three-year relationship, Maddie had considered telling him that everyone knew. She refrained, mostly because his fantasy must have soothed him. Everyone had the right to their own delusions.

His short, blond hair was impeccably styled, and his blue, pin-striped suit fit him like it had been custom made. A lighter-blue, striped shirt was accented with a red-print tie and matching pocket square. He looked like a man modeling business attire, not at all like the other managers, who were mostly average Joes and Janes. Not particularly well paid, most branch managers struggled to support their families in a middle-class style.

Avery, however, went on exotic vacations, owned two Siamese cats whose pictures dotted his office, and made a point of publicly stating that he'd settle down when he found Ms. Right. But even though he was delusional about his own image, he'd been a good friend and confidant. She knew she could trust him, and that meant a lot to Maddie.

"Well, it's been pretty exciting, to be honest. Cody's like a babe in the woods when it comes to her money. It's taken all of my skills to get her to leave it on deposit. I'm afraid one day she'll ask for it all in cash and I'll have to sell my soul to get the Fed to cough it up."

"I still can't believe they gave you a million. How big was the bundle?"

"Big," she said gravely. "I assume it's in her safe deposit boxes, since she can't keep it at home. Did I tell you people dug up her garden to find where she'd hidden it?"

"Don't let her take the money out," Avery warned.

"I'll do my best. I'm trying to establish a good bond with her so she trusts me. She really needs protection."

He blinked slowly. "Not for her. For you! It would look terrible if she moved that money out of your branch. That deposit alone has to be equal to your total assets."

"It was greater than that. Several times greater."

He lowered his voice and spoke like he had when he was her manager. "I'm being serious about this. You've got to convince her to put the money in something where she locks it up long term."

"Avery, I'm not going to trick her into doing something that isn't in her best interests. Don't even waste your time trying to convince me."

"Do you want to keep your job?" he whispered. "They're definitely going to be cutting back. Don't give them a reason to single you out!"

She shook her head, trying not to let his warning get under her skin. "If they want to fire me for protecting my customers, they can. I'd rather go back to waitressing than use Cody's lack of experience against her."

"There's nothing wrong with our investment products. I'm not telling you to have her buy something dangerous."

"I appreciate the advice, but I'm going to give her honest advice and hope she sticks around. That's the only way I can live with myself."

He sat back and regarded her for a moment. "You've been behaving very strangely during this whole thing. Going to visit her was the craziest thing you've ever done. I still can't believe you had the nerve."

That comment irritated her a little, and she counted up the days, wondering if she was about to get her period. "It's not like I went to Afghanistan. They're just people."

"No, they're not," he said primly. "They're hillbillies, and they're a different breed."

"You make them sound like cats! They want the same things out of life that we do."

"No, they don't. Poor people and money don't mix. She'll blow it on junk, or someone will sweet talk her into investing it in something stupid. It'll be gone in a year."

She slapped at his arm. "That's horribly classist."

"No, it's being realistic. Have you ever seen what pro athletes do when they get their first big check? Big cars, big houses, lots of jewelry. It'll be the same for her. Just watch."

"Oh, I'll watch. Worry not." She sat back in her seat as her immediate supervisor took the stage. She'd bet her salary that Cody would have most of her fortune intact for a hell of a lot longer than a year. Thinking of her buying loads of jewelry put a smile on Maddie's face. Unimaginable wasn't a strong enough word for that scenario.

CHAPTER NINE

CODY DROVE OVER TO Aunt Lily's one afternoon, looking for Devin. She was intent on getting him outside again, despite his being so darned tied to the house. Since he'd been home, he only seemed to want to sit in a chair and watch TV. That wasn't good for what ailed hardly anyone.

"Hey," she said as she walked into the house and spotted him in his normal place—directly in front of the television. "Wanna go try out your bow?"

He looked outside and squinted at the bright sunshine. "No, it looks too cold."

"It's not cold. Don't you see the water dripping off the house? It's well over thirty degrees."

"Maybe tomorrow."

Frustrated, she sat down and tried to wait for the commercial to make her pitch. But he looked so lifeless she couldn't contain herself. "Listen, Dev, I know the VA isn't giving you much help. Why don't we try to find a doctor in Huntington, or Charleston. Someone who could help you sleep at night and get you back to your old self."

"What kinda doctor? A psychiatrist?"

"Whatever you need. I can pay for it, Devin. Anything that you think will help."

He shrugged, looking both unconcerned and unconvinced. "Pastor Jackson says the only way to peace is through Jesus. Your money won't help. I've got to work to get closer to the Lord."

That would have been fine if he'd made any improvement. But he'd been home for almost a year and was still only interacting with other people at church on Wednesday night and Sunday morning. That just wasn't enough. "There's nothing wrong with giving Jesus a little help, is there?" She tried to sound like she was joking to keep him from taking offense, which he now did easily.

"The Lord doesn't need our help. We need *his* help."

She sat there, fidgeting. It was a marvelous day, the best they'd had since Christmas. Dying to get outside, she tried one last gambit. "Hey, how about this?"

He turned his head reluctantly, and gazed at her, his eyes almost soulless. "What."

"Maybe Jesus made me win the lottery so I could help *you*."

Shaking his head, he said, "Why would he give it to you? If he wanted me to have it, he would have given it to me."

"No, no, think about it. He knows you're having a tough time. He knows you're not...as...involved with life as you used to be. If you won, you might just stay home like you are now. But he knows we're close, and if he gave me the money, he knows I'd make sure you got some help."

Devin sat there for a moment, then frowned and turned his attention back to the TV. "I'll pray about that. I will."

―――

Cody stopped by the bank one morning, striding across the lobby while Maddie chatted with a gabby customer. Maddie found herself rushing him along to be available when her reluctant millionaire came back upstairs from the vault.

A few minutes later, Cody emerged from the lower level, and Maddie waved and gestured for her to come into her office. "How's it going?" Maddie asked.

"Good. You?" Cody leaned on the doorway, filling it with her casual grace.

"I'm good. Come on in. I haven't talked to you in a while."

She entered fully and slid into the chair. "I told you my schedule's flexible. Just call and I'll be here."

That wasn't a good idea. It was reasonable to have lunch or talk when she came by, but it seemed a little outside the bounds of a professional relationship to be calling her. "I'll bet you've got more demands on your time than you used to."

"Only sometimes. I'm still spending a lot of time driving people to the clinic or taking someone to Fast Money. I drive as much as a long-haul trucker."

Maddie got up and went to the small refrigerator she had in the corner. "Soda? Water?"

Cody chuckled. "I've never had water from a bottle. Let's give it a try." She accepted the bottle, removed the cap and took a big drink. Almost immediately she winced in pain, slapping her hand over her mouth. "Darned nerve."

"Nerve?" Maddie acted like she didn't know what Cody was talking about.

"My broken tooth. It's been two years and it still hurts when I drink anything too hot or too cold."

"You have a tooth that's painful? Why not get it fixed?"

Her dark head shook rapidly. "No, no, thanks. I don't like dentists."

"Do you like nerve pain?"

"No," she said, drawing out the word. "I can't think anyone does."

"How'd it happen?"

"I was carrying someone...probably Adam." She nodded, furrowing her brow, likely fitting events into a timeline. "Yeah, he's three now, so that fits. It was about this time of year, and I slipped on the ice. It was either him or me, and I let it be me." She pointed at her lip, right over the broken tooth. "Hit right here. Got up and spit out half my tooth. Nearly cried louder than the baby."

"You've got to fix it, Cody. You've really got to."

"It's not too bad. Most days I don't notice it."

"Listen to yourself! You don't have to live with that kind of pain. Come on, I'll ask around and see if anyone knows of a good dentist."

Cody looked like she wanted to argue, but eventually gazed at the carpet. "I'm afraid of dentists," she finally said.

"Oh, that's a different thing. Have you ever had nitrous oxide?"

"I don't think so. What is it?"

"Laughing gas. My mom's afraid of going to the dentist, too. She gets nitrous even for a tooth cleaning."

Suspiciously, Cody asked, "And it helps?"

"Oh, yes. It makes her almost look forward to going." She smiled at Cody's doubtful stare. "I swear."

"I don't know..."

"How about this? I have a good dentist in Huntington. Actually, he's the best I've ever had. I'll make an appointment for you for the next time I have to go to headquarters. He can fix it right then and I'll drive you home. You have my personal guarantee that you won't feel a thing and you won't be afraid."

"I'm pretty afraid," she said softly.

"You won't be. Trust me."

After Cody left, Maddie called the dentist and spoke to his helpful assistant. After explaining the whole situation, they made an appointment for two weeks from then. "We're coming a long way. Please make sure Dr. Anderson can fix it that day."

"I've got ninety minutes blocked off. That should do it. If she's been afraid to visit a dentist, she probably needs to have her teeth cleaned, too. Should we do that at the same time?"

"Sure. Why not? Getting her there is the hard part. We might as well get everything done in one shot."

Maddie hung up and dropped her chin into her hand. She was going to have to do some powerful mental gymnastics to convince herself this was part of the Appalachian States Bank customer-service protocol. Damn that Cody Keaton! The adorable scamp was really getting under her skin, and the last thing she needed was to be mooning over a client. Especially one as innocent as Cody seemed. She might have all the experience in the world when it came to the great outdoors, but Maddie would have bet good money that Cody rarely bagged a woman.

They started out from Greenville at seven a.m. The drive to Huntington often seemed interminable, but listening to Cody's observations made the time fly.

"How do you get to be a bank manager anyway? Everybody there seems older than you."

"I guess that's true. I think people come up through different paths, but mine was pretty straightforward. I started out right out of college, and got into the commercial-lending training program."

"I should know what commercial lending is, but I really don't."

"Oh, trust me, there's no need for most people to know what commercial lending is. It's where you lend large amounts of money to corporations and businesses." She looked over and saw that recognition had not fully dawned. "Let's say that The Mountaineer wants to open another branch in Charleston. They might need a couple of million dollars to do that. They could come to our bank for that financing."

"That's not what you do now, right?"

"Right. I did that for about three years, but I hadn't progressed very far. It looked like it was going to take me a couple more years to get promoted. I didn't want to wait."

"You're ambitious," Cody said with a decided note of pleasure. "I can tell."

"I am, to a certain extent. Anyway, I moved over to retail banking, which is the kind of banking most people do. Checking and savings accounts and things like that. I was the assistant branch manager at a branch about twenty minutes outside of Charleston. After three years of doing that, I got my own branch. And that is all she wrote."

With a sweet smile, Cody said, "I think she's still writing. Are you happy?"

"You know, that's not a question that comes up very often."

"It should be."

"I guess it should. But most people are thinking about the next promotion. I'd have to say I'm vaguely happy."

"That sounds vaguely vague. Why aren't you happier with your job?"

Maddie let herself think about her answer for a few moments. "It's not that I'm unhappy, but I would say I'm a little…disappointed. I thought that being in charge of the branch would give me more control, but it really doesn't."

"It doesn't? But it's yours."

Cody made it sound like they'd given her the keys and wished her well. "It's really not. I'm one branch out of a hundred, and all of us are supposed to do things the same way. I have so little discretion that it's starting to wear on me."

"I don't think you could have said anything that would've surprised me more. I thought you were really in charge."

"I am, in a way. But I need permission to do anything even slightly out of the ordinary. I know I'd be happier running my own business, but I don't have that kind of drive, nor the kind of money I'd need to get started."

"What kind of business would you like?"

Maddie considered that for a minute. "That's where the drive comes in. There's nothing that appeals to me enough to throw myself into it. Entrepreneurs always seem to have had a dream to own a restaurant or have a model train store or what have you. I'm not like that. I just want a nice job where I don't have to explain myself every time I make a decision."

Giving her a charming smile, Cody said, "I can find you a good spot in a forest. You might like picking moss. You set your own hours and your salary is one hundred percent dependent on your efforts. You're the president of your own company."

"You never know. Take me along with you one day, and we'll see if I have an aptitude. I wouldn't want to have to fire my own ass if I didn't do well." She cringed when the word came out. How fucking hard *was* it to stop cursing?

They drove down the streets of Huntington, with Cody exclaiming every few moments. "I know that store wasn't here the last time I was in town," she said, pointing at a small appliance store. "It seems like a whole new place."

"How long has it been since you've spent any time here?"

"It seems like forever. Since we can get just about everything done in Greenville, we don't come up here much. I don't think I could ever get used to living in a place this big," she added, sounding slightly in awe.

Huntington was a decent-sized small town. It was big enough for a couple of TV stations and a pair of newspapers, but that was about it. Maddie thought they had about fifty thousand people in the city, and a good bit more in the surrounding towns. But it certainly wasn't the megalopolis that Cody seemed to view it as. What would she think of Pittsburgh or Cincinnati? Hell, Chicago would make her brain short out.

It was just after eight when they got to the dentist. Maddie went in with her to make sure everything was arranged. They were ready to go, and everyone seemed particularly attuned to Cody's skittishness. Still, when Maddie left her, it was a little like taking your cat in to be neutered. It was something that had to be done, but you still felt guilty for being the one to leave a confused, frightened animal behind.

Maddie's meetings were over faster than she'd expected, and she was released before eleven. She headed back over to the dentist, thinking she and Cody could stop to get lunch before going back to Greenville.

When she went into the office, the receptionist said, "Your friend wasn't able to tolerate the mask we use for the nitrous oxide. The doctor had to use IV sedation. She's finished, but still groggy." She escorted Maddie back to a treatment room where Cody lay in a chair that was fully reclined.

"Hi," Cody said, waving her fingers slowly. "I'm waaaay out of it."

"You look it." Those usually perceptive brown eyes had no sharpness left in them. Actually they drifted as they tried to focus. "We can wait an hour or two before heading back."

"No, we can go." She tried to sit up, but looked like a waterbug that had been thrown onto its back, trying to right itself.

"Wait right here, I'll have someone help us."

Maddie and the receptionist worked together to get Cody loaded into the car. Loaded was the operative word. She seemed like she'd had about four drinks too many.

Her limbs were loose and her muscle tone was largely missing, but she was in a lovely mood. The temporary cap the dentist made looked wonderful, and Maddie glimpsed the tooth many times as Cody's liquid smile shone across the car.

"That IV was really nice," she said slowly. Actually everything she did was slow and easy. "I'd go to the dentist every day if I could get that." She took in a long, slow breath. "I might go just for fun. The dentist doesn't even have to be there."

Maddie was extremely happy that she'd decided to give Cody a ride. The woman could be so hardheaded that Maddie wouldn't have been surprised if she'd tried to drive in her current condition. Now she seemed even more like a well-cared-for cat; proud and independent and even a little haughty, but needing protection from harm. "I'm going to have to tell my mom that you said the IV was better. The high she gets from nitrous doesn't last very long."

"Now I know you have a mama. Do you have a daddy too?"

She asked the question with such childlike innocence that Maddie couldn't stop herself from smiling. "Yes, I have a daddy too. I have two brothers also."

"Do you have any kids?"

Maddie glanced at her out of the corner of her eye. "None that I know of."

That was a very lame joke, but Cody thought it was extremely funny. She chortled for a good minute, then said, "Do you have a husband?"

"No, I think I'd notice that too."

"I can't figure why not. You're a really nice lady, and you're smart too."

"That's nice of you to say." Maddie briefly wondered if it would be impolite to stuff one of her gloves into Cody's mouth. Letting someone ramble on when they clearly weren't in control was almost like eavesdropping on them. "The dentist did a really nice job with your tooth. You're gonna be happy with it."

Clumsily, Cody pulled the visor down and looked into the mirror, making herself smile widely. "Just like it never left." She relaxed back into her seat and looked out the window for a moment. "You know who has a pretty mouth?"

There was something about the way she asked the question that seemed fraught with danger. Maddie tried to change the topic. "Did you like the dentist enough to see him again?"

"You do," Cody said, ignoring the intervening misdirection. "Just about the prettiest mouth I've ever seen on a woman. When you smile, it's like the sun shines brighter."

Well, it was nice to know that her instincts had been accurate. A straight woman probably wouldn't wax poetic about the state of Maddie's mouth. But the small amount of pleasure she got from correctly guessing Cody was a lesbian wasn't overridden by the discomfort she felt at being able to hear her thoughts. "Thank you," she said, hoping to put the topic to bed.

"Your eyes twinkle when you smile. Did you know that?"

"Hey! Look at that pretty dog. I saw a dog house on your property, but I didn't see a dog. Do you have one?"

"They do. They twinkle. Just like little stars. So you've got little stars in your eyes and then the sun from your smile…it's like a whole solar system."

This had to stop. Cody was a very proud and very private person in many ways, and it was wrong to let her reveal herself this thoroughly. They were just about to get on the highway, but Maddie wasn't ready to put all of her attention into driving. She pulled over and turned off the car. Looking into Cody's hazy eyes, she said, "You're saying things that you're going to regret. It's almost like you're drunk, Cody. I love to listen to you talk, but you need to be quiet for a while. Now, roll your seat back and just relax."

It wasn't clear what of that she understood, but Cody nodded gravely. She started pushing her torso into the seat back while fumbling for some kind of assistance from the levers. To prevent her from hurting herself, Maddie got out and walked around to her side, opened the door and put her hand on the seat release. She grasped the back of the seat with her other hand and pushed gently, watching Cody go along for the ride. Their heads were very close together, and if she had given her an opportunity, Cody would probably have kissed her. But that wasn't going to happen. She stood up and went back to the driver's side, telling her heart to stop pounding. "Now remember, close your eyes and be quiet for a while."

"I will," Cody said softly. "I'd do whatever you asked." She turned her head and gazed into Maddie's eyes. "Anything in the whole world."

Oh, fuck.

CHAPTER TEN

A WEEK PASSED BEFORE Cody appeared at the bank again. Sitting in her office, Maddie watched her enter, then stop as soon as she got through the door. She was a very cautious person, tending not to move until she had a thorough understanding of the environment. She almost immediately turned towards Maddie's office, and a full, rich, confident smile settled on her lips when their eyes met.

It was only a single tooth, but having it fixed had changed Cody in remarkable ways. She looked years younger, and much less careworn. Maybe she wasn't as old as Maddie had thought. Her date of birth would definitely be in the files, Maddie could just take a look...*No!* That was ridiculous. Besides being an unnecessary invasion of her privacy, it was too personal. They had a professional relationship. Maddie had to focus on *that*.

Cody entered the office and stood in the doorway as she always did. But now she didn't look hesitant. She actually looked like she felt she belonged there and was only trying to decide if she felt like sitting down or not. "I think I'm running out of money," she said, chuckling softly.

"If you didn't buy Virginia, I think you're good."

"I made them an offer," she said, looking absolutely serious, "but they turned me down flat. There's still a lot of bad blood from when we broke away during the Civil War. I'll try Kentucky next."

"I think someone is starting to get comfortable with her money."

Cody walked all the way in and sat down. "Not very. But it seems I'm spending an awful lot more than I thought I would. Almost everybody has one problem or another with their teeth, and after one gets his fixed, the other one wants to go. I really like the dentist you sent me to, but I'd save a lot of gas money if I could talk him into moving to Ramp."

"Dental work is very expensive. Maybe you should look into trying to buy insurance."

Cody held up her hands. "That's way too adventurous for just now. I'll just transfer some more money into my checking account and try not to cry when I'm writing those checks with all those zeros in them."

Okay. She was getting more comfortable. It was finally time to have a talk. "When you first made your deposit, I assured you that the bank was in good shape." Cody's eyes started to widen, and Maddie continued quickly, "It still is, of course. But the way you have things set up is a mess."

"It's not a mess. I've got a little cash stored away at home, a bunch in my checking account and the rest in savings. I can show you a mess if you want to come back up to Ramp."

"I'm not joking, Cody." It was hard being tough with her, especially when she looked at you with those big, puppy dog brown eyes. "You need to do something with your money. If nothing else, you should buy Treasury bills."

A dark look settled onto her face. "You know I don't know what that is."

"A Treasury bill is when you lend the government money and they agree to give you back your money, and a little interest, in a certain amount of time. The federal government issues them, and the chance of them not paying is extremely small."

"But there's a risk. I don't read it every day, but when I stop at the library, I look at the paper. It sounds like one country or another is always going belly up. Our turn could be next."

"No, no, the US is doing fine. Your money would be safe in Treasury bills."

"I don't think so. I'm happy where it is."

"I'm doing you a disservice to let you keep the money here. A tiny fraction of it is insured, Cody. You say you don't trust the government, but I assure you it's in better shape than this bank is."

She shook her head slowly, letting her dark hair move back and forth across her shoulders. "I don't trust them. I trust you."

My God, she was pigheaded! "I hate to be blunt, but that's a bad decision. It's more than bad, it's foolish."

In a flash, Cody was on her feet. She stood there, almost wobbling, then leaned over and Maddie could see the fire in her eyes. "I might not be as smart as you are, and I didn't go to college. I don't have a big job, or an office, or a bunch of people working for me. But I am *nobody's* fool!" She turned and stormed out of the office, leaving Maddie sitting there, dumbfounded.

A week passed, and Cody didn't feel a bit better. She was moping around so badly that going over to see her cousin Devin seemed like a way to cheer up. It wasn't, of course, and the two of them sat, barely speaking, in front of the TV.

"Mama said you were gonna take Bobby's kids to see about getting them braces on their teeth. What's going on with you and that dentist?"

That made her laugh for the first time in a few days. "Nothing. And besides, it's not the dentist. It's an orthodontist, and this one's in Greenville, so I don't have to drive to Huntington *every* day." She laughed softly. "Just every other day."

"Do you stop and see that banker lady when you're in town?"

Just hearing her referred to made Cody's stomach hurt. "No, I'm not doing that. Not anymore." She felt like she'd burst if she didn't tell somebody how she was feeling. Devin had always been the one, and even though he'd changed so much since he got back from the Army, maybe there was still some solace he could offer. "She insulted me bad."

"How?" His dark eyes narrowed. "Did she try to trick you?"

"No, no, she's not like that." Trying to imagine Maddie stealing her money was truly impossible. "She just…insulted me." Devin was still staring at her, all beady-eyed. "She made me feel dumb," she finally admitted.

He rolled his eyes and turned his attention back to the TV. "Did you really think somebody like her would want to be friends with somebody like you?"

That was an awfully mean way to put it, but he had a point. "I did think that. I truly did."

Sharply, he said, "She's got your money, what else could she want?"

"I thought she wanted to be friends."

His laughter felt worse than outright mockery would have. "Friends? She don't want friends from the hollow. Nobody does."

"You don't understand how it was." He looked at her sharply, but she tried to continue. "I don't know how to explain it, but it felt really good to be with her."

For the first time in months, he sat up straight in his chair and showed some true feeling when he said, "You don't need those kind of feelings. Those are feelings you should have for a man, Cody. You need to get you one."

She stood up and walked over to the door, feeling much worse than she had before she'd come. "I don't need her telling me how to invest my money, and I don't need you telling me what kind of friends I can have."

"These aren't my rules. They're God's."

"You can tell God for me that he can keep his nose out of my business too." She walked out and slammed the door, almost glad for the cold rain that was coming down. Weather cleared her mind. She had a lot to clear.

—⁓—

Devin's house was at one end of the hollow, and her uncle Cubby's was at the other. That's why Cody was surprised when she found herself splashing her way down his muddy drive. It was still raining hard, but her new boots kept her feet so dry they cheered her up a little bit. But Devin had really gotten under her skin, or she wouldn't have found herself gravitating to her uncle.

Strangely, Blue and Stripes were tied up outside and they barked their heads off when she approached. After a quick stop to give them each a scratch, she urged them back into their house.

She heard the door squeak behind her; then the distinctive sound of a round being racked in a shotgun made her blood run cold. "It's Cody," she called out, staying as still as possible.

"I figured it was a friend," Cubby called out. "Can't be too careful."

Her hands tingled when she stood up, and she felt slightly light-headed. "Having a gun cocked at your back really gets your blood moving," she said, walking over to the house.

"You here for the dogs? Can't hunt much with this rain," he said, looking up at the slate gray skies.

"No, I was just out wandering."

"Come in," he said. "Lurlene's over at Lucas' place. Now that I have company, I have an excuse to have a beer." He was chuckling to himself as he grabbed two beers and handed one to Cody. Brushing the rain off his shoulders, he sank down into his sofa. "Whatcha been up to?"

"Not much." She took a pull off her beer.

"What's got you down?"

"It's that obvious?"

"It is."

Cody yawned and stretched a little. Talking about things like this made her tired, more tired than she already was, which was considerable. "It's been hard getting used to the money. Everybody treats me like I'm a different person, but I'm not. I'm still me—exactly like I was before."

"Yeah, I can see that. But it'll settle, I'd expect."

"Not fast enough for me." She took another drink. "You and Aunt Lurlene are the only two who treat me just about the same."

"What about that lady from the bank? You went on and on about her last time we talked."

Her muscles itched to get moving, but Cody couldn't very well get up and start doing push-ups. She had to sit there and talk about her feelings. It was embarrassing to repeat what Maddie had said, so she kept it simple. "She insulted me."

"Really? On purpose?"

"I don't know," she admitted, humiliation burning at her. "She told me I was a fool."

"About what? Your money?"

"About how I'm keeping it. She wants me to put it in…" How could she explain what Maddie had said when she didn't understand it very well herself? "Some kind of investment with the government. She says it's safer. But I don't trust the federal government. I trust her. Or at least I did."

Cubby took another drink of his beer, his normally wide eyes narrowed in thought. "Now, don't get your back up at me too, but you might be kinda thin-skinned about this." He looked her in the eye and added, "You're easy to piss off lately, and that's not like you."

"She said I was foolish. Clear as day."

"That's not the same as calling you a fool, girl! Maybe what you're doing *is* foolish. If you trust her, you've gotta let her speak her mind."

"I let her speak her mind," she said, softly.

"Are you sure? Don't sound like it."

Letting her head hang down, Cody shook it. "Maybe I don't. Not all the time, anyway. I suppose I need to apologize."

"You do if you want to be friends. But she's got so much of your money, you could probably slap her in the face and she'd give you a big smile. Is that how you want things?"

"No, of course not. I want her to like me for me, not my money."

"Then you might wanna let her know you can admit when you're wrong."

Cody finally stood up, unable to keep the restless muscles at bay another minute. "Thanks for the talk. I wouldn't have guessed this, but it seems like making friends is harder than having relatives."

"Hell, yes, it is. I'd stay away from friends if I was you, but you've got your own mind."

She grinned, knowing he was at least partially teasing. "I do. And it gets me in more trouble than it's worth sometimes."

—∽—

A busy day at the branch had Maddie running around trying to keep things in order. When her phone rang, she almost let it go, but this week's resolution was to answer her phone if humanly possible. She caught it right before it would have gone to voicemail hell. "Hi, this is Maddie Osborne."

"It's Cody Keaton."

A surprising amount of relief filled Maddie. So surprising she tried to ignore it. "Hi, how are you?"

"I'm all right. Hey, it's almost lunchtime and I'm over at the diner. Is there any way you could see clear to come over and join me?"

Today? It was the day Social Security checks were delivered, and it seemed as if every person over sixty-five came in and had a question or two that only she could answer. Plus, she was meeting a prominent attorney for lunch at one o'clock on the other end of town. But she barely hesitated before saying, "If I stand up I can see you." She waved, and Cody turned away from the public telephone in the entryway of the diner and waved back. "I'll be right there."

Cody seemed as shy and hesitant as she had the first time they'd met. Not as jittery, but just as shy. As they stood in the entryway, Cody started to say something, then stopped. "Is it okay to sit at the counter?"

"Of course." Maddie pushed on the glass door and entered. She sat down on the stool closest to the wall and Cody stood right next to her.

"I want to apologize," she said, leaning over and speaking quietly. "I was very rude to you."

Maddie patted the seat next to her. "Sit down." When Cody did, she leaned over and said, "Don't worry about it. I was going to call you, but I thought...well, you seemed pretty angry. I thought I'd give you some time."

She looked very abashed. "When I get mad, I usually stay mad. But I talked to my uncle and he told me I was being thin-skinned."

Maddie thought that was a pretty good description for Cody, but she wouldn't admit to that. "I don't think that's a fair way to put it. I obviously said something that offended you, and I'm sorry for that. I was pushing my opinion too firmly. That's not my job."

Cody nodded to the waitress to dropped off menus. She surveyed hers for just a moment, then put it down on the counter. "That wasn't it. You hurt my feelings when you said I was a fool."

Maddie gasped in shock. "I didn't say that!"

"You said I was being foolish. That's the same thing."

The hurt was still etched on her face so boldly that Maddie felt the wound as well. She found herself gently stroking Cody's arm when she said, "There's nothing about you that's foolish. That was a very poor choice of words. I was trying to say that I didn't agree with your choices, but I'm only looking at it from a financial standpoint."

"You're talking about money, so a financial standpoint is the one that counts."

"No, not really. Decisions are about a lot of emotional factors too, and you're the only person who can judge how things feel." Now she gripped her bicep and squeezed it. "I'm very sorry."

The waitress came back and they both ordered. Maddie would be asleep at her desk by three o'clock, but it was rude to go visit a client and not eat. She'd have to have two lunches today. The treadmill at the gym was going to get a punishing workout tonight.

"I think I'd feel better if I could read some books about how banks work. Is there anything written for somebody at my level?"

"Of course there is. I'll find some things. And I'm always available to answer any questions you have. I like talking about what I do."

"That sounds like a deal."

When their sandwiches were delivered, Maddie tried to eat her BLT while surreptitiously stripping the B from the sandwich. That had to hold most of the calories. Cody didn't seem to notice, and the waitress would just have to assume God knows what when she realized the napkin was filled with bacon.

"I'm going to head over to the dentist after lunch. He's got my permanent tooth ready."

"Who's going with you?" Maddie asked, alarmed.

Cody gave her a slow smile. "They promised me it wouldn't hurt. I'm going to do it without being knocked out. The next time I go for something serious, I'm gonna to try that nitrous again. Now that I'm not as nervous, I think I could stand to have the mask over my face."

"That's progress. Pretty soon you'll be going without Novocain."

"No, I will not!" Cody looked like she wanted to bolt. "I stopped going to the dentist after having to go to the one guy in town who took Medicaid. I was just a kid, but he didn't give you anything to numb it. He took that big drill and…" She closed one eye and acted like she had a drill in her hand, waving it over Maddie's head ominously. "I almost cried."

"Almost? I'd cry if that happened to me today. I can't imagine having to deal with that when you were little."

"He was a thief," she said dismissively. "He probably got paid for numbing drugs and made more money if he didn't use 'em."

Maddie looked at her from the corner of her eye. It was easy to be victimized when you were poor. Choices just seemed to disappear as your bank balance dropped. It made perfect sense that Cody was skittish and even suspicious of people and their motives. She had good reason to be that way.

"I bet it'll be just around dinnertime when I come through again. Do you eat dinner?"

Sometimes she asked questions with such a straight face that Maddie had to guess whether or not she was teasing. This time she was pretty sure she was. Okay, so two lunches, no health club, and another restaurant meal. What the hell. "I do. I'll wait for you at the bank until you come by. I've got plenty of work to do if you're late." Going out for two client lunches a day had a way of eating up the clock.

———

Something had changed between them. Maybe it was their fight, or maybe they'd just seen each other enough times, but it no longer seemed like they were having a business meeting. They were friends, having dinner together.

Maddie chose the restaurant. She picked the one she hadn't been to yet that day. It was the most casual of Greenville's three sit-down restaurants, which was fine with her.

Featuring large wooden booths stained dark, the place was more of a bar than a restaurant. The entire place had a dark, smoky vibe to it, but that was oddly nice. It was definitely the kind of place that friends, rather than professional acquaintances, would frequent.

Maddie ordered a beer to go with her cheeseburger and fries. Might as well make the day a total blowout. Cody had the same, and they sat there, sipping on their beers for a few minutes in companionable silence. Cody broke the quiet. "You know so much about me, but I don't even know where you're from."

"Right next door. From your mother state."

Cody sat there for a second, frowning, then she nodded and smiled. "You're a Virginia girl, huh?"

"I am. I grew up about an hour and a half outside DC."

"Mmm. The big city."

"Yes, it's pretty big. We didn't go into DC very often, though. It's almost rural around where I lived."

"Almost," Cody said, smiling. "Have you ever been married?"

Almost spitting her beer, Maddie said, "That was a big jump from 'where did you grow up'?"

"I'm so sorry. I don't meet many people…any people…that I didn't grow up around. I'm not sure how you do this."

Maddie chuckled at the way she'd put that. "You have nothing to apologize for. To answer your question, I've never been married. I'm just a swinging single girl, hitting all the hot nightspots in Greenville." She could have gone on, told more about herself, but she thought it was best to stay fairly topical. They had to make the transition from business to personal slowly.

"There are nightspots in Greenville?"

"Not that I've found. One wouldn't guess this, but I was bound and determined to live in a big city. Even DC wasn't big enough for me. But I wound up in Greenville, and I'm still not quite sure how that happened." Laughing softly, she took a drink of her beer. "You never know how things will turn out."

Giving her a surprisingly open look, clearly showing her feelings, Cody said, "I'm really glad you wound up here."

That seemed a little intimate. Maybe it wouldn't in a week or two, but it felt that way right now. Maddie tried to back away, saying, "What about you? Have you ever been married?"

"Hardly," Cody said, chuckling. "I've never really been interested in anyone."

That seemed unlikely, but Maddie didn't think she should follow up. Switching topics seemed like a better idea. "Would you mind if we cleared the air a little bit about business?"

Cody didn't reply with words. She just shrugged.

That wasn't much of an invitation, but Maddie chugged on. "I'm not sure if I've ever made this clear, but it looks good for me to have your money in my branch."

Those big brown eyes shot wide open.

"Your money was many times more than our total deposits the day you came in. So it looks like I massively increased our deposits in just a few months. That looks good for me."

Hesitantly, Cody said, "I'm glad. I want you to look good."

"I'm just telling you that because I want you to understand that I'm not interested in looking good at your expense." She reached across the table and put her hand over Cody's. "I'm concerned. You really should hire a financial manager and let him or her guide you."

Cody's head shook decisively. "I'm not comfortable with that."

"Okay. We've already talked about Treasury bills. The next safest thing is to break your money up into two-hundred-and-fifty-thousand-dollar batches and open a savings account in every bank in the state. Actually, there probably aren't enough banks in the state. You'd have to roam."

"Nope."

Maddie placed both of her hands on the table and said, "Okay. I'm finished."

"Good. Spring turkey season is pretty soon. Do you hunt?"

She was quite deft with the *non sequitur*. "No, I grew up indoors." She laughed at how that sounded, adding, "I'm not exaggerating much. I've never been near a gun."

"Bow hunting?" Her eyes showed she was teasing.

"No, I clearly eat animals, but I take the easy way out and let other people kill them."

This time she looked deadly serious. "You don't fish?"

"I wouldn't know which end of the pole to put the…bait on. It's called bait, isn't it?"

"You might not like hunting, but everybody likes fishing. Come to Ramp and I'll show you."

Maddie took a long pull from her beer and said, "I've grown fond of my wheels. Would I be able to bring them home with me?"

A wide, toothy grin smiled back at her. "Guaranteed."

When Maddie had a free moment one afternoon, she called her friend Avery. She hadn't found anyone to confide in at her new job, and old friends never wanted to hear about work or clients. Plus, he was usually pretty good at telling her when she was doing anything too risky for her career.

"Avery," she said when he answered. "Got a minute?"

"Of course, principessa." She wasn't sure why he referred to her as an Italian princess. She was neither. "What's the big news from Greendot?"

"Not much. I had dinner with my reluctant millionaire the other night." She held her breath, waiting for him to react.

"Not a good idea, girl. You're showing too much interest. I saw a picture of her, and I'll admit she's cute, or that you'd think she's cute, but she's a nonstarter."

"I'm not interested in her in that way," she insisted. "But I think she's a lesbian and…" And what? Did all lesbians have to congregate?

"It'd be bad enough if she were a man. But snuggling up with a woman…" He let her imagine the consequences on her own. "Don't risk it."

"I'm not doing anything, Avery. Even if I liked her as a…whatever…I don't want to stay here one minute longer than I have to. I'm not going to get tangled up with a local."

"You thought Charleston was too small," he snickered.

"Hey, I thought I was lowering my standards to look for jobs in Pittsburgh. When I got out of college, I had my heart set on New York, San Francisco, or Los Angeles. Chicago was my fallback if none of the big three came through."

"Funny what having to live at home with your parents for two years can do to your requirements."

"Yeah, that was funny all right. Waiting tables and begging every bank in the western hemisphere for an interview gave me a whole new perspective."

"You've gone from small to smaller, Maddie. There's a trend. You might as well start shopping for a bride in Greendot."

"I'm not averse to being in a relationship. Far from it. But it wouldn't be Cody—even if she wasn't forbidden fruit."

"I think you're lying. She's exactly your type. Oh, hell, I could convince myself she was my type. Her bank balance would make me completely forget she didn't have a penis."

That would have been the oddest pairing ever. "I guess she would be my type, but I don't think she's ever been kissed. Her town has about six people in it, and she's related to all of them. And *please* don't make any incest jokes."

"I wouldn't stoop so low. I know small towns, so it doesn't surprise me if she's as pure as an angel. Gayness is as foreign as a good Chinese restaurant."

"That's probably true. It's a shame," she said, finally letting her guard down. "She's the kind of woman you could trust with your life. But I'm not the kind of woman who'd take a frightened lesbian's virginity. One of her relatives would show up on my doorstep with a shotgun…and I don't mean that in the figurative sense."

CHAPTER ELEVEN

EVERY TIME MADDIE HAD seen people fishing in movies or on TV they were sitting on verdant green grass, and butterflies were flittering around in the dappled sun. They were always barefoot, and usually had their tootsies in the water to stay cool. Shivering by leafless trees on ground just barely cleared of snow didn't have the same allure as those mental images, but given the forty-five degree temperature, barefoot toe-dipping seemed unlikely.

Cody, however, assured her this would be a perfect day. Given that Cody was able to wear a light jacket in the coldest weather the mountains could throw at her, she might not be the best person to judge by. It was clear and sunny, though, and the blue sky stretched out before Maddie as she drove over the winding country road.

Finding the trailer was much easier this time, since Cody had tacked a cardboard "Welcome" sign to a big tree by the road. Pretty cute. That was probably the only "welcome" sign in the county, but maybe Cody would start a trend.

As soon as she pulled in, Cody bounded out of her home, wearing... new clothes!

Maddie got out and whistled appreciatively. "How many guns had to be held to your head to get you into those?"

"Just one." She laughed. "My cousin Mandy went with me to the outdoor store for my weekly ammo run." A dark scowl covered her face. "My cousins like shooting at cans more than getting their butts out of bed and hunting something worthwhile." She shook her head and took in a slow breath, as if she had to clear the thought of her cousins' wastefulness from her brain. "Mandy said people would start to think I was mentally ill if I kept wearing Devin's old stuff."

"That's all it took to convince you? You've got a whole ensemble there."

Cody looked fantastic in the clothes that fit her slim, wiry frame properly. Maddie hadn't realized how long and lean her legs were, or how trim her waist. She must have been staring, because Cody started to explain her outfit. "They said you can wear lighter stuff if you dress in layers. So I got this little jacket," she tugged on a gray, close-fitting garment, "and a vest, and a waterproof shell." She chuckled. "I don't know why they call a rain jacket a shell, but wearing all three keeps me warmer than the huge hunting jacket I used to wear. Plus I don't look like a little girl wearing her brother's clothes."

Maddie marveled at how put-together she looked. But she didn't want to get too enthusiastic, afraid she'd make Cody feel like she'd looked ridiculous before. "Those slacks are really nice. I love that dark grey color."

"That's stone," she said, wrinkling up her nose. "I wanted all dark brown that wouldn't show dirt, but Mandy wouldn't allow it. I'm glad I let her talk me into different colors."

"It all looks really nice. What color is that shirt?"

"Pewter." Cody looked like she'd just come up with the right answer on a big test. "It was hard for me to buy clothes that expensive, but I've got to get over thinking I have to save every penny." She fingered the material of her new pants. "These resist water and stains, and the shirt is supposed to repel bugs. If I'm not covered in mosquito bites this summer, I'll be a very happy woman."

Maddie put her hand on the shoulder of the thin vest. "How does it feel to have something that fits well?"

"Odd. Very odd. But I'll get used to it." Her eyes settled on some spot in the distance and her voice grew soft. "It's only been the last few years that I stopped caring about my clothes."

How did you respond to that? "Uhm…what changed?"

"We never had much, but my mama kept us afloat. Besides gathering moss, she could sew a little. My clothes were homemade, and looked it. Not because my mama didn't do a good job, but I wore slacks and blouses while the other kids wore jeans and T-shirts. Still, I looked all right."

"I bet you did." She could picture a young Cody in homemade slacks and a simple shirt while everyone else wore brand-name gear with logos. Kids were cruel to anyone who looked even a tiny bit different from the norm. She must have been taunted constantly.

"After high school, I decided I didn't care to go to the trouble." She showed a sad smile. "Ever since then people have given me their stuff right before it goes into the rag bag." She ran her hand down her sleeve, almost caressing the fabric. "I'm turning over a new leaf."

"That's the spirit. I know you'll never throw money away just for the heck of it, but you deserve to be warm and dry and have things that fit."

"Everybody deserves that, but I can have it now, and I'm going to try to get used to it."

"Excellent. So…where do we go?"

"I thought we could go to a place I really like, but it's wa-a-ay deep in the forest. We'll need some assistance."

Her racy grin compelled Maddie to hop in the Jeep and hold on tight.

———

They had to stop at two different places to collect them, but they eventually sat astride borrowed four wheelers, ready to take on whatever the forest could throw at them. Maddie was a neophyte, but Cody insisted she'd get the hang of it quickly. "Just follow me and don't let yourself get too far off horizontal."

"I don't want to be at all off horizontal!"

"You'll be fine." Cody took off, fishing gear strapped tidily to the remarkably filthy four wheeler she drove. Maddie wasn't sure where the vehicles had been, but they would have weighed ten pounds less if someone had washed the mud off them.

She had to concentrate intently to keep up with Cody as they crossed over creeks, massive roots that shot out of trees, and every other kind of vegetation a forest could sustain in late winter. Their four wheelers made quite a racket, but the forest was otherwise devoid of man-made noise. A few hawks and other chatty birds called out, but the engines blocked everything softer.

Given how Cody seemed to love the peace and quiet of the woods, it was surprising they were riding rather than walking. But after they'd been jolted and jarred over hill and dale for a half hour, Maddie silently thanked Cody for her foresight.

They reached a clearing where Cody stopped and turned off her engine. "We can walk the last bit. It's pretty level from here on." A charming grin appeared. "I didn't think you'd appreciate the terrain up till now."

"Oh, I appreciated it. I appreciated not having to walk over it."

Cody carried everything, holding a fishing pole in one hand and slinging a gear bag over the opposite shoulder. Then they started out, quickly being enveloped once again by the woods. The wind was very mild, with just the tops of the tall trees moving about and making a strangely appealing sound. It was like the big trees took the brunt, protecting them as they walked. "This is nice," Maddie said. "I've never been in a forest. It's a whole new world for me."

Cody stopped abruptly, staring, open-mouthed. "You're not serious."

"Yeah, I am. Completely. I wasn't kidding when I said I grew up indoors."

"But...why?"

"You don't have to look that sorry for me," Maddie teased. "I told you I had older brothers. They were both really involved in sports, mostly basketball and wrestling. So I spent a huge part of my youth going to their games and matches and things."

"But that didn't take every minute...did it?"

"Well, no, I guess not. But we just tended to do things indoors." She shrugged, having little insight into the reasons for her family's habits.

"What about you? Did you play any sports?"

"I did rugged, outdoorsy stuff like student government and yearbook. I also worked backstage on some plays the drama department put on. All indoors," she added with a wink.

"Remarkable. Don't you get...itchy being inside?"

"Uhm...no. Itch free." They continued to walk, with Cody floating along, seeming to know where every dip and rise was without looking. Maddie carefully put each step down precisely, treating the forest floor like a warren of ankle sprains just waiting for her. "Is that how you feel when you're inside too much? Itchy?"

"Yeah. I like being warm and dry as much as the next person, but I'd rather freeze and shiver than be inside all the time. I don't see how people can stand it."

"I can stand it easily. Freezing and shivering are two of my least favorite words," Maddie said, smiling back when Cody turned and gave her an indulgent grin.

They continued to walk, and Maddie tried to let herself experience the foreign environment. It was remarkably peaceful…yes, that was the word for it. But the peace came mostly from the absence of man-made noise. That was kinda awesome.

The forest was actually full of sound…but only from chirping birds, skittering creatures of some kind, and the sharp snap of a stick breaking— whether from the wind or an animal, she didn't know. If she'd been alone, Maddie would have been jumping out of her skin every time an odd sound hit her ears. But Cody seemed so…at home…that she found herself relaxing more and more. Who would have guessed you could leave the hustle and bustle of Greenville behind that easily? Okay, it was only big enough for bustle. Still…

They finally reached the spot Cody had in mind. The sound of rushing water had reached them a few dozen yards away, and now they were almost at the banks. "Oh, Cody, this is lovely," Maddie breathed.

A slow moving river lay before them, the short, thin plants along the banks vivid green and unusually lush, especially for late winter. Big, old trees with moss hanging on some of the branches dotted the banks. "I'd normally shimmy up there and reduce that by about twenty-five percent," Cody said thoughtfully, pointing at the kelly green plant clinging to a thick limb. "But we're here for fun, not work."

Maddie wanted to ask whether Cody was planning on continuing her career in the moss business, but thought the question might be impertinent. Collecting moss was probably more than a job to her, although what that additional element might be was anyone's guess.

Cody put her finger to her lips and started picking her way down what looked like a rough trail…probably created by her own footsteps. They walked quietly, and Cody held up her hand when they were about twenty-five feet from the water. Then she pointed at a…thing…some kind of assemblage of sticks and twigs and good-sized branches. The structure damned up a branch of the river, making a good-sized pool. As they watched, a beaver popped his head out and looked around. Maddie flinched, and grasped Cody's shoulder excitedly. "Look!" she whispered.

Cody turned around and gave her a look that said, "That's why we're here," but she politely didn't add words. Another beaver popped out from under the dam, then another. These two were smaller and looked younger than the first, and their heads continually peeked out of the water after diving for goodness knew what.

They stayed right there, watching the beavers work or play or whatever they were doing, for a long while. Maddie tried to keep a list of questions organized in her head, but this not speaking thing was hard.

Finally, the big beaver disappeared, and the smaller ones didn't show themselves for a few minutes. Cody turned and pointed to the left, then got in front and led Maddie away from the scene.

"That was fantastic!" Maddie enthused. "I've never, ever seen anything like that in my entire life!"

"You've never seen a beaver?" Cody asked suspiciously.

"I've never seen a river!" Maddie said, laughing at the doubting look Cody gave her. "Well, I've seen rivers, but I've never walked up to one."

"I'm…" She stood there, looking absolutely stunned.

"I know it sounds odd, but we went to the mall on weekends, not to the river. Those *were* beavers, right? Not otters or something like that?"

"No, those were beavers." She still looked amazed. "What…what's it like seeing one for the first time?"

Maddie had to think about that. "It's…kinda magical," she admitted. "I've never felt so…naturey."

"Naturey, huh? I like that." They walked over and stopped by the far bank of the river, and Cody pointed to a series of pools created by boulders. "Those are just deep enough, and just cold enough to be the best skinny dipping spots in the county. When it's hot and humid and you're sticky from sitting in the sun fishing, or climbing trees—can't be beat." She paused and blinked. "You've been skinny dipping, right?"

"Only in a swimming pool. Does that count?"

"Nope. Not even close."

―――᷽―――

They kept walking, eventually stopping at a glade near the river. Cody produced a tarp from her pack and shook it out. "I normally sit on a tree stump, but I wanted to make sure you were comfortable."

Maddie sat down, waiting expectantly.

"Lunch," Cody proclaimed.

She produced a few foil wrapped bundles and handed one to Maddie. If this was something weird…like snake or raccoon…she was going to have to struggle to be able to give it a polite bite. When Cody unwrapped hers first, Maddie saw that it was good, old-fashioned ham and cheese. Realizing she was starving from the exercise, she hurried to uncover hers and take a bite.

They sat there near the quiet river, letting the squawks, squeaks and caws from unnamed animals serenade them. "This is really the nicest time I've ever had outdoors," Maddie said.

"Sounds like it might be the *first* time you've had outdoors." Cody's dry delivery was awfully cute, and the way her eyes revealed her teasing topped her delivery on the cuteness scale.

They finished their sandwiches, and Cody produced something dark and flat. "Venison jerky," she said. "Made it myself. This one's sweet and spicy."

Venison. That was deer, right? Like Bambi? No, like Bambi's *mom*, killed by a hunter. Maddie could still make herself tear up when she thought of the scene from the movie. But you couldn't refuse homemade food, even if the thought of it did turn your stomach. Maddie reached out and took a small piece, chewing delicately. "This is good," she said, amazed. "It's really spicy."

"I use cayenne pepper along with molasses and brown sugar. Some of my cousins don't like spicy food, so I make it as hot as I can stand." She grinned mischievously. "Then I can keep more for myself."

Maddie didn't think she'd ever consider it one of her favorite foods, but it wasn't gamey…which had been her fear. The spices and sugars took care of that.

"You know what I've been wondering?" Cody asked, now stretched out on the tarp as if she were on a comfortable sofa.

"No, I don't. Tell me."

She pointed at Maddie with her remaining jerky stick. "I've been wondering what you do for fun."

"Fun?" Maddie took a few seconds to ponder. It wasn't a good sign that nothing came to mind immediately. "Well, I usually run after work…" She trailed off, thinking that was more work than fun. "I go to see some old friends in Huntington or Charleston if I have the whole weekend off." Shrugging, she said, "That's a small list, isn't it."

"Yes, it is." She chewed thoughtfully, gazing at Maddie with hooded eyes. "What kind of friends do you visit? Like…romantic friends?"

"Romantic…oh!" All right. This was the moment of truth. She was clearly asking who you date. Tell her. "Uhm, no, not really." Damn, why was this still hard after so many years? "One of the people I see is an ex-girlfriend, but the others are just people I know from working there."

"Ex-girlfriend? Like a friend you don't like any more?"

"No. Like a woman I used to date." There. Done and done.

Cody's eyes were as wide as they could get without popping from her head. "You're a…?" She clearly couldn't even make herself say the word.

"Yeah," Maddie said, chuckling. "I'm a lesbian."

She looked very suspicious, then laughed nervously. "You're pulling my leg."

"No, I'm not." Oh-oh. It was a long, long walk home if Cody didn't cotton to lesbians. "Aside from some weak attempts to date boys, I've identified that way since I was in high school."

"Identified?"

What in the hell was she asking? "That's when I came out…to myself. I told my family right before I went to college."

"I can't tell if you're being serious," Cody said, her eyes narrowed. "Are you really?"

"Yes, Cody. I'm not sure why you're amazed, but yes, I'm gay."

"You don't look it. At all." Her dark head shook vigorously.

"This is how lesbians look," she said, framing her face with her hands. "You don't agree?"

"That's not what I...thought. You wear lipstick and makeup on your eyes."

"Yes, a lot of other lesbians do too. Where are you getting your examples from? Do you know any lesbians from around here?"

"No. Well, there's one woman who everyone says is. She's a little bitty banty rooster, old as the hills, and she has a crew-cut and chews tobacco. People steer clear of her. Mean," she added, ominously.

"We come in all shapes and sizes. You really can't assume lesbians look a certain way." There was some...yearning...some need so stark it was almost visible. It was probably too soon, but she asked anyway. "What about you? Who're you attracted to?"

The question in those dark eyes was snuffed out in a second. "No one." She shook her head and stood, then started to pack up their things. "I've never been interested in anyone."

Maddie stood as well, then made herself say, "Does my being a lesbian...bother you?"

"No, no, why would it?" She displayed a very artificial-looking smile. "I'm just surprised, since I've never met one...that said that's what she was." She winced. "I don't mean to make it sound like you're a thing. You know what I mean, don't you?"

"Yeah, I think I do." But she didn't. Not really. Was Cody afraid of her own sexuality? Or of Maddie's? One way or the other, something was making her look like she had ants in her pants and desperately needed to put the conversation far, far behind her.

———

They started off again, continuing down the bank of the river. Cody seemed at ease once more when she steered the conversation away from sex. "Tell me more about your family," she said as they walked along, side by side.

"We're pretty average, I'd say. Both my parents work for a company that makes advanced weapon systems for the military."

"Really? That sounds...hard."

Laughing, Maddie said, "They don't design them or anything. My dad operates a computerized tool and die machine and my mom's the person who puts that 'inspected by Number 88' sticker on finished parts."

"I don't know what that is…"

"Someone does a final inspection when a part comes off the assembly line. My mom does quality control."

Cody's eyebrows were raised up high. "She works a line?"

"Yeah. They were at different factories until about five years ago when my dad's shop closed down. Luckily, a big defense contract came in and he was able to get on at the place my mom works."

"That's amazing," she said slowly. "I thought you'd be a doctor's daughter or something like that."

"No, we're blue collar."

Cody's impish smile showed. "We're no collar. Maybe no shirt!"

Maddie was sorely tempted to take her hand. Cody was just plain adorable, making those little jokes and showing rapt interest in Maddie's life. It was ridiculously nice to have a woman be interested in what you had to say.

"We're shirt-wearing people, but we've been blue collar for a long time. Both my grandfathers worked in Navy shipbuilding yards."

"I'm still trying to make that fit with how you seem. I thought for sure you came up rich."

"No, not a bit. But even though my parents were working class, they made it clear they wanted us to be professionals. They thought we'd be more secure that way."

"Are you?" Cody looked like she was slightly afraid to hear the answer.

"Mmm, not really. The bank's always the target for takeovers from the big guys. If that happens, they'll close a bunch of branches." She shrugged. "At our last monthly meeting, they said they were considering having one person manage two branches."

"Two? How could you do that?"

"I'm not sure," she said, chuckling wryly. "You might be able to do it if both branches were in the same town, but not out here. It's forty minutes to the next closest location."

"Does anyone have a safe job?" Cody asked, sounding rather forlorn.

"Politicians!" Maddie smiled brightly when Cody turned and scowled.

"Please don't ruin my day."

They stopped at an achingly beautiful spot, where the river took a gentle turn and the water cascaded over big rocks half submerged in the rapidly flowing stream. "My God, Cody, I can see why you'd want to live outside if you could be here."

"This is one of my favorite spots. For fishing. In late winter and early spring."

"I have a feeling you have an awful lot of favorite spots."

"You need to. Every place has a little something different to offer."

"I guess I assumed people went outside mainly in the summer. You know, when it's nice out."

Cody laughed at that. "There's less going on in the summer than any other time of the year. I love fishing, so I love summer, but fall and winter are when things are really popping out here." She put her gear down, and started to assemble the rod and reel, talking while she did. "Since you don't have a license, I only brought one pole. If there's a game warden anywhere around here, it'll be a first, but it's best to be careful. If we get stopped, you're just observing."

"I can get a license."

"Yes, you can, but there's no sense if you don't like fishing." She grinned, a confident, almost cocky smile that made Maddie's knees weak. "Although who wouldn't like fishing is beyond me."

Cody proceeded to talk at length about all of the myriad regulations the state imposed on fishing. The type of fish one could catch, the size, the number, the season, the kind of bait, lures, and other items too arcane for Maddie to even begin to grasp. Then she started in on proper technique. Maddie must have looked as puzzled as she felt, for Cody finally said, "Just watch."

She walked from rock to rock until she was standing tall on a flat topped one almost in the middle of the stream. Her wrist snapped, and the reel let the fly soar balletically into the air and land softly in the water many, many yards ahead. She stood there, jiggling her rod for a while, then reeled it in and started over again.

Maddie dearly wished she'd had a camera to record the graceful movements Cody made when she stretched and flexed her body to get the fly to do what she wanted. It took a while, but Cody purred contentedly when her line snapped taut. Reeling the fish in while she hopped from one rock to the next, she jumped onto the bank and pulled the squirming fish from the water. It was remarkably beautiful, flipping wildly in the air, with the sun showing a wealth of colors on its smooth skin. Maddie was certain she didn't have the stomach to kill it.

Luckily, Cody took a pair of pliers from her pocket, cut the hook and had the fish back in the water with an amazing economy of movement. "He'll live to fight another day," she said, sounding a little disappointed.

"Why'd you do that?"

"I figured we'd catch and release." She smiled like an indulgent adult helping a child do something mildly frightening. "We'll take a baby step."

"We don't need to do that. I feel like I'm hurting your enjoyment. Go ahead and keep the fish if you want."

"I'm having a fantastic time. Come out here with me and I'll show you how to do it." She held a hand out and Maddie took it. They jumped from rock to rock, finally standing side by side on the big boulder in the middle of the river. The water flowed by, making tinkling sounds against the rock as it sped away.

Cody stood behind Maddie and showed her how to hold the rod, then held her arm and demonstrated how to snap her wrist. She was sure she was making a very poor copy of Cody's form, but it was still fun. Having Cody's reassuring presence right behind her was nice, too, and made her forget she could fall and drown in about two seconds. Her swimming skills left something to be desired.

A fish caught the fly and the reel started spinning. "Help!"

Chuckling, Cody put both arms around Maddie and calmly let the fish play the line out for a moment, then slowly reeled him in. When Cody held him up in front of her, Maddie wanted to touch him, his flesh shining in the muted light that filtered through the canopy of trees. But he was back in the water, swimming away before she could ask. "I'm loving this," she said, amazed at how true it was. "I don't want to take them home, but it's really nice pulling them out for a visit."

—∞—

They kept at it, leisurely casting for a long time. Cody seemed almost tranquilized, and Maddie thought there'd be fewer prescriptions written if everyone had this kind of beauty to relax in. "When did you know?" Cody asked, standing so close her breath tickled Maddie's ear when she spoke.

"Know…?" Ahh. The lesbian question was back. "I think I knew…in one way or another…all of my life. Even as a little girl, I was always interested in other girls. I don't think I ever had a true crush on a boy."

"But you said you…tried to like them?"

"Yeah, I suppose I wanted to fit in. I figured that maybe I hadn't given them enough of a chance. So I tried to make myself interested, but no matter how much I tried, it wasn't right for me."

"That's interesting. Did your parents…were they…upset?"

"I don't think it was a surprise, to be honest. When your daughter's life revolves around one girl after another, and she never seems interested in boys, a perceptive mom just knows. My dad was puzzled, but he got over that pretty quickly."

"Somebody told my mama I was qu…lesbian," she said quietly. "Some nasty little polecat from grade school and her mama came up to mine and said the other girls were calling me queer."

"Oh, Cody." Damn, did she have *any* uplifting stories from her past? "That must have been upsetting."

"It was fine. My mama told her to keep her nose out of our business, and if they didn't like how I was they could stick it." She chuckled softly at the memory. "I think she wanted to say something stronger, but my mama didn't swear."

"Did she talk to you about it afterward?"

"No. The whole thing made me feel funny, though, and I tried to avoid talking to people who weren't from here."

"Kids can be very cruel."

"Yeah, they can. I thought about it over the years, though." She seemed so shy and tentative it was heart-rending. "You know?"

"Yes, I know." Well? Get to it, woman!

"I figured out I was asexual. I looked it up, and that seemed to fit."

"Hmm. I suppose some people are. But maybe you just haven't had many opportunities to explore your sexuality. It's hard to pick what you like when the shelves are only filled with relatives."

"Maybe," she allowed. "But that's what I think."

Maddie was sure that Cody Keaton was as much a lesbian as she was. She was also sure that her identity frightened or at least confused her. But she wasn't going to be the one to try to lure Cody out. She was so sweet and unspoiled, it would have been like hitting on a fifteen-year-old. No, as attracted as she was, Maddie had to keep her thoughts…and her hands off the breasts that occasionally pressed into her back when they moved together to let the fly zoom through the air. Damn it all to hell!

—⁓—

They stood in front of Cody's house, both of them seemingly unwilling to let the day end. "Do you have dogs, or not?" Maddie asked, looking at the empty doghouse.

"Oh. Yeah, kinda, but we all share them. They're supposed to be hunting dogs, but they don't really know it."

"Are they…pets?"

"Pets? They don't come inside if that's what you mean. They're just a pair of mountain curs, one brindle and one blue."

"Mountain curs? Is that a breed?"

"I suppose. They're just hunting dogs. Everyone around here has one or two."

"I'd like to meet them. I like dogs."

"Then you'll have to come back. I'm not sure where they are, but they'll turn up eventually. You'll just have to time it right."

She was absolutely adorable when she teased like that, and Maddie purposefully broke their gaze and got into her car. The urge to hug her was acute, but no good could come of that. "I had a spectacular day. Really. It was fantastic."

"Same goes for me." She put her hands on the door and leaned on it for a moment. "Don't be a stranger."

—⁓—

The sun had just gone down behind the big hill to Greenville's north when Maddie got near. She'd been along the road many times before, but had never stopped long enough to take a good, long look. There was no traffic, there never was on a late Sunday afternoon, so she pulled over to do just that.

It looked like someone had threaded a string through a few dozen houses and placed it carefully along a ridge. The houses lined up, single file, then looped back and down, heading for the floor of the valley.

The valley itself was very narrow. At one point in town it felt like you could reach out and touch the hills that bracketed the main street as they started to climb.

Aside from the two main strips of houses, and two commercial streets, that was the whole town. When you stood on Main Street, a big hill loomed in front of you and filled your field of vision. It was an odd place, very insular, and much smaller and more rugged than any place Maddie had ever been. But when she looked at it from a distance, she could easily see why people had decided to settle there.

It was only when you got close, and saw that many of the shops and restaurants had closed that it could feel small and stultifying. People claimed the town was thriving and vibrant in the fifties, but that was an age ago. No, the commercial aspect was dismal. The natural beauty—that was impressive. All she had to do was concentrate on deadening her focus on the man-made things and sharpening it on nature's gifts. Damn! She was beginning to sound like Cody!

CHAPTER TWELVE

MAYBE SHE WASN'T EXACTLY asexual. But she would have confidently made that claim just a few months ago. Now…now…things were different. The throbbing between her legs was like a drumbeat whenever Maddie was close. She had a feeling asexual people didn't focus on one particular woman and burn with need whenever their bodies touched.

Cody was adrift with unanswered questions. She could hardly ask Maddie, and her only other sources for romantic advice were her aunts. Her aunt Lurlene might have been very happy to talk about the birds and the bees, or just the bees…Cody wasn't sure which one was the female… but she couldn't have considered asking her. Some things just weren't done. Besides, this was deeply private stuff. Something she should have put some energy into resolving years earlier.

It had just seemed like a waste of time and energy. She'd never really had a reason to put herself in one camp or the other, and letting it ride had let her think of herself as just a single woman in an area with few marriageable men. The hollows were full of single women, since men around there were loath to be tied down—but most of them had a kid or two. A young cousin had asked why she didn't have a baby of her own, and it had been easy to say she couldn't afford another mouth to feed. That excuse had flown out the window when her fortune had flown in. She couldn't use the poverty excuse any more, and having money probably made people wonder if she was marriageable.

The money would let her branch out now, seek out what she wanted and go get it. Her car worked, she had some nice clothes, her smile was back in place, and she didn't technically have to spend twelve hours a day gathering moss. It was time to figure this out.

As she almost always did when she wanted answers, Cody went to the library. There were two that she frequented. The big one, in Greenville, home of the county library, and a smaller branch in Twined Creek. Both had internet access, and the one in Twined Creek was usually only frequented by mothers and their kids going to story time, and old folks, neither group using the internet much.

She headed over a few days after Maddie had come to fish. It was rainy and a cold wind was blowing through the hollow, making it less than ideal for any of her favored pursuits.

When she went to the library she tended to keep a low profile. The librarians seemed nice enough, but they were kinda snooty, and she always felt they looked down on her in her too roomy army uniform.

Now she wore a pair of jeans that fit close to her skin and a snug, long-sleeved T-shirt that was supposed to be the first layer in what they called a system. If she'd known how warm and comfortable shirts like this were, she might have longed for one before. But all things had their time, and now was hers.

It made her feel good to see the sea-foam green shirt peeking out through her new jacket. She walked with a certain pride as she cruised into the small, squat building. Wearing color was a luxury she'd never had, but she thought she could easily grow used to it.

Both computers were available when Cody went over and signed in. For reasons she couldn't understand, you could only get access for a half hour at a time. Then you had to go back and ask for more. The librarian always gave permission, as long as no one else was waiting, but it seemed dumb. Why not let you use it until someone else asked for it? She would have asked, but she'd learned that people liked rules—just for rule's sake, she supposed.

Starting off slowly, she poked around, finally typing in "how do you know if you're a lesbian?" in the search box. She got what seemed like a million hits, and clicked on the most promising ones. Forgetting the time, she found herself engrossed in suggestions like "think of how it would feel to touch someone of your own sex." That was nice. Especially when she pictured Maddie smiling at her when she put her hands on her shoulders and let them slide down her arms.

Then the site said not to be confused just because you had an attraction to a particular person. It was normal to have a fantasy about a friend or a celebrity. It suggested you think of people other than the one you usually focused on to see if your attraction was more general. She looked around. There were a few young mothers and their kids. Nothing. The librarian? Nope. She looked like a less pretty version of her granny. No, Maddie was the one she was interested in. But maybe it was only a crush or a fantasy. The site said there was a difference between having a thought and wishing you could act it out. Well, that was easy. She'd act it out with Maddie right that second if she had the chance.

The screen went dark, and she sighed and went back to the front desk. "Can I have another half hour please?"

The woman looked at the big clock, then at the signup sheet. "You still have time." The counter swung up and she stood next to Cody. "That one's been acting up." Before Cody could stop her, she walked over and started playing with the cord and the screen glared brightly again. The woman took a glance down and her eyes widened when she saw the image on the screen. The article Cody had been reading showed a thumbnail photo of two young women kissing. She'd clicked on it because one of them looked a little like Maddie with her golden hair and shining eyes. The woman she was kissing didn't look a thing like Cody, but she'd closed her eyes and tried to think of how it would feel to have Maddie pressed up against her like that.

Seeing that image now, with the librarian right next to her, made her want to climb into a hole. Her face heated up and her ears burned when the librarian leaned over and hissed, "We have children in this library, young lady. They don't need to be exposed to this kind of"—she sputtered when she spat—"filth."

Making a mad dash for her coat, Cody scurried from the library, certain she'd never set foot in the place again. She jumped into her car and peeled out, shame burning in her like a harsh flame.

—⁓—

Cody was mortified, and the embarrassment wore at her for two whole days. It wasn't even the thought that the librarian might have told other people about it—even though that was possible. It was being singled out and made fun of. That was the thing she hated more than anything on earth. Like she was different in some important way, and other people were better.

There wasn't a soul she could talk to, so she kept to herself, not even heading over to her cousin Melissa's house for Caleb's birthday party. Since he was only a baby, he wouldn't know, but she rarely stayed away from family celebrations.

She sat in her trailer, trying to read, but the words kept merging into one another. It was Friday night, almost suppertime, and she didn't have a thing in the house other than canned goods. She'd often had beans or potatoes for dinner, but she wasn't in the mood for pure sustenance. Might as well skip dinner altogether.

When her phone rang, she hoped it wasn't her aunt chiding her for skipping the party. "Hello?"

"Hi," Maddie's cheerful voice said. "What's going on in Ramp today?"

"Oh!" Hearing that sweet tone made her heart race. It felt like Maddie could see what had been going on, and somehow knew how troubled Cody was.

"Cody? Is everything all right?"

For possibly the first time in her life, she broke down in tears in front of someone other than her mother. "No," she sobbed. "I…"

"I'll be there in an hour," Maddie announced and hung up.

Oh, Lord. How was she ever going to explain this?

True to her word, Maddie was there in a little less than an hour. She'd obviously gone home after work, since she wore dark blue jeans and a salmon-colored, V-necked sweater. Cody had seen a lot of her clothes, but she was sure she'd not seen this particular sweater. There was no way she'd forget the way it caressed Maddie's womanly body, showing off the curves her business suits generally covered. "What's wrong?" she asked, her pretty blue eyes scanning Cody carefully, as if she'd show some visible sign of her distress.

"Nothing. I'm…sorry. I'm just having a bad day." She looked around, trying to think of a reason she could be having a tough time. "I'm probably hungry."

"Hungry?" Maddie gave her a very puzzled look. "Okay. Let's go get dinner. I haven't eaten either."

"Uhm, there isn't anyplace…"

"There has to be something in Twined Creek, isn't there?"

"Yeah. There's a roadhouse and they have nachos, I think."

Maddie made for the door. "Then we'll go have some nachos. I'll drive."

They didn't talk a whole lot on the long drive to Twined Creek. Cody twitched around in her seat, trying to think of what excuse she could make for causing a scene, but she came up empty.

They pulled up in front of the roadhouse, already packed early on a Friday night. "Disability checks came today," Cody said, nodding at the filled parking lot.

They went inside and were assaulted by the sound of country music playing loudly, dozens of people wedged in next to one another, plenty of beer flowing, and thick cigarette smoke hanging like fog over the room. Most people seemed to know one another, or the beer had made them instant friends, and they gathered in knots near the bar. A few people yelled over the music, a woman's high-pitched voice squealed with laughter and a couple of big men stood with their arms around each other—bosom buddies until the money ran out. Maddie pointed at the sign hanging from a neon beer advertisement near the corner of the bar. "Nacho machine is broken."

"Greenville?" Cody asked.

Maddie headed straight for the door. Once they were in the car, she said, "A person could starve to death around here."

"I know. The grocery closed when I was in high school. There's a gas station with snacks, and you can buy a few things at the clinic, but that's all. People go to Greenville and stock up. Or go hungry."

"Is that really why you were crying?" Maddie asked gently. "Because you were hungry?"

"No, not really. I had a…bad experience earlier, and I'm still smarting from it."

"What happened?"

It was dark, and the lights on the dash only gave a cold glow to the interior of the car. Talking about it now would save the embarrassment of doing it face to face.

———

After Cody'd finished giving the blow by blow, Maddie sat there for a few seconds, then said with a quiet rage, "If I could get my hands on that woman…"

"Hey, don't be mad. I'm sure she thought she was protecting kids."

"From what?" Maddie demanded. "From information? Screw that! Sanctimonious bitch!"

It truly didn't sound like dirty words belonged in that pretty mouth. Every time she swore, Cody started. She just hoped it wasn't obvious, because she'd do anything to avoid hurting Maddie's feelings. "I guess she thought I was looking at something dirty."

"There's nothing dirty about sex." She stopped, then chuckled. "Well, that's not always true, but there's nothing dirty about love, or desire or attraction." She turned and looked at Cody, empathy almost glowing in her eyes. "Tell me about your feelings. You can trust me."

"Uhm…well, I…"

"Have you ever acted on them?"

"Yes, I…have. Not often, but I have." Thank the lord it was too dark to see the embarrassment that colored her cheeks.

Maddie didn't say anything else. Her eyes were fixed on Cody, but she didn't seem like she was in a hurry to hear more. That made it easier to spit it out.

"Uhm, the first time was right here at the roadhouse."

"Really?"

"Uh-huh. I was probably fifteen or sixteen. I'd gone down to pick up one of my cousins, who'd gotten so drunk total strangers took his keys from him." She chuckled at that. "Mama sent me for some reason, even though I didn't have a driver's license. I got there and my cousin was out cold. An older woman helped me get him into the car. We stood there, cooling off, it was hotter than blazes that night, and she turned around and kissed me."

"A total stranger? Damn, Cody, you were just a girl!"

"No, I wasn't. I looked about like I do now. I'm sure she thought I was over eighteen. Of course, she was plenty drunk. I guess I'm not sure what she was thinking."

"Was that it?"

"I didn't know what to do, so I stayed right there. She kissed me a few more times, but..." She thought of the experience, still fresh in her mind. "Like I said, she was drunk and smelled of cigarettes and gin. I wanted to stay...but I wanted to leave too."

"That's not a very nice story," Maddie said. "That could put you off experimenting for years."

"I had some...experiences with boys, too. Just a few. But they didn't like it when I..." She tried to collect her thoughts, unsure of the dynamic. "It's like they wanted me to sit there and wait for them to decide what to do." She shook her head. "That wasn't appealing."

"No, I can see that wouldn't be your style." She reached over and put her pretty hand on Cody's leg. "Let's go have something decent to eat. I was going to make a salad for dinner, and I've got enough for two. Interested?"

"In going to your house?"

"My apartment, yes." She cast a quick glance Cody's way. "Is that good?"

"Sure." *Oh, Lord.*

———

They had salads, filled with all of the fresh vegetables that Cody knew the local store carried at this time of year. "This is good," she said, pointing at the bowl. "This summer I can make you a vegetable salad that will make your head spin."

"I'd like that. Finding fresh produce isn't easy in Greenville."

"Was it easier in Huntington?"

Maddie shook her head. "There's a reason it's the city with the largest percentage of overweight people in the country. Aisles and aisles of junk food, but not a great selection of produce."

"I'll grow extra this year. You'll have beans coming out your ears."

Maddie took their bowls into the little kitchen, and Cody got up to wander around. It was a stark box, with another box for a bedroom and a smaller box for a bath. Maddie hadn't done much decorating, like she didn't expect to stay long. The walls were beige, the sofa dark brown, and the side chairs brown tweed. Nothing about it seemed like Maddie. Cody would have lost her mind if she'd had to live in a place that cold and soulless.

"It was furnished," Maddie said, coming up behind her. "I bet you're wondering about my lack of taste."

"No!" Dang, she was like a mind reader!

"It's okay. I'm just here so little, and I never...well, hardly ever entertain. Still, I should get busy and put some personal touches in."

"It's nice," Cody lied. "It's clean and everything."

"No, it's not very nice, but there wasn't a lot to choose from. It was this building or the spare bedroom in someone's house." She laughed softly. "I didn't want to scandalize the lady with my lesbian ways." Leading Cody back to the sofa, Maddie sat next to her and said, "I think you have more to say about your past." She patted her on the leg. "Do you?"

Shrugging shyly, Cody admitted, "You know where we had burgers in town?"

"Sure."

"I got a little drunk there one night and found myself in the storeroom with a waitress." Just thinking about it made her blush.

"I see," Maddie said. "Was that your idea?"

"I don't know. Maybe. It's kinda hazy in my head."

"Anything else?"

Cody held up a single finger. "The big one." She took a breath. "A woman at the roadhouse again. Drunk, in the bed of a pickup truck."

"Wow." Maddie smiled, but she looked strangely sad. "That sounds like the big leagues."

"I think she might have been a prostitute," Cody admitted. "At least that's what I hear. She didn't charge me or anything," she hastened to add, "but I think she's gotten to know a lot of people in the area."

"That's the whole roster?"

"Yeah. That's it." She sat there, waiting for Maddie to comment.

"It doesn't sound like you're asexual, Cody." She looked her right in the eye. "It sounds more like you've just not had enough opportunities to decide who you are."

—⁓—

Poor, poor Cody. Sometimes her life sounded like a Dickens tale. Maddie had an image of her, in the middle of the nineteenth century, working in a shoe-blacking factory alongside other dirty-faced children. But this was the twenty-first century in America. She had opportunities. Plenty of them. She just had to be more proactive.

"You have to take some risks," Maddie insisted. "No one can tell you who you are. Only you can do that. But whoever you are, you need to own it. Even if the people closest to you don't like it." Maddie leaned over to force Cody to look into her eyes. She looked so earnest, so willing to take any bit of advice. Maddie considered her words carefully. "You deserve to have a sex life. You deserve it, but *you* have to claim it."

As if the words leaving Maddie's mouth compelled Cody to act, she gently grasped Maddie's shoulders and pulled her close, whispering, "*This* is who I am."

Then her lips pressed against Maddie's, shocking the very fibre of Maddie's soul. Who was this? Where was shy, tentative Cody?

"I don't…" Maddie managed to say as she slowly pulled away. "I don't think this is a good idea."

"Yes, it is. It's the best idea I've ever had." She boldly put her arms around Maddie's shoulders and pulled her into her body.

Cody's warmth enveloped her as muscular arms encircled her in a protective embrace. Then soft, sweet lips found hers and pressed urgently, seeking entrance.

Maddie's brain sent out commands which her body blithely ignored. This couldn't go on! Cody wasn't even sure she was gay, and Maddie wasn't going to be her testing ground. Logical, well reasoned arguments demanding that Maddie pull away were rebuffed, first by her mouth, which opened and gratefully welcomed Cody's tongue. Then her arms rebelled, wrapping themselves tightly around Cody's body, moving with her, responding as though they were one.

Opening herself to Cody, Maddie lay in her arms, letting fervid lips trail down her throat, up near her ears, across her cheeks, returning again and again to her lips. It was like Cody'd done this hundreds of times—not just once or twice in a storeroom or a truck bed.

Thinking of those grim circumstances made Maddie try for control once again. "We shouldn't," she moaned when Cody kissed and nipped along her collarbone.

"Yes, we should." Cody's voice was clear and firm, as if she'd been given orders she was merely carrying out. "This is exactly what we should be doing."

Maddie ceased all resistance, letting her hands tangle in Cody's dark hair, pulling her hard into her body when she began to stray. It was a thrill she hadn't had in years...or ever. That primal, thrumming need that couldn't be resisted no matter how foolish it seemed.

Then Cody slinked her hand between them and palmed Maddie's breast. That simple act seemed to break whatever spell she'd been under, and Maddie put both hands on Cody's shoulders and firmly pushed her away.

Cody's eyes were half-closed and she looked a little drunk, but she pressed hard against Maddie's hands, murmuring, "More. Let me."

"No, *no*," Maddie said, fighting the need that filled her body to overflowing.

Cody's eyes opened wide and she blinked slowly. "Did I hurt you?"

Now she was back. This was the Cody she knew. Sweet, shy, concerned, always thinking of others. "No, of course not. But we have to talk about this."

The rakish grin came back, transforming her once again. "Talking is for later. This is for now." Then she pushed past Maddie's weakened arms and placed a sizzling kiss upon her lips. Her hand went to the waistband of Maddie's jeans, where decisive fingers gripped and pulled the zipper.

"No!" This time Maddie leapt to her feet, making sure to stay several feet away from the forcefield that was this new Cody. "You're a client!"

"I know," she said calmly. "That doesn't matter."

"It does." She forgot why it did, but she thought that was the correct answer. Perching on the edge of a chair, she said, "You don't understand. I don't belong here. As soon as I can, I'm going to move."

"As soon as you can?" Cody looked stunned, like she'd never considered the idea.

"Yes. I need to live in a bigger place. A place with a football team, and lots of movies, and ethnic restaurants, and golf courses. I *need* that."

"You need a football team?" she asked, blinking confusedly.

"No, not specifically. But I need a big town. It's what I've always wanted." She leaned over, close enough to make her point but not so close she got pulled back in. "I can't be casual with you, and I can't afford to get involved. I'll have to leave and it'll be too hard. We'd both be hurt…"

That seemed to register. Cody sat up and straightened her shirt, then ran her hands through her hair. "I understand," she said quietly. "You want more."

"No, not more…just something different." A place where you didn't have to drive for a half hour to find out the nacho machine was broken!

Cody got up and walked over to the window. The view was of nothing but the backside of a house, but she stared at it for a long time. "If I'd ever had something more, I might want it too." She turned around. "But this is all I've ever known."

"I know that." Maddie felt empty. Like there was nothing inside her but a dark void. Feeling Cody's hands on her body had sparked a warmth that Maddie hadn't felt in years, but she was purposefully snuffing it out. Images assaulted her brain. The one that rose to the top was of Cody, her soulful eyes filled with tears as Maddie got into her car to leave the Greenbrier Valley. She couldn't be the person to break that pure heart. She just couldn't. "It's not all I've known" she said, feeling herself mist up. "I miss the things we don't have here. I don't want to give up on getting them again."

"Okay." Cody walked over to the entry table and picked up her coat. Turning, she revealed a sad smile. "You helped me a lot tonight. I think I know who I am now." As she put her coat on she added, "Someone from the hollow will be at one of the places on Main Street, and I can catch a ride. I'll see you."

Then she was gone, leaving Maddie with an ache in her heart and a lump in her throat.

The next day Maddie sat in front of the computer in her office. The bank closed at noon on Saturday, and everyone else had gone, letting her work in private. She scanned the list one more time. Every decent-sized bank in every city in America with a professional sports team and an ethnic makeup of more than one race was listed. She hit the Print key and watched envelope after envelope spit out. She had to get out of there, and soon. No good could come of her staying.

CHAPTER THIRTEEN

CODY SPENT THE WHOLE day walking in the woods. She didn't carry a gun, a fishing pole, or a bag for moss. Nothing but her thoughts accompanied her wanderings.

The feeling of Maddie's lips on hers so filled her mind that she thought the sensation might remain for the rest of her days. Not that she minded. Those kisses were the best things that had ever happened to her, and she desperately wanted to call Maddie and thank her.

Given what she'd told Maddie, it had probably seemed that Cody'd just leapt to a conclusion about being gay last night. But now that she'd faced the truth, Cody had to admit she'd been ignoring the signs all along. She'd honestly been too afraid to think about it and had never been pushed to take a risk. Maddie had helped her break out of the fog. She owed her a lot for that. The question was how would Maddie think about her now? They *had* to stay friends. It would kill her to lose the only outsider she'd ever been able to open up to.

But how did you get your mind off a woman once she'd gotten under your skin? That was a darned funny expression, and one that she now realized was completely apt. Thoughts of Maddie had gotten inside her, had burrowed into her skin and made her whole body thrum with feeling. It was gonna be a huge hurdle to get over, but she'd have to learn to live with it. There was no other way.

A few days later, Cody paused and took account of where she was. She'd been gathering moss since not long after dawn's first light, and had wandered a good ways away from home. You could pick any time, really, but she liked the forest best when it was waking up. That's when it was filled with promise. Anything could happen, and just might.

She knew people thought she was stupid to keep picking moss, but she'd been doing it since she was a girl. Some of her fondest memories were of her mama showing her how to do it right. Even though he was older, Cody had always bested her brother, but she thought that might have been because he never took to it. Keith didn't waste his time on things that didn't come easily or please him. Maybe that's why he was gone. Cooking up drugs seemed very easy, but it hadn't been. He'd paid the price, that was for sure. She shuddered just thinking about it.

Thinking about Keith always took the shine off a day, and she was heavy-hearted when she finally got to her drive. Then her senses alerted her that something was wrong. It didn't take long to see what. Her door was open and her stomach turned when she saw that she'd been invaded once again. Going inside, her heart sank when the absence of her guns hit her like a punch. The house had been turned upside down, but at least this thief didn't rip everything apart. Probably too lazy. She kicked at the door, sending it slamming into the jamb. *What did they want from her?*

Still seething, she growled, "Hello," into the phone when it rang.

"Cody? We got robbed," Aunt Thelma said. She sounded frightened, and that made Cody see red.

"I'll be right there."

She drove, pulling up at their trailer just a few minutes later. Chase and Brett were there, along with a couple of Chase's kids. They were old enough to know their grandparents had been robbed, but too young to understand why everyone was so upset. That made them fussy and whiny, and that made the whole situation worse.

"Austin, quit that whining or I'll *give* you something to cry about," Shooter threatened.

That, of course, made the boy cry all the worse, as he took shelter behind his grandmother, who shot her husband a lethal look.

Their place had been treated about the same as Cody's. Everything had been overturned and pawed through, but nothing of value had been taken. Her uncle had been out squirrel hunting, and had his new gun with him. At least they didn't get that.

Cody guided her aunt and uncle outside so they could talk without the children hearing.

"I guess you can't take nothin' when there ain't nothin' to take," Shooter mumbled.

"We don't have to sit still for this," Cody said. "I'll buy you an alarm or a...camera...or a guard dog. Whatever you think will help."

"That ain't it," Shooter snapped gruffly. "It's just...it don't feel safe here no more...with you."

"With me?" She stood there in shock, amazed at what she was hearing. "You think this is my fault?"

"Whose else?" He had a bad temper, and it was high. She knew she should back off, go home and let him calm down, but she was getting hot too.

"It's not my fault these thieves are too stupid to know we don't keep any money in our houses."

"We don't *have* no money," he snarled, sticking his jaw out. "You're the one with the money, and they think you give it to us. We're getting robbed and such for nuthin'!"

She felt like steam would blow out of her ears. "I've paid for anything you've asked for!"

"Now, Cody," her aunt said, putting a comforting hand on her back. "Don't pay him no mind."

"No, no, he's got something to say. Say it!" She glared at her uncle, daring him to continue.

"We're sufferin'...for nuthin'," he repeated slowly.

"How much will it cost me to live in my home?" she demanded. "How much do you want? Tell me!" She was red with rage and her cousin Chase ran out of the trailer and pushed her hard, backing her up, a little cloud of dust gathering where her feet skidded.

"Don't get all up in his face," he warned. "You know he'll hit you."

"He's already told me to leave the hollow." She poked her head around Chase's big frame, glaring at her uncle. "Kicking me in the face couldn't hurt worse!"

Her aunt squeezed in front of her, stroking her cheek. "Don't get like that, Cody. He's just mad at them who did this. Not you."

"No, it's me," she insisted. "I haven't done enough for him. For anybody."

"That ain't it," Thelma insisted. "He just…we all thought there'd be more."

"I bought you everything you asked for. Everything! Doesn't anybody remember going shopping?"

"We thought that was the *first* day," her aunt said. "Not the *last* day."

Her breath came in pants as she tried to get her heart to slow down. It took an effort, but she finally took in a breath and said, "Have everyone come here at seven. Bring a list of what you want." She started to walk away, then turned and added, "Whatever it is, you can have it."

—◦◦—

Cody stood on the sliver of space she'd carved out of the sea of bodies on her Uncle Shooter's living room floor. His place had always seemed big enough, but when you got the whole group inside, most of them sitting cross-legged on the floor, there wasn't a lick of space left.

Every set of eyes old enough to care stared at her. The young ones played and poked each other, but even they were a little sedate. She cleared her throat and said, "It seems you all aren't happy with the way I've been handling my money."

"I didn't say that," Shooter said, his eyes dark and moody. "But you have been cheap."

"That's not true. I've paid for every single thing anyone has asked for." She could already feel her neck heating up, and they'd only just started.

"We don't like having to *ask* all the time," Merry said. "It feels like we're always at the well."

That was true, and there was no reason to say it wasn't.

"That's a fact," Shooter said. "A couple of us been talkin', and we think it'd be best if you just split it up. Give us each our share and be done with it."

She almost snapped that they had no share, but she managed to control herself. She *had* to stay calm. "Do you have any idea how small your share would be if I broke this up? There's forty people in the family. That'd be…" She did the math in her head as quickly as she could, not used to figuring sums this high. Dang, now that she had the number she had to admit it was pretty high. They'd want it for sure. "A lot less than you think."

"It'd be heaven to have some real money," Lily said wistfully. "I'd never have to worry about nuthin'."

"Think how fast some people could go through it," Cody warned. "How many times have we watched shows about people blowing through millions and millions and then going broke. I've spent an awful lot in the last few months, and all we have is better teeth and some clothes."

"But we'd only be spending on ourselves," Merry reasoned. "You're spending on all of us. Of course it goes fast."

"Okay. Think of this. Someone will run through whatever money they get like a dose of salt through an old maid." She had no idea what the expression meant, but her grandfather had used it, and she'd always liked the sound of it. "When that happens, and it *will* happen, who'll want to give up the money they've been careful with when the broke one needs something bad?" She looked around the room, secretly pleased when a few people cast suspicious glances at Ricky and Brett, the two most likely to blow every dime they could get their hands on.

"Then just split it between you and your mama's brothers and sisters," Amber said. "That's fair. Five ways'd give everyone a big chunk and they'd know best how to spend it for their own."

"That ain't fair!" Ricky howled, jumping to his feet. His temper was the worst in the bunch, and people near him leaned away in case he started swinging—or kicking. "Aunt Merry's only got Amber. My mama's got..." He made a face when he counted, "Seventeen to buy for."

"I've got two babies," Amber said, glaring at him. "There's four of us if there's seventeen of you."

"You can argue about it all night," Cody said, raising her voice, "but it ain't gonna happen. There's no way to do it and not have you at each other's throats. If I keep it you can all be mad at me, but at least you won't be jealous of each other."

"We'll take our chances," Brett said. "I want to have my *own* money. Not have to go ask like a baby."

"Then you'll have to get your *own* job," Cody said, staring at him unblinkingly.

"If there was jobs here, we'd have 'em already. I'm sure as shit not gonna drive an hour to get a job washing dishes in Greenville."

He had a point, but she wasn't in the mood to get sidetracked. "The simple fact is that this is *my* money, and it's staying mine. When I got paid for picking moss you all didn't think I should come home and divide that up. This is no different. I gave to whoever needed then, and I do now. If you need something, ask me and I'll give it to you."

"I want a house," Shooter said, staring lasers into her. "I want a real damn house, not some ticky-tacky, ass-busted trailer."

She almost gagged, but Cody calmed herself and nodded slowly. "Figure out what you want. I'll pay for it."

"A house?" Cubby said, his voice so high he sounded like a boy.

"Yes, a house," Shooter snapped. "Cody said we could have anything. I didn't hold a gun to her head."

"It's okay, Uncle Cubby," she said soothingly. "Uncle Shooter's right. I made a promise."

"I want one, too," Jaden said, after waiting just a second. "I got five damn kids staying here. I need my own place."

His kids were with three different women, and tended to stay over just because he was too lazy to take them home to their mamas, but Cody didn't argue. "Fine. Do the same. Figure out what you want and how to get it. I'll pay."

Lucas and Ricky joined the list, and Cody said, "Where do you want these houses? Greenville? Charleston? Paris, France?" Being sarcastic wasn't wise, but she was quickly running out of patience.

"Right here," Lucas said. "We've each got enough land."

"You don't have *any* land," Cody said. "Your daddy does. You'd best make sure he doesn't mind you plucking yourself down wherever you please."

"I need a car," Bobby said. He looked around at his cousins for support. "We *all* do."

"Nobody's ever missed anything important because of a car," Cody said. "But if you want them, you can have them." Her heart was slamming away in her chest, amazed at their nerve. At their *gall*. "Just remember the money you spend doesn't come back. Every well runs dry if you take too much water from it."

"I want a damn satellite TV," Shooter said. He was still staring daggers at Cody, and she had to remind herself that his moods could last for days. Once he got mad, he stayed it. "Every other hillbilly in the hollow has one. I'm so sick of watching that grainy crap we get off the antenna, I'm about to go blind."

"We all need that, too," Bobby said, clearly comfortable speaking for everyone. Cody noted that no one contradicted him.

"I've got my own satellite," Cubby said quietly. "I don't need a thing."

"Ain't you just too proud of yourself," Scooter growled. "Well, the rest of us don't have it, and we want it."

Cody jumped in. "You can have it. Find someone who can do the work and let me know." She looked around, glad to see some of her relatives show a measure of discomfort. Whether from their greed or their discomfort about the tension brewing, she wasn't sure. "I think that's enough for one night."

She started to thread her way through the bodies when Brett said, "We wouldn't have had to do this if you'd offered."

Cody continued to tip-toe, stepping on a few feet as she went. When she got to the door, she faced him and said, "You should have told me right away. Waiting until you were fed up was little of you." She got her hand on the knob and added quietly, "I thought you were happy with how things were before. I was." Stepping outside, she filled her lungs with cold, fresh air. She *had* been happy, very happy before she'd won. How was it humanly possible to be less happy when you had money to burn?

It was still pretty early in the evening, but Cody had no idea what Maddie's schedule was. She might have gone to bed as soon as it got dark, or stayed up until three. But she needed to talk to someone…someone who didn't want her to buy them anything.

"It's Cody," she said when Maddie answered her phone. "It it okay to call you?"

"Sure. Of course. I just got home."

"From work?"

"No, from the gym."

"Where's there a gym?"

"Out on the main road, you know, by the tire store and the auto repair place."

"There's a gym?"

Maddie laughed. "It's not much of a gym. The guy who owns the tire store had a room upstairs that he fitted out with free weights and things for muscle-heads. But he also put in a treadmill. I go there to run most nights."

Cody was speechless. Running was okay, she guessed, but why would anyone want to do it inside?

"I bet you've never been to a gym," Maddie teased. "Even though I've never seen anyone with a body better than yours."

The thought of Maddie noticing her body was enough to make her blush, but what was she supposed to say? "Uhm, thanks," she managed. "Uhm, I had some things go on today that… Well, I didn't have a particularly fine day. Will you listen to me complain for a while?"

"Oh, of course I will. I'm going to get a bottle of water. Then I'll sit down and listen all evening long."

"Really?" Cody was suddenly anxious. "I'm not stopping you from doing anything you'd rather be doing?"

"Not at all. After I run, I come home and zone out in front of the TV. My life is about as boring as you can imagine."

"That's why you want to leave," Cody said softly.

"Well, that's part of it. I'd love to be able to see a show or a good movie. Even going to lectures or finding unique restaurants would be a nice change. All of the things big cities have." She paused for a second, then added, "I've never had that, and I've always wanted it."

"Never? Where'd you go to college?"

"Virginia Tech."

"That's not too far from here! Heck, you know it's rural when I've been hunting near there. Why didn't you go somewhere like…" She didn't actually know many colleges, but she knew some of them had to be in the kinds of cities Maddie would like.

"I wanted to go to NYU or Columbia or UCLA, but I didn't have the grades to get an academic scholarship. And I couldn't see saddling myself with the kinds of loans I would have needed just for tuition." She laughed, and Cody could imagine how the corners of her mouth turned up when she did. "Plus, my girlfriend was going to Tech, and I had to be with her. Of course, she dumped me the week before school started."

'Dumped *you*?" Who in the world would not want to be with Maddie Osborne?

"Yeah. Hard to believe, isn't it?" She giggled the way she did when she'd said something she thought was particularly funny. "She didn't want to be tied down. It's easy to think your first is the best. But she rarely is. Don't forget that lesson, Cody."

No one could convince Cody that Maddie wasn't as good as they got, but they certainly weren't girlfriends. "Will do. Now let me tell you how being robbed again was the best thing to happen to me today."

———

Cody described the whole evening, sharing her hurt, her disappointment, her dismay. Maddie was outraged, then started ticking off ways to make sure the family didn't gang up on her again. But as she listened, Cody didn't feel a bit soothed. She realized she didn't want advice, mainly because Maddie didn't understand them. She was as nice as pie, but she didn't understand hill folks at all. This wasn't the worst fight they'd ever had. It probably wasn't in the top ten. Maddie acted like the family would be split apart, but that wasn't how it was. They were kin, and they were together until the end. You fought and squabbled, but you stuck together like flies on a glue-strip.

Feeling more lonely as the minutes ticked past, Cody realized what she needed. She wanted sympathy, not solutions. Tenderness was what she craved. Maybe you couldn't get that from a friend, but she still wanted it more than she could say.

———

Cody was about to set off the next morning, when she heard an engine sputtering as it got closer. Sticking her head out the door, she saw Uncle Cubby puttering along before stopping right in front of the door. When he turned off the engine it coughed and argued a bit, but it eventually died down. Cody walked out to meet him.

"I came to apologize," Cubby said.

"For what? You're the only ones who didn't get in line for a house or a...jet," she said, still smarting from the family meeting.

He looked genuinely ashamed when he said, "I'm apologizing for my kids. I know I didn't do a very good job of raising those boys, but it wasn't for lack of trying."

"You're a good father," she said. That was generally the truth. He'd loved his boys plenty. His problem had always been discipline. The boys did whatever they wanted, and all Cubby ever managed was to quietly tell them to be better. With high-spirited boys and lots of bad influences, that wasn't nearly enough.

"Time will tell on that, I suppose, but I'm still sorry mine were the ones causing the most ruckus last night. I don't know where Jaden gets his nerve."

"It's all right. Really."

"No, it's not. You don't have to give my kids anything. They've done fine so far."

That wasn't true, but most of their problems weren't caused by a lack of funds. "I've got money, Uncle Cubby, and I really want to help those who need it. If Jaden needs a place for his kids, he can have it. The same goes for you and Aunt Lurlene. If you need anything..." She eyed his woebegone vehicle, "I'm happy to buy it for you."

His big brown eyes were filled with emotion when he said, "I promised your mama I'd look out for you. Taking money from you just ain't right."

She descended the stairs and gave him a quick hug. "You've done a good job looking out for me. But I've got enough money for all of us to enjoy. We just need to figure out how to do that without tussling over it."

"I'll leave that to you," he said, getting back into his car. "I have no idea how to keep the boys from fussing and fighting."

———

About a week after the big family meeting, Shooter came by Cody's house just before dinnertime. His mood had cleared up, and he seemed in good spirits again. "Thelma made you a pie," he said, holding it out awkwardly.

"Thanks," Cody said. "Much appreciated." He came inside and started to sit on the sofa, but must have realized she still didn't have cushions on it.

"You gonna get a new one?" he said, gesturing at the cushions no longer there.

"Maybe." It was silly, but she hated to have anything new. Having people come and traipse through her old stuff was bad enough. But if she'd bothered to buy a nice, new sofa and it got wrecked…she didn't want to think of her reaction.

He had some papers in his hands, and he thrust them at her. "I talked to this builder guy in Greenville. He didn't seem too excited about coming out here, but when I said we had that lottery money, his eyes lit up."

"I'm sure they did." Great. Now another leach could grab on and start sucking. "What are you looking at?"

"He says we need about three thousand square feet. Does that sound right?"

Cody had roughly three hundred, so three thousand seemed a little generous. "What will you do with all that space?"

"It's not that much. Four bedrooms, a dining room and a family room. He says it'll cost about a hundred dollars a square foot." He locked his dark eyes on her. "You *said* you'd do what I wanted."

"I will. You don't mind if I ask around to see if he has a good reputation, do you?"

"No. You do what you need to." He got up and put his hand on the knob. "I'm sorry I was mean to you. I don't mean no harm."

"I know that, Uncle Shooter." She went to him and gave him a very quick hug. They weren't an affectionate people, but she wanted to make sure he knew there were no hard feelings. "Thank Aunt Thelma for the pie, okay?"

"All right." Then he was off, roaring down the drive in his ancient truck…undoubtedly on the list of vehicles that had to be replaced.

Cody was going to talk to Maddie and see if she had any ideas about getting a house built, but she decided to wait a bit and see if the family would give her uncle a slap to the head before she did too much work.

By the end of the next week, every aunt from each branch of the family save for Shooter's had called to complain about the "mansion." Cody patiently explained that she was merely doing what she said she would. If everyone wanted a big house—the money would be gone and they'd have to find some way to pay the real estate taxes in the future or the government would take them away. Simple as that. She heard every variation of "You can't let people run wild," but she maintained her motto. "People can have what they want."

—⁓—

On Friday evening, Cody headed over to Aunt Thelma's for dinner. A formal invitation was rare, making the get-together take on added meaning. There was no doubt what the agenda would be. She just didn't know if they'd dug their heels in or would be swayed by family sentiment.

Dinner was Aunt Thelma's truly delicious tuna casserole. The recipe wasn't difficult, but it tasted so much better than when Cody tried to imitate it. None of her cousins were around for a change. Mandy and Melissa had their own places, and Chase and Brett were off doing god knew what. With no grandkids running around, it was strangely quiet. So quiet you could hear the wind whistling through the door that had never had a proper seal.

"I've been doing some thinking," Shooter said, "And I don't think having a house built from scratch is a good idea. A guy over where I got my hair cut says the only thing we should ever have is modular." He waited a beat. "That's like trailers, but better."

"But you said you didn't want a trailer."

"No, I don't. But this guy says modular is way better. You can have a real foundation put down. They bring the whole thing in on a truck and just plunk it down. Nobody has to come all the way up here every day for months, either."

"Okay. I'll check and see if there's any good ones made. You don't want another house where it always feels like you're wearing cheesecloth underclothes."

That made her uncle smile, and Cody relaxed enough to have a second piece of pecan pie.

CHAPTER FOURTEEN

CODY HAD AN HOUR or two to kill in Greenville, while her uncle Shooter finally had his appointment with the eye doctor. He'd been squinting for years, but hadn't had the money to get his eyes checked. Now that Cody was footing the bill, he'd finally made the appointment.

The need to see Maddie was fairly constant, but Cody had managed, through great pains, not to go trotting into the bank every day just to look at her. This time it had actually been almost two weeks, but not having anything save for a doctor's office to keep her occupied made her resolve falter. Maybe she'd just mosey over to Main Street and take a look around. There was a chance some good sense would come over her on the way and stop her from lurking around the lobby like a stalker.

It didn't. It was early afternoon, and the branch was almost empty. That was nice in a way, because Maddie might see her and call her in for a chat. But it also let the employees, especially that evil Goodwin girl, keep an eye on her. Not allowing herself the luxury of even turning her head, Cody went straight down to the vault, where she removed one of her safe deposit boxes.

The privacy room was small and stuffy, but she still managed to waste a good twenty minutes there, playing with stacks of bills. She'd gotten good at weaving them together, letting the interlaced packets climb to a fairly impressive height. This was nearly the only time she actually enjoyed having a ton of money. It was all security and potential when it was nicely arranged in towers. Eventually even that got old and she put the box back to head upstairs.

Her body tingled when she nearly smacked into Maddie, who was just walking away from her assistant's desk. "I thought that was you scampering across my lobby," she said, her lovely smile sculpting her face into contours so beautiful they made Cody's heart ache.

"Yeah, I had a little…business to take care of. How are things?"

"Good. Hey, I had an idea or two and wanted to talk to you. Is this a good time?"

"Perfect." Cody followed along, wishing she could just walk behind Maddie for a few hours every day. They wouldn't even have to talk. She settled down in the chair in front of the desk and tried to make herself focus on Maddie's words, rather than her beautiful mouth.

"I've been thinking about your family situation," Maddie began.

Cody's stomach turned sour just hearing the words. "It's a situation, all right. They're lining up for houses and cars."

"Do they have their own houses now?"

"Most don't." She stewed for a second, then decided to just tell the truth. "You can't buy a house, even a cheap one, without some kind of credit. Not many of them have ever had a real job."

"None…at all?"

"Well, all of the boys but Devin have a record." Admitting that was painful. Deeply painful. "Mandy'd have one too, but most of her scuffles were when she was still a minor."

"Scuffles?"

"She has a temper," Cody said, leaving it at that. "Like I've said before, there's not many jobs, and there's nothing for a guy with a record. Some of 'em are still on probation, and can't even leave the county. Last year they were hiring in the mines in Higgins County, but they can't travel to get there." She shook her head, ashamed and downhearted.

Thankfully, Maddie didn't look or act shocked. Instead, she tried to get to the heart of the matter, without moaning about the details. "Maybe they're asking for a lot because they don't have any money of their own for day-to-day things. Have you given them anything?"

"I fill their freezers and buy their kids' clothes and take them to the doctor and pay for their prescriptions and their gasoline and their…"

"No, no," Maddie said, shaking her head. "I know you pay for a zillion things. But have you given them any money…no strings attached?"

"No."

Smiling again, Maddie said, "That was a very short answer. Do you want to expand on it…just a little?"

"No, ma'am," Cody said, unable to keep a grin off her face. "I haven't."

"Do you know why you haven't?"

"Because it's not theirs."

"Okay, then why are you paying for everything?"

"I don't know," she said, feeling grumpy. "I want to help, but they don't think of the money like I do." She dropped her head, supporting it with her hand. "I know it's small of me, but I don't trust them to use it like I think it should be used."

"And that's how?"

"For security," she said with feeling. "I want to go on like before, but use the money to take the pressure off. Do you know what I mean?"

"No, I don't think I do. Pressure from…bills?"

"Yeah. From feeling like the county could kick us off our land for not paying our taxes, from knowing I had to learn to live with pain because I couldn't afford to have my tooth fixed, from having to put duct tape on the kids' hand-me-downs. I wanted to make things better…not different."

Maddie shook her head slowly, her eyes closing briefly when she did. "Things have changed, Cody, and your family is ready to embrace that change. You're going to have constant battles, and they're going to be angry with you and resentful if you don't let them enjoy this money a little bit."

"They'll enjoy it all right," she said sourly. "They'll enjoy it until it's all gone."

"You don't have to let that happen. But you have enough to buy everyone a big house and a couple of cars and give them all a couple of hundred thousand dollars a year. You could do that easily, but you're acting like you have to watch each cent. That's just not so, and I'm begging you to get over that mindset."

"It's really hard," she said, feeling like she'd tear up. "I loved my life before. I want it back."

"I think it's gone," Maddie said softly, empathy coloring her tender tone. "But you can still live like you want to. Just let the rest of them go a little crazy."

"How little?"

"I see that smile trying to hide. Come on now, let's look at this logically. Why not give them each a sum of money…maybe twenty-five thousand…and let them buy what they need themselves? Then you don't have to be responsible for filling their freezers. Take yourself out of the godfather role. Let them figure out how to manage a little bit of money."

"That's not a little bit of money. That's a lot of money," she grumbled.

"Not compared to how much you've got sitting in my vault. I don't want to hurt your feelings, but you own a huge bakery and you're telling everyone you'll decide when they get a cookie. That *has* to lead to resentment."

Feeling the air go out of her argument, Cody nodded. "Okay. How do I do it?"

On Friday evening, Maddie arrived at Cody's trailer just as it turned dark. Cody was skittish and obviously unsure of her decision, but Maddie was proud of her for at least giving it a shot.

It only took a few minutes to get to Cody's uncle's place, and Maddie wished she had an extra minute or two to compose herself when she caught sight of it. Cubby had a real house, not a trailer, but it was a lethal mess. The kind of house you'd imagine only someone with great physical or mental disabilities would be stuck in. Maybe "sentenced to" was the better term.

It was small, made of clapboard and brick halfway up. Judging from the outside, it was well under a thousand square feet. But size wasn't the issue. Cubby had probably never truly thrown anything away. He'd just opened his front door and tossed it outside. Old appliances, car frames, wheels, broken swing sets, tires suspended on ropes from tree limbs, a vile mattress lying on its side and toys…every kind of broken toy imaginable. What was it with poor people and toys? Maddie didn't think it possible to say a word, but Cody came to the rescue.

"Do you see why I worry about giving everyone a bunch of money?"

"Yeah, I do," Maddie managed, her heart beating hard and fast. This was more than she'd bargained for, and she was desperate to not look as disgusted as she felt. It was no shame to be poor, but it was deeply shameful to live like this.

When they went inside, about a dozen sets of suspicious eyes landed on her. Standing there in her business suit and long wool coat, she felt like an item on exhibit in front of a group of people who regarded her as entirely alien. The interior of the house wasn't as bad as the exterior. It was dusty and messy and all of the furniture was worn out or ruined. Toys in various states of ruin covered the floor, but the kitchen was pretty clean and it didn't smell. Small favors.

"This is Maddie Osborne," Cody said. "She's going to explain how you're going to get your money." She started pointing at people. "My Uncle Cubby and Aunt Lurlene, and their kids Lucas, Jaden and Ricky."

"Pleased to meet you," Maddie said. Ricky had a cast on his arm and stitches across his chin. Cody hadn't mentioned an accident, so his injuries were probably not from helping old ladies across the street. Now that she looked carefully, another of the cousins had a black eye and still another had a bandage over his ear, with an unsightly bald spot where his longish hair had been shaved. Everyone, even the women, was almost glaring at her, and she felt her temperature rise from the pressure. Then it dawned on her that it was the actual heat in the room that was so oppressive. She was about to pass out, but didn't see anywhere she could put her coat and have it come back clean.

Cody must not have noticed her discomfort, for she kept going with the introductions. "My Uncle Shooter and Aunt Thelma, and their kids, Chase, Mandy, Melissa, and Brett."

"Nice to meet you," Maddie said, receiving nods in response.

"My Aunt Merry and her daughter Amber, and Aunt Lily and her boys Bobby and Devin. There's a few kids in the back bedroom, but we tried to keep this to adults."

"Good idea," Maddie said. She had to take her coat off. Putting her briefcase at her feet, she let the coat slide down her arms where Cody caught it.

"I'll put this…" She stood there for a second, then walked back to the door and hung it on the knob. The bottom of it lay in small clumps of mud by the entryway, but that was about the best she could do.

"Okay," Maddie said. "We're going to open checking accounts for all of you, and Cody's going to deposit twenty-five thousand dollars in each account."

"Why not do it the easy way, and just give it to us?" a cousin asked.

Maddie fielded that one. "Since many of your houses have been broken into, it's clearly not safe to have cash lying around. I promise this will be better and safer than having actual cash in your homes. You'll each get ATM cards and checks, so you'll have access to your money when you need it, but it won't be lying around for people to steal."

"I'd rather take my chances with thieves I know than thieves I don't know," a cousin Maddie thought had been identified as Jaden said.

"Shut up," Cody snapped hotly. "The people at the bank aren't thieves."

"Sez you," he grumbled. "For all you know you've got ten bucks left."

"I trust them with millions," Cody said, glaring at him. "You can trust them with twenty-five thousand."

"Okay," Maddie said, trying to sound cheery. "I brought the new account forms with me so you don't all have to drive to Greenville." She started handing them out, having a few of them snatched roughly from her hand by a surly-looking cousin or two. This was a damned tough crowd!

⁓⁓⁓

It took quite a while to get all of the forms filled out properly, and having people show their driver's licenses was a little bit of hell, but they were finally finished. Cody and Maddie walked out into the cool, clear night and Maddie let the fresh air cleanse her lungs.

"See why I balked at opening accounts for them?" Cody asked, finally showing a small smile.

"Yeah, I don't think I made any friends tonight. But at least the money's safe this way."

"Until a few of them spend it in one card game," Cody grumbled.

⁓⁓⁓

Maddie came in to have a cup of cocoa and they talked for a while. But Cody couldn't get over the humiliation of having Maddie see her aunt and uncle's house. She kicked herself for not having thought of how bad it looked, but it had always looked like that and was now just a part of the fabric of the Montgomery family.

Maddie stood out so starkly in the filthy house, it was hard to even think about it. It wasn't just the dirt, either. Her creamy skin and fair hair seemed to sparkle next to the Montgomery mens' dark, lank locks and sallow complexions.

Cody sat there, trying to lift herself out of her funk, but her mind kept straying to thoughts of her mother. She'd wanted out of the hollow so badly she'd run off to Greenville when she was only sixteen. Even though she deeply loved her family, she couldn't abide their laziness or slovenliness. They'd had all of the pride drained out of them. The only way to have a chance at something better was to get away. That's why moving back had been so devastating for her. She'd been duty bound to do right by her kids, but had failed.

It had been horrible knowing her mama was ashamed of their life in the hollow, but she'd never let that influence her own view too much. There was good in both the land and the people. Pride buried beneath the dirt and rot. Cody'd believed that firmly until tonight when she saw it through Maddie's eyes. It was going to be very hard to put the sheen back on after seeing those pretty blue eyes squinting in disgust when they walked into Uncle Cubby's house. This had been a very bad idea, in every way.

On Monday afternoon, Lucas and Ricky Montgomery sauntered into the Appalachian States Bank and stood in front of Lynnette. "We want our money," Lucas said, staring hard at the teller.

Fortified by the secure barrier that separated her from her customers, as well as her own ample nerve, Lynnette said, "What money? You two don't have any money."

"I told you they'd steal it," Ricky said, punching his brother in the arm.

"Lay off," he growled. "Where's the lady who runs the place?"

"She's not available. Now take off before I have the guard throw you out."

Lucas leaned over the barrier, fixing Lynnette with his nearly black eyes. "I want my money," he seethed. "And I want it now!"

Maddie heard the last word, since it had been shouted. She scampered from her office and stood right next to the men, immediately intimidated by their size and menace. "Hi," she managed, her voice breaking. She stuck her hand out. "Maddie Osborne. We met the other night."

Neither man offered his hand in return. "We want our money," Lucas said flatly.

Her stomach was doing flips and Maddie worked hard to make her voice sound normal. "You want...some of it?"

"All of it," he said, and his brother nodded. "It's ours."

"Yes, it most definitely is." She tried to smile, but knew she wasn't pulling it off. "I assume you want it in cash."

"Hell, yes!" Lucas growled.

Sweat was running down her back, but she tried to sound confident. "We don't keep that much cash on hand. I'll have to arrange to get it from another branch. How about tomorrow?"

"Today," Ricky said, narrowing his equally dark eyes. "It's ours."

"Yes, it's definitely yours," Maddie agreed. "But it's going to take a while for me to get it." She took a few quick breaths, with her head spinning. "Wait here and I'll see how long it will take."

A pair of elderly ladies walked in, saw the Montgomery boys standing there, turned and headed back out so fast they almost sprinted.

Maddie got on the phone, making call after call. Finally, she had the cash lined up. After seeing another three customers come in and depart quickly, she called the men into her office, just to remove the menace from the lobby.

They walked in and towered over her desk—big, burly bodies, black hair hanging over their eyes, and square jaws set for a fight.

"I'll have the money in a couple of hours."

"Hours!" Ricky looked like he'd pick up her desk and drop kick it into the next county.

"I'm really sorry, but we can't keep large amounts of cash here."

"It's a god-damned bank," Lucas sneered. "Why isn't it here?"

There was no way she was going to have this conversation with every Montgomery. Having it with Cody had taken enough out of her. Besides, she wasn't ever going to have a long-term customer relationship with these two, so it was a waste of time trying to placate them. "It just isn't. Now you can go home and wait for me to call or...go over to the Tap Room. As soon as the money comes in I'll come get you."

"We need *some* money," Lucas said. "Give us something."

"No problem." She got up and went over to Lynnette. Taking two blank checks, she filled the forms out with their account information and gave them to Lynnette. "You have a thousand dollars in your drawer, don't you?"

"Yes," she snapped, scowling at the men.

"Then please cash these checks for our customers." She smiled tersely at the boys and said, "I'll come over and let you know when I can complete the transaction."

As she started to walk away, she heard Lynnette call out, "Maddie, what's going on here?" She chose to ignore her, going back to her office and closing the door. Then she pulled a cord and twisted the dowel on the blinds, lowering them for the first time since she'd started at the branch. Closed off from view, she put her head on her desk and tried to order her thoughts. She was going to need cash. Lots and lots of cash. And she was going to need it soon.

CHAPTER FIFTEEN

LUCAS AND RICKY HAD come on Monday. Mandy showed up on Tuesday, with Wednesday bringing Chase and an unrelated woman who seemed very eager to get her hands on some greenbacks. Maddie had another fifty thousand in the vault, and she was fairly sure it would be gone by the end of the week, if not the day.

Her head ached, not only from the cartwheels she had to perform to get that kind of cash in a branch as small as hers, but from the gnawing in her gut over the secret she had to keep. Even though they were the worst customers in the history of Appalachian States Bank, the Montgomery cousins were still customers and deserved their privacy. But Cody would never understand. Maddie was as sure of that as she was that the cousins having large amounts of cash would lead to nothing good. But she was powerless to do anything about either situation—except worry.

Her prophecy didn't take long to be fulfilled. On Friday afternoon, Cody came roaring into the bank, stormed across the marble lobby and stood in the doorway to Maddie's office, face flushed, ears beet red. "My cousin was almost killed today, thanks to you!"

Maddie grabbed at her throbbing temples and lightly beat her head against her desk. "Fuck, fuck, fuck!" She looked up at Cody's furious expression and felt a flash of fear course through her body. There wasn't a huge difference between Ricky and Lucas and Cody at that moment, and it was spine-chilling. "What happened?"

"Someone knew that five of my cousins had cash. Every one of them had their places torn up. The idiots had hidden money in jars and under mattresses and in the toilet tank and it was all taken. But Ricky..." She was breathing so hard and fast it looked like she might pass out. "Ricky was at home when they kicked in his door. He said he didn't have any money."

She paused for a beat. "Until they put a gun to his brain and cocked it, that is. Then he remembered."

"Shit." Maddie couldn't compel herself to lift her head from the desk. "I'm so sorry, Cody. I can't even tell you…"

"Sorry!" Cody held the doorframe and shook it, making the entire office vibrate. "You're sorry? You made me lose a hundred and twenty-five thousand dollars, and almost got my cousin killed…and you're sorry?"

"I…I can't…what else can I say?"

"Nothing. Thanks for nothing." She turned and stomped out, with Maddie jumping to her feet to follow her.

"Wait, Cody, please!"

Every eye in the bank followed them, like they were watching the most exciting movie ever made. The pair flew from the bank, with Maddie running to catch up with Cody, who ate up sidewalk with her long, loping gait. "Please, Cody, please let me talk."

"You've talked plenty," she growled. Then got into her car and roared away, her new engine doing a fantastic job of peeling out fast enough to leave long stripes of rubber on the pavement.

Maddie turned and headed back to the bank, rolling her eyes when she spotted every one of her employees gathered on the front steps, avidly watching the drama unfold.

—⁓—

Everyone scampered back inside by the time she entered, but none of them even tried to act like they hadn't been watching. They all stood at their posts, looking at her like she'd have something momentous to say. Instead, she went into her office and grabbed her coat and briefcase. On the way out, she said, "You can take bets on where I'm going, but only a fool would bet on anyplace other than Cody Keaton's house. I'll see you on Monday."

—⁓—

That hadn't been the most professional scene in her nine-year career, but given her new clients, she figured there'd be at least that much drama another time or two. Still, she was sick with worry and anger at the whole situation. It was almost impossible to provide reasonable sums of money to people who'd never had two nickels to rub together and expect them to know how to handle it wisely. It also wasn't possible to maintain harmony when you had millions and refused to share. Cody was really in a bind, and Maddie hadn't helped matters one bit. And for that she was sorry, deeply sorry. She just had to hope Cody could forgive her. If not today, then soon.

———

When Maddie pulled up in front of Cody's trailer, she sat in the car for a few seconds, trying to stop her hands from shaking. A few moments wasn't nearly enough time to calm herself. By the time Maddie was out of the car Cody stood on the front step. "Was it worth getting fourteen new accounts?" she asked bitterly. "Everyone told me you were after my money. I'd never believed them…until now."

"That's bullshit!" Maddie's anxiety flipped over to anger in a heartbeat. "I might have made a mistake in telling you to give them money, but I didn't do it for selfish reasons. That's utter bullshit, Cody, and you know better than to even accuse me of that!"

"Everybody knows you can't trust hillbillies with money!"

"That's bullshit too! You're doing a great job with your money. You haven't wasted a dime!"

"I wasted a hundred and twenty-five thousand dimes…dollars," she corrected. "And you talked me into it. You could have done something to stop this…" She stood there for a second, then her face grew dark. "Did you know they'd taken the money out? Did you?" She was shouting at full bore now. Every bird had gone silent, each one waiting for the danger to pass.

Maddie was sick to admit it, but she had to be honest. "Yes, I knew."

Cody turned and slammed the door, cracking the thick, old glass in the tiny window. Then she kicked something hard, the sound reverberating through the clearing. Maddie was nearly paralyzed with anxiety, but she marched up to the steps and opened the door. Cody was standing in the kitchen, gripping the counter. Slowly, she turned and stared malevolently.

"You have to hear me out."

"Get off my land," Cody growled.

"No." She dropped down onto the sofa, cursing herself for wearing a pencil skirt to the hollow. When would she learn to dress for conditions?

"You can't accuse me of cheating you and expect me to just run away with my tail between my legs."

Cody stood right where she was, staring at Maddie with narrowed eyes. She took that as an invitation to speak. "I owe every one of my customers their privacy. I was sick when I had to pay them out, but I had to Cody, it's the law, for God's sake!"

"The law doesn't say you can't tell me when they're doing something stupid."

"No, you're right. That's not the law. But it's the bank's policy, and it's my policy. I'm sorry you didn't know, but I'm not sorry I didn't tell you. I'm deeply sorry this went badly, but I just didn't have the option to warn you."

"Fine. Then who told?" Cody moved over to her rocking chair and sat down, still staring hotly. "Only the cousins who took their money got robbed."

"I don't know," Maddie said, quietly. "If I find out it was someone at my bank, I'll fire them immediately."

"That Goodwin girl did it."

"She might have," Maddie admitted. "But the guard might have told someone or one of your cousins might have let it slip. Ricky and Lucas were over at the Tap Room for a couple of hours waiting for me to scrounge up fifty thousand dollars. They were far from sober when I went over to tell them the money was ready." She shrugged. "Do you think they just talked about the weather?"

"You're blaming them, but it's your fault!" Cody was on her feet again.

"It's as much your fault as it is mine. You know your cousins better than I do, why weren't you keeping an eye on them?"

"Get out!" Cody pointed at the door. "Get your ass out of my house!"

"No." Maddie folded her arms across her chest. "You owe me an apology. I opened those accounts to keep your family safe. I spent hours of my time coming up here and getting those damn things open. I went in on Saturday to do the paperwork so none of my employees would see the new accounts and ask questions. I did everything I could to make things easier for them and for you." She was heating up now, her anger at Cody bubbling up from her chest. "You owe *me* an apology, damn it!"

Cody loomed over her, dark and threatening. "Get out," she said, her voice breaking. "Get out or I'll throw you out."

"No." Maddie looked up at her, seeing the anger almost radiating from her body. But Cody didn't frighten her any more. She could see she was frightened herself. Frightened by the violence, by the burglaries, by her cousins' recklessness. She just needed to vent her anger and they'd work it through.

Cody stunned her by leaning over, grasping her elbows and easily lifting her to her feet. They stood, toe to toe, with Cody now whispering, "Get out."

"No," Maddie said one last time. "I care about you, and I can't leave until you believe that."

A single muscle flexed, a small one near her lips, and Maddie could see the angry facade start to crumble. "I don't know who to believe..." she began, then closed her eyes tightly as her jaw began to quiver.

"Believe me," Maddie begged. "Believe I care for you." She placed her hand over Cody's heart, feeling the beat, rapid and strong. "I would *never* intentionally hurt you." She reached up and ran a hand through her silky hair. "Believe me, Cody."

Cody released her hold, then slid her arms around Maddie's body, locking her in a tight embrace. She didn't utter a word, but her eyes searched Maddie's for some sign, the smallest indication that she was feeling the same heat. All Maddie could do was stare at her mouth, willing it to claim her.

Tightening her hold, Cody kissed Maddie hard, covering her mouth while her fingers pressed into her back.

Maddie grasped her head, pulling Cody into her body, not allowing her to even consider letting go.

Growling with what sounded like a mixture of pleasure and angst, Cody's hands were everywhere, peeling Maddie's suit jacket off while she continued to kiss her possessively.

Holding onto Cody's shoulders with both hands, Maddie gripped tight enough to bruise as she felt the room spin and realized they were banging their way along the hallway. She grabbed Cody's shirt, pulling it from her body, yanking it over her head as they spun together like a pair of punch-drunk boxers, lurching and grappling from wall to wall as they made their way to the bedroom.

Maddie's blouse was gone and Cody struggled briefly with her bra, the assault of kisses unrelenting. Breathing hard, she slipped the bra from Maddie's shoulders and filled her hands with her breasts, squeezing them until Maddie growled with a mix of pain and pleasure that only sex could bring.

Now Cody's kisses were like fire. They tumbled to the bed, with Maddie kicking her shoes off before digging into the mattress with her heels, trying to gain purchase. Cody slid her hand up Maddie's thigh, not stopping until the tips of questing fingers brushed against her panties. The pencil skirt was nothing but a hindrance. Cody grasped the fabric with both hands and eased it up, freeing Maddie's legs which opened in invitation. Cody slowed down dramatically, trailing her fingers along the waist, then the leg of her panties, teasing Maddie's skin with her touch. She was about to combust when Cody shifted to lie on top of her, pinning her with her body.

They kissed as if the merging of their lips was the life-force that kept their hearts beating. Maddie had never in her life been this hungry for a woman's mouth. It was like the whole world resided in that small, warm, wet space and she craved those kisses like a drug.

Cody's fingers never stopped teasing. They traveled along Maddie's hip, her belly, the inside of her thigh. Anywhere but where they were desperately needed. Her legs spread wide with unquenched desire. "Touch me," Maddie breathed.

With a quick snap of her wrist, the panties disappeared and Cody nipped at Maddie's lip the moment her decisive fingers found her sex. Maddie let out a low, hungry moan when Cody's cool, smooth fingers hit her hot skin like a salve. Maddie had to have more. More touch, more pressure. Just *more*.

She pressed against Cody's fingers, riding them until they got in sync. Then she lay there, wide open, and let Cody's glorious hand send pleasure through her entire body. It was rough, and sloppy and fierce, and Maddie had never wanted anything more than she wanted Cody Keaton at that minute.

She wanted to hold out for hours, but Cody was too demanding. Fingers slid to her opening, spreading the evidence of lust all over her sex. Cody lavished attention on her clit while probing Maddie's mouth with her tongue, capturing her moans. Wrenching her mouth away, Maddie shivered roughly. "I can't stop…" she tried to say, but collapsed onto the bed as spasms shook through her body.

Cody was right with her, kissing her head, her face, her lips, as Maddie continued to gently thrust against her hand. "Oh, my God," she finally breathed. "That's was"—she pried her eyes open and looked at Cody's earnest face—"amazing."

Maddie was stunned by the whole episode. She'd been sure she was making the right decision in keeping their relationship friendly, not romantic. But here she was, lying on the bed, naked from the waist up, her skirt a wrinkled, bunched up mess. And a very assertive woman was lying beside her, grinning.

Cody must have sensed that she'd recovered, because she leaned in and started nuzzling against Maddie's neck. What in the hell was Cody thinking? They'd been ready to come to blows just a few minutes before and now they were half naked and wet with sex. Maddie wanted to reflect, to figure out how they'd gotten here, but then Cody's kisses had a little fire behind them, and Maddie started to lose her train of thought. Cody was so deadly sexy, it was mind boggling. The woman who stood on that rock in the middle of a stream and cast her rod with utter confidence was here… lying beside her…and Maddie was smitten.

Cody grasped Maddie's hand and put it between her legs, thrusting her hips against it. Way to go! Don't be afraid to take your pleasure. Really good instincts!

Even though Cody had the courage to ask for what she needed, Maddie didn't need encouragement. Her mouth had been watering every time she looked into Cody's half-closed eyes and saw desire radiating from her. Cody was blazing hot—for her—and that made her own drive kick into high gear.

"Why do you have all of these clothes on?" Maddie asked, running her hand along Cody's flank.

Cody didn't need to be asked twice. Sitting up, she reached behind herself to remove her bra.

"Let me," Maddie said, shooing her hands away. Undressing a woman was always a turn-on for her, and doing it for the first time was a special treat. When they were both massively turned on…it was heavenly.

Maddie leaned into her and kissed her lips, while her hands played lightly over Cody's back, teasing her. A sound like a gentle purr came from deep within Cody's chest. She sounded like a cat relaxing in the sun, stretching out her muscular body—it made Maddie's clit throb.

Unfastening the hooks, Maddie let the bra dangle from her shoulders while she tickled the skin that had just been freed.

"Really nice," Cody growled.

Her voice was lower than normal, and a hell of a lot sexier. Just a few syllables sent chills down Maddie's body. She wanted to make her talk more, but she also needed to keep her mouth attached to Cody's sexy lips. The lips won, and she knelt astride her to get a better angle.

Now she could cup Cody's breasts, letting them fill her hands while she kissed her hard. On the few occasions she'd let herself fantasize about being with her, she'd always pictured Cody as pliant, accepting, even trembling from a gentle touch. Maddie thought she'd have to handle her like a frightened kitten. But that's not at all who Cody was. She was decisive, hungry, and bold. Like she'd done this a few thousand times and was going to mold Maddie to her needs. It was divine.

Showing her decisiveness, Cody tossed her bra away. Maddie got to work on Cody's slacks, dealing with them quickly and efficiently. The time for teasing was past. Impediments to pleasure had to be removed. Then Maddie realized her skirt was still bunched up around her waist. Deciding she'd never wear another tight skirt when Cody was near, she shimmied out of it, shivering when the cool air hit her heated skin.

Now that she was naked, it was Maddie's turn to take over. Cody had unleashed her assertiveness; she went for what she wanted. Burying her face between those strong legs wasn't an option…it was a command.

She wanted to open her up and savor her, so she slid off the bed to kneel next to it. Cody's confused, questioning gaze lasted only a second. When Maddie firmly planted Cody's feet on her shoulders, those brown eyes got wide, then her head dropped onto the bed and she lay there in anticipation, quivering with need.

This was just how Maddie wanted her. Open, hungry, and ready for anything. She dipped her head and breathed in deeply. She wasn't sure what hormones were activated when she savored a woman's arousal, but they worked instantaneously. Cody's scent made her pussy throb so much, she almost diverted a hand to touch herself. But her need to explore Cody was stronger than her own desire. Opening her fully, she leaned in close and watched her flesh twitch for a few seconds. Cody's body was coiled with tension as Maddie finally dropped her head and tasted her.

"Mmm," she growled. It was primal. Way beyond what your logical brain could ever understand or make any sense of. This drive—this need to suffuse yourself in another woman's scent, to press your tongue against her pulse—was beyond words. It was a need that could only be answered by diving in, and Maddie dove in without fear.

She tenderly explored Cody's secrets, keeping her touch light and easy. Cody was shaking with such desire, that Maddie could have easily brought her to climax in just a few strokes. But this was probably the first time Cody had ever had anyone explore her this way, and Maddie was going to make it memorable.

Cody had other ideas. She'd obviously not learned that patience could be rewarding. Grasping Maddie's head, she tried to force it onto her clit, but Maddie refused to bend. She knew things Cody had yet to learn. She was the guide who would gently show her the way.

"Move just a…" Cody let out a frustrated grunt when Maddie danced away once again.

"Relax now," she said softly. "Breath and relax and let me please you." She pulled away and touched her gently with a finger, swiping fluid up from Cody's opening, which opened and closed rhythmically. Maddie was intrigued, and she traced around the flesh, watching it flicker. But when she tried to slide inside, Cody stiffened. She didn't say a word, but she might as well have said, "No thanks."

That was a little surprising, but Maddie reasoned everyone had their favorite things.

Then Cody's hands were on her shoulders, tugging her up, demanding she join her. Maddie got up and lay next to her, wondering if she'd breached some boundary. But Cody grabbed her roughly and started to kiss her again, working herself into a frenzy. She was panting with desire when her hand went between Maddie's legs and she slowly, tentatively slid a finger inside. That was adorably Cody! If Maddie had touched her that way, she must have wanted it. Since Cody hadn't done it earlier, she had to get at it right that minute!

Maddie only had a second to process how delightfully earnest Cody was. That probing digit got her going again and she slid her hips back and forth, urging Cody to move with her. As if Maddie had verbally instructed her, Cody responded immediately. Her fingers filled Maddie exactly the way she needed them, making her swoon. Maddie growled and slid over to straddle her, sitting up to let Cody's fingers probe her thoroughly. A neophyte would never be able to figure out the delicate geometry of doing several things at once, so she braced herself by putting a hand on Cody's shoulder, then touched herself with the other.

Cody's fingers started to move faster, and she reached up and forcefully tugged on a hard nipple. "Oh, damn, that's good," Maddie gasped. They were nearly in a frenzy, the sweet sounds of sex filling the room. Maddie bent over to change the angle, and that simple movement sent her over the edge. She cried out and collapsed onto Cody, those devilish fingers still buried inside her. Her pussy clamped down on them, and Cody knew to stay very still for a minute. Then Maddie came to her senses and started to pull away. Cody snaked a hand around her neck and pulled her down for a hot kiss. "I *loved* that," she murmured.

Gathering her strength, Maddie promised, "You'll love this more." Then she turned around, spread Cody's legs and dove in. This time she devoured her. No gentle nuzzlings. No slow exploration. This time she was going to make her come—hard.

It didn't take long. Cody's hands cradled Maddie's head, not letting her move an inch. It was an unnecessary effort. Maddie was savoring every sensation and wouldn't have traded her spot for any place in the world. Cody almost bucked her off when her body started to spasm, but Maddie stayed with her through her shaking, shuddering climax. She moved her head just far enough away to be able to gently blow on Cody's overheated pussy, and as soon as she stopped shaking went back for more.

"I don't think…" Cody started to say, but then she gurgled a moan and opened wide. "Yeah, that's…so good," she breathed.

Maddie pulled climax after climax from her, not stopping until Cody was limp and her own tongue was numb. Then she swung a leg over her and scooted around until she could collapse next to her, spent.

"I had no idea…" Cody began, then trailed off.

With the last of her strength, Maddie propped herself up on an elbow to see her face. "Better than the bed of a truck?" she teased.

Cody blinked slowly. "What? Oh, that was just kissing…and some rolling around. I've never had anyone touch me inside my clothes."

Maddie shot up and stared at her. "I thought you'd had sex with the prostitute!"

"I didn't say that. I'm *sure* I didn't say that."

"But you said something that made me think…something about it being the big one or something?" Her heart was pounding in her chest.

"Oh. Probably because she grabbed my…" She looked down shyly. "You know. She frightened me and that made it seem like a big deal." Grinning, she added, "If I knew then what I know now…" She whistled slowly, then dropped her head onto the bed. "My stars!"

Both of them were running on fumes, the long, emotional day taking its toll. "Do you want me to sleep here? Or…" Cody pointed towards the hallway.

Good God! They'd practically seen each other's viscera and now she was tentative about sleeping arrangements? "Do you want to sleep together? I can leave if you don't…"

Smiling happily, she twitched around in the bed they'd trashed. "This is good. Great, in fact."

Maddie jumped to her feet. "I'll be back in a minute. I've gotta…you know…brush my teeth." Brush her teeth? With what? An imaginary toothbrush? Maddie stood in the bathroom, her pulse hammering away, making her woozy.

She'd been the only person to ever touch Cody's sweet skin. The only person to ever see her naked. She'd taken the woman's damned virginity, and she'd taken it hard! *God damn it!* They'd been writhing around like rabid animals, not at all the way she would have treated her if she'd known.

She paced in the small room, claustrophobia making her sweat. Okay, this was dumb. What in the hell *was* virginity anyway? This wasn't feudal times when you had to be sure your line was carried on in your offspring. They'd had sex the way Cody'd wanted to. Maddie was sure of that.

She opened the door to find Cody sound asleep, lying on her belly with her back exposed to the cool air. Seeing her lying there, so trusting and open, made Maddie's heart clench with emotion. She tenderly covered her with the sheet, then walked over to stand at the window.

Maybe Cody'd only been aggressive because that's how she'd been treated by those other women. Oh, fuck! That was probably it! Each one of them had been rough with her. It didn't sound like there'd been any lead-up—just a random woman grabbing her and wrestling her into submission. Just like Maddie had done to her. She squatted down, legs too shaky to support her. She'd been like those other women…the ones who'd frightened or confused her. Damn it to hell. *Damn it all to hell!*

———

Early the next morning, Cody gazed across the bed, watching Maddie sleep while she reflected on their adventure. It was absolutely stunning to finally understand how sex made you feel. No wonder people ruined their lives chasing it!

It was a tremendous relief to finally feel settled. She was a lesbian. A real lesbian, who'd had real lesbian sex. There couldn't be more to sex than what they'd done!

Strangely, watching Maddie sleep was just about as nice as having sex with her had been. Cody lay there, letting those warm feelings wash over her, when from the depths of her memory, an image hit her, making her stomach clench. Chelsea Bracken. Seventh grade. They were in the same class, but Chelsea was one of the rich kids, and paid Cody no mind. Actually, she was at the top of that little upper class group, and made it clear to everyone beneath her that they belonged there. But Cody's mama had gone over to Chelsea's house to do some last minute alterations on a dress for Chelsea's mom. It was a store bought dress, but Mrs. Bracken had gained a few pounds and couldn't get it zipped. For some reason, Cody had accompanied her mama that day even though there were a thousand places she would rather have been.

Cody didn't recall either mother instructing them to speak to each other, but Chelsea must have been bored or grounded or something. She was actually friendly, and spent a good hour amazing Cody with her dazzling displays of books, tapes, and trophies she'd won in gymnastics. It was a magical hour. The only time she could ever recall being let into the inner sanctum of a popular girl. But on Monday morning, the spell had been broken. Chelsea looked right through her when she'd waved a friendly hello outside school. Normally, that kind of behavior would have made Cody march over and slug her. She'd never been able to tolerate being put down. But in this instance, she'd understood. There was a chasm between their social classes that was impossible to breach long term. A popular girl could spend a few hours in the enemy camp, but if you were caught you could be drummed out of the corps.

Cody looked at Maddie, a woman who made Chelsea Bracken look like poor white trash. Maddie was classy, educated, successful, and just passing through Summit County on her way to someplace much, much better. Cody had to face the facts and face them full on. Maddie'd lost her head yesterday, but she wasn't about to be caught sleeping with the enemy.

Watching the slow rise and fall of Maddie's chest, Cody let another fact enter her heart. Maddie would never turn her back like Chelsea had. They'd be able to stay friends. Cody would have staked her life on that. Maddie'd just gone a little haywire last night, and now that Cody knew what sex felt like, she was amazed anyone could control themselves at all. The heat of their argument had gotten the best of them. Now they'd have to move on and chalk the night up to the full moon.

Maddie opened her eyes, sure she'd been dreaming about a magical evening of sex. She gasped when Cody's big, brown eyes were gazing at her from just a few inches away. "God!" she panted, her heart racing. "I didn't know where I was."

"Wanna go fishing?" Cody asked, her sweet grin firmly in place.

"Uhm…I don't know." *Fishing?* They'd spent the night despoiling her virginal body and she wanted to go fishing? Cody must not be a lesbian, because she didn't have the angst instinct. They were supposed to talk and talk and process and cry and all sorts of other emotional things. But she wanted to fish. "I don't have any fishing clothes…"

"Hmm. My jeans will be too long for you, but you could roll them up." A flash of insecurity zoomed across her face. "If you want to, that is."

"I'd love to." She put her hand on Cody's cheek, a jolt of pain hitting her hard when she flinched under the caress. "Do you want to talk about last night?"

"Talk? Like how?"

Oh, she was definitely a different kind of lesbian. "Well, I thought you might want to talk about how you felt. It was your first time and everything…" She wasn't even sure of what she was after. It just seemed impossible that Cody had nothing to say on the matter.

"I liked it," she said, an earnest, uncertain smile settling onto her face. "A lot."

"I did too." Maddie sucked up her courage and said what she wished wasn't the truth. "I think we got a little carried away." Cody's smile vanished. "Not that I regret it!" Ignoring Cody's skittishness, she put her hand on her shoulder and gave it a tender squeeze. "But what I told you before is still true. I'm trying to get to a big or at least bigger city…"

"Oh, yeah, I know that." The sunny smile came back. "So you're not sorry we…" She looked down, eyeing their bodies, covered with just a sheet.

"No, of course not. But we probably shouldn't…"

"I understand." Cody nodded somberly. "I don't expect to."

How awkward could a conversation be? "Okay then. Uhm, do you drink coffee?"

"I do. Be right back." She jumped up and started to put her clothes on, then padded into the kitchen. Maddie lay there, about to jump out of her skin from the awkwardness that it seemed only she felt. Feeling the slight soreness that came from energetic sex, she got up and went into the shower to wash the scent of their lovemaking from her body. When she emerged from the bathroom, wrapped in a towel, Cody held out a pair of jeans and Maddie's own blouse and underwear. She snuck back into the bathroom and got completely dressed, then came out and gratefully accepted the coffee.

"My turn."

Cody was definitely a variety of lesbian that Maddie was unfamiliar with. For the first time in her life she kinda missed exploring and discussing every nuance of a burgeoning relationship. With a start, she shook her head, trying to hurl that thought out of it. They were *not* in a relationship. Nor would they ever be.

⸻

While sitting on a log next to a nearby stream, chosen because of Maddie's inadequate footwear, Cody let herself think of everything that had transpired.

What did Maddie do when she went to visit her friends on the weekend? There had to be women in Huntington or Charleston that she saw for sex. Anyone would want to have sex with Maddie if they had the chance. That only made sense.

She thought of how she'd behaved the night before. Fairly confident she hadn't embarrassed herself, she was equally confident she hadn't been great at it. Even though Maddie'd obviously enjoyed herself, it had to be better with someone with more experience. It was probably like fly-fishing. You could catch a trout your first time out, but you had to fish for years to learn their secrets. Women had to be like that, and since Maddie was really, really good at it, there had to be practice involved.

It wasn't gonna be easy, but now that she knew who she was, Cody would have to find a woman. Maybe more than one. There wasn't any rule that said you had to take the first one you tripped over. Of course, she'd never get anyone like Maddie again. Heck, there weren't other women like Maddie. But there'd be someone. She just had to put her mind to it and buckle down.

⸻

It was late when they got back to the trailer, and Maddie was toast. She was sure they were outside, sure they'd fished, but she was so massively preoccupied, she wasn't sure of anything more than that. Cody, on the other hand, seemed fresh as a daisy. She walked Maddie to her car, and with a big smile and clear, happy eyes said, "The weekend started out pretty rough, but it got a heck of a lot better." Her grin grew impossibly brighter. "Everything…everything about last night was remarkable, and I want to sincerely thank you." She hesitated for a second, looking like she was going to reach out for a hug. But then she practically skipped to her front door and walked in. Maddie sat there for a second, wondering what universe she'd time-traveled to. Idly, she brought her fingers to her nose and sniffed. Despite her shower, despite the hours that had passed, the delightful scent of Cody Keaton lingered, infused onto Maddie's skin.

CHAPTER SIXTEEN

A FEW DAYS AFTER the robberies, Maddie got home after a long run on the treadmill. She would never have guessed it, but running inside had lost its charm. Going on a brisk walk in the woods was far superior, but she didn't think it wise to tramp about in the forest after dark. She was stuck with her lot.

After changing into her robe, she flopped down on her sofa to while away the hour she had to spare before bed. She'd obviously had the local independent station on the night before, and when she turned the TV on she rolled her eyes when the omnipresent news anchor said with standard breathless alarm, "Authorities frustrated by lack of witnesses in Little Egypt conflagration."

Conflagration? Really? Who pulled out the thesaurus for that one? She was about to change the channel when they showed an exploded map and she noticed that Little Egypt was on the other side of Delilah, which came right after Ramp. Summit County didn't have a large population, but it covered a lot of land. And the little corner where Cody lived never made the local news.

They played a clip of the sheriff standing at a lectern and interspersed that with images of a burned out truck, along with several felled, incinerated trees. The sheriff was a rotund, somber man, whose voice showed little but resignation. "A gas can was found a few feet away from the truck, which was purchased with cash just yesterday by an Alma Winterspoon, eight-two." He stared hard into the camera. "Mrs. Winterspoon has been living in an assisted care facility for the past three years." He looked down at his notes. "Mrs. Winterspoon would not respond to questions today, saying 'Don't come back without a warrant.'" He cleared his throat and continued. "I think it's clear this bedridden woman did not buy the truck for her own use, since it was found twenty miles from her residence. A grandson of Mrs. Winterspoon, one Dervis Gamble, resides in the mobile home next to where the truck was found, but he claims no knowledge of the vehicle, nor to have noticed the fire which claimed seven trees and could have easily gotten out of control were it not for the able assistance of our county fire protection agency." He took a breath and added, "Summit County Hospital reports that Mr. Gamble was treated for a gunshot wound to his…backside yesterday. How his injury might be related to the fire is not clear at this point." He had a few papers and he snapped them sharply onto the lectern. "The sheriff's department is eager to pursue crimes like this, but it's an impossible job when no one, not even the victim, is willing to come forward."

The camera cut back to the anchorwoman, slowly shaking her head in disgust. "If you have any information about this crime, please contact the Summit County Sheriff's Department."

Maddie turned off the TV and sat motionless for a few minutes. There was enough of the truck left to show it was a big, powerful one. The make and type were still visible and she got on her laptop and looked it up. A truck like that cost over forty-five thousand dollars, a sum she knew was greater than the value of any house in Summit County. Where would a person get nearly fifty thousand dollars—in cash? Her churning guts knew exactly where the money had come from, and she thought that Dervis Gamble was lucky all he had lost was a truck, some trees and a bit of his butt.

Maddie was walking down Main Street the next day, when Cody got into step beside her. "Hi," Cody said, grinning happily.

She looked just as pleased as she had after they'd had sex. What in the world was going on in her mind? "Hi. Going my way?"

"No. I'm in town taking my aunt to the diabetes doctor. She wanted me to go get her some postal money orders. I'm headed back to the hospital now."

"So we just met by accident?"

"Yep."

It probably wasn't wise, but the issue was burning a hole in her head. "Hey, speaking of accidents, I saw something on TV last night about a big fire in Little Egypt."

That open, friendly face closed like a heavy book being slammed shut. "Yeah, I heard about that."

"It sounded bad. Like the forest could have caught fire."

Cody looked down at the sidewalk. "Yeah, I suppose it could have, but not at this time of year. Everything is still pretty wet."

"Yeah, I guess you're right about that." She waited a beat, but Cody was mum. "Hey, have you heard anything from the police about your robberies?"

A slow head shake was the only answer.

Maddie was like a dog on a bone when something was bothering her, and this had her plenty bothered. "The sheriff said a lot of people don't report crimes…so I was wondering if you had…"

"I didn't ask if anyone called the sheriff." She didn't say another word, but her chin stuck out a little, as if daring Maddie to continue. "I don't like to ask too many questions."

That was sufficiently rude. Maddie gave her a tight smile and said, "Okay, then. Back to work for me. Good to see you."

She turned but Cody put a hand on her shoulder, stopping her. Her expression was now gentle, open, trusting. "Hey, I did want to call you or come by at some point. I guess I wanted things to settle a little, and I think they have." It wasn't clear if she was nervous or shy, but she had trouble maintaining eye contact. "I really had the best time with you last weekend." She reached into her pocket and extracted something. Extending it, she said, "I bought you a fishing license. It's not much of a present, but I wanted to make sure you knew how much I appreciated everything you've done."

Maddie nodded dumbly. "That's…very nice."

"Okay. Bye."

Maddie watched her lope down the street—cool, calm and confident. *What the fuck?*

When they walked in, Maddie was on the phone. She hung up so fast she wasn't sure she'd even said "goodbye." Lucas and Ricky Montgomery were standing in the middle of the lobby, looking just as impressively threatening as they had during their last visit. Maddie scampered up to them before they could reach the teller's window. "Hello," she said breathlessly. "Can I help you?"

"We need to make a deposit," Lucas said. He dug into the pocket of his jeans and pulled out a huge wad of hundred dollar bills. "This." He dropped it on the table and backed away.

Maddie scooped up the cash to allow the other customers to start their hearts beating again, then walked directly into her office, followed by the brothers. She carefully placed the money on her desk, then sat down and tried to slow her heartbeat. "Okay. So you want to make a deposit. Do you want a checking account like last time?"

Both men shrugged. "We don't care. We just don't want it around." Ricky elbowed Lucas and he added, "You were right. It's not safe at home."

Maddie was almost afraid of handling the cash, worried she'd be duty-bound to alert the police if it smelled like gasoline or fire. But she made herself count it and put it in neat thousand dollar piles. "Twenty-eight thousand. Right?"

"Right. We…spent some," Ricky said, his brow creased in thought. "Make it half in each."

"I can do that. We'll open two new accounts and put fourteen thousand in each."

"I oughta get more," Lucas grumbled. "I'm the one who got it…"

Ricky slugged him hard in the arm. "Half in each," he repeated. "Please."

"No problem." Maddie couldn't fill out the forms quickly enough. When she went out into the lobby, Lynnette was glaring at her and the men, so she marched over to her assistant manager, Geneva. "Will you make a couple of deposits for me? Lynnette seems…preoccupied."

Later that day, three other new accounts were opened. She added up all five deposits when she had a free moment, and saw that they'd gotten seventy thousand back. Given that each cousin had deposited the same amount, they'd obviously decided to share in the loss equally. She was fairly sure the guy who'd stolen it had been terrorized in ways she didn't care to know about, but she had to concede that seventy thousand was a heck of a lot more than the police would have been able to recover. She shivered, and locked up for the night, carefully looking up and down the street before dashing to her car. Doing business with this particular group of Montgomerys was not beneficial for the bank or her nerves.

―~~―

Cody's freshly-minted lesbian identity had to go on the back burner. It would have been nice to spend hours online trying to find an available lesbian in Summit County, but she'd been goofing off. The requests were piling up, and she had to do her homework to keep up with the hard work of giving money away. After working doggedly in the Greenville library for a couple of days, she finally admitted defeat. Swinging by the bank just before they were scheduled to close, she organized her questions, trying to take as little of Maddie's time as possible. As soon as she walked in the door, that mean woman, the Goodwin girl, hissed at her. "She's not here today."

Cody took a quick look, seeing Maddie's desk neat and nearly empty of the usual papers that crowded it. "Is she sick?"

"That's not any of your business, is it."

Cody turned and was out of the building before she could be insulted again. She didn't have to put up with people like that any more. Maddie wouldn't be able to prove it, but Cody was sure the Goodwin girl was the one who'd told about her cousins getting hunks of cash. She'd give anything to have Maddie fire her, but knew that wouldn't happen without evidence. Maddie wasn't the type.

Heading back to the library, she called Maddie's number, getting voicemail. Where was she? What if she was sick and needed help? She got into her car and drove by her apartment, seeing the parking spot for 2D empty. If she was sick, she'd taken herself to the doctor. Or someone had— Cody shook her head sharply, trying to dislodge bad thoughts. Then she went back to town, found another rare pay phone, and left a message this time. She hung around town until late, then drove by Maddie's one more time. Nothing. Her gut was worked into knots, but she had to remind herself that Maddie had a real life with people Cody knew nothing about. She'd just have to wait and hope she turned up before Cody had to hire a private detective or buy her own helicopter to find her.

The next evening Maddie called. "I'm sorry I wasn't home last night. Did you need anything special?"

Cody waited a second, thinking Maddie would say where she'd been. But that didn't happen. "Uhm, yeah. I need some help. My uncle wants a modular house."

"I'm not sure…"

"That's a trailer that doesn't have wheels, near as I can figure. Anyway, I looked at all of the manufacturers and saw nothing but complaints from folks. If you want to read tales from a whole raft of really disappointed people, look it up."

"No, I trust you. Hmm…let me think about it, will you, Cody? I'm going to be behind at work, but I promise I'll get to it as soon as I can."

"Uhm, would you…should I come by your work when I have questions like this? I don't want to…"

"No! Don't be silly. We're friends. I just wanted to let you know I might not have time tomorrow. I want to do some research before I send you off on a wild goose chase."

"If you're sure…"

"I'm totally sure."

"Okay. And if you've never chased a wild goose…don't waste your time. Only a gun will do. Those suckers do *not* want to be caught."

It took until Thursday to hear back from Maddie, but she had a bucketful of information. "Here's what our mortgage financing people tell me," she began.

"I don't need a mortgage. I can pay cash."

"I know. But I thought they'd know what modular homes are worth. Not much," she added. "The guy I spoke with said over half of all people who bought them register complaints. That's a really, really high number. But he's going to talk to someone and see who the best manufacturer is. Are you sure that's the way you want to go?"

"Well, I don't want to pay over a hundred dollars a square foot to have a house constructed on site. I can get one of these for fifty thousand, total, and it's a good size. Three bedrooms, with a family room."

"The price is right. But you don't want shoddy construction."

"That's the word I saw more than any other on those sites where people congregate to complain. Shoddy seems like it's everywhere."

"How about this? The guy I spoke with suggested you look into super energy-efficient, 'green' homes. There are a few of them out there, and, even though they're not very traditional looking, they don't hurt the environment."

"That'd be nice. I'm not sure how you mean, but I like the environment." She hoped Maddie knew she was teasing.

"Look them up," Maddie urged. "I know you're good at using the internet. Search for 'green modular homes.' They're more expensive, but I think many of them are better made. Most of them are designed by architects who are trying to come up with good, inexpensive houses, not just builders looking for the highest profit."

"Okay. I guess I don't mind paying more to get more. Thanks for doing this." She paused, trying to think of a way to slide into an invitation. "Doing anything this weekend?" That was smooth.

"Nothing in particular. I was going to go to Charleston, but you could talk me out of that. What's on your mind?"

Cody thought she'd better not say what was really on her mind. She didn't know much about women, but telling one you kept thinking about how it felt to have her breast in your mouth was probably not a good idea. Just because your blood was running high and you fell into bed with someone didn't mean a darned thing in the cold light of day. There was no sense in even discussing it.

"Cody?"

"Oh! Well, I was going to go fishing. Nothing special…"

"If you're inviting me, I'd love to come. Saturday morning?"

"Sure. Any time. I'm always up."

"I just bet you are."

—⁓—

The whole thing was crazy. Cody acted completely normally, giving off no indication that she thought they'd done more than have sex. But that was so *odd*. Especially for an adult who'd barely been touched. Maddie was the one who should be cool and calm about the whole thing, but she found herself thinking about Cody several hundred times a day.

She didn't want to live in Greenville—or Twined Creek or Delilah or Little Egypt or Ramp or any other squiggle on the map! And there was no way Cody would, or even could, live in a big city. Then why obsess about her? They'd had a wonderful roll in the hay, and she should put that experience in her masturbation bank and be done with it. But she couldn't let it go. Here she was, canceling plans just to go fishing with the woman she refused to fall in love with. Really smart, Maddie. Excellent long-term planning.

She got up and closed the blinds, sat back down, then folded her arms and rested her head upon them. A gnawing sensation lodged in her gut; it had been growing since she'd left Cody's bed. Spending more time with her was stupid. Plain and simple stupid. Besides all of the other issues, she was from a family teeming with felons! But Maddie couldn't help herself. She had to go with her gut—which was probably going to lead her to a bad end. Her track record wasn't exemplary, and given how things were unrolling, it wasn't going to get much better.

Cody sat at the biggest car dealer in Huntington, trying to get her hand to move. She knew she could write a check…she'd done it dozens of times. But this check was for an astronomical amount of money. The kind of money it would have taken her ten years to earn doing odd jobs and selling moss. But Brett had been the first to decide what he wanted, and he wanted the most expensive, gas-guzzling, all wheel drive SUV ever made.

Brett. The one she knew had gotten Keith involved in drugs. He and Ricky both rolled around town with drugs on them, selling Percocet or Oxycontin or Vicodin to one poor soul or another. Usually people who let their babies go hungry so they could deaden their brains for a few hours. It made her sick, but she couldn't turn them into people she could be proud of. They were lost.

She didn't think anyone in the family had ever had a brand new car, and it galled her to think Brett would be the one. But he sat there, unashamed, while she wrote the biggest check of her life. It made her guts roil, but she'd promised, and she'd never go back on a promise—no matter how stupid it now seemed.

———

Brett's siblings, Chase and Melissa, had ridden to Huntington with them. On the way back, Melissa chose to ride home with Cody, instead of in her brother's new car. When they skirted by Greenville, Melissa said, "Let's stop and have a beer. The kids are going to their daddy's after school."

"All right." Melissa was probably the most stable of Cody's female cousins. Her kids were all from the same man, her legally married husband, no less. Her ex-husband worked some, and didn't have any obvious bad habits. Actually, he seemed so unoffensive Cody couldn't imagine divorcing him. But Melissa was particular, always going her own way.

She and Melissa were close in age, with the three years that separated them seeming like nothing now that they were adults. But it had been a lot when they were kids, and Melissa had complained frequently when Cody'd followed her around. Now she was definitely one of the people Cody relied on; not as close as Devin, but still close.

They stopped at the Tap Room, the place she'd gone with Maddie. It wasn't likely for the bank manager to be sitting in a dark bar in the middle of the afternoon, but anything was possible and Cody scanned the place carefully, hoping for a sighting.

They got beers and went to sit in a quiet booth. Melissa played with everything she could get her hands on, acting so fidgety that Cody finally slapped a hand over hers . "What's on your mind?"

"Oh, shit," she said, clearly embarrassed. "I didn't realize how antsy this makes me." She took another big sip of beer. "I saw Brett parked out by the old plant. A guy was leaning into the car, obviously buying drugs. He's gotten really brazen, and I'm afraid of what's going to happen when people see him flying around hell and back in that big car. Somebody'll kill him for it or for the money they guess he has."

"That could happen," Cody said sourly. "But I can't mother him. He's got his own for that."

"My mama don't say a word to him," Melissa said. "You know that. But I'm damn glad you didn't give us too much. No matter how much you gave us, Brett would spend his and want mine. And Mandy's."

"I know that." She sat there quietly, thinking. "I'm disappointed in all of them, to be honest. Lucas and Jaden have boys in high school. Why didn't they ask for money to send them to college or trade school? Everybody just wants cars and houses." She slammed her beer down, forcing a ounce or two to bubble up from the neck. "Don't they want better for their kids?"

"I want better for mine," she said, sounding defensive. "But what happens if they go to college? Where will they work?"

"Not in this county," Cody admitted. "There will never be jobs near us. All we can produce is hillbilly heroin."

"It's a damn crying shame, but it's the truth. I know my kids'll take off, but I still want them to go to school." She gave Cody a narrow-eyed look. "I didn't know I had to get in line already if I want tuition in ten years."

Cody felt that chiding look like a slap. "I'm sorry. There's no rush. But two of the kids *are* getting to the point where they have to start applying to colleges. No one says a word about it. Did they even take the SATs?"

"No one's said. I'll ask."

"Try to drop some hints to the boys' mamas, will you?"

"They're mad they ain't got any money yet," Melissa admitted, snickering. "I'd steer clear if I was you."

"I'm clear, and staying that way. If I have to give money to all of the boys' ex-girlfriends, I'll be broke in a month."

"It's not that bad, is it?"

"No, it's not," she admitted. "But you know there's not enough money in the world to keep everyone happy. If they had a big pile of money some of the boys would just go have another bunch of babies." She shook her head. "They're so damned irresponsible."

"Could I..." She dropped her head, a little shame-faced. "I know I could get by without one, but I'd dearly love a car of some sort. I've still got a lot of the money you gave me, but I thought that was supposed to be for regular living expenses. A car would take all of it and then I'd be asking again."

Cody started to speak, but Melissa was still going.

"It doesn't have to be new, or even nearly new. But I worry about needing to take the kids to the doctor and not being able to get there. I'll be lucky to *see* the inside of Brett's car again. I'm not even gonna think I can count on him."

Cody smiled at her indulgently. "Why should you be the only one with a beat-up car? Decide what you want, and we'll go shopping."

Cody'd been in the house just seconds when her phone rang, "Cody?" Maddie's anxious voice asked.

"Yeah? What's wrong?"

"I got a call this afternoon from a car dealership in Huntington. Did you buy something huge?"

"Oh, yeah." She laughed at the thought of Maddie running over to the car dealer to see who was impersonating her. "Should I tell you before I do something like that? I'm gonna have to do it about ten more times."

"Write checks like this?" Her voice was a whole lot higher than normal.

"Not that big, but that was the first of the cars they want. The list is getting a lot longer."

"Cody," Maddie sighed heavily. "Please let me have a financial planner talk to you. I know you can easily afford what you're spending, but without a plan…"

"Everyone will calm down, and if they don't…then I don't have to worry about it any more."

"Have you even replaced your sofa yet?"

"No, but I'll get around to it. I just put my bed pillows on it when I want to use it. That works fine."

"I'm sure it does, but look at what you're doing. You're spending remarkable amounts on cars…My god, please tell me this was for more than one car."

"No. Just one."

"How is it even possible to spend that for an American car? Mine was a fifth that much!"

"This one's nicer than yours," she said, chuckling. "And you're not a stupid hillbilly without the good sense god gave him."

"Did you pay list price?"

"I paid what Brett told me it cost. I was outside while they were shopping."

"Okay." She could hear Maddie take in a breath. She'd obviously upset her, but wasn't sure why. "Here's what I'd like to do. I'm going to contact the woman who runs our auto loan department. She'll call and give you some tips on how to buy cars. You have to negotiate, Cody, and you have to do your homework before you go shopping. It's the only way to not be taken advantage of."

"Once they know I won the lottery, they all take advantage."

"That's not true," Maddie said insistently. "They can't take advantage if you don't let them. Believe me, they'd rather sell you a car for a fair price than not sell it at all. I've got to go now to catch this woman before she leaves. See you tomorrow!"

CHAPTER SEVENTEEN

MADDIE PULLED INTO CODY'S drive at eight a.m. It was early for her, but worth the extra effort since Cody so enjoyed sneaking up on the fish.

She was outside by the time Maddie'd gotten just a few feet down the drive. Cody walked over to the car and opened the door when it stopped. "The fish are ready for lunch," she teased.

Maddie hopped out and stood there for a half second, deciding whether to offer a kiss or a hug. She had no experience in how to treat a woman she'd had sex with once—given they were not girlfriends. Choosing to avoid the issue, she reached into her back seat and took out her carryall. "I've got bug spray and a change of clothes in case I fall in."

"Bug spray, huh? I've never used it. Does it work?"

"Let's both use it. Then we'll find out."

Cody took the can Maddie offered and scanned the label. "No, you use it. Then if I get bit and you don't—we'll know it works."

"I guess that's the more scientific way. Mind if I put my bag inside?"

"No, not at all. But it'll be safer in your trunk. I don't lock the door anymore. Heck, I might as well leave it wide open. A new lock costs more than anything I have right now, given that my guns are gone."

"Cody, you've got to replace them. Don't suffer when you can easily afford them."

"I'm not suffering. It's not hunting season right now, so I'm biding my time, waiting for a sale." She looked proud of herself, and Maddie wasn't going to argue. It wouldn't do a bit of good.

"Hey," Cody said seriously. "I've got some money hidden that I want you to know about."

"Me? Why me?"

"'Cause I know you won't take it," she said, winking. She led the way down a well-used path, then pointed at a tall tree with a big y-shaped crotch. "That looks like a good place to hide money, doesn't it?"

"I suppose. You could probably climb up there if you were good at that kind of thing."

"Right. And that crotch would be a good hiding spot. But that's not the one. It's that one." She pointed at a tree father away, not easily reachable from any other. "You can't tell from here, but that one has a hollow spot way up at the top. I've got all my cash in there. If anything happens to me…it's yours."

"Oh, Cody, I couldn't take money from you. And nothing is going to happen to you!"

"Stuff happens to people," she said quietly. "It just does." She brightened when she asked, "Want me to climb up to show you exactly where it is?"

"No, don't bother," Maddie said, laughing. "I'd have to chop it down to get at it, anyway. I don't have your tree climbing skills."

"Well, if you don't want to climb it or cut it down, tell Devin. He can climb trees better than I can."

"I won't need to, but I'll remember."

After Maddie applied a thorough coating of bug spray, they left, on foot this time, for a spot Cody swore was close by. Maddie assumed her vision of close and Cody's would be different, so she pledged to not care if they walked for hours.

Cody had obviously changed her mind about fishing, for she carried nothing. Maddie thought to question her, but she honestly preferred hiking to taunting fish, even though she wouldn't admit it to Cody.

They made their way through glades of mountain laurel, so pink and vibrant that Maddie's breath caught in her throat. "Yeah, that's nice," Cody said, dismissively, "but I'm on the lookout for another one." After another half hour of fairly aggressive hiking, Cody stuck an arm out, stopping Maddie short. "Right there," she said, as though she were pointing at an animal who might scamper away. The plant was definitely pretty. Low, rich green and filled with leggy flowers that were nearly maroon, each perfect and delicate. "Bubby blossom," she said, looking proud.

"It's gorgeous." Maddie moved closer and inspected the plant.

"It's rare, that's for sure. Sometimes we don't get any at all. But this year was good for it with the rain we've had. I assumed we'd find some today." She grinned toothily, like she'd gotten the upper hand over someone. "You'll only find this up high when the soil's moist. Some people grow it…in their yards and such." She made a dismissive gesture. "But it's only wild up here. Take a sniff."

Maddie leaned over and inhaled deeply. "What in the hell?" she said, then slapped herself lightly on the mouth. "I mean, gosh! It smells like… pineapple…or strawberries. It's tropical!"

"It is. It reminds me of bananas too. The whole thing has a scent… even the roots. It's best when it's warm out, near sunset. It can make you want to lie down and soak your senses in it."

She looked so remarkably happy—the way people looked when they got a fantastic surprise present. No one on earth could have appreciated her environment more than Cody Keaton, and Maddie found that trait delightful. Cody was possibly the only person she'd ever known who was as happy with a flower as she was with a new car…or a cushion for her ass! That was a tough one to accept. But having a new sofa wasn't a priority. This was. This pretty, fragrant, unique, rare flower was her priority, and Maddie was very grateful to be able to share it with her.

She knew she shouldn't do it. Being physical would send the wrong message. But Cody was so adorably happy that Maddie needed some of that glow to rub off on her. She grasped her arm and hugged it to herself. "Thanks for sharing something so special with me."

"My pleasure," she said, then almost scampered away, leaving Maddie to wonder what made Cody so damned skittish.

They reached a beautiful little pond next to a narrow, fast-moving river. "The pond is real good," Cody said. "Deep and cold. Fish love it. The river's good, too, but I didn't want to carry much."

"You have to carry *something*," Maddie insisted. "We don't have poles, and I'm not sure I want to jump in and wrestle with 'em. Maybe when it gets warmer…"

"You're very funny," Cody said, only smiling slightly. "Don't worry. I'm not going to do any hand-fishing." She reached into her pocket and removed a sharp-looking knife. It wasn't one of those fancy, multi-purpose things. Just a long blade in a worn wooden handle. "If you can't make your own fishing pole…well, I'm not sure what that says about you."

Maddie was going to offer that you could get by quite well without being able to make your own toast, much less your own fishing pole, but Cody's view of the world was pretty well set.

Going to a long branch, Cody snapped it off near the trunk, the crack ricocheting around like a shot. Then she cleaned up the wound, cutting away the bark neatly. She held out the six foot long branch and made a few more cuts, trimming off the stray mini-branches. "River willow," she commented, while working. "Bamboo's better, but we don't have much of that."

When she was finished, she held the pole out to Maddie, fat end first. "Your pole." Then she repeated the exercise, selecting an even longer one for herself.

"Now I've got some old fly line," she said, pulling a neat bundle from her pocket. "I'll just snell a hook on here, and we're ready to go." She worked quickly, amazing Maddie, who stood silently by, watching carefully.

"Wanna find some worms or caterpillars while I finish up?"

"No one's ever asked," Maddie said, setting off to give it her best.

She was still digging away when Cody walked over. "Need help?" Without waiting, she turned over a big rock with her boot, then pointed at a dozen fat, squirming creatures. "Sorry that was so tough," she said, snickering.

"I can balance a checkbook really fast! I'm not without skills."

"You've got a million. And once I teach you how to fish, you'll have a million and one."

———

This time, they didn't release the poor things. Cody said you should never kill more than you needed, and you had to do it quickly and painlessly, but if Maddie would eat fish, she shouldn't be squeamish about catching them.

Well, Cody could have all of the dictums she wanted, but Maddie wasn't crazy about the whole thing. Cody had to take each of the two fish she caught and string them to a line, after gently chiding Maddie for being yellow.

Cody only took two herself, even though Maddie was pretty sure she could have had more. They weren't huge fish, and they got smaller when Cody took her knife out, gutted them and removed their heads. It was only through avoidance of embarrassment that Maddie didn't upchuck.

Cody then proceeded to build a fire. It took no time at all, and when she had twigs and broken branches arranged to her satisfaction she took out a piece of cloth and sprinkled the contents onto the kindling. "I take wood shavings and pour melted wax over them. Makes the fire just jump at you." When she lit a match it did jump, and Mattie stepped back a pace. "It'll take a while to simmer down. Take a rest."

Maddie sat on a rock and watched the fire burn. She'd never been so thoroughly steeped in nature, and she had to admit it felt wonderful. Her senses were somehow sharper, and she was aware of movement and sound and even shapes in ways she usually ignored. This was such a vacation from her world that it seemed like she was hundreds of miles away. But this was all just an hour from her. Well, two and a half if they'd walked straight up the hill—which she had no idea if they'd done. Still, it was remarkably close, and all free.

"Is this legal to do?" she asked.

"Sure. I told you about the limits and all of that."

"No, is it legal to fish *here?*"

"Oh, sure. This is public land. I'm no fan of the government, but if we didn't have some public land we'd be shooting each other over every fish. It'd be like England in the bad old days when people starved even though they lived right next to a forest filled with wildlife."

When the fire was close, Cody got up, threaded the fish along a green branch she'd sharpened, then held the stick over the fire. Soon the entire forest was filled with their scent. "That smells so good," Maddie said. "I can't believe how hungry I am."

"Too bad we've only got fish, but it's too early for berries. We'll have to wait until July, at the earliest, for those." A big smile creased her face. "There's nothing better than wild berries. You wait and see."

When the fish were done to her satisfaction, she pulled the stick from the fire and let them cool until she could handle them. Then she pushed the top one off into Maddie's hands, then the next, until they were piled up. She took the cloth she'd had her wood shavings in, and spread it on the ground, then took the fish and placed them on it. "Dig in," she said. She took the top fish and delicately peeled the skin from it, dropping big pieces into her mouth. Maddie mirrored her, chewing the first chunk. "Hot damn, this is good!" Rolling her eyes, she said, "I can't stop cursing around you."

"I don't mind. And I'm glad you like the fish."

"Like it? It's the best I've ever had."

"The freshest, for sure. Fish doesn't like to wait to be eaten."

"I think you are one hundred percent correct, and I'm only too happy to accommodate their wishes."

It took a while to douse the fire and clean up their campsite. Surprisingly, Cody said they should leave the guts and bones. "Someone needs them," she said, starting to walk away. "Nothing goes to waste."

They walked back via a slightly different way. "It'll start to get dark by five, and I want to be closer to the road," Cody said.

It was only three, but Maddie wasn't about to argue. They set off, scampering over rocks and vines and tiny creeks that bubbled up from seemingly nowhere. It still seemed like they were deep in the forest, but Cody's expression turned grim when she said, "Hold your breath if you can."

"What?" Then it hit her. Something very offensive was close by. "What in the heck is that?"

"People dumping." They walked on, and finally came to a ravine that was right next to the road. They hadn't heard a single car, but this was obviously a popular spot. It was nearly filled with every kind of trash a human could create. Cans, bottles, paper, plastic, and what seemed like a million disposable diapers had been dumped. Much of it wasn't even in a bag. People must have just filled the back of their truck, turned it around and shoved it all out.

"Nobody did this to us," Cody said quietly. "We did it to ourselves."

"But…why?" Maddie asked. "Why go to this much trouble?"

Cody turned and looked at her, eyes dark and sad. "The dump's all the way in Greenville, and you have to pay. Lots of folks can't afford it."

"You have to pay to throw your trash away?" Who ever heard of such a thing!

"Yeah. It used to be free, but the county ran out of land. They hired some big company to run it privately. They're there to make money. You pay too. You just might not know it."

Maddie assumed her rent covered trash pickup, but still… "How can you have pride about your home when it looks like this?"

"You can't. Most don't. They live here, but they're not proud of it. Look at my uncle's house."

"Is…does he…is he unable to pay to take his stuff to the dump?" That was a damned tough question to ask gracefully.

"No, he's just slovenly." She turned and started to walk again, moving quickly now, probably to get away from the smell and the thoughts associated with the disgusting mound of trash.

—⁂—

Cody's mood was back to normal by the time they reached her house. She stood just inside, looking around aimlessly for a second. "Hey, my Aunt Merry brought me some apple pie. Want a slice?"

"No, I don't think so. But I'll watch you eat some." She'd put on five pounds that winter, having to be polite and nibble on the treats that an amazing number of people brought to her and her staff. Five pounds wasn't much, but she was determined to take it off. Trekking all over West Virginia with Cody was a good way to do it, and eating pie would negate the day's effort.

Cody plunked herself down onto the sofa, allowing Maddie the chair. She took a big bite, let out a happy groan and said, "If you like pie at all, you need one bite."

"Oh, I like pie plenty. It doesn't like me much though."

Cody just cocked her head, then extended the fork. Maddie placed her hand atop Cody's and guided it to her mouth, where she urged the bite inside with her tongue. "God damn, Cody. How am I supposed to refuse pie when it tastes like that?"

"You're not supposed to refuse pie. You're supposed to savor it." There was Cody…sitting on a bare sofa in an ancient trailer…and she was as happy as a woman could be. Proud and strong and honest and perfectly content—with or without money. Maddie must have allowed her tender feelings to show, because Cody leaned over, slipped a hand behind her neck, held her there for just an instant, then pulled her in for a kiss.

Divine. Apples and sugar and cinnamon and Cody. A sweet, sweet combo. Maddie sighed with pleasure, then Cody had her by the shoulders and pulled her to her feet. It was all Maddie could do to stay upright before Cody unleashed the drive she'd been doing a fantastic job of hiding. Or her drive had only two settings—way off and way on. Either way, it was on now, and Maddie struggled to catch her breath.

"I'm gonna do everything to you that you did to me," she growled huskily. Then she had what must have been a moment of indecision. Her eyes moved jerkily around Maddie's face, as if she had to work to focus. "You want to, right?"

"Yeah, yeah, I want to," Maddie panted. "I *really* want to."

⁓

Cody tugged at Maddie's zipper, her hands shaking so hard it was tough work. It was amazing…remarkable…stunning, really. Who would have ever thought she'd get to do this again? Thank god she hadn't been wrong about the look Maddie had given her. That would have been awful! Heck, she would have dug a hole and climbed in if she'd pushed too far. But the look Maddie had given her tonight was exactly how she'd looked the first time they'd done it. Like she wanted to climb right into Cody's mouth. That was a wonderful, wonderful look.

Kissing Maddie possessively while undressing her took a lot of coordination, but Cody found that pressing her up against the wall helped a lot. Once she had her still, she could let her hands roam all over her gorgeous body, cupping her breasts, her ass, touching that soft skin as the clothes fell from her body. This time she was going to leave her bra and panties on for as long as possible. She didn't know where Maddie got her undies, but it wasn't in Summit County. There was definitely no place close that sold the sexy things that covered her most delectable parts. She let her fingers trail over the detailing that flitted along the edge of the bra, knowing that full, sexy breast was just waiting for her mouth. Filled with so many emotions, she was lightheaded. But pressing her lips against Maddie's centered her and made her feel anchored. Anchored to a woman she knew could never, ever be hers. She tried to focus on a goal, so she wouldn't get lost in the feelings that enveloped her. The odds of ever being here again were pretty darned slim, and Cody did not want to waste a golden opportunity. She was determined to divine every trick that Maddie could teach her about sex. That pretty head was just filled with information Cody might never be privy to again.

Maddie had never seen Cody hunt, but she knew just how she'd be. Quiet, careful, patient to the core. But once she had the prey in her sights, she'd pounce and slay it without a moment's hesitation. Lying on the bed, with Cody looming over her, Maddie could empathize with the hapless doe who'd barely heard a twig snap before being felled.

Maddie had never been with anyone with the rabid intensity Cody lavished on her. It seemed like her hands touched every part of her body at once; caressing, squeezing, palpating her flesh so thoroughly and rapidly that her brain couldn't keep up. Cody's hand was clearly grasping her ass, but her breast still throbbed with sensation, begging those determined fingers to return and caress it again.

They'd only been on the bed for a few minutes, but Cody was ready to get down to business. She slithered down the bed, a sexy smile on her lips as she settled down between Maddie's legs.

It was remarkable. The woman had never gotten near another person's private parts, yet Cody's smile was beyond confident. Spreading Maddie open, she gazed at her like she was looking at a fantastic Christmas present she'd longed for and now held in her hands.

In the moment before Cody's mouth touched her, Maddie was struck with the thought that she'd never been more aroused in her life. It wasn't about experience or technique. Seeing a woman look at you like you were divine was what did the trick. When you could almost see the heat pouring off another woman's body when she touched yours, there was no way in hell to be dispassionate. You needed to jump right in with her, and that's what Maddie did when Cody delicately kissed her.

Her hands threaded themselves into Cody's silken hair, but she resisted the urge, the need to pull her in tight. Cody had to go at her own pace, even if it killed Maddie…which she thought it might.

Soft moans escaped her lips and she gently thrust herself against Cody's warm, wet mouth. She couldn't help it. No human could have lain there passively when she was being caressed that enthusiastically.

All Maddie had to do was move an inch, moan a little louder or grow silent and Cody responded. She was so rigorously aware of Maddie's needs that it seemed they were sharing the same nervous system. Cody tried everything, experimenting with pressure, motion and tension. She made her tongue pointed, then velvety, then used just her lips to drive Maddie absolutely wild.

Finally, Maddie was near collapse. She'd been taken so close to the edge so many times she was desperate for release. "Please," she whimpered. "You've got to let me come."

Cody looked up with such a teasing grin that Maddie feared she'd back off and leave her to beg. But her generous nature showed through and she lowered her head and focused, gently sucking Maddie into her mouth and applying just enough pressure to pull a shuddering climax from her enervated, grateful body.

It took a few seconds to come back to earth and Maddie finally realized Cody was earnestly trying to urge another orgasm from her.

"You've got to let me rest for a bit," Maddie said, stroking her head tenderly. "I can't shoot them out as quickly as you can."

The dark head popped up abruptly. "You can't? Why?"

"I don't know why. I just can't." She quirked a finger. "Come up here and kiss me."

Cody climbed up and got to work, her buoyant enthusiasm back in full force. She kissed like she was in a bit of a hurry, and so very, very excited about what she was doing that she really had to get at it. It was remarkably endearing, and Maddie found herself stroking her head like she would a pet.

"I like it when you do that," Cody said, slowing down to pull away and gaze at Maddie for a second. "It's gentle. Nice." Then she dove back in, ratcheting up the passion again.

Maddie hadn't yet gotten anywhere near Cody's erogenous zone. Maybe pleasing others was *how* she got pleasure, but she still needed to relax and have a woman focus on her. There were selfish lovers out there, and Maddie didn't want her to encounter one and be left high and dry.

She got Cody onto her back and started to explore her. They'd been so rushed the first time, she felt like there were dozens of things she didn't know about her luscious body. Running her fingers up and down her cleft, she stopped and spent a moment playing outside her opening.

Cody didn't freeze like she had last time, but there was still no "come on in."

"Do you not like penetration? I'll leave you alone if you're not into it."

Looking down, clearly puzzled, Cody said, "I haven't had sex before. Remember?"

"Yeah, I remember." Maddie giggled when she saw that Cody was teasing. "But a lot of women like to have a finger inside when they touch themselves…no partner involved."

"Really?" Her brow was furrowed, and she looked like she was expecting a trick. "Why?"

"There are plenty of nerves in there. Wanna see?"

"Sure." She grinned. "Why not?"

"I admire your adventurous spirit." Maddie focused on her task and delicately tickled the skin just outside.

"That's nice."

"There's more." She took her index finger and, sensing no resistance, slowly entered. Cody was narrow, but so wet that Maddie slid in easily. "How's that?"

"Okay, I guess."

"Now we add something." She bent her head and delicately laved all around her labia, then probed with her tongue. She could feel Cody's body grow tense, like a really good sensation was coursing through her and she didn't want it to stop. Meeting her eyes, she said, "Any good?"

Her face was scrunched up in thought. "I can almost forget you're in there."

"Is it uncomfortable?"

"No, it's not that." She frowned, looking like she was testing theories. "I suppose I'm just not used to it. I guess you develop a routine or a habit…"

"That makes sense." Maddie moved her finger, gently stroking in and out. "It feels good to me to stretch the skin. I started doing that when I was young and figuring things out, so I guess it's a habit."

"Yeah, I don't have that habit." She paused for just a second. "But if you like doing it, go right ahead. I'll get used to it."

Laughing, Maddie moved up alongside her. "I like being inside you, but it's not a requirement."

"Show me how you like it." Cody circled her finger all around Maddie's opening.

"Okay." She guided her hand, keeping it from going in too deep. "Some women like to be fucked deeply, but that's not my thing." She kissed the addictive lips so close to her own. "I like it slow and shallow."

Cody moved to partially trap her, a sensation Maddie was quickly becoming reliant upon. Then she slowly moved in and out, adding another finger as she watched Maddie's reaction with the utmost fascination.

"You're doing me again," Maddie teased, hearing how slow and syrupy her voice had become. Cody could turn her to jelly in seconds. "It's *your* turn."

"I know what feels good to me. It's you I'm interested in."

It took all of her fortitude, but Maddie regretfully stopped Cody's hand. "And I'm interested in you. Now lie back and let me do what you like, the way you like it." She teasingly patted her sex. "We're playing according to type. You like the outside and I like the inside, where it's nice and warm."

That determined hand tried to sneak back in. "I like *your* inside."

"Let me have some fun and I promise you can come back in later." She swiped her hand away. "It's time to stay outside and play."

They'd gone back and forth for well over an hour, with both of them thoroughly sated. It was still early, and since Cody didn't seem too sleepy Maddie got to engage in one of her favorite things, lying in bed and talking after sex. Barriers were broken down, and even deep conversations always seemed easier.

She'd been wondering about something, and the afterglow was a perfect time to bring it up. Cody was lying on her back, grinning happily. Maddie ran a finger across her chest, tracing her sternum, her collarbones, anything that protruded.

"You're memorizing me," Cody said quietly. "Like you want to remember where everything is in case you have to take me apart."

"I'd never take you apart, you silly thing. You're perfect just as you are." She leaned over and kissed her breast, the nipple immediately standing at attention. "See? Even your nipples are perfect. They know what to do with no instructions."

"That's funny."

"No, I mean it. You're body is very responsive. But your brain could use a little…freeing up."

"My brain? Like what?" She rose up on an elbow, her expression somewhere between alarm and suspicion.

"Nothing to worry about. Lie back down and let me make a point." She flicked at her softened nipple, giggling when it hardened again. "I don't think you let yourself dream."

"That's not so. I dream like everyone does. Most of my dreams are really nice too."

"No, not when you're asleep. I want to know about your dreams for yourself…your life. What your goals are. Things like that."

Lips pursed, Cody shook her head quickly. "I don't do that. No good ever came out of sticking your head in the clouds. I just try to stay on my toes and handle what I can handle when it comes."

Damn, she sounded like she was waiting for the trials of Job! "Come on." She continued to pet her, rubbing her belly gently. "I know there are things you want…even if you don't think you can have them."

Cody's body continued to gain tension. "No, I don't like to want things I can't have. It's not smart."

"But you can have everything!" She patted her belly firmly.

"No, you can't. And it just hurts worse to lie to yourself. Some things are out of your reach." Her eyes had taken on the flat, cold look they had every time they talked about money.

"You can buy anything in the world, Cody. You can live anywhere, do anything. Travel, go to school, learn to paint, take people fishing... anything."

"Oh. Yeah, that's true." She relaxed a little, surprising Maddie. Usually this was tough going, and it had seemed so until just a second ago. Maybe the reality took a bit to sink in every time she thought about it.

"So tell me about your dreams." She kissed her cheek, still flushed from sex. "What would you have if you could have anything?"

"If I could buy anything..." she mused. It took quite a few minutes, but she finally said, "I'd like a house on top of the hill."

"The hill?"

"My hill." She frowned when it was clear Maddie didn't get it. "The hollow is a sharp valley. There's a big hill on one side, and a littler one on the other. I'd like a place on top of the big hill."

That was so adorable! She could have anything in the world, and she wanted to move about a mile away.

"I'm happy here, of course, and if I could grow a better garden I'd never want to leave. But we get a lot of fog in the summer and that can ruin everything that needs a lot of heat. I'd love to grow melons, too, but they need an awful lot of sun and warm nights. I think I'd have a chance on top of the hill."

That was it. That was all she wanted. A way to grow things you could buy at the grocery store. So cute!

"You can have that. You can have what you've dreamed of. Winning the money can give you what you couldn't have had before."

"Dreams can be scary," she said, shivering.

"They don't have to be." She snuggled up next to her and stroked her lovingly, tenderly. "Let yourself dream, Cody. Take off the brakes and let your mind roll."

Maddie woke to the sun pouring in on her, slapping her right in the face. "What in the heck…" She sat up, and immediately realized she was at Cody's. "Am I alone?" she called.

"Not hardly." Cody was dressed and ready to take on the day. She held a cup of coffee in her hand, and when she sat on the edge of the bed she offered it to Maddie. "Milk and sugar."

Maddie took a sip, then wrinkled up her nose. "Just milk for me. Plenty of it."

Cody went and made another cup, then brought it back and handed it over. "I thought about what you said about buying what I wanted. I think you're right." She walked over to the window, looking out on the trees just a few yards across the drive. "I'll be up where I want, and I might lead the vultures away."

"Vultures?"

"Yeah. Sometimes an animal will see its young is going to be caught. It'll divert the predator's attention and offer itself up. It's the bigger animal, so the predator always goes for it." She shrugged. "I'm the bigger animal now and if I leave, the vultures might leave my family alone. Especially if they think we're on the outs. Heck, the thieves'll spend a year digging this place up, I figure. They might strike oil while they're at it and be happy with that."

Maddie slipped out of bed, realizing she was stark naked. She was usually quite at ease with her body, but things were different with Cody. There was still some odd sense of formality between them, and she felt strange being naked. So she quickly dressed, then stood close, needing to see her eyes. "Are you sure this is what you want? I know leaving here would be hard for you."

"It would be. It will be. But I'll keep the land. Because this was my Granny's place, it'll always be special to me. I'll plant her favorite things and keep this as my cool weather vegetable plot. Maybe I'll put lights in the trailer and use it to grow things from seed. I'll have the height and the hollow."

It seemed like there would be more to it than what vegetable to plant where, but Cody seemed resolved. "If that's what you want, you should get it."

"I'll start looking for land," she said firmly.

"I'd love to go with you."

"Then I'd love to have you. Now get ready and we can do a little fishing. I've got a place where I can teach you how to catch rainbow trout. Hurry on, now! Haven't you learned fish don't like to wait?"

———

Maddie drove home that night, still full of rainbow trout. She would have to bring a vegetable or something to not overdose on protein on their hikes. Or wait until berry season, which was still months away. Cody would know where the best berries were, of course. They might be at the Ohio or the Virginia border, but they'd be be worth it.

Cody. The sex they'd had was…wonderful. Cody was full of energy and enthusiasm and wasn't afraid to try anything. And she was so focused on pleasing that she almost had to be forced to lie still and accept pleasure. So what was missing? It seemed silly, since they'd explored every inch of skin, but even last night the intimacy had been scant and…elusive.

It was pretty clear Cody wasn't very comfortable with affection. She never offered a hug or a kiss outside of bed, and she danced away from the most casual touch. Strangely, hugs were a little off limits, but cunnilingus was a snap, and she went at Maddie like burying her head between her legs was the most natural thing in the world. So maybe intimacy was going to be a problem for her. Of course, some women would be perfectly happy merely being fucked hard and well, so that might not be a liability. But Maddie needed tenderness, something she hadn't gotten much from Cody.

Still, it was hard, very hard…okay, impossible to get her off her mind. She wasn't worldly, had little experience in the ways of average city people, and could be strangely prickly about odd things. But what a heart she had! She was giving and generous and loyal to a fault. Those were traits that could make up for a wealth of deficiencies, and she certainly didn't have more than a few. No, Cody was as good as a woman could dream of. Maddie just hoped she found someone who'd love her hills and hollow as much as she did. That would be one very lucky woman.

Cody sat on her steps, sharpening her knife. Both dogs sat at her feet, obviously hoping something exciting was going to happen. It was almost dark, and in a month she'd not be able to sit outside at night without being eaten alive by bugs.

Late winter was the perfect time of year in her view. The early shrubs were in bloom, the fish were biting, and everything smelled green and fresh. There wasn't much to hunt, but she'd have plenty in the fall. She could wait.

She let her mind wander and, like it did whenever she let it, her thoughts roamed over Maddie's body, caressing her in her imagination. Goodness, but she was a beautiful woman. It still amazed her that Maddie let her touch her the way she had. She'd been so open...so willing. There was no doubt she was the sexiest woman alive. No one even came close. So why'd she have to ruin everything with her talk about dreaming?

Sharply swiping her knife down the stone, Cody almost nicked herself. She put the stone down and sat there, trying not to dream. It was so tempting...so very, very tempting. But it wasn't in the realm of possibilities. Women like Maddie Osborne didn't take up with hillbillies. They might have sex with them, but that wasn't the same as telling everyone you knew that you'd chosen a girl from the hollow as your own. That just didn't happen, and dreaming about it was a surefire way to lose your mind. Her brother would still be alive if he didn't have dreams that he could never reach. If he'd just settled for what he could have had, he'd have plenty of money now and could chase his dreams anywhere he wanted. But he got greedy and let his desires overtake his sense. That was the biggest danger. Letting your desires rule you. A person had to be realistic to be happy.

Even if Maddie wanted to do it again, Cody didn't think she'd be able to, and that was a crying shame. It was Maddie's fault, but she didn't mean any harm. She couldn't know how much dreams like that cost a woman like Cody. She just didn't know. She *couldn't* know. But once that thought had invaded her mind...when it was just a tiny shoot coming out of the frozen ground...it was already too late to put it back. Maddie had gotten into her heart, and having sex with her wasn't worth what it cost to have her jump into her little car and head home. Cody would give anything to stay friends with her—but sex was too tempting and it was too, too painful to act like it meant nothing. The spell was broken.

CHAPTER EIGHTEEN

THE BIGGEST SOCIAL EVENT of the year was the annual Ramp Festival. The wild onions were beloved by the people in the hollow, and they put up a respectable event, held in "town," which was really just a flat spot of land where the post office and gas station sat.

It was a very low-key affair, with tables set up for local folks to sell crafts, and have a contest for best pickled ramp, ramp pie, and other culinary delights. No one minded that the hollow and most of its inhabitants smelled of the strongest possible onion for much of the spring. In fact, the aroma was almost a badge of honor. They didn't award prizes or anything formal at the festival, just bragging rights. But it was a nice way to commemorate spring and the end of a pretty wicked winter.

As Cody was walking by with a few cousins, she stopped short when she saw Maddie, dressed in a blue sweater and khaki slacks, standing behind a booth her bank had set up. Ramp was nearly an hour from Greenville, and no one from the bank had ever acknowledged the town's existence, much less tried to encourage people to do banking business. Until Maddie took over. Things were different now.

Trying to stay out of her field of vision, Cody did her best to observe Maddie without anyone catching her. She was as pretty as a woman could be. And very friendly and comfortable-looking even when most people stayed about ten feet away from the booth. Only Stumpy Grimshaw had the nerve to stand right in front of her, eying Maddie like she was on display. His having given her a ride that winter's day must have made him think he had a claim on her.

Cody stood by old Mr. McCracken's homemade bird houses, surreptitiously trying to keep an eye on Maddie, when those pretty blue eyes locked on her. She felt like a coyote who'd been hit with a laser sight. Her body tingled and a warm glow suffused her chest. With a furtive wave, she dashed over to stop Cassidy from breaking a bird house. Holding the squirming child in her arms, she looked over to see Maddie still watching her. It was rude to stand there like a statue, but that Goodwin girl was in the booth, glaring at her. She'd just have to apologize for not being friendlier. No way would she let that snooty woman make her feel small.

—∿—

"Appalachian States Bank. This is Maddie Osborne."

"Hi, this is Cody Keaton telling you to expect a call from a car salesman asking if I really have any money in my checking account. Tell him I'm a pathological liar and to hold me until the police get here." She laughed hard at her own joke. "I'd love to see him cry if he thinks he's wasted the whole morning with us."

"Us? How many of us are there?"

"We're knocking off four today. All different, but similar. Everyone has scaled back their expectations, thank the lord. Each car was under twenty-five thousand. I think they're waiting to see if anyone picks Brett off before they take a chance of sticking their heads too far out of their holes."

"You sound very upbeat for spending a lot of money. Is it getting easier?"

"It is when I feel like I'm doing the right thing. That woman you put me in touch with was great. She told me about all sorts of sites I could use to figure out what I should pay."

"Really? I'm so pleased."

"It was great. I gave everyone a sheet showing the options for the car they wanted, then added it all up. I figured out my top price, then went to the guy here in Huntington who sells all of the ones we wanted. I told him I'd give him X amount of money for those cars with those options." She chuckled evilly. "He didn't like to do it my way, but I told him we'd just sashay over to Charleston, and, just like you said, he figured he'd rather have a little profit on four cars than a lot on none."

"That's fantastic! It must be great to have a little control in these kinds of situations."

"That's exactly what it is," she said thoughtfully. "I don't want to spend the money, but if I've got to, I've got to do it wisely."

"Exactly true. If you're thoughtful about it, it's much easier."

"Oh, my cousin Melissa helped by asking for the cheapest car made. Only thirteen thousand."

"Wow. That must have been nice. She's respecting your sensibilities."

"Yeah, I suppose she was. I made her step up and get the more expensive model though. I can afford it, and the bigger model is rated better for crashes."

"That was nice of you. I'm sure she appreciated it."

"Yeah, she did. And I appreciate all that you've done. You've helped me a lot, Maddie. Thank you for everything."

"I'm proud of you. You're handling a huge amount of pressure and expectations, and you're doing it beautifully. I hope you're proud of yourself too."

"Pride goes before the fall and I'd rather steer clear of one of those. But I'm happy you're proud of me. That's plenty." She cleared her throat nervously. "Sorry I didn't get to talk to you at the Ramp Festival. I was busy chasing kids."

"Yeah, I could see that."

Maddie didn't say another word. What was she thinking? Was it normal to have hours of fantastic sex and never even mention it? It must have been, because they'd done it twice and had barely brought it up again. "It was nice of you to be there. No one from the bank has ever come."

"We can't get people to use us if they don't think we want them. I'm just trying to make sure everyone knows we'd like a chance to do business with them."

"I think you've got Stumpy's vote. A marriage proposal probably isn't far behind."

She waited a beat, then Maddie laughed, making the hairs on the back of Cody's neck stand up. She had such a beautiful laugh. Just beautiful.

Maddie looked out at a swath of bored-looking youngsters, and briefly wondered if she was wasting her time. She'd been mentoring a group of kids at the high school since just after she'd arrived in town, but it wasn't going like she'd hoped.

She always had to go to work early and skip lunch to be able to get over to the school by three, and now she wondered if they'd all be happier if she sent them home.

But she'd put in over fifty hours on this project, and hated to have it all for naught. The kids were just very...bored. That had to be what they were. Or maybe they were tired. Whatever they were, they looked at her like she was the only thing keeping them from a good, long nap.

Future Businesspeople of Summit County, indeed. This group would be lucky to be mattress testers. "I know it's late in the day, and you're all tired," she said, trying to show some enthusiasm. "But we need a spring project. We need to do something to show folks we have some"—she smiled brightly—"sprite."

"What's sprite?" A particularly dull boy asked. At least that's what she thought he asked. His head was lying on his arm, which was draped along the desk in front of him, and his mouth was obscured by his books.

"Enthusiasm," she said, her own draining quickly. "No ideas from anyone? Does anyone have anything to say about any of my suggestions?"

"Why don't you just decide?" the most helpful girl said. "That's easier."

"Well, it might be, but if you want to be in business, you need to lead...to have ideas for ways of making your community better. I won't be there to help you at that point."

"Since when does a business do anything for people?" someone asked. "They just want our money."

"Not everyone in business is like that," Maddie said. "I'm not, and my bank isn't."

Mitchell, a boy who looked much older than a high school student should be said, "What's your bank done for us? They don't even give out suckers to kids anymore."

Good lord. It had been her idea to stop giving out candy, given the rampant tooth decay and obesity the county experienced, and that simple decision had been a source of endless complaints.

She looked at the kids again. They were nice, well-mannered and wanted to better themselves. That had been clear during the individual talks she'd had with each of them. But when they were in a group, they clammed up and seemed afraid to voice anything close to a suggestion. It was honestly like they were all afraid of taking a risk—something she never would have considered in kids this young.

They weren't able to stretch themselves yet, but she wasn't going to give up. A wild thought popped into her head, and she put it into words. "You know what? Mitchell makes a good point. Let's show the people of Summit County that we care about this place. Let's make a clean sweep of the stuff that's weighing us down, and start fresh." That garnered zero enthusiasm, but she kept going. "I was up in the mountains not long ago, and almost choked when I got near a big dump. We can't have things like that if we want to feel good about our home. I'm going to commit the bank to funding a county-wide cleanup project, and I want our group to lead it. Who's with me?" She thought she'd been fairly stirring, but only one hand went up. It was a start.

It took a lot of arguing, but Maddie finally convinced the VP in charge of her region to approve spending a few thousand dollars to buy T-shirts, signs and a tiny bit of advertising for the first of their clean-up days. It took all of her patience not to roll her eyes when he insisted balloons were a must. The irony of adding more trash to the town was lost on him. So she agreed, and decided to tell him the balloon-maker went out of business if he were to find out she hadn't bought them.

The club members started to show a little initiative. A committee of them guilt-tripped the county government into paying for the first big clean-up event, which was, not coincidentally, in Greenville where the county board met.

An impassioned plea to the school board freed up the buses to drive people to the various sites, and the drivers volunteered their time. A week before the first event Maddie was feeling remarkably confident about the whole thing. She was in her office, the glass partition obscured by a big "Make Summit Sparkle" sign, when Cody popped her head in. "Got a minute?"

"Yeah, of course. Come on in."

Cody did, carefully reading all of the signs and materials that covered every flat surface. "I didn't know you were involved in this."

"Yeah, I've been working like a dog to get it all ready. It's really a school project, but we're paying for a few expenses."

"School? What school?"

"Your alma mater." When Cody looked even more confused, Maddie said, "I'm an advisor to a group of kids who want to be business people." She could feel her smile brighten. "I've finally gotten some life into them."

Cody sat down, still letting her gaze roam slowly around the room. "That's...really, really nice of you. To give your time and such."

"Oh, I like it. They're a nice bunch of kids, and now that they're actually doing something, they're getting pretty resourceful."

"It's next week?"

"Yeah." Maddie grimaced while pulling her blouse away from her neck. "The pressure's building. I think we might have a hundred people show up to help. Excellent, huh?"

"And you're gonna...pick up trash?"

"Yep. We found two spots just outside downtown where people dump illegally. We're hoping if those sites get cleaned up by their fellow citizens, people might feel bad dumping there again."

Cody scratched her head. "I don't know about that. I think they might get over their bad feelings pretty quickly."

"Come help us. The county's paying for the dumpsters. All we have to do is fill them."

Standing up, Cody took a few flyers. "I will be there. And I'll do my best to bring some help."

The next Saturday morning, Maddie was pleased, and charmed, to see Cody pull up at the high school with nine of her relatives. Eight were jammed into a big, black SUV, and Cody rode with her menacing-looking cousin Devin. Her shotgun-wielding posse. Maddie didn't have time to run over and say hello, but she waved and smirked to herself when Cody very discretely waved back. It was like she didn't want her relatives to know how friendly they were. That was a little odd, but not too odd for Cody.

The first site was close by, just up a short hill outside of downtown. The street dead-ended because of the steepness, and Maddie had learned that a dead-end street was a favored place for dumping anything you couldn't or wouldn't take to be disposed of in the proper way.

They filled three buses with volunteers. She was enormously proud of her kids for busting their butts in getting volunteers not just to promise— but to show up.

It wasn't easy work. The bank provided money for a few dozen pairs of heavy work gloves and people snapped them up quickly. The stuff in the gully was not something you wanted on your hands.

The students figured out how best to organize, and they had things sorted out well. Then it was just hours of good, hard work. Cody was, not surprisingly, one of the people who volunteered to take a big manure shovel and pitch piles of rubbish into a dumpster. She had a bandana wrapped around her nose and mouth for protection from dust and dirt— and probably for a slight reduction of smell.

Cody looked so damned cute, working away without complaint. She had on Devin's army T-shirt, and his old camouflage pants, and Maddie thought she should throw the ill-fitting things into the dumpster with the last shovelful. But, knowing Cody, she couldn't bear to get too much dirt on any of her new clothes. Few people took better care of their things than Cody did.

Cody's female cousins pitched in just a vigorously as Cody did. Other than Devin, the rest of the gang was young teenagers, none of whom Maddie had met. They played and tussled more than they worked, but that was pretty common for their age group. At least they'd showed up.

Devin worked right alongside Cody, matching her shovel for shovel. Of the dozens of times she snuck a glance at her, Maddie never saw Cody talk to her cousin, but they looked very symbiotic—like they were communicating without words. One time, when a load had been too tough for her, Devin turned and snatched part of it right out from under her, without a request or an acknowledgment of his action. There was a job to be done, and no time for excess socializing.

Maddie had a hundred things to do, finding herself running from one minor problem to the next. By the time the big group had loaded the last of the refuse into the last of the dumpsters, it was late afternoon, time to get the thank-you party rolling.

Everyone headed back to the high school, where several other student groups were waiting with punch and home-baked cookies and brownies. Since she'd organized the event, Maddie had to socialize, thank dozens of people and make sure the snacks were set out properly. As soon as she had a free minute, she sought Cody out. But all she saw was the group getting into their cars and heading back to Ramp.

―⁓―

Maddie was miffed. She spent the next hour trying to pull herself out of her funk. Genuinely thrilled with how the day had gone, she was even more pleased by how accomplished the kids in the club seemed to feel. This was real progress for them, and she was thankful just to be a part of it. But having Cody ignore her had really gotten under her skin. First the Ramp Festival, now this.

The last of the volunteers straggled out of the gym by six o'clock. One more round of sincerely expressing her thanks to all of the kids, then Maddie walked to her car. Where a clean, new-clothes-wearing Cody sat on her bumper. She'd been reading a book, and she slapped it closed when Maddie got close. "Tired?" she asked, grinning happily.

"Where the heck did you take off to? I wanted say hi to everyone. I've never even met the kids."

"Oh, they're just kids. You've got to be related to give a darn about 'em."

"I'm serious." She really was. Hurt, too.

"To be honest, Devin's not much for socializing, and Melissa had to get Brett's car back to him before he had kittens. We'll have more time when we do the next one." She hesitated. "There *is* gonna be a next one, right?"

"Uhm…yeah. But the county's out of money already. We're going to have to raise funds to pay for the dumpsters. It probably won't be until next fall."

"No, that won't do." Cody took Maddie by the arm and led her to her car. "We're gonna go have dinner, in case you're wondering."

"I was, kinda," she smirked.

"Well, I'm hungry, so I know you are too. Over dinner you can tell me how much it's gonna cost me to pay for those darned dumpsters." She glowered playfully, leaning close to Maddie. "'Cause you're bringing those folks to Ramp. Soon."

They went to the most formal of Greenville's restaurants, even though Maddie insisted she was too grubby to be seen in public. But Cody insisted she needed a good meal, and was going to have it.

Over their roasted chicken dinners, Cody leaned over, the flickering glow of a candle illuminating the lovely planes of her face. "I want you to know how much today meant to me. I know you did it for the town and the county and even the bank, but you did it for me too."

"I did," she admitted. "I know how much you love your home, and seeing your neighbors wreck it has to test your last nerve."

"My very last one," she admitted, nodding her head gravely. "But what means so much to me is that you're not one of those city people who feels sorry for us and tries to figure out why we're so screwed up." She looked like she wanted to spit or curse, and Cody never cursed. "But you don't do that. You just try to find a way to make the bad things better." She sank back in her chair. "That's righteous."

Maddie had never had a compliment register so thoroughly. If one day Summit County, West Virginia, was as clean as Switzerland, she wouldn't feel as good as she did right that minute, all because of a few words from a woman whose opinion meant the world to her.

They stood out in the parking lot, and Maddie tried not to be too obvious in her flirting. She ached to have Cody come to her apartment, but was a little shaky on how to ask. "Are you tired?"

"Beat. I worked my tail off today. How about you?"

"Oh, I have a little gas left in my tank. We could…have a drink or something…if you want." She tried to be subtle, but only managed to look at Cody's mouth like she wanted to suck the lips right off her. *Nice move, Maddie. Subtle as a freight train.*

But Cody was either really tired, or really oblivious, or both. She yawned, stretching her arms out. "No, I'd roll right off the road if I had a drink when I'm this tired. It's a long drive back to Ramp."

"You could stay…with me…if you're tired."

"I think I've got enough energy to get home. But just barely. Thanks again for everything." She almost made a move to offer a hug, but shook her shoulders and got into her car. With a quick wave, she was gone, leaving nothing but the trail of her lights and a sick longing in Maddie's heart.

———

An hour later Cody pulled up in front of her house, went inside and put on the magic shirt that was made to keep mosquitos away. She hadn't seen any yet, but they had a habit of appearing all at once. Then she went back outside and sat on the steps, just needing to breathe the night air.

Her mind was a jumble of thoughts, but it was her body that demanded attention. Maddie had wanted sex. Even with Cody's scant experience she recognized the look. The *look*. And Cody had intentionally ignored it. How in the name of god had she managed to do that? Just thinking about those beautiful eyes landing on her mouth made the pulse between her legs throb. She could have had her. Could be having her right at that very minute. She couldn't help it; she had to give herself just a minute…a few seconds of dreaming about her. About those soft, full breasts. How Maddie's hips swayed when Cody went down on her. The way she tasted. Nothing in the world was better than putting her mouth on Maddie and making her squirm. The sounds that came out of that woman when she held her by the hips and sucked her into her mouth…

Like a slap, she sat up straight and let reality hit her. She *loved* Maddie Osborne, and savoring her body would never, ever be enough. It might kill her, but she'd never let herself touch her again. She only had one heart and Maddie'd already taken too big a chunk out of it. She couldn't let her break it in two.

———

It was time to get it done. The entire foundation of the family had been eroded since she'd won the money. Uncle Cubby wasn't really the head of the group any more. He'd silently slid back down to equal with his brother and sisters, leaving them leaderless. Cody was the one everyone relied on now, but she hadn't taken his place. She was the money pit, not the leader.

Now that she was planning on moving high up the hill, their cohesiveness was being fractured. And Uncle Shooter's "green" modular home was going to sit at the edge of his acreage, so he could use the solar panels that could be added to the flat roof. That took him and Aunt Thelma out of the center of their branch of the family, upsetting things even more.

Everything was in flux, with two cousins still itching to move from their parents' into their own places, and new cars changing the amount of time they spent together. Cody hadn't driven anyone into Greenville since she'd bought the bunch of cars for her cousins. She had to admit she missed the hours they used to while away together.

Since everything was in flux, now seemed a perfect time to make what was probably an open secret an open truth. It was time to come out. Once it was set in her mind, it seemed like hiding something to keep it to herself. Not that she wanted to discuss it in any depth. It was like finding out that she was able to read minds. That was a pretty important thing to learn, and not mentioning it to your closest relatives would have been strange. Besides, she wasn't going to just hope some woman showed up on her doorstep. The only way to stop obsessing over Maddie was to find a woman of her own. It was only polite to tell her family she was going hunting before she carried her prize trophy home. The thought of slinging some woman over her shoulder and plopping her down in front of the whole crew made her laugh. And if the woman wasn't local, seeing the Montgomerys stare at her would make her take off like a scalded cat.

She wasn't nervous about making the announcement. They weren't the kind of people to get all hot and bothered about sex. Her cousin Lucas was only fifteen when he got a girl pregnant and people acted like he was merely announcing he was going on an unexpected trip. It caught everyone's attention, but no one made a big to-do about it.

Still, she started off easy, with her Aunt Lily, figuring she'd work her way up to the more vocal relatives. Cody went over to her house one afternoon when she knew she was likely to be alone. After knocking politely, she opened the door and walked in—Montgomery style. Actually, no one else knocked, but she thought it was the right thing to do when someone was home alone.

Her aunt was sitting in front of the TV, working on a big jigsaw puzzle. "Hi, Aunt Lily," she said, walking around to face her.

"Hey, Cody! Have a sit."

She sat down and considered a few time-wasting gambits, but decided to get it over with. "Aunt Lily," she began, "I want to talk to you about something important…and personal."

"What is it, honey? Are you well?"

"Yeah, I'm fine. I've been doing a lot of thinking, and I'm confident that I'm…" What word to use? She hadn't thought about the particulars. "I'm attracted to other women. I'm a lesbian."

Aunt Lily's eyes popped open and she dropped the puzzle piece she'd been holding. "Don't you go listenin' to what Bobby and them boys say. You're no such thing, honey."

So, Bobby had been talking. Who else? Probably everyone.

Her aunt continued to speak, her voice getting louder and more insistent. "Don't be discouraged, honey. If you set your sights on a boy, I'm sure you could get him."

"I assume I could find a man if I wanted one, Aunt Lily. What I'm saying is that I don't want one. I want to find a woman to love."

"To *love*," she said, as if chewing the word over. "I don't know, Cody. I don't think that's something you ought to try."

She wasn't about to say she'd tried it and loved it. Her personal life was still intensely personal—and always would be. "It might take a while for you to get used to it, but I *am* a lesbian. No one made me think it. It's just the truth."

"Well, I don't know about that. I think you'd best spend more time thinking about it. People can be very cruel about that kind of thing, honey. Don't go asking for trouble."

She stood up and headed for the door. "I'm not asking for trouble, Aunt Lily. I'm just telling you who I am. It'll all be fine in the end."

—∞—

It went about the same for each of the other three branches of the family. No one offered hearty congratulations, but no one threw the Bible at her—literally or figuratively. Thankfully, only one person in the whole clan was particularly religious, and she knew she'd have to have a separate conversation with Devin. She'd happily do that—when he came asking for it. There was no sense in bringing it up yet. His mama could do the hard work and Cody'd clean up the mess.

—⁓—

It didn't take long. The next afternoon, Devin showed up, walking into her house and standing at the front door like he was going to block her from leaving. "Why now," he demanded.

That was a surprise. She knew his pastor was hot against gays and abortion, so she expected him to start citing chapter and verse. But he seemed to be questioning her...timing?

She could have played him for a little time, to get her feet back under herself. But that wasn't how they were with each other. Neither had a lot of patience for verbal games. "Because now's when I knew."

He walked further into the house, then perched on the sofa arm. "No, that's not so. You knew before now." He was nearly scoffing at her. "Everybody knew."

"Thanks for telling me my own mind." She went to the refrigerator and took out two beers, then handed him one as she passed by to sit on the chair. "When exactly did I know?"

He opened the beer and took a long pull. "High school. Thereabouts. Maybe a little earlier."

"I wish you would have told me." She drank some of her beer, briefly thinking about the years she could've been doing something about being gay if she'd been sure.

"Come on, don't lie to me. I'm not gonna hit you over it."

That got her dander up. She stood and glared at him. "You won't do it twice. Count on that."

"I said I *wouldn't*," he complained. "I don't go around punching every sinner in town. My hand'd fall off. I just figgered...you might think I'd be hard on you."

"Do you think you're being particularly understanding? You've got your mind made up about something, and I can't figure out what it is."

"Something's made you get up the nerve to tell everyone. I think I know what...who that is."

Oh-oh. She really didn't want to involve Maddie in this. People in town would not be overjoyed about having their local banker be a lesbian. Devin knew a lot of people from that church…No, there was no way she'd talk about Maddie.

"Whether you believe me or not, I'm telling people now because I just figured it out now. Maybe I'm slow, but I'm certain."

That dark-eyed Montgomery stare that made people run for their mamas ran right through her. "What *changed* to make you certain? Something had to happen."

"I did research on the internet." That was true.

"What *made* you do the research?" The stare peeled the skin right off her, exposing her thoughts.

"Nothing made me. I just…I had an idea I might be gay and it seemed like it was time to decide."

He stood and gulped the rest of his beer down, swallowing it like he could just open his gullet and take it in. Then he put the empty bottle down and stood over her. "Here's how it is. Every once in a while, a girl gets a touch of mountain fever and thinks it'd be fun to have sex with somebody from the hills. They come up to the roadhouse in Twined Creek or some such place and act all interested. It's not real, Cody. You're a dirty pleasure for her. Don't you even *think* you're good enough for the likes of her. You're not."

She stared up at him, blank-faced. She would *not* let him see her shiver. "I don't know what you're getting at, but I suppose I should thank you for caring enough to warn me…about something you think's important."

He wasn't buying it. Devin leaned over and pinched the fabric of her shirt. "I saw how you look at her. *Stop it.*" He snapped his wrist, making the fabric rub roughly against her neck. Then he went to the door and stood there for a second, still glaring at her meanly. "It's a sin to covet what you can't have."

Cody sat in her chair for a good hour, going through the whole conversation over and over. She had no idea what had gotten into Devin. Everything about it had been weird…very off. She'd wanted to reassure him that she knew what she could have and what she couldn't have. But that really was none of his business. None of it was, but why had he focused on Maddie, rather than his belief that being gay was sinful? He seemed to think trying to move out of their social class was the sin…which was just…strange. That damn war had made him a very strange man.

Cody got up to divert her attention from the depressing topic. Grabbing a book, she stopped for another beer, needing a little tranquilizing. She wasn't the type to dwell on the past, or lament her circumstances. But if she would have let herself, she could have spent a good long time stewing about how it hurt every bone in her body to want something she could never, ever have.

CHAPTER NINETEEN

THE NEXT WEEKEND, CODY called to go fishing again and Maddie had to beg off.

"I wish I could, but I'm going to go see my parents. I haven't been in weeks."

"How are you going?"

"I'll drive."

"Drive? Really? How far is it?"

"About five hours. It's not too bad. I leave after work and I'm there by bedtime."

"You know, I've never been anywhere near...where exactly do you live?"

"Culpeper."

"That's right. Culpeper. I wonder if I'd like it? I should go some weekend...maybe drive. But I'd like to have company. I'm like that, you know. I hate to be alone."

"I can't believe how bold you've gotten, Cody Keaton," she laughed. "Be at my apartment at five o'clock on Friday. If you're late...I'll wait."

Maddie stared at the phone after she hung up. What in the hell? She was trying to avoid lusting after Cody, and here she was taking her to meet her parents! And there was no way in hell her mom wouldn't know something was going on. She was like a bloodhound once she got on the trail. This was just stupid. But she couldn't refuse the chance to be with Cody. *Damn her!*

When she walked into the apartment on Friday afternoon, Cody looked good enough to eat. She must have gone wild at the clothing store, because she wore yet another new outfit.

Dark slacks not only fit her waist, they were the proper length. And an emerald green fleece top made her look as cuddly as a teddy bear. She even wore shoes! Not boots, regular shoes…although once Maddie looked carefully she noted they were the kinds of shoes one could wear hiking or clambering up a tree to fetch a nice patch of moss. "You look nice," Maddie said, trying to sound merely friendly. "Emerald is your color."

"It is?" She looked a little uncertain, the way she always did when something came up that she didn't immediately understand.

"I just meant it works well with your skin tone. It shows how beautiful your eyes are too." Oh, this was a textbook example of how to not sound interested in a woman. Doofus!

"Oh, thanks."

"Did your cousin take you shopping again?"

"No, I bought everything at once. Four pairs of slacks, two pairs of jeans, six shirts, three sweaters, three pairs of shorts and underwear. My underwear is part of a system," she said, with either pride or puzzlement, it wasn't clear which. "Is this okay?" She extended a cardboard box.

"For what?"

"I didn't have anything to put my clothes in. Is it okay to use a box?"

She was so cute! Her drive to learn how other people lived was nonstop. "Sure. But I could lend you a bag if you'd like. I have a carryall that would work perfectly."

"Carryall. That sounds like a great bag." She giggled. "It must be *huge*."

Maddie smiled at her lame joke. "It's misnamed. It should be 'carry a little.' I'll get it."

―――

They got into the car and started heading to the interstate. Right before the entrance ramp, Maddie pulled over to get gas. As she got out, the attendant walked out and said, "My credit card machine's broke. Do you have cash?"

"I don't think so." She reached into her pocket to check, but he waved her off.

"Will you be back this way?"

"Sure. I live in Greenville."

"Then just come by and pay me next time." He turned and went back inside, leaving Maddie to stare after him.

When she returned to the car, Cody was laughing at her. "You coulda caught flies with that mouth hanging open like that. Hasn't anyone ever trusted you for fifty bucks?"

"No, they definitely have not!"

"I told you West Virginia is a great place to live. Try that in New York City."

Maddie snuck a glance at her, seeing Cody looking smug. It was nice to feel that your little town in the middle of nowhere was better than New York City. Delusional, but nice.

—m—

Because they stayed on the interstate the entire trip, they didn't get to see any towns or much of anything, really. But Cody watched the scenery avidly until it was pitch black out. "This is beautiful country," she sighed, when even squinting didn't reveal much.

"I suppose it is. I could see you living deep in the Blue Ridge."

"Yeah. My people stayed in what's now Virginia for a hundred years before they made it over the mountains. They settled Ramp about twenty years after the Civil War. Boy, it must've taken some brave people to do that."

"Like you. I could see you taking off in a wagon, with just a shotgun and a knife."

"Yeah," she agreed, chuckling. "I'd probably do something like that. I can be brave when I need to be."

Maddie spent a good long time thinking of Cody, dressed in homespun buckskins, traveling across the Blue Ridge mountains, seeking some elusive treasure in West Virginia. It was strange, but she fit in the fantasy better than she did in modern times. The woman was made for the frontier.

—m—

An hour before they reached the Osbornes', Cody had slumped against her door. God knew what time she usually got up, but it was early.

Pulling into the wide drive of her parents' home Maddie sat for a second and assessed it, trying to see it as Cody would. If you didn't know better, you'd think they were rich as Croesus. Their house was good-sized, about seventeen hundred square feet, located in a development that had sprung up out of the fertile farmland in the mid eighties.

Her parents had paid a lot for it, over two hundred fifty thousand, but it was worth a lot less now. Still, she was sure they loved the town and were glad they'd moved there. The schools had been good, and they were the kind of parents willing to stretch to make sure their kids got a good education. Sadly, now they were stuck with a place bigger than they needed, and their entire investment had vaporized. But they could pay the mortgage, as long as they kept their jobs—which was far from assured.

The houses were all on quarter-acre lots, generous for many parts of Virginia. When they'd lived in Newport News, she had been able to see into their neighbor's kitchen when she was at the sink. Not so in Culpeper. There had been room to breathe, to stretch out a little, and she was grateful for the opportunities their town had offered.

Her parents had changed jobs, losing years of seniority, and added an hour to their commute to make a better life for her and her brothers. She realized she'd rarely thanked them for that, and pledged to correct that omission this weekend.

Cody lifted her head from where it lay pressed against the window. "Are we there?" She sat up and gawped. "It's a mansion!"

Tim and Sara and a golden retriever emerged from the house, making a bee line for Maddie. "There's my best girl," Tim enthused when he wrapped her in a big hug.

"Mom should be your best girl," Maddie teased. "But I'd love to be second best." The dog jumped up on Maddie, standing with his paws firmly against her thighs while his head lolled back gazing happily at Maddie's parents.

"Calm down, Thumper, you need to behave for our company." She kissed and hugged her mother. "This is Cody."

The dog's paws hit the ground and he dashed over to Cody. He started to jump on her, but for some reason he stopped, sat, and stared at her uncertainly.

"You scared my dog," Maddie teased.

Cody reached out and shook hands with Tim, then Sara. "Pleased to meet you. Thanks for having me." She snapped her fingers, and the dog approached. Then he wagged his tail like a maniac when she scratched under his chin. "Good dog," she cooed. "Good boy."

"Come on in," Tim said. "If you like the place, you can buy it." He laughed and slapped Cody on the back. "Maddie told us about your good fortune. Congratulations."

"Tim," Sara said, scoldingly. "Don't embarrass the girl." She looked at Cody. "Don't mind him. He thinks he's funny."

"He is," Maddie said, taking her father's arm to walk back into the house.

———

Maddie's room was very much as she'd left it when she'd moved to West Virginia. Her parents weren't overly sentimental, but they didn't need the space for any other purpose, so they'd left it as it was.

She and Cody sat on her twin bed, Maddie in pajamas and Cody in a pretty, green, snug-fitting top and Devin's army sweatpants. The outdoor store must not have sold pajamas.

Thumper was on the floor, watching them ardently. He'd always insisted on being right on the bed, but he seemed less assertive around Cody. Maybe he could tell she didn't mind dispatching animals from their earthly realms.

Cody was so full of questions that Maddie couldn't keep up with them. "Yes, that's the first headline I got published in the student newspaper. I was sure I was going to be a journalist and break massive stories all over the world." She shook her head. "That's not how the wheel of fate has turned."

Looking so earnest it was touching, Cody said, "You're not unhappy, are you?"

Maddie patted her lightly on the shoulder. "No, not at all. Most people don't have jobs they're crazy about. I work because I have to, but my job isn't bad. Not at all," she emphasized when Cody looked doubtful.

"I couldn't stand it if you were unhappy," Cody said, her eyes so intense that Maddie's breath caught. Damn, she was a kind, caring woman.

Why couldn't she be a nice, experienced lesbian from San Francisco? No such luck.

Cody pointed to a photo of Maddie's entire senior class standing on the steps of the Capitol. "Is that in Washington or Richmond?"

"Washington. We got to meet our local representative. It was kinda boring, but we got a day off school."

"What's it like?"

"Getting a day off school?"

"No. Going to Washington. Is it really nice?"

"You've never been?" Damn, Cody grew up half a day's drive from the nation's capitol. Everyone within twelve hours came at some point in their youth, didn't they?

"No. Huh-uh. I've always wanted to, but I couldn't talk anyone into going with me, and didn't want to go alone. It seemed too...big," she admitted shyly.

"We'll see if we can fix that."

The next morning Maddie sat with her mother, drinking coffee in the kitchen, while Tim showed Cody his elaborate model train setup in the basement. "I don't think you've ever brought a client to visit," Sara said, smirking. "Is that a new customer-relations technique?"

Rolling her eyes, Maddie said, "We're friends."

"Friends?" Sara said doubtfully. "Nothing more?"

"We're not...I don't really...we're not...involved." She could feel her cheeks turning pink. That sounded so stupid!

"I know I should mind my own business, but I'd love to see you find someone who appreciates you. Not like that...Dawn."

Maddie's ex was no longer on the Christmas card list. Her mother was her staunchest defender and believed any woman who didn't commit to her was somehow lacking...or evil. "I'm not looking for a relationship now, Mom. You know that. When I get to a city I want to stay in, I'll start looking."

"Just because a city is bigger doesn't mean the people you'll meet are better, honey."

"I know, I know."

"I just worry about your always talking about where you're going to go next. The years have a way of catching up with you, honey. If you want children…"

"I read every article you send about a woman's reproductive abilities crashing into a wall about two seconds after she turns thirty." She smiled at her mom's chiding look. "If I find a partner and she wants to have kids—we'll do something about it. If not—I've got my nieces and nephew. That's plenty."

———

Maddie went to get ready for the day, thinking over her talk with her mother. Her mother was a little delusional, but she really believed Maddie could have everything—a spouse, kids, a great job, plenty of money, and opportunities galore. It must've been hard to have your kids not reach the goals you'd hoped they'd easily make, but reality had a way of interfering with the best laid plans.

Still, it was important to keep plugging away. Her parents had made many sacrifices to help her take a step up the socio-economic ladder. It seemed a betrayal to just sit in Greenville hoping to hang on to her job. There were bigger fish to fry. She couldn't just let the years roll by, she had to keep striving.

———

The four of them strolled around the old town center, took in a couple of Civil War battlefields, and even stopped at a winery or two. Maddie did her best not to laugh at the look on Cody's face when she sampled a local wine. It was obviously a new, and not particularly pleasant experience for her, but she tried so hard to fit in that it was beyond endearing.

They had dinner at a not very authentic Chinese restaurant, but it was good quality and Maddie lusted for ethnic food whenever it was available. She noted that Cody mirrored her order, as she always did when she was uncertain. Their appetizers were delivered and Cody surreptitiously watched all of the Osbornes pick up chopsticks and dig in. Maddie put the sticks in Cody's hand and patiently worked with her to get a pot sticker into her mouth. Soy sauce dripped down Cody's chin and Maddie sat there giggling at her determined efforts to get another bite of food before it was all gone. Looking up, she caught a knowing smirk on her mom's face. *Busted!*

―⁓―

On Sunday afternoon, Cody sat watching a colorful HO gauge train run around the track. She didn't flinch when Maddie put her hand on her shoulder and shook it lightly. "We've got to get going."

When she turned, she looked up from under the bill of the engineer's cap Tim had graciously let her wear. "So soon?"

"You don't have to go yet," Tim said, waving his hand dismissively.

Maddie kissed his thinning hair and squeezed his shoulders. "Yes, we do. I've got some things to take care of."

"Aw, darn," he said, glumly. "I hardly ever have a pretty woman over to play with my trains."

Maddie slapped at the back of his head. "I play with them. Watch yourself."

―⁓―

Cody effusively thanked the Osbornes for their hospitality, and after a long goodbye, they took off. When they got to the interstate, Maddie headed north.

"I don't mean to tell you what to do, but you're going the wrong way."

"No, I'm not. We're only fifty miles away. It's time you saw where some of your least favorite people work."

Cody was thrilled. Beyond thrilled. She kept asking if Maddie was sure she could take a day off with no notice. "Yes, of course I am. Don't worry about a thing. I called my assistant, and she'll take over. And I got us a hotel room." She waggled her eyebrows. "My treat."

"No! You have to let me pay."

"No, I don't. This was my idea, and you're my guest." She let the slight Southern accent she had come to the fore. "My mama raised me right."

―⁓―

Cody was seriously awestruck. She barely spoke as they slowly drove around Washington with Maddie pointing out all of the sights. It was dusk, and the lights were just coming on, illuminating all of the bone-white monuments against the deep blue sky. "It's amazing," she breathed. "And so clean." She turned to Maddie. "How do they keep it this clean?"

"Your tax dollars at work," Maddie teased.

"This is worth it," Cody said. "This is a place we can be proud of." A half-smile settled on her face. "Too bad it has to be filled with politicians."

———

Maddie made a game of collecting hotel points by opening and closing credit cards and doing whatever else she could to rack up the points. As a result, she'd been able to book a nice room in a good hotel not far from the Mall for no charge.

They checked in, and Cody set herself up in front of the window and didn't budge. They had a great view of Washington, and even though she'd been there many times, Maddie had to admit it was special. But it was dinner time, and she was starving. "If you won't leave, we'll have to order room service. Once you see what they charge for that—you'll lose your appetite!"

———

After an enjoyable dinner watching Cody's hesitant experimentation with Thai food, they again stood by the big window, with Cody watching cars whiz by as avidly as she had the train set. Maddie was going to go get dressed for bed, but Cody draped an arm around her and pulled her close for a hug. "This means more to me than you'll ever know."

It felt so damned good to be close to her. It was particularly nice to have Cody offer a touch that wasn't the first step in a bold leap towards bed. "Aw…it's my pleasure." She leaned her head against Cody's, and they stood just like that for a few minutes. Asking questions that could produce disappointing answers probably wasn't wise, but Maddie couldn't let it go. "Why…" She turned and faced Cody full on, seeing the slightly wary look she always adopted when Maddie said anything out of the ordinary. "Why don't you want to be close any more?"

"Close?"

Maddie could actually see her swallow. All of the color drained from her cheeks and she leaned against the wall for support. "You know what I mean," Maddie said, never letting her eyes leave Cody's. "I haven't asked you point-blank, but you've ignored some pretty obvious flirting." Her heart felt like it had raced up to lodge in her throat, but she had to get this out. "Did you lose interest so fast?"

"God, no!" Cody grabbed her shoulders and held on tightly enough to hurt. But she looked so sincere Maddie's pulse slowed down and she could breathe easily again. Cody wasn't the type to put on a show to avoid hurting her feelings.

"Then why?"

Cody's hands dropped and Maddie felt their loss. Any time they touched it felt like she'd connected with some important sense or feeling that she'd been missing deeply.

Cody walked over to a chair and sank down into it. "I can't really say."

She looked away, consciously ignoring Maddie's intent gaze. Good luck with that! Maddie walked over and sat on the wide arm of the lounge chair. "Maybe you *won't* say, but you can."

With lips pursed, a stream of emotions passed through Cody's dark eyes. "I just don't think it's a good idea. We're…well, we're not looking for the same thing. I don't think." Her hand went to her face and she shielded her eyes.

"I don't know what you're looking for, Cody. You've never told me."

Looking up through her splayed fingers, she said, "I don't know that I want to."

"God damn it!" Maddie stood and marched over to the window, staring out while trying to control her temper. "You've swooped in and knocked me off my feet twice, and I don't even merit an explanation for why you're done with me?"

Cody leapt to her feet, standing behind Maddie in a second. "I'm not done with you," she said quietly. "But I can't have you get inside my heart and then leave town. I can't *do* that," she said, her voice filled with emotion.

Maddie turned and gazed into her eyes. "You aren't…you're not tired of me?"

"Tired of you?" She laughed bitterly. "I could never be tired of you. But I can't have you and…being with you for a little while isn't enough."

"Who says you can't have me?" Maddie turned and put her hands atop Cody's shoulders, her eyes closing at the comfort that suffused her just by that simple touch.

"You did," she said emphatically. "You told me you were gone as soon as you could get out." Her eyes darted across the room, like she couldn't make them settle on Maddie's face. "I might not have any experience, but I read a lot. I know that people use excuses instead of saying hurtful things. You made it really clear you put your job hunt ahead of anything." She paused and looked down at the floor. "Or any*one*."

Struggling not to cry, Maddie tightened her grip. "I know I did that. That's how I felt then. But now…I'm more confused than I've ever been. I can't stop thinking about you, Cody. I try to convince myself I need to move, to make more money and get more experience…but all I can think of is you, and how wonderful it feels to have your arms around me." Like magic, those arms slid around Maddie's back and enveloped her. Breathing in deeply Cody's soothing scent, Maddie lay her head on her shoulder and snuggled close. "Like that," she sighed.

"Then be with me." Cody placed her hands gently on the sides of Maddie's face, holding her still while looking deeply into her eyes. "Just be with me." Leaning forward, their lips met and they kissed, softly and sweetly. "Be with me."

Maddie tightened her hold, feeling the buoyant surge of confidence that washed over her whenever Cody held her. Her life, her future, and her dreams all centered around this beautiful woman and the emotions that filled her at that moment. Being with Cody was the answer to any question.

Then Cody's sure, steady hands were working at her blouse, deftly opening each button. Thoughts swirled through Maddie's mind, with warning bells and caution signs popping up repeatedly. But Cody's warm mouth captured her breast and all cogent thought vanished. Maddie's world revolved around that warm, gentle mouth and the sensation that pulsed in her breast, obscuring, then erasing every stray thought. There was only Cody.

———

Later, they lay in a tangle of sheets, bodies covered with a sheen of perspiration. It was time to talk. The sex had cleared her head and now Maddie's brain nearly burst with questions and lists of problems she'd made over the past months. But Cody looked at her with soulful eyes and said, "Can I hold you?"

Once again, she was lost. The caution signs were bowled over and she cuddled up to Cody's side. She tenderly rubbed her hand over Cody's belly, the warmth from their lovemaking still flushing her skin.

"I love to be held," she sighed, then felt herself falling into the void of sleep.

———

Cody lay on her side well before dawn, looking at Maddie's sleeping face. There was only the light of the city to illuminate her, but this little corner of Washington had more brilliance than all of Ramp and Delilah and Twined Creek put together.

The whole night had been stunning. Maddie wanted her. She wasn't sure what that really meant, but there was no doubt that Maddie wanted to be with her. For now at least. God only knew what the future would bring. But there was no way every word Maddie had spoken, every sigh she'd uttered, every kiss she delivered hadn't been one hundred percent genuine. She was leaning heavily towards staying. Cody just had to be ready to catch her if she leaned far enough.

———

Things were only slightly uncomfortable between them when they finally woke. That was very common in Maddie's experience. Revealing yourself thoroughly to another person was always a little embarrassing, so a slight tension was normal. But there was a bit more this time. She hadn't been forthright enough. There were issues…big issues…and she should have spoken of them before they'd made love. But Cody had been so assertive, so dominant, so sexy. How did anyone ever say no to anything she asked for?

They got dressed and went to a coffee shop to get a little fuel before they lit out for their exploration. Maddie's stomach ached at the thought of discussing all of the things she should have said, but she had to get them out. Cody was sipping her coffee, and seemed tense too. Anxiety was contagious.

"I uhm…had a long list of things I wanted to talk about last night, but…we got a little carried away," Maddie began.

"We do that," Cody said, nodding gravely.

"Yeah." She sat up straight and cleared her throat. "I meant everything I said last night. I really want to be with you, but I'm conflicted."

"About leaving?"

She searched Cody's eyes for understanding. "Yes. If we'd met in Chicago or Los Angeles, I'd be chasing you like you chase…whatever's in season. But I'm not sure I can be happy here long term." She reached across the small table and held Cody's hand tightly. "But I'd like to try." She looked into her eyes. "Do you want to try?"

"Yes," she said firmly. "But what does that mean?"

"I like that you say 'yes' first and ask questions later." Maddie leaned over and kissed her soft cheek. "I'd like to date you. To spend a lot of time together and see what we have. I can't decide to stay or go unless I know what's holding me here."

"So…girlfriends? Would we be girlfriends?"

"Yeah, that's a good term."

A storm of concern passed across Cody's eyes. "Would you just be *my* girlfriend?"

Confused, Maddie stared at her for a minute. "Oh! Are you asking if we'll be exclusive?"

"Yeah, I guess."

"*I* will be. I hope you will be." She laughed at the stunned expression on Cody's face. "I assume you will be. You don't seem like a two-timer."

"I'm not gonna go looking for some mangy coyote when I've got a gorgeous doe in my sights." She laughed, her eyes crinkling up with happiness. "You're the prettiest doe I've ever seen."

Maddie put her hand on Cody's shoulder and squeezed, making sure she was listening before she spoke. "I want to be *clear* that I'm not sure I can stay in Summit County. I'm gonna try, but…"

"I understand," Cody said gravely. "Now that I've seen just a bit of Washington, I can understand even better. Especially since you were raised inside…like veal."

"Yeah, that's part of it." She cleared her throat, ready for the next hurdle. "I have to make sure we can be intimate, too. I need that, Cody, and we haven't had much of it."

Her brow knit and she sat there quietly for a second. "I'll get better with practice. I'll really try…"

"No, no, not sex. That's been fantastic. But we don't touch or hold hands or even hug when we're not naked. That's not enough for me."

Blanching, Cody said, "I just thought…I assumed you didn't want…I thought sex was…you didn't ever…" She slapped her face with her hands. "I…I thought you only wanted sex."

"Why would you think that?"

Cody shrugged. "I'm not sure. I guess I was waiting for you to show me what you wanted." She briefly glanced at the floor again. "That first time…as soon as we were done you were kinda…done. You didn't kiss me or anything the next day. You didn't even touch me when we slept." Her dark eyes met Maddie's, the hurt still visible. "I figured you just wanted that."

Maddie gripped her hand tightly. "No, I'm not like that at all. But I can be shy…or tentative. That's the right word. I wait to see what the other person wants."

Cody sat up straight and smiled at her. "One of us is gonna have to stop that or we'll never get anywhere." Her grin grew brighter. "I'll try to say what I want. That's my natural way."

"You've got a deal. But I'll try too. Let me start now. I want to know you feel affectionate towards me. I know you're into me sexually, but I need tenderness."

With a grin wide enough to show her teeth, Cody took Maddie's hand, brought it to her lips and kissed it. "If all I could ever do was hold you and stroke your hair, I'd be happy."

"If we were back in the room, we'd be having sex right now," Maddie said, the hungry look in Cody's eyes heating her up again. "I think you need more than hair stroking."

"I *want* more, that's for sure. But I'd be happy holding you. That's the God's honest truth."

"I believe you. I think I'd be happy with the same, but I couldn't look at you when I was holding you. You're sinfully sexy."

"I didn't say I'd be looking at you," Cody agreed, laughing. "It'd be tricky, but the best part of being with you is just being with you."

"Very well said. So, girlfriend, are you ready to explore Washington?"

"I am."

"We're gonna walk our asses off today, so I hope you're ready." She got to her feet and pulled Cody up, then hugged her tenderly.

Cody looked around, eyeing the other patrons. "Is it okay to do this here?"

"Fuck 'em if they don't like it," Maddie said, giggling. "By the way, I'm giving up on my campaign to not curse around you. I fucking admit defeat."

"I think it's cute. Just try not to do it too much around my aunts. They'll think you're cheap."

"I am, but they don't need to know that."

CHAPTER TWENTY

THE FIRST WEEK OF their new girlfriend status was kind of tricky. The last thing Cody wanted to do was be too pushy or assume too much. Maddie said they'd date. Which meant…darned if she knew. It was probably best to give Maddie room to make up her mind about things. Nothing would be worse than to influence her and have her change her mind a year or two down the line.

Cody waited until Tuesday to drop by the bank. Once in town, she stayed in her car for twenty minutes, waiting until it looked like no one was in the lobby. Maddie was right where she belonged: sitting at her desk, leaning back in her chair, talking on the phone.

She wore a light blue sweater that was just tight enough to make Cody's mouth water. Even before she'd seen her naked, Cody had been reduced to a weak-kneed mess when she allowed herself to think about the curves that lurked under those snappy business suits. But once she'd seen Maddie in her sexy bras and panties…it was time to surrender.

Cody wasn't sure if Maddie liked wearing her bra a little tight, but Cody certainly liked it. It was just snug enough to make a swath of the nicest breasts in the world spill over the edge, and seeing that bit of flesh striving for freedom made Cody want to march in there and liberate them. But just because things were different in their real lives, Maddie was still at work and nothing had changed in that arena. Actually, Cody was bound and determined to pull back a little to make sure no one at the bank could tell they'd gotten so close.

Cody stood by the door, waiting for Maddie's invitation to sit. Maddie signaled her, then made a face at the phone, showing she was sick of listening. Finally, she wrapped it up and put the phone back in its cradle. "I hope you're here to kidnap me," she said, smiling wryly. "I'm begging the clock to move, but it won't listen to me."

"I wish I could kidnap you, but we probably wouldn't get far. Everyone here knows me. Even the sheriff would be able to track me down, and he couldn't find his butt with both hands."

"Are you going to hang around until I'm done and come to my apartment? Please? Please?"

That stung. She should have made some plans, not just dropped in. Dumb! "I wish I could, but I'm just taking one of the kids to the orthodontist. Even though his daddy has a new car and no job, he can't manage to come down here. I should have arranged to have more time or something..."

"No, don't worry about it." Maddie waved a hand dismissively. "I'll see you...when?"

Was this a test? "Saturday, right?" That was when the next cleanup was. If Maddie wanted something different, surely she'd say so.

"Sure," she said, looking a little disappointed.

"I'll have a bigger crew for the Delilah cleanup, since it's right next door. Let's see if I can get one of the boys, other than Devin, to break a sweat."

"I don't care who comes, as long as you're one of them."

That was as nice as a kiss, Cody decided. Affection was very highly underrated.

―――

The Monday after the cleanup in Delilah, Cody popped in at the bank. She sat down, wincing a little when she did. "Got a minute?"

"I'm always going to have a minute for you, so you don't have to keep asking." Maddie looked at her closely, noting that Cody was favoring her left side. "Did you hurt yourself?"

"Not much." She reached around and let her hand hover over her ribs. "I guess I get out of shape over the winter. Sitting around reading isn't very strenuous."

Maddie couldn't imagine what "active" meant if Cody thought she'd been sitting around all winter. "You need to let the men do the heavy work. You're taking jobs too big for you."

"I can keep up. I tried to scoop up a bag that looked light, but wasn't. Must've had rocks in it."

Maddie wasn't sure if she was teasing. Cody looked far more serious than usual, making her a little anxious. "Are you in town to go to the doctor?"

"Doctor?" She shook her head. "No, I'm alone."

"I meant for you." Maddie touched her own ribs. "For whatever you did there."

"Oh, no." Cody laughed, showing a little of her usual lightness. "You don't go to doctors for sore ribs. They can't do anything. Other than charge you a lot of money." She sat up straighter, wincing again when she did. "No, I came to talk to you." When their eyes locked, Maddie's pulse quickened. Cody had such a soulful stare, like she could see right into her.

"You've done so much for me, and I've been pigheaded about the one thing you've asked me to do."

"I don't remember asking you to do anything…"

"Sure you have. You've asked me to talk to someone about my money." She put her hands on the desk, as if waiting for instructions on what to do next. "I'm ready."

"Are you really?" Maddie was delighted. This was a huge development! Cody was finally ready to face the burden of having a great sum of money. It also showed that Cody finally trusted her about something momentous, which was equally huge, and more meaningful.

"No," she said, looking down. Maddie could almost feel her confidence begin to slowly deflate. "But it's the one thing you want, and I can't keep saying no."

"Yes, you can. You don't need to do what I think is best."

"You never tell me how to fish," she said, letting a small grin peek out. "I shouldn't tell you how to think about money. Let's get it done."

Maddie touched her keypad to bring her computer screen to life. "I just happen to have the name of someone who comes very highly recommended." She took a notepad and wrote down the particulars. "Do you want me to call her and pave the way?"

"No, this won't be hard," she said airily. "It was the decision to go that was tough. I know you'd only send me to someone good. I can handle it."

With a twinge of disappointment, Maddie said, "Okay. But if you change your mind…"

Cody sat up and gazed at her intently. "Do you *want* to go with me?"

"Yeah, I would."

With a charming smile, Cody said, "Then why didn't you say so? You were supposed to be working on not being tentative."

"Working," she said, grinning back, "implies a process. It's gonna take me a while to change."

"I suppose that's fair. I'm still sitting on a sofa with no cushions." She stood up and said, "Make whatever arrangements work for you. As I've said before, my schedule's flexible."

Maddie got up and walked her to the door. The urge to kiss her was palpable, but she had enough inquisitive sets of eyes watching nearly every thing she did, and adding public displays of affection might have brought on at least one heart attack. She stood there, trying not to look as smitten as she was. "I know I shouldn't play favorites, but you're my very favorite client."

Chuckling, Cody said, "I darned well ought to be. You're sitting on a ton of my money, and you pay me next to nothing!"

———

They set up an appointment for the next week, and when the day came, Cody came by the bank to pick her up. Maddie knew she was asking for gossip when she grabbed her coat, told Geneva she'd be gone for a few hours, and walked out with Cody, but Maddie didn't much care. People gossiped about the people they worked with; living your life to keep them quiet was impossible.

Cody was quiet on the drive to Huntington, but that wasn't that odd for her. She was the kind of person who could be perfectly content watching a bird sit in a tree or just listening to frogs croak. Maddie briefly wondered if Cody's capacity for stillness came from not having a computer or a cell phone for that matter. She laughed to herself. Cody didn't have a friggin' TV! Listening to frogs *was* her version of cable!

———

The investment advisor, Miss Norman, as Cody insisted on calling her, outlined a good dozen alternatives for her to consider. Maddie, who had a very good working knowledge of investments, was a little overwhelmed, so she knew Cody would be as well. Still, she was anxious to know how she felt and she squirmed with excitement as they walked back outside.

"So? What did you think?"

"I've got to let it settle," Cody said slowly. "But I hope you know how much I appreciate the trouble you went to to find Miss Norman for me. She seems really smart and she's a good listener. I liked her a lot."

"I'm glad for that. Having someone you like and trust is really vital."

Cody held a hand up. "I didn't say trust. That'll come. You can't rush that. It's gotta be earned." She headed for the car, giving Maddie a bigger grin. "How long did it take you?" She chuckled, "I'm gonna go drive up to the top of the hill tomorrow and look for land. If you want to come with me, I'd be on my doorstep by eight." She stopped at the car door and looked over the roof, giving Maddie a heart-melting smile. "Unless you'd rather come tonight. I've got a spot all picked out for you in my bed."

"I think I can make it. Actually, I'd hate to be the idiot who tried to stop me."

They took off, soon settling into companionable silence. Maddie used the time well, daydreaming about Cody. She thought they'd be all but merged by now, but Cody seemed perfectly content to get together on the weekend. She hadn't once come into Greenville to stay over, and Maddie tried not to be hurt by that omission. But it was tough. She itched to get her hands on Cody, thought about her most of the day, and longed for her body at night. But she didn't at all feel that Cody was doing the same.

She was a little embarrassed to admit it, but she was used to being chased. Even though she hadn't had many lovers, she'd always been able to hold back and decide whether to say yes. The inequality she felt with Cody was unsettling, even uncomfortable. But when they were together she had every bit of her attention. Cody was definitely into her. She just seemed able to stay on an even keel and not let their new relationship change her routine. And that sucked.

———

Cody stood on the very top of the tall hill that hugged her hollow, breathing in the air. It was decidedly different from the air near home, even though it wasn't even a mile as the crow flew. The trees were different, a bit thinner and taller, and the air smelled like it was from another place.

There wasn't a house in sight, which was a thing of beauty in itself, but she was loath to be the woman who knocked down a copse of trees at the summit just to plant her butt down on virgin ground. There had to be a better way.

She and Maddie had inspected every big plot of land available on the mountain, and she'd intentionally saved this one for last—thinking it would be the best. It was smaller than she wanted, only twenty acres. She'd hoped to be able to buy fifty, just to make sure no idiot could move right next door and start a band in his garage. But twenty was nothing to sneeze at. And having this view…

She turned in a complete circle, taking in the view from every perspective. It was perfect. On one side was the valley, and if she tried she'd be able to pick out her current home. It'd be easy to find each relative's plot and keep her eye on the whole bunch…like a mother hen.

To the other side was the first bit of a state-protected forest. There wasn't a cut, or even a bruise on that land from where she stood. It was all trees, without a road to be seen. She'd been hunting in there dozens of times, and knew there were plenty of access roads. But they were hidden from view during the springtime, when everything was green and vibrant and full of promise.

"I think this has to be it," she finally said.

Maddie had been standing a few feet away, staring carefully at the valley. "I might be totally wrong, but I think I can figure out how we came up here. And I think I can see roughly where you live." She pointed at what Cody was sure was the correct spot.

"Nice job. You could be a mapmaker."

"If you put your house right here," she said, stomping her foot, "you could see the whole family."

"That's true." Cody started to walk in the opposite direction, with Maddie following behind. They scampered down a slick path, with Maddie landing on her butt twice before they got to a relatively level spot at least two hundred feet from the summit. "But I'm thinking I'll put it here." She held up her hands, making a frame. "I can just picture how the big window in the front will be."

"You don't want to look at your home?"

"*This* will be my home." Merely saying that felt good. "I'll keep as many trees as I possibly can, and I'll definitely leave the top of the hill untouched. I don't want to stick out and have a place that you can see for miles away. I wanna blend in."

"What kind of house will you build?"

"Log. And I'm going to do it myself." Maddie had been right. Dreaming about this felt as good as anything she'd ever done. It was all possible...not just folly. "My view will be of the forest. I want to see this land like the first Montgomerys did. Like the whole place would look if we'd been more gentle with it."

"You're gonna love it here," Maddie said, sounding about as cheerful as she'd ever sounded. "I'm so happy for you."

"Thanks." She turned and saw how bright those pretty blue eyes were. Maddie's lips were pink and soft and as sexy as homemade sin. When Cody tilted her head to kiss them, she was sure she'd never been as happy as she was at that moment. She'd have a new home, a new view, and a new girlfriend. Life couldn't get better. Unless Maddie decided not to stay, of course. She cut that thought off with a mental slap. Dreaming about the future wasn't smart. Maddie had promised nothing, really. Just that they'd date each other and see how things went. That was a heck of a long way from forever.

On Monday, Maddie spent hours on the phone, trying to get out of something she'd tried hard to get into. "Maddie, I know I could send someone, other than you," her boss said, "but you're the one who most needs mortgage lending instruction. You begged me for a month to send you to Arizona, now I can't figure out why you're trying to skip it."

"I don't want to skip it," she said, although that's exactly what she wanted. "I've just got a full plate with our cleanup program. Plus, Geneva's got some personal matters that might require her to be out of the office for a few days. She doesn't really have a backup."

"That's something you should have taken care of before now. The classes start on Monday, and you'd better be there."

"I will be," she said, then hung up, feeling sick. When your new girlfriend was starting to build a house, you needed to be there. Too bad you couldn't be honest with your boss about anything that really mattered. Why had the darned classes seemed so important at the time? Oh, that's right. They were B.C. Before Cody.

———

That night Maddie spoke to Cody on the phone. "I couldn't get out of my classes in Phoenix," she groused. "But I could skip the second week I'd planned on spending in LA."

"You planned this trip a long time ago. Your friend is counting on you."

"I know, but I didn't have a new girlfriend when I made the plans. Doesn't that change everything?"

Cody laughed. "It does to us, but I don't think other people think of it the same way. You go ahead and go. You've never been to Los Angeles, even though it's on your list of places you want to move to. You owe it to yourself to check it out, Maddie. You really do."

Cody was right, of course. Her friend from college had taken a week off work so they could see all the sights. It would have been amazingly rude to just blow her off. But her thirst for Cody was unquenchable, and being away from her for two weeks seemed like a lifetime.

———

The worst part of the trip was not hearing from Cody very often. Since there was no service up in Ramp, she didn't have a cell phone. She also didn't have a computer, and had to go all the way to Greenville to use the internet, making it a huge undertaking merely to dash off an email. As a result, they only got to speak twice in two weeks, a near eternity for Maddie.

Mortgage school would have been interesting if she hadn't been focused on wondering what Cody was doing. Images of her invaded Maddie's brain so often she had to pinch herself to keep her focus anywhere near the intricacies of lending money.

Los Angeles, on the other hand, was a massive disappointment. She'd had this image of wide, open spaces, orange trees, clear skies and plenty of sun. But her friend lived near Pasadena and the smog was particularly bad that week. Something about an inversion layer, whatever that was. After just a day her lungs hurt when she took a deep breath, something she couldn't imagine everyone ignored. But they seemed to.

Karen, her college roommate, had a good job with a stable company, something Maddie would have jumped at just a couple of months ago. But Karen had to drive over an hour in heavy traffic to get to work. Maddie had to admit she whipped up to Ramp, also an hour trip, at the drop of a hat. But the drive was pretty and she was often the only car on the road for twenty minutes at a time. That drive let her relax and daydream about Cody. Karen's drive seemed like an extra hour of work—at both ends of her day.

Disneyland was fun, that was for sure. But getting there had consumed an hour and a half of stop-and-go traffic. Karen said you got used to it and listened to books on tape or found radio shows you learned to love, but Maddie had her doubts. She didn't mind driving, but she liked to get somewhere. Idling in traffic to go just twenty miles seemed like a little bit of hell. And where were the damned orange trees?

—∞—

She got home late on Sunday night, calling Cody as soon as she had a good cell signal. "I'm back in civilization," she announced.

"I thought you'd been in civilization," Cody teased.

"No, I've decided I don't care for Phoenix or Los Angeles. Too hot, too dry, not enough green, not enough trees, too many cars, air's too chewy."

"Chewy?"

"It's hard to describe. But I can't wait to fill my lungs with sweet, rich Ramp air."

"I can't wait to fill mine with sweet, rich Maddie scent. When can I see you?"

"I'll be swamped at work all week. I'll try to drive up after work, but…"

"Don't worry about it. It's such a mess, you need four wheel drive to get to the site. You'd have to park out on the road and walk in. I'll come see you on Sunday. If I'm away from here, I won't be tempted to work."

"Sunday? What's wrong with Friday night?"

"Don't you have to work on Saturday?"

"Yeah, but only until noon. You could lie in bed for hours, like you love to do, and keep it warm for me."

"I wish I could, but I've gotta work on Saturday. I've got so much to do it isn't funny."

Maddie sighed. Having a girlfriend wasn't all a bed of roses. Speaking of which, why hadn't she seen roses in Pasadena? Did they have to truck them in for the parade?

―⁓―

Saturday brought a powerful thunderstorm, which had Maddie as happy as a clam. Being stuck in her apartment wasn't usually a joyful occasion, but when it brought Cody down the mountain to nest with her, all was right with the world.

―⁓―

The next Saturday marked the one month anniversary of purchasing the land. When they turned off the main road, Maddie knew what Cody was referring to when she said you still needed four wheel drive to get in. Her Jeep struggled and strained and surged to clamber over the remnants of the trees that had formerly filled in the approach to the plot. Then a clearing opened up and Maddie saw a beautifully placed site staked out, with bright orange paint demarking it.

"How did you know…where did you learn…"

Cody jumped out and stood there, smirking, arms crossed over her chest. "I did some research, and found a guy in Bluefield who builds log homes. He's been up twice, and he'll be back after I get the foundation laid. It's impressive, isn't it?"

"It's amazing! How did you decide where to put it?"

"That was the hard part. I want to blend in, so we really had to work to find a spot big enough, and level enough to work. Then we had to plot out the drive, which was tough too. It's a long way up here from the road, and you've got to get the slope just right or the darned thing will wash out with the first big stump soaker."

"Stump soaker…?"

"Rain," Cody explained. "We worked really carefully and managed to fell all of the trees we'll need without making it look like an earth-mover came in here and ran roughshod."

"You...felled your own trees? Built your own drive?"

"Who else would? I told you we've been going gangbusters."

"But you didn't say specifically what you were doing." She scanned the site, still amazed.

"You didn't ask. Not that I minded. To be honest, I didn't want you to ask too many questions. I love to surprise people." She grinned her toothy grin.

"It's amazing. Truly amazing. I can't fathom figuring out how to lay out the drive."

"Remember when I brought you up here to see the raw land and you almost lost a few teeth crawling over the last few hundred yards? I can't have my girlfriend come to visit me and need to hike in, so I had to get it done, lickity split."

"Your girlfriend thanks you for that. But how did you know which trees to take?"

"There's quite a technique. Luckily, I only had to fell them and skid them over there." She pointed at a flat spot covered with plastic tarps. A few dozen logs lay there, naked and waiting.

"How did you *do* it?" Maddie asked again. She wanted details, not generalities.

Cody led her over to a big tree and, after craning her neck to gaze up at it, slapped its trunk sharply. "This one would be fine. It's tall, and straight as an arrow. You chop it down, like you would any big tree, then take it to where you can work on it. Then you skin it and cut it into logs." She held her hands up, as if she'd just explained how to open a can of soda.

"But how do you know how big the logs should be?"

"Oh, you have to have a plan for that. I've *got* a plan," she said, nodding firmly. "I know exactly how many logs I need, how long each of them needs to be, and where each of them will go. They're already marked." They walked over to the big pile of wood, and Maddie bent over to read the markings Cody had made on them with a yellow wax pencil.

"Astonishing," she said. "Truly."

"It's been going really well. The pile over here is odd lengths that aren't long enough for exterior walls. I'll use them to build cabinets and for this and that. I'm gonna do my best to not waste any of it."

"You're not doing the foundation yourself, are you?"

"Jimmy, the guy who's teaching me, says I could, but I decided to give a local guy the business. Then I'll hire another local guy to do the drive. I felled the big trees and cut down the scrub, but I don't have the equipment to turn that into a proper road. I'm going to hire someone for plumbing and electrical too, even though Jimmy says it's all easy." She grinned. "Maybe I'll do the next one entirely by myself."

"The next one?" Maddie was almost seeing stars.

"Not for me! But someone around here will want one when they see mine. I did a lot of handywork around here, you know. People know me."

"And I bet they respect you. If you did a project for me, I know it'd be right."

"That's the only way to work. Do it right, or stand aside and let someone do it better."

They stood on the site, looking at the beautiful, protected land straight across from them.

"My house is going to be made just like my relatives would have built when they first came to Virginia. They'd probably moved on from log cabins by the time they settled Ramp, but I like to think of how I'm doing the same darned thing those first hard-headed, Scots-Irish Montgomerys did...and how it's just as good a building technique as it was then. That's remarkable, when you think about it."

"I can't believe you've done this much in just a month. How did you even get a permit that quickly?"

Cody laughed. "There's no backlog, since no one hardly ever gets a permit for anything on the mountain. You just build stuff and dare someone to tell you to take it down."

Maddie patted her shoulder. "I'm glad you're a little more amenable to government regulation."

"Just a little. I don't like having to ask permission, but I'd be darned if I'll do all this work and have some county man come up here and order it destroyed. I don't want to go down, guns a blazin', in Cody's Last Stand.

Maddie walked over to the orange lines. "Is this...the garage?"

Cody laughed. "No, that's the whole house. I don't need much."

"How much don't you need?" She could feel the blood rushing to her head.

"It'll be a little bigger than my house now, but not much." She stuck her jaw out—a sometimes cute, but more often frustrating, show of her tenacity. "All I need is a good-sized bedroom, a nice kitchen and a bathroom. Then the rest will be open space."

"What rest?" Maddie tried hard not to express her dismay, since Cody had clearly not asked for any form of advice.

Slinking an arm around her shoulders, Cody said, "It'll be plenty big. The smaller it is, the easier it is to keep it toasty warm in the winter." She moved over to a spot and said, "I'm gonna put a big stone hearth here. I've been meandering around, looking for stones. I'd really be happy if I could find them all on site."

She looked so damned happy that Maddie couldn't say a word that would spoil her joy. She sorely wanted to, but this was Cody's house and if she wanted to live in a matchbox—she had every right. It was ridiculous and shortsighted, but Maddie didn't think she had much of a chance of changing this hard-headed Montgomery.

⸺

Cody had prepared well for Maddie's visit, and when they went back to the trailer she went to her remarkably narrow refrigerator and produced a sauce pan covered with foil. "I made something I think you might like," she said.

"I'll like anything you've got in there. I didn't get lunch, since I was in such a hurry to lock up the bank and drive like a bat out of hell to get up here."

"You'll like this because it's ethnic," she said, waggling her eyebrows. "I had to go to Higgins County, but I found a little store in a town over there with a lot of Mexican immigrants. They had spices," she added dramatically.

"Spices? What kind of spices?"

"The kind to make mole."

Maddie paused, thinking, then laughed softly. "Two syllables. Accent on the first." She grabbed Cody and hugged her tightly. "I can't believe you went to a different county to make molé for me!"

"They're the only ethnics we've got, so I hope you like it. I can't guess where I'd have to go for Chinese or Thai spices."

"We can stock up the next time we're in Virginia. People from all over the world live around my parents." She kissed Cody tenderly, holding her close. "This means a lot to me. Going so far out of your way makes you an excellent girlfriend."

"You might want to wait to see if I made a mess out of it. I've never had Mexican food more complex than tacos, and that was only in the school cafeteria."

"I don't care if it tastes like dirt, which I know it won't. You're the best girlfriend ever."

—※—

The chicken in molé sauce was about as good as Maddie had ever had, and the lovemaking afterward reached as lofty a height. They lay in bed cuddling afterward, sated physically and emotionally.

"Hey," Maddie said quietly. "Have you given any thought to telling your family about us?"

"I meant to ask you about that, but it keeps slipping my mind. I was going to tell my uncles and Devin last week, but I wanted to make sure you won't have trouble if word gets back to the bank."

Maddie sat up abruptly. "Last week? You were going to come out to your family last week?"

The slow, sly smile that made one corner of Cody's mouth rise appeared. "No, I came out to them a while ago. I was going to tell them I've got a girlfriend." She placed a sweet, soft kiss on Maddie's lips. "'Cause I do."

The words sputtered out. "You already came out? And you didn't even mention it?"

Shrugging nonchalantly, Cody said, "It wasn't a big deal."

"Yes it is," Maddie said, staring at her. "It's a very big deal for... everybody!"

"Not me. My people are pretty accepting of whatever comes along."

"And were they? Accepting?"

Another shrug. "Yeah, pretty much. My aunts all tried to convince me I could get a man if I tried really, really hard." She chuckled at that. "But I told them I didn't want a man. They didn't say much more than that."

"I'm…I'm flabbergasted." How did a woman give almost no thought to her sexual orientation for years and years and then come out like it was of almost no importance?

Now Cody sat up and looked at Maddie with a guarded expression. "Are you mad I told them?"

"Of course not." She took in a few slow breaths, reminding herself to try to understand things from Cody's perspective, not her own. "I guess I'm a little hurt that you didn't tell me. Coming out is a big deal, Cody. It just is."

She blinked, clearly not getting it. "But it wasn't for *me*."

There was no way to bridge this gap. Cody had her own way of viewing the world and it was so far from Maddie's that it sometimes felt like they were from different galaxies. Willing herself to let it go, she lay back down and tugged on Cody until she nestled up against her body. "I believe you. It was a big deal for everyone I know, but that doesn't mean it has to be for you. Now tell me how they reacted." She pinched her, making Cody squeal. "They *did* react, didn't they?"

"Yes," she said, rolling her eyes. "I don't think it was a surprise to anyone. Two of my aunts begged me not to let the boys convince me I was gay, so they'd obviously been talking about it for a while. I guess it was a family secret no one let me in on."

"Do you feel good about it?"

"Sure." She sat up and gave Maddie a look that was hard to decipher. "Maybe we're different because of the stuff that's happened to us. We've had some very bad things go down. You can't get all up in arms about something as puny as who you sleep with."

Oh, damn. Maddie couldn't avoid talking about one particular bad thing. It was time to come clean about what her least favorite employee had told her all those months earlier. "Uhm," Maddie cleared her throat and shifted nervously. "Right after we met, someone told me about something bad. Something very bad…"

"My brother," Cody said flatly.

"Yeah. I heard that he was killed."

"He was." Cody slipped out of bed and walked over to her dresser. Searching through the top drawer, she extracted something and walked back to the bed. Instead of getting in, she sat on the edge and handed the folded newspaper to Maddie. "It's all in there."

Maddie held the paper in her hands, wincing when she read "RAMP MAN KILLED IN EXPLOSION" and beneath that "Police Suspect Methamphetamine Laboratory." There wasn't one part of her that wanted to read it. She folded it and handed it back to Cody, who cocked her head in silent question. "I don't care about the facts. I just wanted you to know that I'd heard about it, because I don't want to have secrets between us."

Head dropped, Cody quietly said, "I thought you'd be interested…"

Maddie wrapped her in a tender embrace, and nuzzled her face into Cody's shoulder. "I'm interested in you, and your feelings. Do you want to talk about it?"

"No, not really. It won't change anything."

"Then put that away." Cody got up and walked back over to the dresser. "If you ever want to talk about it, or anything else, I'm here for you. I promise that."

Cody returned and sat on the edge of the bed again, quietly gazing into Maddie's eyes for a few minutes. Maddie couldn't guess what was going on behind those sad eyes, but she didn't want to push her. Finally, Cody leaned over and kissed her gently. "If it's all the same to you, I'd prefer to think about the present."

"I think the present's pretty darned good, so that seems like a fine idea."

That slow smile appeared again. "I think so too." She lay back down, grasped Maddie and tucked her up against her body. "I know so."

CHAPTER TWENTY-ONE

MADDIE'D BEEN PUTTING OFF having the conversation, but she had to go to Huntington for her monthly meeting, and decided it was time to come clean with Avery. They went to lunch at a little Italian place they used to frequent. The owner was very effusive, lamenting their absence and asking why they didn't visit more often. Maddie got the impression he thought she and Avery were romantically involved, and she would have dissuaded him, but the image was so funny she played along.

She was very tempted by the breadsticks, but she was still trying to lose a few pounds. Getting them out of her field of vision helped reduce their lure. "So," she said, placing her hands on the table dramatically. "I have procured for myself a genuine girlfriend."

"Not Cody Keaton!"

"Indeed it is."

"You did not!" He looked like he couldn't decide if he should slap her or hug her. "You've taken up with a real, live hillbilly."

"I have. And I'd complain about you using that term, but I'll give you a pass since she doesn't seem to mind."

"I'd tie you up and hold you captive if she wasn't rich," he said, snickering. "But you can help her hang onto a few hundred thousand of her many millions of dollars."

"Uhm…" She wasn't about to complain, but a few things had been irking her enough to at least give voice to them. "She's not really interested in my advice when it comes to money."

He slapped his face with both hands. "Oh, god, is it gone already?"

"Of course not! I'm telling you, Cody's not like that. She's very, very, very prudent with her money. We saw a financial advisor who had some good advice, but Cody hasn't brought it up since the day we visited."

"That's because the money's all gone!"

Lord! He could be so dramatic! "It's not gone Avery. She's not a spender. But her family isn't as prudent, and she gives them an awful lot of rope. I'm afraid someone will hang themselves."

"Of course they will! You've got to get on her, Maddie. Don't let her fritter those millions away."

"*We* don't have much control... She's pretty independent," she said, thinking that was the best term for it.

"Screen her calls. Don't let the moochers onto the property."

"We're not living together. We only see each other on the weekends most of the time."

"What? Are you not lesbians?"

"Yes, we are," she said, rolling her eyes. "But she's never been in a relationship before, and she's used to being very independent."

"I sense trouble in paradise, and you've barely entered the Garden of Eden."

"No, not trouble..." She thought for a moment. "I thought we'd at least discuss things before she does them. But she's building a house and it's nothing like I would do."

"Oh, God, what is it? Twelve bedrooms and a twenty-two car garage?"

"Hardly. One bedroom, one bath, and a main room."

His mouth gaped open. "You're shitting me," he said flatly.

"No, I wish I were. That's a much smaller house than I'd like if I decide to stay in town..." She shook her head. "It's not the space. It's that she just does what she wants without even informing me. She came out to her family weeks ago and didn't mention it."

"She's no lesbian," he declared dramatically.

"I'm fairly confident she's a lesbian. Want me to tell you what she's best at?" She made her eyes big. "It's something you've never, ever done."

"No!" He put his fingers in his ears and spouted some gibberish to not hear.

She held up her hands in a "time out" signal. "I'll behave."

"You'd better. Now tell me all about her horrible faults. I love to hear that people in relationships are less happy than I am being single."

"Thanks," she said, giving him a sickly smile. "She doesn't have horrible faults. It's just that she acts like she's still entirely single, but I'm acting like we're serious about each other." She slumped down in her chair and sat there glumly. "Sometimes I feel like I'm more into her than she's into me."

"Well, you don't have millions of dollars…"

She grabbed a breadstick and hit him with it before taking a big, crunchy bite. "That's not it at all. I know how much she cares for me. She's just not obsessed with me like I am with her and that…hurts."

Avery sat back in her chair and gazed at her for a minute. "I'm sorry you're having a rough patch, principessa. She'll come around. You're the one people should be flocking to. Your charms are worth a lot more than her millions."

—⁓—

The foundation was poured, the drive had been graded, trucks full of shredded rubber had been dumped, raked and sealed to make the driveway, and Jimmy was back on site, ready to lead. He and Cody stood by the pile of logs early in the morning, while he clearly laid out the plan of attack.

A vehicle roared up the hill, and Cody stalked over to the drive, smiling, despite her annoyance, at how quiet the rubber made the approach. There was only one reason to come up that high, and that was to be on her land. Her skin prickled in irritation, but when she caught sight of her Uncle Cubby, she relaxed. Walking over to his old, battered truck, she leaned on the window. "If you're here to help, let's get started. If not, come back after five. I'm paying this guy by the hour."

Cubby laughed. "You've got the money to pay someone to do all this, you know."

"I know. But I want it done right. And right means my way."

He got out and reached into the back of the truck, pulling out a worn, leather tool belt. "Tell me where you want me. I can saw, plane, cut and level. But I don't do ladders."

"We don't have one." She led the way back over to Jimmy, grinning like a possum eating grapes.

The next day, her uncle Shooter was in the truck when it strained its way to the top of the drive. They'd gotten the vapor barrier and underfloor heating installed the day before, now they were going to put up the first course of logs. Shooter walked around, exclaiming over this and that, until Cody said, "We'll chit-chat during lunch. Now's the time for work."

On the third day, Lurlene and Thelma arrived before noon, carrying a basket full of Lurlene's famous fried chicken.

It was so delightful to sit down on a log and eat the best fried chicken in the county after a long morning's work that Cody felt like she'd died and gone to heaven. She munched on a thigh, her favorite part, while eying Aunt Thelma's berry cobbler. It struck her hard that this was the first family project they'd ever done. At least in her memory. She'd heard tell of many of them in the past, but this was it for her. She almost teared up from the tender feelings she had for her family at that moment, but that chicken wasn't going to eat itself, and the cabin was just as lazy.

Cody pulled into her drive late that afternoon, tired but happy. They'd gotten a huge amount of work done, and her uncles seemed not just willing, but interested in the details and even the planning.

Her skin prickled with anticipation when she saw Maddie's little car near her front door. She drove right up next to it, and hopped out. Maddie strolled out of the forest, waving when she caught her eye.

"If you weren't here by six, I was gonna drive up that hill until I ran out of real estate," Maddie said.

"What were you doing out there? You don't have a gun, so don't even think about bagging a deer."

Maddie chuckled. "You've made me prefer walking around to sitting. How would you like me to treat you to dinner?"

"I can ask the same question, and I bet what I've got is better than what you're offering." She reached into her car and took out a basket. Waving it under Maddie's nose, she said, "You might not be able to smell it, but that's the smell of perfection."

"Let's do it. I love perfection."

"Do you have any of that bug spray on you?"

"I'm lousy with it. Why?"

"We're gonna have a picnic. I'll go put on a fresh shirt and grab some napkins."

They didn't go far at all. Actually, the lovely spot Cody chose was only fifteen minutes away. "You've dragged me all over West Virginia, when you have this pretty spot so close?" Maddie demanded in playful outrage.

"The fishing is terrible here. But it's a darned nice place to sit and think. Or eat." She spread out the blanket she carried, sat down gracefully and started to reveal the contents of her basket. "Fried chicken good enough to make you cry," she announced.

Maddie took a piece and bit into it. She rolled her eyes. "I'd weigh a thousand pounds if I had constant access to food this good."

"You don't wanna know what it tastes like fresh out of the pan."

"I think you're right." She savored another bite. "I've had fried chicken hundreds of times. But this is better than every other time…rolled into one."

"My aunt keeps chickens. That's half the battle."

Holding the piece away from her mouth, Maddie said, "So this is a pet? Did it have a name?"

"Yep. That's Delicious. Eat up." She took a piece and started to devour it, almost making sparks fly. "I get godawful hungry when I work like I have been. It's a wonder I don't gain weight, but I can barely keep my pants up. I'm gonna have to get a pair of suspenders like Uncle Shooter wears."

Cody did look thin. Well, thinner than normal. But she also looked tanned and healthy, with a lot of color in her cheeks. "You look good. You should probably wear sunblock, but I assume you won't listen to that piece of advice."

"No, I don't need it. We all tan easily."

"You don't have the same skin tone most of your cousins do. They're kinda swarthy."

"Yeah, that's the Montgomery side. I got Keaton skin. Even though I don't get dark like my cousins, I've never been sunburned bad. Even if I get red, it fades by morning." She rolled back the sleeve of her T-shirt, showing paler, but still brown upper arms. "See? That was pink yesterday."

Maddie saw the muscle that Cody was developing on top of the muscle she already had. The urge to climb onto her lap right then and have those strong arms wrap around her was remarkably powerful, but she could wait until after dinner. She hoped. "You look good. But mostly you look happy. Everything's going well?"

"Better than well. My uncles have been up every day to help, and my teeth about fell out when Devin showed up yesterday.

"That must have made you feel great."

"It truly did. We're going gangbusters. Uncle Shooter is like a pro with mortar. He's whipping along right behind us when we set a log. Teamwork," she said, proudly. "And if they both help for the whole project, they'll each lose a few pounds and maybe a few points off their high blood pressure."

"Don't make them work too hard. If they've been inactive for a long time…"

"Oh, yeah," Cody teased. "They could drop dead. But better at a job site than in front of that infernal TV."

"Heartless, but pragmatic. That's what I like about you."

"I think you like my…" She stopped short, an adorable blush coloring her cheeks. "I'm glad you like whatever it is you like." She was so damned cute. They'd had each other in every way imaginable, and she was still too shy to say anything even mildly racy. She was a peach.

—⁂—

They walked carefully back to Cody's in the twilight. It was like picking your way through a field of land mines, with depressions, dead tree limbs, little piles of leaves hiding god knew what, and a thousand other impediments. Maddie stayed right behind her, watching each step and trying to mimic it.

They got back at eight, and Cody stopped right at the door to Maddie's car. "Drive home tonight? Or an extra hour in the morning?"

Maddie put her arms around her, feeling the soft curve of her breast and the taut muscles of her lower back. What a combination. "What?"

Cody leaned over and kissed her gently. "Would you rather go back tonight or tomorrow morning?"

"Neither." She tightened her embrace. "I hate to leave you."

Stroking her hair, Cody dropped kiss after kiss on the crown of her head. "I feel the same. I'd come down to see you every night, but I've got to have my wits about me. Some of the stuff we do is very tricky, and I've got to be sharp."

Maddie smiled up at her. She'd walk to Ramp to see her, but she had her pride, and begging for Cody's attention wasn't gonna happen. Her powers of denial were good enough that she could ignore the fact that she'd come up uninvited tonight. "Banking's easy. I can be a dullard. Let's go play. I'd rather be well loved than well rested."

———

Devin was not only willing to be outside all day working on the house, he was never in a hurry to take off at the end of the day.

They started early, had lunch early, and stopped early. By four thirty, Jimmy went to the cooler and took out a beer. That was the equivalent of blowing a whistle at the end of a factory shift. Then they all sat wherever they could and talked about their progress. Jimmy knew more about log cabins than Cody could ever hope to learn, and he was very generous in sharing his experiences. He loved to talk too, and she greedily soaked up the bits of knowledge he imparted through his stories.

Devin was his new, sullen self most of the time, but he was showing up and working hard. That was a big hurdle.

Once Jimmy, Cubby, and Shooter took off for home, that left Devin, who didn't have much to say, but also didn't seem to want to leave. Cody took him down to Twined Creek one day, spending a quiet hour having a beer and eating nachos, and when he eventually got into his old, beat-up Jeep to head for home, she said, "Bring your bow if you come tomorrow. We can practice."

He brought it, and she brought hers and they shot at targets until it was too dark to see. "Nighttime coyote season lasts until the end of July," she said as they were putting their gear away.

"Nighttime?" he stared at her in the gloaming. "*Night* time?"

Laughing, she nodded. "We've been hunting a thousand times at night. Why do you act like I'm talking crazy?"

"I didn't know you hunted coyote to start with. Why bother?"

She actually had no interest in killing coyote. You couldn't eat it, and the animals did a pretty good job of keeping their own population in check, so there was no reason to cull them. But that was the only thing legal right now, and she assumed they'd never bag one if they went bow hunting. Those suckers were hard enough to catch with a good rifle. Actually, she would have been happy to just sit and talk with Devin, but they'd always interacted best when hunting, and she needed to know what was going on in his head. "I just like to hunt," she said, figuring that was good enough.

"Fine. I'll go, but don't cry when we come home with nothing but chigger bites."

She flicked him on the back of the neck, then danced away when he tried to retaliate. "If I gave you a dollar for every time you've seen me cry, you couldn't buy a gallon of gas."

Everyone said you should carry a red or amber light to shine in the coyote's eyes. That let you lock 'em in while you got off a shot. She didn't have one, and Devin didn't either, making their improbable quest even more improbable. Now that they were going, she was even more determined not to kill. It would make her look like a fool, but if Devin got one lined up, she was going to push him or do something to upset his aim.

There were coyotes on her land; she knew that for sure. She'd heard them when she was at the site late, and had to admit their yodeling sometimes gave her the willies. But she wasn't afraid of them in the least. They were like dogs, and she'd never met a dog she couldn't handle. All you had to do was make them think you were both unafraid and bigger than they were, and they'd leave you alone.

They decided to just take off down the hill and see what they could find. Cody didn't have a store-bought call, but Devin could imitate a wounded rabbit better than anyone she knew, so they had everything they needed.

Since she wanted to go home *without* a coyote, she let herself talk in near normal voice. "I remember the first time we went hunting together," she said. "My daddy took us. Remember those puny little guns we had? You could barely put a dent in a sparrow with those things."

"Yeah, I remember," he said. "You talked too loud then...just like you do now."

"I know when to shut up. Don't worry about it."

"I'll admit you fit in better than anyone thought. Even in Huntington, you were hill folk." He chuckled at the memory. "When you'd come up here in the summer, you'd be talking like us by the end of the first day. No shoes, squattin' in the woods, eatin' anything we threw at you." His laugh grew louder. "You were a real hillbilly."

"I still am. Keith never was though."

"No," he said quietly. "He never was. I think he had too much Keaton and not enough Montgomery."

"Maybe. But my daddy could hunt with the best of 'em."

"Yeah, he could, but being hill folk is about more than huntin'. Keith needed...something...and he couldn't get it here."

"He definitely needed something." They trudged on for a good long while. The forest was quiet, just a few birds singing their night calls. Very little scrambled around on the forest floor, and there wasn't even a hint of a coyote.

"I don't think I'll ever be able to shoot a gun again," Devin said, making Cody stop in her tracks.

Good lord, it took guts for him to admit that. A Montgomery who couldn't hunt was just about a waste of resources. But at least he'd said *something* that was on his mind. "Then we'll just have to be the best bow hunters we can be."

Devin didn't say another thing, but a tiny bit of the darkness that followed him seemed to leave his eyes. Maybe it was her imagination, but maybe it wasn't. Getting outside and opening up, even a little, had to help.

They kept walking, going slow and keeping their senses sharp. After a while they reached a bit of land that jutted out, allowing them to look down into their valley and see the lights of houses dot the landscape.

"I hope we never have another boy think he has to join the Army just to get the paycheck. They took Keith and almost took you. That's enough."

"The Army didn't take Keith. Prison might have though."

"Well, if he hadn't deserted, he wouldn't have been to prison. And if they hadn't tried to send him to Iraq, he wouldn't have deserted."

Devin shook his head. "Where in the hell did he think they'd send him? Hawaii?"

"I have no idea. He signed up without telling a soul. He saw how mama was struggling and…you know how it is. You did the same darned thing."

"No, I wanted to go. It wasn't just for the paycheck. I thought I could learn a good trade." He put his bow down on his boot and leaned back to gaze up at the first stars. "If you need a man to search for IEDs, call me first."

"You're making progress," she said, finally feeling that was the truth. "You need to do the things that used to make you happy. Sitting in front of the TV was never for you."

"No, you're right. I'm just tired most of the time."

"That's depression, Devin. You've gotta fight it, and the only way is to get up and keep going."

"I'll keep coming to help you. That's been good."

"It's been really good for me." She almost put an arm around him, but that would have shown she was treating him different, and that was the last thing she wanted.

"Let's go back up, I'll blaze a different trail. The one you picked didn't have diddly."

They started back up, using the moonlight to guide them.

"Hey, I've done a lot of thinking about your…what we talked about."

"My lesbianism?" she asked, unwilling to avoid the name.

"Yeah. Well, Pastor Jackson told me I was playing with fire to keep seeing you. He told me to shun you, and if I didn't, I was giving you permission to sin."

"Everybody in the county could shun me and I'd still be a lesbian. I don't mean to speak badly about somebody you respect—"

"Hear me out," he interrupted. "He's a man of God, and I respect him an awful lot. But he's a man, not God, so I decided to go to the source. I read the Bible for days and couldn't find one passage where Jesus shunned a sinner. He did just the opposite. So, I'm not going to walk away from you, Cody. I'm gonna pray for you," he said, smiling.

"Thank you." She managed to smile back. If it made him happy to try to pray away her gayness, he could do it until his knees bled. "Let's leave it at that, okay? You do your thing, and I'll do mine."

"My thing won't lead me to eternal damnation," he said, the fire of the converted burning in his eyes.

"I understand you believe that. I've heard your warning. Now, be like Jesus, and accept me, sins and all."

He looked like he had a quick retort, but Devin just smiled and shook his head. "I'll try," he said, then started leading them back up the steep hill.

CHAPTER TWENTY-TWO

THE NEXT SATURDAY, MADDIE was scheduled to work until noon, but she didn't expect a very busy day. Because she'd given Geneva, her assistant, several Saturdays off during the winter, she had no qualms about choosing today as a mental health day. She called Cody at seven a.m., trying to make sure she caught her before she went hunting or fishing or snake charming. "Hi, I was thinking of driving up to see your progress. Is this a good day?"

"Mmm…" Maddie could almost hear her making up an excuse. "It'd be okay, but tomorrow would be better. That's what we planned on, right?"

"Right." What the fuck? What in the hell did Cody have going on?

"Uhm, if you give me a couple of hours I might be able to change things around today. You know I want to see you."

Damn, she was such a dear woman. There was no need to make her jump through hoops. "No, don't do that. I'll come up tomorrow."

"Or tonight. Come tonight. You don't have to call first. Actually, come up to the new place. There's no sense in stopping here."

"You won't be out hunting?"

Cody laughed. "There's no good hunting in the summer. You can't even take a squirrel until mid-September. Summer's for fishing." She sounded content just saying the word. That woman *loved* to fish.

"I'll see you tonight or tomorrow, depending on how my day shakes out. Have fun today."

"I will. It's nothing big," she said hastily. "I'm just having some of my relatives over to see the construction."

"Oh." Maddie waited, assuming there would be more. But Cody didn't add a word. What in the hell was going on? Why wouldn't you ask your god-damned girlfriend to come over to a family party? "All right. See you." She hung up, steaming mad. Cody either couldn't read her mood or preferred to ignore it. Either way pissed her off massively. But there was no way she was going to be stuck inside steaming all day. She'd been dressed for a day in the woods, and she decided not to waste it. The Hatfield-McCoy Mountains were not far at all. She got into her car, set the GPS, and took off. She didn't need Cody Keaton to have a nice day.

―⁓―

Every member of the extended Montgomery family gathered at the site of Cody's new house that afternoon. She'd borrowed her Uncle Cubby's truck and had filled the bed with every card table and folding chair she could borrow, then wedged in two big coolers filled with ice and soft drinks.

Now they were all eating the fried chicken, cornbread, bean salad, and potato salad that her aunts had made. The babies were playing in a sand pit she'd made just for them, and the bigger kids romped in the "slip and slide" she'd rigged up with a couple of plastic tarps and a hose.

Everyone had their rifles, shotguns and pistols and Cody got a huge charge out of their excitement when she brought out the trap thrower she'd bought. Watching them shoot at cans was getting old, and the clay wouldn't be dangerous for the kids to run around in, the way those decimated aluminum cans could be. And there was some added technique needed to trap shoot. The boys could spiff up their skills. Game tended to move around, unlike a Coke can.

Playing around and blasting three hundred dollars worth of shot didn't even hurt. Maybe you could get used to literally blowing money. Actually, this kind of day made the troubles she'd had with the money fade from her memory. It seemed like old times, with everyone having fun and no one holding a hand out, expecting hundred dollar bills to fall into it. The only difference from their past ways was they were at the top of the hill, in the sun, and Cody hadn't had to scrimp to buy a half keg of beer. She reflected that being poor hadn't ever been horrible for her, since she had access to food and her living expenses were so lean. But being able to provide fun for her family—pure fun with no payback—was awfully sweet. Money didn't have to be the root of all evil. That was an expression someone who didn't want poor people lusting after his money had probably made up.

―⁓―

Maddie parked her car in a big lot next to a visitor's center. It was such a nice day that people had flocked to the park, and she got one of the last spots, even though it was still early.

After a quick visit to the center, she figured out which trail would cover five or six miles and took off. It was...odd. Having the trail marked so clearly was a little formal, given what she was used to. And, even though it was clean compared to a city street, there were still crushed soda cans and paper napkins lying just off the path. There weren't hundreds of them, actually just a few, but they were there, making it clear the trail got a lot of use.

She supposed she could have taken off on her own, but she didn't know the area and had no interest in having to be rescued. Besides, Cody would never stop laughing if that happened, and she couldn't have that.

Maddie hiked for a long time, encountering few people along the way. That was nice, and she almost forgot she was near others until she reached a promontory that looked out over a pretty valley. She stood there, taking it all in, until a gaggle of kids ran up beside her, chattering like magpies. It was great that kids got out of town to learn to appreciate the wilder side of West Virginia, but she had a real taste for solitude...well, maybe one more person would be nice. But that person was enjoying her family, and that family clearly did not include Maddie.

—⁓—

Three hours traipsing around the mountains cleared Maddie's head and allowed her to vent almost all of her anger. But the hurt lingered. Having this kind of thing between them wasn't wise on any level, and she decided she wasn't going to let it fester. It was time to gut it up and tell Cody how she felt.

Her first instinct was to call, but, as usual, her cell service was nonexistent. Then she recalled that Cody was at the new house, and she didn't have a phone there. The only other option was to drive up to the job site and do it in person. Cody had invited her, so she wasn't just storming up there to cause a scene. And if her relatives happened to still be there... so much the better.

—⁓—

She must have driven faster than she'd planned, because Maddie turned off onto Cody's road when it wasn't even five o'clock.

Turning onto the long drive Cody had constructed, Maddie marveled that it looked like a thick bed of rubber. Cody'd sworn she wasn't going to have a rutted, muddy drive for the first time in her life, and cruising up it gave Maddie one more reason to believe every word that came out of that pretty mouth.

Even though the drive was silent, some kind of gun was blasting away at fairly quick intervals. God only knew what Cody might be shooting at, since she claimed there wasn't anything to hunt at that time of year. Maybe Maddie would have to paint her car hunter's orange not to have it mistaken for the world's largest deer.

Cars, trucks and Jeeps stretched out down the drive, and Maddie stayed at the back of the pack, pulling off onto the unpaved shoulder. When she got out she heard the guns still firing rapidly, and a chorus of deep voices and kids' high-pitched ones shouting and whooping and hollering. For the first time, she paused and made herself consider what she was getting into. Besides needing a moment to think, she was a little afraid of being killed…unintentionally, of course, but you were just as dead if your girlfriend shot you by accident.

She got back into her car and rolled down the window. The delightful smell of something being cooked on the grill drifted down to tickle her nose. It might be worth getting shot for some of that fried chicken… She shook her head, forcing herself to stay on topic.

In reality, her family and Cody's had been on the same path. But for a few bad breaks, they could have…should have been in the same economic bracket. Cody's parents had been blue collar factory workers just like her own, but they hadn't had the resources to pick up and follow the work when it left the area. That's something that her own parents wouldn't have let happen. They would have moved to Houston or North Carolina or Alaska to keep working, but that's not what Cody's people did. They were tied to the land and to each other in ways that Maddie was entirely unfamiliar with. Accepting that bond would be part of the deal. That was obvious. Cody was part of the landscape, and trying to take her out of it would be a huge mistake.

But fitting into Cody's world was not going to be easy. The gun culture was really going to take some getting used to, not to mention Cody's need to hunt. But the bigger issue was money. No matter how little

Maddie had, she would always have more than Cody. Not in reality, of course, but Cody's mindset was of a very, very poor person, and having money thrust at her as an adult would never change that. It had taken Maddie months to get that through her head, but it was now clear. Cody would learn to spend, but it would never be easy for her. And that might be tough to live with.

The other issue was Cody's family. Maddie didn't know what had landed the boys in jail, but you didn't get sent there for being really nice. Just being around a few of them made her more than uneasy, and that wouldn't go away anytime soon. But you had to take the whole package, and she'd have to get used to having petty drug dealers and thieves and arsonists and god only knew what else in her extended family. Not great. Not great at all.

Why couldn't it just be the two of them, enjoying Cody's money in a lovely setting where Cody could still hunt…like about an hour outside of New York City? She chuckled to herself. That would never happen. She'd have to take Cody as she found her, or move on. It was time to face the music…of the staccato booming of guns. The only way to know if she could learn to live with the extended Montgomery family was to hurl herself into the middle of it. She got out of her car and started up the drive, hoping they had the sense to aim away from their own new cars.

When Maddie reached the top of the rise, the drive opened up to a nice-sized clearing with two log walls gleaming in the afternoon sun, already standing tall and proud. She hadn't noticed a group of teenagers loitering near the drive, smoking grass and drinking beer out of plastic cups. Well, that was…different. "Who're you?" a boy asked, already having mastered the dark, suspicious Montgomery glare.

"I'm Maddie Osborne," she said, finding herself shivering, even though it had to be eighty degrees. "A friend of Cody's."

"She's shootin'," he said. "Steer clear." He pointed to a spot well away from the cabin.

"Will do. Can I…go behind…that way?"

"I suppose."

She started to walk across the clearing, noting so many changes to the land that she almost stopped to take a closer look. But a group of people, mostly Cody's aunts and some of her female cousins, were sitting on chairs and picnic tables, staring at her like she'd dropped down from the sky. This was not going to be an easy group to breach.

"Hi," she said, waving when she got close. "Maddie Osborne. We met at your house," she said, directing her gaze at Lurlene, thanking her lucky stars she was good with names and faces.

"I remember," Lurlene said, a ghost of a smile on her weathered face.

"I came up to see Cody," Maddie said when no one offered a word.

One of the cousins, named…Melanie or…no, Melissa got up and said, "She's over shooting. I'll show you."

They walked around behind where the house would eventually fill out. Seven or eight big men, and two older, bigger, wider men stood there, shooting at whatever you called the targets you launched into the air and blasted to bits. Cody was taking a turn. She raised a rifle to her shoulder and called, "Pull!" An orange disk flew into the air. She tracked it for a second, then squeezed the trigger. After catching just the edge of it, she shook her head and lowered the barrel of her gun. "Winged it," she grumbled loudly, probably because of the ear protectors she wore.

Melissa went up behind her, tapped her on the shoulder and stepped back, instinctively knowing to give a person holding a gun a wide berth.

Cody and all of her cousins and uncles turned and stared, with only Cody's mouth dropping open.

Maddie hoped to God she was imagining it, but Cody looked… embarrassed. She moved quickly and stood in front of Maddie, her gun cocked or whatever it was called when it looked broken in half. "I thought you were coming up tonight."

"Want me to wait in the car?" Maddie asked, trying but not managing to avoid sounding testy.

"No! I'm just…surprised. Uhm…you've met everyone, I think."

Maddie nodded to each of the men, receiving nods or quiet "hellos" from the more outgoing ones.

"Let me get you a beer or something." She handed her gun to Devin, who was staring daggers into Maddie. He might have been Cody's favorite, but he was creepy. That was the only word for him. He looked like he'd sneak into your house and strangle you while you slept…just for fun.

Melissa stayed back with the men, probably to discuss the invasion of the banker, and Cody led the way to the spot where she'd set up a keg of beer. Her hands were shaking slightly when she took a cup and poured a cold one for Maddie. "I'm glad you're here," Cody said, looking anything but. "Uhm…what should I tell people? Should I say you're here for…I don't know…you've got something you want me to sign?"

"Can we go someplace to talk? Alone?"

"Sure. Sure." She poured another beer and took a gulp, probably to calm her nerves. Then she led Maddie around the front of the house and down a path through a stand of trees.

They walked at least a few hundred feet, then came to another clearing, this one large enough for a big, well-organized garden. "I've been keeping this a secret," Cody said. "No one knows about it yet." She shrugged. "I don't know why, but I like to have little secrets."

"Yeah, I know that about you." Maddie walked around, surveying the neatly laid out square plots. Each one was flanked by a log, flat side up, that one could use to walk through the space. "Why don't you want your family to know about us?"

"Why don't *I* want…?" She grabbed Maddie by the shoulders. "I didn't think you'd want anyone to know. Your job…" she said, trailing off.

"I'm able to handle myself, Cody. We're not talking about my job. We're talking about your family." She stared at her hard. "Are you embarrassed about being with me? About being gay?"

"No, not a bit." She pulled Maddie into a fervid embrace. "I'd understand if you were embarrassed to be with me, but I'd have to be out of my mind to be embarrassed about you." She pulled away and locked those puppy dog eyes on Maddie. "If I tell my family about us, everyone will know. *Every*one," she stressed. "It'll get back to the bank in an hour."

"Fuck the bank," Maddie said, clearly snapping off each word. "I don't live my life for other people's comfort. I've never come out to my boss, but that's only because he's never asked me a personal question." She put her hands on Cody's hips and gazed into her eyes. "I have nothing to be ashamed of. You're my girlfriend, and I'm damned lucky to be able to say that."

With a smile so sunny that the shoots on the ground could've grown a good inch, Cody tucked her arms around Maddie again and kissed her head, then her face, then her lips repeatedly. "I'm sorry I didn't ask you how you wanted to handle things. I just didn't think…"

"I should have made it clear." She leaned back and said, "I'm entirely comfortable with my sexual orientation. You have my permission to tell anyone about us. Anyone on earth."

"I'll do that right now." Cody started to lead way back to the group, but Maddie tugged her to a halt. "You can't show me your secret and not spend a minute telling me about it. It's awesome, you know."

"I think so," she admitted, grinning happily.

"How do you water it?"

"I've got a water tank over there," she said, pointing to a spot behind the house. "And I put drip hoses in so I don't waste a lot." She walked along a log, surefooted as expected. "I'm gonna have a good crop of tomatoes if it kills me," she said, putting her hands on her hips and glaring at the plot. "Cucumbers, beans, squash, okra, corn if I'm lucky, and melon if I'm very lucky. All of the salad plants are down at my trailer." She pointed to orange X's painted on the dirt. "That's where I'm going to put the posts for the deer fence I'm building. I like my deer well fed, but they're not gonna eat my vegetables."

"I feel like you've made years of progress in just the couple of weeks since I've been to visit."

"Has it been that long?" She looked puzzled, like someone had messed with the calendar.

"Yeah, it has."

"Time's getting away from me. I work so hard I can't keep track of the days."

Cody took her hand and they walked back to the group of women and kids in the front of the house. A few sets of eyes looked like they'd pop from various heads, but Cody didn't hesitate. "You know how I told you all I was gay?"

A few heads nodded mutely. "It didn't take me long to find a girlfriend." She held their linked hands up, and showed a charming grin when she kissed Maddie's hand. "Surprised?"

More heads nodded. Only Melissa had the ability to say, "You could knock me over with a feather."

"I'm not such a bad catch," Cody said, now seemingly at ease. "I'm rich, if nothing else."

"I don't mean about you," Melissa said. "I never would have guessed that…" she looked to Cody for advice. "What should I call her?"

"Maddie," Cody said, chuckling. "You can all call her Maddie. That's her name and all."

After giving Cody a mean glare, Melissa continued, "You don't look like a…gay…person. Is that rude to say? I don't know much about this kinda thing…"

"No, that's fine," she said, even though it was kinda rude. "I was gay before I met Cody. Her money didn't turn me," she added, but the joke fell flat. Only Cody laughed, which was all Maddie needed.

"Let's go make some eyes bug out in the back yard," Cody said, leading her around the house.

"Can you make sure no one has a gun ready to go?"

"They didn't shoot me when I told them I was gay, and there's no way adding you to the mix would aggravate anyone."

They rounded the corner and Maddie felt her heart thump hard when she saw Devin glaring at them. *Oh, this is fun!*

"I have a girlfriend," Cody said when there was a pause in the shooting.

"What?" Brett had just taken his turn, and his hearing protectors had obviously been working well. He laughed hard. "I thought you said you had a girlfriend."

"I do." Cody casually slung an arm around Maddie's shoulders. "She's my banker and my girlfriend. I'm crazy about her and she has a little interest in me." She elbowed Maddie. "Get it?"

"Yeah, you're really knocking them out of the park today."

There might have been more awkward encounters in the history of the world, but Maddie certainly had never been part of one. Again, no one said a word, they just looked at Cody like they were waiting for the punch line.

"Congratulations, Cody," she said, looking from man to man. "Nice to have you, Maddie. Something like that would be nice."

Cubby was the first to speak. "Glad to have you around."

It wasn't much, but at least he'd spoken. The other guys mumbled words that Maddie couldn't make out, but they at least didn't throw things at her.

"We're gonna go get some food."

They walked away and not another shot was fired. Cody made Maddie a plate of food, then sat beside her and tried to engage her relatives in conversation. It was slow going, but they seemed to try. A few of the teens came over, clearly plastered. "Who gave the kids beer?" Cody demanded.

"It won't hurt 'em," Jaden said, limping over to the table. "We was all doin' the same at that age."

"No, we weren't," Cody said, scowling.

"Everyone but you was," he amended.

Instead of arguing, Cody dropped it immediately. That seemed to be her way. She made her point and then moved on. That was probably nicer than having someone harangue you, but Maddie doubted the gentle approach worked on most of her renegade cousins.

It was after six, with the sun sinking along the horizon just enough to make the kids who'd been playing in the water start to shiver. "I wish I had warm water, but that'll be a few more weeks," Cody said.

"We ought to be getting home," Mandy said. "But we'll help you clean up first."

"No, don't bother. Maddie's really good at cleaning things up. She's gonna do the whole county."

The last of the Montgomerys departed by seven, leaving Cody standing with her arm around Maddie's shoulders, waving at the final car.

"That was...kinda awkward," Maddie said. "But I'm glad we got it done quickly."

"They'll be fine. But it'll take a coon age to have them treat you like you're from around here."

"I don't know what a coon age is, but I assume it's long."

"Yup. Real long."

As they walked back up to the house, Maddie asked, "Did Jaden hurt his leg? He had a heck of a limp."

"Oh, yeah. A long time ago." It took her a second to add, "Some genius told him he could get disability if he shot off a toe or two."

Maddie's mouth dropped open.

"He shoulda used a pistol, but he didn't have one at hand so he used a shotgun." She shrugged. "He doesn't tend to think things through. There might've been alcohol involved."

"That's…" What did you say to that kind of situation? I'm sorry your cousin's an idiot?

"There's a doctor almost on the Kentucky border that'll write up any kind of disability for five thousand dollars."

"Five thousand dollars! He takes bribes like that from people who don't have a dime?"

"Yup. You have to give him the first few checks you get or he tells the state he made a mistake."

Maddie couldn't decide if the hard and dark look in Cody's eyes was from anger or from embarrassment about what she was revealing.

"They didn't learn about him until after Jaden messed up his foot, but my aunt Merry hightailed it over there and got him to convince the state she was mentally ill. And my uncle Shooter has high blood pressure, but not as high as the doctor writes on the reports." She grabbed a trash bag and started filling it with the detritus of forty people partying. "It's stealing, pure and simple. I guess it's better than knocking over a liquor store…which Ricky did two years in jail for…but it's still stealing."

"It makes you sad, doesn't it," Maddie said, stopping to face Cody and capture her in a hug.

"Yeah, and it's embarrassing. They know better. My granny raised them better than that."

"It's all right," Maddie said, holding her gaze. "What they do doesn't reflect on you."

"It does, but I hope it doesn't make you think too badly of them."

"What I think of them isn't nearly as important as what I think of you." She tightened her hug and kissed Cody's cheek. "And I'm constantly impressed by your work ethic and your morality. You're a very good person, and I respect the hell out of you."

"Thanks." She was always skittish about being complimented, and she quickly slid out of the embrace and got to work.

They made their way around the property, filling bag after bag. As Maddie was picking up cups from near the foundation, she stood there for a second, perplexed. "Wasn't the footprint supposed to be over there?" she asked, pointing at a smudge of orange on the scrubby grass.

"Yeah, but Jimmy convinced me to go up, rather than out. It's cheaper to have a second floor than a bigger foundation and more roof. So the bedroom will be on the second floor, and the first will be all open. The only walls will be around the bathroom."

"That's nice. I hate to go in public."

"It's gonna be sweet," Cody said, grinning like a child. "And doing it all by myself was the best idea I've ever had."

She was clearly building it herself. With no discussion, no input, and no assistance from her alleged girlfriend. Maddie tried hard not to sulk, but it wasn't easy. The last thing she wanted was to be a nag; that determination made her hold her tongue when she probably should have spoken up. But Cody clearly had an independent streak a mile wide. That was a core element of her personality. If Maddie didn't like it, she'd have to move on because Cody wasn't the kind of woman who changed easily.

"How was work today?" Cody asked after another few minutes of picking up cans and cups.

"Skipped it. Instead, I went on a very long hike in the woods. First time I've ever been alone in nature. I kinda loved it."

Cody beamed a smile, held a hand up and slapped it against Maddie's. "Of course you loved it! Nature's inside all of us. We just have to let it out."

"But there was something I didn't like about it."

"What's that?"

She almost laughed at herself. "People. I like it so much better to walk around with you and never see another soul."

"Oh, yeah." Cody nodded energetically. "You have to go wilderness trekking for that. Can you read a compass?"

Maddie stared at her for a second. "That can't possibly be a serious question. The mall has a map. A compass isn't required."

"Oops. Sorry." She led the way over to a picnic table and sat down. "Devin and I made this the other night," she said, inclining her head. "I hope the varnish is dry."

Maddie jumped up to feel her pants, but Cody just laughed at her. "It's dry. Your butt was on that very seat hours ago."

"You're such a tease!"

"Hey, did I tell you my uncle Shooter wants me to cancel the order for his new modular home?"

"Cancel it?"

"Yep. He wants a log cabin." She grinned with pride. "And he wants to build it himself."

"That's great! You're setting a very good example."

"I hope so. I assume my cousins will want log homes after they see mine. I'll help them, of course. That'll also save me a ton of money." She showed her evil grin, which Maddie found remarkably alluring.

"Are you going to *offer* to help them? I mean, will you make it clear that building a new house is an option?"

That dark head shook. "No, I'd rather wait for them to decide they're interested."

"But if they don't know it's an option..."

"They should know." She nodded briefly, her mind clearly made up. "I've told them I'd buy them what they wanted."

"But building your own home is a different thing. Doing that would encourage them to be active participants, instead of just taking money from you. Don't you want that?"

Her expression hardened. "*They* should want that. I can't make them have a work ethic. If they want to sponge off me, I have to let it go."

"No, you really don't," Maddie heard herself say. Cody's eyes widened slightly. "You're being kinda passive aggressive about your money, and I don't think that's doing anyone any favors."

"How am I doing that?"

"You're almost daring them to ask for things they don't really need. It'd be so much better to give them some guidance, to let them know what's best. Offering a good, reasonable option is a lot better than letting them just pull ideas out of thin air."

"Mmm, I don't think so. I like to do my thing without anyone telling me what to do. They're the same."

Maddie reached over and took her hand. "That's not always a good thing in a relationship."

"What'd I do?" she asked, eyes wide.

Sighing, Maddie brought Cody's hand to her mouth and kissed it gently. She sucked at keeping her feelings to herself. "I wish you would have talked to me a little bit about the house. It hurts to think you don't even want my input."

"But...why would I want..." She stopped, bit her lip and started again. "I'm always interested in what you have to say. But I know what I want. I did the research and worked with Jimmy to make the best use of the land. I didn't think I needed help."

"When I do something important, I like to talk about it while I'm planning it."

"Yeah," Cody said, nodding, clearly confused. "I do that too. I talked to Jimmy. Do you know how to build a house?"

"No, I don't know a damn thing."

"Then..." She looked as puzzled as it was possible for a human to be. "Did I make a mistake? I don't really know..."

Wow. She didn't have a friggin' clue. "Don't sweat it. I'm just feeling a little fragile."

Cody went to her side of the picnic table, pulled Maddie to her feet and held her close. "Tell me about it. I don't want you to ever feel fragile around me."

"It's fine. I'm better now."

"If you ever have anything to say...any advice or anything...I really want to hear it," Cody said. "I just don't always think to ask."

"Okay. I'll try to say what's on my mind." She stood there, relishing the feel of Cody's embrace. It would take a long time for her to have the confidence to ask why the fuck Cody wasn't making plans for them as a couple. But she had no intention of shoving that concept down her throat if it wasn't something that Cody had the sense to consider. There was only so much you could force on a woman.

—⁓—

On Monday morning, Devin arrived at Cody's trailer a good half hour before she was planning on leaving for the worksite. She opened the door and stood in the doorway, watching him tromp across the drive and brush past her. As if he'd been expected for breakfast, he went into the kitchen and poured himself a cup of coffee. Then he sat on the ultra-low sofa and looked up at Cody. "She'll never stay with you," he said flatly.

Cody had already poured her own coffee, and she picked it up before sitting on her rocker. "Thanks for the...what would you call that...advice?"

"You can call it whatever you want to call it. It's a fact."

"I think I know Maddie better than you do, Devin. Maybe I should be the one worrying or not worrying about our relationship."

"I don't know why she got stuck in Greenville," he said, as though she hadn't even spoken, "but she couldn't have chosen it. She looks like one of those girls selling shampoo on TV. She don't belong here."

Cody thought about his observation for a moment. Maddie did have beautiful hair. But if she was gonna model, she should go for bras. That woman could fill out a bra like nobody's business. She had to work to force herself back into the conversation, shooing images of Maddie's breasts from her head. "She didn't choose to be here," she admitted. "But she's here now and I'm going to work to make sure she doesn't want to leave."

"She'll just break your heart."

"She might," she admitted. "But not on purpose. She's a damn good woman, and she'll only leave if she can't manage to stay."

"That's bullshit," he said bitterly. "No one comes to the hollow. People *leave* the hollow. It's a one-way road." His eyes narrowed and he added, "You only come here when you've got no choice." He was obviously referring to her mother, and that made her want to pop him one. He was right, but that didn't make it hurt less.

"I hope you're wrong. There's nothing I've ever hoped for so badly in my life." She leaned over and got nearly nose to nose with him. "But even if she leaves, I won't regret being with her. Maddie's worth risking everything for. *Everything.*"

He took a big gulp of coffee and put the mug down hard. "Are you ready?"

She went into her room and got her boots on, then followed him out to his Jeep. He turned and looked at her for a second. "I know I promised not to bring this up again, but I have to say one thing."

"Go ahead," she said, rolling her eyes.

"Lying with a woman is gonna send you to hell. Lying with *that* woman is gonna make your life on earth a living hell."

"I heard you," she said, trying hard not to let his words reach her heart. "You couldn't be more wrong, but I know it's important to you to be able to speak your mind. Now honor your promise and keep your thoughts between you and the God you believe in. The one *I* know doesn't punish people for loving each other."

He shot her a look, but then turned and got into the Jeep, not adding another word.

CHAPTER TWENTY-THREE

IT HAD TAKEN MONTHS of dogged effort, and Maddie had been forced to suffer rejection after rejection. But she had finally reached the goal she'd been seeking for nine years. And she didn't want it. At all.

Pulling up to park in front of the trailer, Maddie sat in her car until Cody popped her head out and waved. "Hi," she said, brightly, approaching the car. "Did you have a nice drive?"

"Sure." She got out and started to take her carryall from the backseat.

In the few seconds they'd stood there, Cody's smile dimmed. "Are you okay? You look…not quite right."

"Oh, I'm fine." She tried to up the wattage of her smile. "I had a tough week at work. So, what's on the agenda for today? Fishing?"

"We can if you want. But I thought it'd be nice to hike around and explore. We might find some surprises."

"That sounds great. Where should we start?"

Cody opened her door, deposited Maddie's carryall, picked up her own pack, then slung it over her shoulder. "Right here is good." She led the way, and they set off for points unknown. At least from Maddie's perspective. She assumed Cody could find her way out of Burma without a map.

After a good two hour trek, they came to a fairly dark, damp glade. "Come to mama!" Cody dashed over and grasped a branch, shaking it at Maddie. "Blueberries! Finally!"

Maddie walked over and watched as delight suffused Cody's whole being. She picked a few berries, popped them into her mouth and moaned like she was being stroked. "You've gotta have some."

Maddie picked and tasted a few. Cody wasn't exaggerating. "That's crazy good," she said, picking a few more.

"Few things better. Don't bother taking any that aren't perfect." She walked slowly, eyes scanning all around her. "There's more here. We've just gotta find 'em."

They hunted until they found another type of berry bush that Cody called dewberries. These were just as good, if a little less sweet, and the vines had a ton of fruit ready to be eaten.

Finally, they hit the big one…a stand of red, ripe berries just waiting to be picked. "Have at it," Cody announced. "Take as many as you can stuff in your cheeks."

"Are these raspberries?"

"We call 'em wineberries, but they're close to raspberries. And gooood."

Maddie loaded up, filling a cloth Cody handed her. Then they walked until they reached a clearing, with a big patch of long, lush green grass that the rain had knocked down into a carpet. Maddie started to sit, but Cody urged her to wait. "I brought a tarp. The last thing you want is chigger bites." She unfurled it and they both sat down, then dug into the berries.

Cody lay on her back and popped them into her mouth one at a time, seemingly savoring each. Maddie watched her, lying there in the sun, looking as happy as a cat with catnip. She almost chickened out, but she had to get it out. Do it *now*.

"Uhm…I got some good news the other day," she began.

Cody rolled onto her belly and gave Maddie her full attention. "Yeah?"

"Yeah. I uhm…went to Pittsburgh a couple of months ago to interview for a job."

Cody's smile disappeared. Her eyes grew wide, and she didn't move a muscle. "You never told me that," she whispered, her voice shaking.

"I didn't think anything would come of it. Plus, we hadn't been intimate…"

"You could have told me *after* we'd been intimate."

Maddie looked down, ashamed. "I should have. I'm sorry I didn't."

"Well, you wouldn't bring it up now if something hadn't happened."

"Something did. They called to offer me the job. It's…a good one…I think. In the headquarters of a much bigger bank. It'd probably be a little more secure than what I have now…"

A few seconds ticked by, then Cody swung around and sat up. "Tell me more about it."

"Well, there isn't a whole lot to tell. It'd be doing what I'm doing now, but one step up the ladder. I'd be responsible for six branches in north suburban Pittsburgh."

"That's a whole lot."

"Yeah, I suppose it is."

"Are you…What are you…?"

She couldn't bear to see the terrified look in those lovely brown eyes. "I want to take it. I want to live in a real city, with plays and good restaurants and a football team." She dropped her head into her hands for a moment. "But I want to be with you."

Her voice was almost dispassionate. Only someone who knew her well would hear the pain Cody tried to hide. "Then you have to make a choice."

"I want both." Maddie looked into her eyes, seeing the flat, cold, distant gaze Cody had shown when they'd first met.

"You can't have both." Cody scooted across the tarp on her knees, grasped Maddie by the arms and hauled her up until they were face to face. "I will love you with all my heart if you'll stay with me. But I can't go with you. I'd never make it in a city."

"You love me?" Maddie asked, fearing she'd imagined the words.

"Of course I love you." She pulled Maddie close and kissed her with such emotion that the only thing Maddie could think of, could feel, was Cody's warm, sweet mouth. Breaking the kiss, Cody whispered, "How can you not know that?"

"You've never told me…"

"I show you. And you show me. Every time we're together, Maddie. You show me how much you love me. I've just been waiting for your words to catch up to your actions."

"You know? You know I love you, but you didn't say anything?"

"I didn't want to push you."

"I wasn't sure you did…" she murmured, on the verge of tears when she thought of the nights she'd spent wondering how deep Cody's feelings went.

"Not sure?" Her voice grew louder. "Not sure? How could you not know?"

"You don't seem as…obsessed with me as I am with you. I thought maybe you were…" She closed her eyes, feeling more confused than she ever had. "I don't know what I thought, but I was afraid…afraid you weren't ready."

"I'm ready," Cody said, intensity burning in her eyes. "I'm ready to love you for the rest of my life. But you have to choose me, Maddie. I will not bind myself to you if I'm going to have to worry you'll take off the first time someone in New York offers you a job." She shook her gently. "I will *not* do that."

Maddie wrapped her arms around Cody as tightly as she could. "There isn't a city on earth that could make me happier than I am when we're together."

Cody cocked her head, as if she had to strain to hear. Then her lips moved silently, the way they sometimes did when she was figuring something out. "Do you mean that?"

"I do." A sense of peace filled her, like she'd been granted every wish she'd ever had. "I do, Cody. I would turn down a job in any city in the world to be with you."

"Any city? Any job?"

Joy filled her whole body as Maddie lunged at her, kissing her face, her neck, her lips. "*You're* my dream," she whispered. "Nothing on earth can match the time I spend with you."

"It can't?" Cody looked like she was hearing words from a foreign tongue.

"Nothing! You're worth more than New York, London, Paris, Beijing and New Delhi all rolled into one. You're my universe."

Cody pulled away just a little bit. Their faces were just inches from each other, and Maddie could see the uncertainty in the brown depths. "You love me enough to give up your dream?"

"Yes. Yes. Yes. I love you more than anything on this earth." She leaned forward and kissed her, breathing in the scent of her body, of the glade, of the fresh grass, of the sweet berries. "I love you."

Cody almost collapsed. She sat, legs splayed, her face a mass of confusion. "You're sure you can be happy in Greenville?"

Christ! Did she have to be dragged to every logical conclusion? "No, damn it! I can't live in that crummy apartment by myself. I want to be in Ramp, with you."

"You want to live in my house?"

"Don't you want me?"

"Of course! I just never, ever thought you'd be able to be happy here."

"But I told you I was going to give it my best. Didn't you believe me?"

"Yeah, but I didn't think you'd be able to do it."

Maddie grabbed her shoulders and stared into her eyes. "What did you think would happen?"

"I didn't let myself think any farther than knowing we were falling in love. Things just...trailed off after that."

"They trailed off?"

"I've told you before, I don't let myself get lost in thoughts about the future. I just try to stay on my toes and deal with what comes along."

That was it. She'd been telling Maddie how she was from the very beginning, but it had only now become clear. "Did you ever, even once, think of us living in your house together?"

"No." Cody's dark head shook slowly. "Never."

"You never had one image of us living in your new home?"

"Not one," she said somberly.

Maddie put a hand on her shoulder and pushed her gently. "No wonder you didn't ask for my input!"

"I thought you'd visit me, and stay overnight like on the weekends... but that's all."

"Oh, Cody. I'd give anything for you to be able to really dream, to plan, to hope..."

"That's never been very helpful in my experience," she said, looking away.

"Well, I dream about living with you, and in my dreams we have more than one bedroom! I want a place where my family can come to visit."

"I'll fix it," Cody said firmly. "Give me a month, and it'll be right."

"A month? I'll give you the rest of my life!"

Cody sat there, looking numb. "The rest of your life. You really want to be mine."

"I do, I do, I do. I've never been happier than when we're together."

"Even in the country?" she asked, clearly dubious.

"Especially in the country. When we're out stomping around together I'm as happy as I've ever been. I'm a country girl. It's surprised the hell out of me, but I'm a country girl."

"And you want to be *my* country girl. Mine alone."

"Yours alone. Forsaking all others." She grasped her shoulders and pulled her close for another kiss. Then, quick as lightening, the Cody'd who'd first swept her off her feet was back.

Cody scrambled to her feet and, grasping both of Maddie's hands, pulled her up. "I've tried hard to think about today…only today," she said, staring right into Maddie's eyes. "But I can't control my mind when I sleep. I've had a dream that haunts me." She closed her eyes and when they opened she whispered, "It doesn't have to ever haunt me again." Her smile blossomed and grew until it covered her entire face. "It can come true!" Without another word, she abandoned the tarp and her pack, and took off, leading Maddie by the hand as they scampered down narrow paths. They walked so quickly Maddie was panting, and even though they were deep in the forest it was hot and making her hotter from the effort.

Maddie was just about to beg for mercy when she vaguely recognized the place they'd first been fishing. Cody led her to a quiet spot and sat her on a boulder to begin undressing her.

Looking into her eyes, Maddie saw nothing but confidence. Sexy, devastatingly sexy confidence. "You look like you've got a plan." She rested her hands on Cody's shoulders, letting her work unencumbered.

"I do." One eyebrow went up and she smirked while she made quick work of Maddie's clothes. Then Cody shucked her own clothes, standing before Maddie naked and proud. "Every time I've been in this pool, I've thought about how wonderful it would be to share it with someone I loved. With someone who loved me." She whisked Maddie off her feet, making her giggle wildly. Then Cody took one sure step, then another, slowly lowering them into the clear, cold water.

Maddie shivered and squealed, but Cody held her tightly, not giving her a chance to get away. Not that you could have pried her away with a crowbar. Being held in Cody's arms was the best feeling on earth, and if she had to be doused in a cold pool to feel that—it was well worth it.

Cody dunked them, both sputtering when she popped up again. "We're born again," she called out loudly. "We're *us* now, Maddie. Not you and me. Us."

Hot tears fell to Cody's cheeks, warming her chilled skin. They were the happiest tears she'd ever shed. The ones that blessed their new life—their oneness.

When Cody carefully helped Maddie onto a smooth boulder it hit her like a truck. Everything was different now. Her body ached with desire, but they weren't playing any more. They were lovers.

Her focus went haywire for a second, almost like it had when she'd won the lottery. How did you make *love* to a woman? It had to be different than just having sex. It *had* to be. But what was the difference?

Maddie looked down at her, the beautiful smile melting Cody's heart. Her heart. That had to be it. It was time to stop protecting her heart. Time to let Maddie know how much she meant, how much she'd longed for her. How ridiculously happy she was at that very moment. It was awesome. Truly awesome.

Cody wrapped her arms around Maddie's incredible body. Nothing had ever felt better in her whole life. Nothing ever could.

Slow down. She closed her eyes and commanded her brain to focus. Love. This was love. Her body was humming with desire, but her heart had to speak too. Running her hands down Maddie's back, tenderly letting her fingers stroke her smooth skin helped center her. *Take it slow.* Maddie leaned into her, breathing deeply when her face pressed into her neck. That was just how *she* felt! Like she had to imprint Maddie's scent onto her brain. Like she could somehow pull her into her body by scent and touch alone.

Cody had so many urges, so much to say, so many questions. But her heartbeat settled into a slow, easy rhythm when she held Maddie in her arms. It was like they formed some kind of loop—where Maddie's scent and the sensation of holding her connected to Cody's heart, smoothing everything out. She felt like she could stay right there, simply holding her, for the rest of her life, and die a very, very happy woman.

Delicate eyelashes tickled her skin when they fluttered. "I love you," Maddie whispered.

Cody placed her hands on either side of Maddie's sweet face and gazed at her for the longest time. The water she stood in was cool, almost bracing. The scent of the earth was lush, rich and filled with life. The air bristled with the songs of birds. And the most beautiful creature of them all looked up at her with love-filled eyes. *Perfection. True perfection.*

Maddie sat on the boulder, looking into Cody's beautiful eyes. The eyes that had captured her heart months earlier. They'd done nothing but hold each other for the longest time, but Maddie was sure she'd never get tired of the sensation. Simply holding the woman she loved was as soothing a sensation imaginable.

Trailing her hand down Cody's back, she felt her shiver. "I think you're going to turn blue," she murmured into her perfectly shaped ear.

"I don't mind." When she lifted her head the smile she revealed was luminous. "Not a bit."

"Maybe we should dry off. I'd never forgive myself if you caught pneumonia." She slapped her hand onto the boulder. "And my butt's getting numb."

Cody laughed and put her hands on Maddie's waist, picking her up and settling her on the floor of the pool. "It *is* a little chilly. I stopped noticing a while ago, but that might be because I can't feel my feet."

They climbed out and tried to dry each other, using their clothes. It was ungainly and inefficient, but a heck of a lot of fun. Once dressed, they walked, hand in hand, eventually getting back to the clearing where their gear was.

With a devilish look in her eyes, Cody asked, "Have you ever made love outside?"

"No, I can't say that I have. I'd like to, though. How about right this second?"

In moments, they were naked, and Maddie reflected that she actually did feel born again. Her skin was cool and clean and all of the concerns and worries of the last weeks had floated away. She felt as innocent as a new baby, ready to begin what would undoubtedly be a fantastic life with the woman she loved.

Cody knelt, tugging Maddie down with her. Then they kissed, slowly and deliberately, as if they each needed every kiss to be memorable. Eventually, they tumbled to the ground, lying on their sides as they kissed with a growing intensity.

Pulling away just a few inches, Cody breathed, "I will never stop loving you. *Never.*"

"I know that." And she did. Cody would be her only love for the rest of her life. She would have staked her life on that promise without a second thought. "I feel the same. Exactly the same. Forever, Cody."

Tears showed in those warm, brown eyes and Maddie choked up as well. She would never tire of showing Cody what was in her heart, or learning her secrets. They were a pair. They were inviolate.

Her heart had been given free rein for a long time. Now every other part of her needed to vent. Cody purposefully let her body speak. She roamed over Maddie's body as if to devour her. Kissing every bit of skin, nibbling on her ears, her neck, her breasts. Every part was tender and divine. "I can't get enough of you," she murmured, her head swimming.

"It's overwhelming. But so, so nice."

Cody looked up and met her eyes. "It is. Nicer than I ever could have dreamed."

"Let yourself dream," Maddie soothed, stroking Cody's hair. "Let it in, baby. Let it in."

Cody opened her heart and let her dreams come true. Every one was lying right in front of her, and she dipped her head once again, filling her senses with the beauty of their love.

It took hours to get home. Maddie knew it was going to be a long trip when Cody stopped not fifty feet from the glade and pulled her to her chest, holding her tightly for a minute or two. "Do you still love me?" Then, without letting Maddie reply, she giggled. "Just checking," she said, her shy smile making an appearance.

"I'm not going anywhere," Maddie assured her.

"Yeah, but I might have hit my head and dreamed all of this. I need to keep checking until any possible damage has been resolved."

Maddie kissed her cheek, then took her hand and started off again. This time they got a few hundred yards before Cody pulled her to a stop.

Stopping every few hundred feet to kiss and giggle and share their excitement didn't get them home quickly, but it was too much fun to forego.

When they finally made it to the trailer and stood inside, a bit of the spell was broken. They both looked about nervously, unsure about what to do next. "Are you as hungry as I am?" Cody asked.

"I'm not sure. Could you eat squirrel?"

Smiling slyly, Cody said, "I love squirrel. Stewed, braised, fricasseed…"

Maddie put her fingers to her lips. "Then, no, I'm not as hungry as you are." She wrapped her arms around her and squeezed tightly. "But I'm still starving."

"Everything I have is frozen solid and I don't have a microwave."

"If I don't get something soon I'm gonna eat one of your books."

"Then it's on to Greenville."

Maddie reached into the properly repaired bookcase and picked out a big, hard-backed novel. "Just in case the grocery store's closed."

After Cody packed a change of clothes in a paper bag, they got into Maddie's car and headed out. "I remember the first time I saw you open your car doors," Cody said. "I thought that little beeper thing was about the neatest thing I'd ever seen."

Maddie spared a quick, loving glance. "I remember that very day. That's the day I saw your cousin, sitting in the front seat, glowering at me while holding a shotgun across his lap. I almost wet myself!"

"We were a pair," Cody admitted. "I was so nervous I didn't have the sense to realize a guy with PTSD wasn't the best choice to ride shotgun. He would've blown somebody's head off if they'd looked at us cross-eyed."

"I'm *so* glad I don't know how to cross my eyes." They laughed at that, both lost in their memories of those early days. Those sweet early days that had led them right to where they needed to be.

———

They stopped at the grocery store, then zoomed back to Maddie's place. Both very hungry, they made sandwiches like they were in a race, throwing cold cuts and cheese at the bread while giggling. "I need mustard and mayonnaise and pickles,"Cody said as she poked around in the refrigerator. "Where's your mayonnaise? And your pickles? No horseradish?"

Maddie shrugged her shoulders. "Sorry?"

"I might have to reassess. I don't know if I can love a woman who doesn't love condiments."

"I'll start." She headed for the door, grabbing her keys on the way. "I'll buy every condiment they have and be back before you know it."

Cody ran for her, wrapping her in a bear hug. "No way. You might come to your senses and never return. I'll give up condiments before you." She picked up a sandwich, dressed with only mustard, and held it in front of Maddie's mouth. "Bite," she instructed. Then she took the next bite and they traded off, demolishing the snack in scant minutes.

Even after eating, Cody felt just as much at loose ends as she had at home. The newness of the situation had her off her pins and feeling skittish.

"I think you and I would fit really nicely into my shower," Maddie said, eying Cody slowly. "Wanna try?"

"Race you." Cody took off, blocking the door with her hip when Maddie tried to scamper past her. "I win!" She grabbed Maddie and started to peel her clothes off, getting her naked in seconds. "Now I *really* win."

Maddie returned the favor, removing Cody's shirt and unzipping her shorts, her temperature rising as the pants slowly fell to the floor. Then she put her hands on her ass and squeezed. "I love these strangely girly camouflage shorts," she said, chuckling. "I've never seen pink camouflage."

"I guess that's what I get for letting my cousin's ten year old daughter go shopping with us."

"The kid has good taste."

Unable to keep from giggling, Cody explained, "They're part of a system. I've got these boy shorts, and long underwear, and base layers...I had no idea underwear had advanced to such heights.

"They look great on you," Maddie purred, palming her butt repeatedly. "And even better off you."

Cody was blanketed with chills. Having Maddie's hands roam all over her body made her skin come alive in ways that were entirely new. Entirely new and remarkably wonderful. "I think I'm gonna have to make love to you again," she said, trying to sound serious. "I'm just gonna have to."

"I would argue...but I'm not crazy. Let's go!"

———

They were sparkling clean, fairly well fed, and sleepy when they finally climbed into bed. But Maddie jumped up, dashed back into the living room, and returned with something hidden behind her back.

"A present?" Cody asked.

"Yeah. For me." She presented Cody with a copy of *A Tale of Two Cities*, taken from her trailer.

Cody took the book, turning it over in her hands. "What...?"

Maddie climbed in next to her and rested her head on her chest. "I want to go to sleep every night hearing you read to me. I know you love Dickens, and I want to love him too."

Sweet memories filled Cody's head and she couldn't stop the tears from falling. "I wish my mama could have known you." She kissed the top of Maddie's head and felt a bit of warm liquid trickle onto her skin. Maddie was crying too. "Mama loved this book. I think it was her favorite."

Sniffling, Maddie whispered, "Then it's the best one to start with."

Cody cleared her throat and began, "It was the best of times..." She choked up again. "It *is* the best of times," she murmured. "The very best of times."

CHAPTER TWENTY-FOUR

CODY LEANED AGAINST THE back of the straight-backed chair that Maddie kept by a little desk in her bedroom. She'd been awake for a while, and when she couldn't lie in bed another minute she got up, put her shirt and underwear back on, then straddled the chair.

Yesterday was still shining like a bright new dime in her memory, and she hadn't been able to get her mind around the whole thing. Maddie loved her. Was *in* love with her. She rocked back and forth, agitated by the thoughts that roared through her mind. How in the world could that be? How could she possibly keep a woman like Maddie happy?

Slowly, Maddie's arm started to move, and her hand went to the empty space next to her. "Cody?" she called out, her voice thick from sleep.

Cody could feel a big smile settle onto her face. How could you not smile when you heard that voice? "Yeah?" she sat on the bed next to Maddie and scratched her back, getting a chill when Maddie stretched like a cat. Watching her body move around under the thin sheet was as erotic an image as Cody could imagine.

"Why are you awake?"

"Just habit, I guess." She idly patted Maddie's back, then decided to stop wasting time and put it out there. "I've been thinking."

She must have sounded serious, because Maddie flipped over and those pretty blue eyes looked up at her wide with alarm. "Is everything okay?"

"Oh, sure. Sure." She kept touching her gently, finding the solidity of her body reassuring. "I'm just feeling…kinda…amazed, I guess. Yeah, that's a good word for it."

A slow, satisfied smile crept onto Maddie's lips. "It's amazing I didn't realize this months ago. Amazingly stupid."

"You knew…months ago?"

"The first time we spent the day together," she said thoughtfully. "If I would have concentrated on how I felt, instead of what I should do and where I should work and all of that crazy stuff…I could have gotten to the good parts a hell of a lot sooner."

"But why?" Cody got up the nerve to ask. "Why do you love me? We're so different…"

Maddie slipped out of Cody's embrace and sat up. Putting a hand on each shoulder, she looked at her for a long time. "We're ridiculously similar. We both like simple things, simple pleasures, and honest, loyal people. Everything else is details. Inconsequential details."

"But I've never done anything. I've never been anywhere, gone to college, been to a real shopping mall. Nothing!"

"I've been to enough malls for both of us." She placed a soft kiss on Cody's lips. "If you really want to go, I'll take you to the one in Charleston."

"Be serious now." She put her hand on Maddie's cheek and looked into her eyes. "We didn't have running water when I was a little girl and I spent my summers with my granny. We used outhouses. Think about that. We're *country*, Maddie. As country as can be."

Maddie put her hand on Cody's cheek again, and stroked it tenderly. "I didn't plan on falling in love with a woman from the mountains. But I'm betting you didn't expect to fall in love with a city girl. We match, Cody. We just do."

"That's really enough?" She wanted to believe more than she'd ever wanted anything. "You really think so?"

"I know it is." Her hand slipped down and she held it over Cody's rapidly beating heart. "It's what's in here that matters." She took Cody's hand and put it over her own heart. "And mine is bursting with love for you."

"What about your job? It's a long way to Greenville."

"I've been worried about that," Maddie admitted. "That's a sticking point."

"I understand. When you have an important job, it must be hard to even think about leaving it."

"Oh, God, that's not it! I'm worried about you feeling like I'm another mouth you have to feed. I'd quit my job in a hot second if I could be sure you wouldn't feel I was taking advantage of you."

Cody lunged for Maddie's cell phone. "Call them and quit," she demanded. "Call them right now."

Maddie started to laugh, the sound so massively beautiful, Cody got tears in her eyes. "I don't need to do that. We'll figure something out. I don't really want to drive that far, but I don't want to sit around and watch the grass grow, either. I need to do something with my time."

"I can keep you busy. You just follow along beside me and you'll be able to hit a squirrel from a hundred paces within the year."

"Yeah. About that…" She hugged Cody close. "We need a different plan."

"I was teasing. But I'd be very happy to have you waiting for me when I got home from wherever I was traipsing about. That would be a fine way to end the day."

"Waiting isn't my thing. We'll have to work on a plan," Maddie said, smiling serenely. "Together."

They stood in front of Cody's trailer on Sunday evening, holding each other so tightly they seemed to be welded together. "Are you sure you can't come back to Greenville with me?" Maddie asked.

"No, I've got Jimmy coming back first thing, and my uncles and cousin show up early. I'd have to leave so early you wouldn't know I'd been there."

"Oh, I'd know. But I don't want you to be driving that much anyway. I just want you to know how welcome you are."

"I feel pretty welcome," Cody said, kissing Maddie's cheek. "I've never felt more welcome."

Maddie pulled away and stroked her face with her fingertips. "I've got everything memorized. Don't change anything." She got into her car and immediately rolled down the window to offer one last kiss. "I love you with all my heart." She gazed up at her, feeling as lovesick as a woman could be.

"I love you just as much. Now promise me you'll drive safely."

"I will. Promise me you'll go right to bed. I can see how tired you are."

"I will." She leaned in and placed one last, sweet kiss on Maddie's lips. "I love you."

Maddie sighed and put the car in reverse. She was physically ill, her stomach turning in knots at the thought of leaving. But she had a job to do, and so did Cody. For now, they'd have to continue to live for the weekend.

―――

The next afternoon, Jimmy put his hammer down at four thirty and went to grab a beer. Cubby and Shooter were right behind him, then Devin ambled over and took out a cold one. Cody watched them, trying to think of a way to get rid of the whole bunch of them. Even though she and Maddie had agreed to wait until the weekend to see each other, there was no way she could hold out. It didn't matter if they only had an hour or two together—she just had to see her. This was what being in love must be like —a craving for togetherness, the likes of which she'd never had.

It was actually a little uncomfortable, and she knew she'd fall off the roof if she kept daydreaming like she had been all day. But thoughts of Maddie filled her head like a hive of bees had gotten inside. Buzzing, buzzing, buzzing with thoughts and images of her spectacular girlfriend.

Grabbing a beer just to be sociable, Cody sat on a log and tried to keep up with the conversation. But she could only think of one thing… Maddie in her business suit, sitting at her desk. Looking pretty…and smart…and clever…and…

―――

Cody was in such a hurry to get to Greenville that she almost skipped stopping at home. But she was sweaty and dirty and couldn't imagine she'd make a very good impression covered in sawdust.

She ran for the shower, scrubbing the dirt away as quickly as her washcloth would send it down the drain. Grabbing the first pair of shorts she found, she hopped into them while looking for a clean shirt. Her shoes were on but untied, and she was running a comb through her wet hair when she stepped outside—to hear a familiar engine creep down the drive. Maddie.

Cody stood on the step, grinning like her face would split. "I forgot to put on underwear," she chuckled as Maddie got out of her car. "I was so hot to see you I almost skipped taking a shower."

Maddie walked over and put her cheek up against Cody's chest. "I could stand here all night just listening to your heart beat." She tilted her head up and smiled. "I'm gonna lose my job if I can't concentrate better than I did today."

"Did you stay until closing, or just wander away?" Maddie looked utterly confused. She was cuter than a bug's ear.

"I think we were closed." She chuckled. "If not, I locked people inside."

"Come on in. The least I can do is feed you."

Maddie gave her a look that no earthly woman could have resisted. "I can eat at home." She put her arms around Cody, letting one hand trail down and cup her ass. "You've got something much better than food to fill me up with."

—⁘—

They lay together in the warm bedroom, hoping for a breeze. Maddie didn't know how Cody had lived for so many years in this small space, with few windows and no air conditioning. Maybe she'd developed a unique body temperature regulatory system, since she wasn't even sticky.

"Do you feel really different now?" Maddie asked.

"Different how?"

Sitting up and bracing herself on an elbow, Maddie gazed at the lovely planes of Cody's face. Some new drive made it impossible not to touch a part of her, so she satisfied her need by gently trailing a finger along each feature. Examining Cody's eyebrows, she said, "You seem a lot more…intense. Yeah, that's the word. Like your emotions are in another gear."

"It feels completely new," Cody admitted. "The minute you told me you loved me, everything changed."

"Not for me. Telling you how I felt was more incremental for me. It was like a step. A really good step, of course, but a step I thought would come."

Cody laughed. "It was like jumping off a cliff for me. I thought I was crazy about you before, but that was just playing. It's like you've taken over my brain!"

Maddie leaned over and kissed her tenderly. "That's how it feels to be in love. You were holding back before."

"I didn't know that. I truly didn't."

"I was hoping you were holding back," Maddie admitted. "I was starting to feel like I was a lot more into you than you were into me."

Cody's eyes grew wide and she lost a little of her color. "That's not true! That was never true!"

Patting her gently, Maddie said, "Maybe not. But I felt that way and it was starting to worry me." She draped herself along Cody's body and held her tightly. "This is much better. I feel very, very loved."

"If anyone loved a woman more than I love you…" She grinned. "No one ever has, so I don't have anything to compare it to."

"I love you," Maddie whispered. "More than I'll ever be able to tell you."

"Can I talk about us? I'd like to watch a bunch of jaws drop when I tell everyone we're in love. They probably assume you'll move away and I'll go for that little old banty rooster I told you about."

"Go right ahead. I woke my parents up to tell them last night."

Eyes wide, Cody said, "Did you really?"

"Heck, yes! Neither of them can take calls at work, and I couldn't wait until they got home today." She put her hands on Cody's shoulders and playfully tugged her back and forth. "Being in love is big news!"

"Uhm, what if our big news reaches the bank?"

"Well, West Virginia doesn't have employment protection for sexual orientation discrimination. I suppose I could lose my job." She shrugged, realizing she didn't care. "But I'd rather collect moss with you than hide who I am."

Cody tickled under her chin. "I could probably float you a loan if you get into trouble."

"No, thanks. I need to work, Cody. The more I think about it, the more sure I am. You need your things and I need mine, and I don't have any in Ramp."

"We could…" She sat there for a minute, looking like she was searching hard for ideas. "Open some kind of business. Then you wouldn't have to work for anyone else."

Maddie tenderly stroked her cheek, then placed a soft kiss there. "No, I'm really not the type. I'll keep doing my job and see what happens." She started to get up, but Cody grabbed her and placed her on her lap, kissing all over her neck and chest.

"If anyone says one cross word to you, I'll take every cent I have out of that bank. Then I'll buy the building and evict 'em!"

"I like the way you think."

They lay together and touched and kissed, just enjoying the closeness. But it was after eight, and Maddie had to get home. Driving an hour in the morning was not appealing, even though sleeping with Cody certainly was. "Help me find my clothes, I need to get back to town. You undressed me so quickly I barely knew what hit me."

"Get used to that," Cody said, slapping Maddie on the butt when she got up. "That too," she added, letting her devilish smile show.

They both got dressed. Cody put on jeans and a sweatshirt, then she stepped into and laced up her boots. Maddie understood about the boots. Cody had convinced her that going barefoot wasn't a good idea, given the wide variety of things in the area that bit, but she was wondering what made a woman wear jeans and a sweatshirt when it was hot and a light jacket when it was bitterly cold. It was beyond her ken.

It was clear Cody didn't want her to leave, but Maddie just couldn't function if she had to get up at five. That extra hour of sleep somehow made a big difference. "Hey!" Cody said brightly. "I just had an idea. Let's go somewhere to celebrate!"

"Celebrate?"

"Being in love." Her eyes were shining and she looked like she'd wag her tail if she had one. "I really want to." Cody took off, jogging down a dark path, Maddie carefully trailing behind her.

"Where are you going? How can you see?"

"Easy. I've been walking around here forever." She stood in front of the tree she'd pointed out weeks earlier. "Give me a second." Then she wrapped her arms around the trunk and started to climb. Maddie stood on the ground, mouth wide open in amazement. Cody climbed like she was five years old and weighed forty pounds. Her body moved steadily, pushing up with her booted feet, and grasping further up the tree with every push. When she reached the right spot, she dug around for a minute, then grabbed something and dropped it, almost hitting Maddie on the head. "Sorry," she called out, then quickly came back down, once again grasping the trunk with her feet and shimmying down gracefully.

Maddie was still standing exactly where Cody had left her. "I'm....I've never seen an adult do something like that."

"The moss doesn't just jump off on its own," she said, with her own brand of logic.

"So you just go from tree to tree? Climbing all day?"

Cody laughed. "Most moss is on the ground. It does best on a rock by a stream or a pond." She was still chuckling when she reached down and picked up the packet, then carefully tore off the plastic grocery bags she'd wrapped around it. "I can't believe you thought I had to climb trees all day," she chuckled quietly. Finally, she held a stack of bills in her hand, then bowed and handed them to Maddie. "Decide where you want to go. Do it up big. I want you to spend every dime."

Maddie fanned herself with the bills. "No...really?" She had never wanted Cody's money, but having a big pile of it in her hand was a bit thrilling.

"Yep. If that's not enough, let me know." She pulled Maddie close and kissed her, lingering as she slowly pulled each lip in and raked her teeth over it. "You're giving up every big city in the world for me. The least I can do is pay for us to go places you'd like to see. I don't want you to have one need that isn't met, Maddie." The determination in her eyes was actually startling. "Not one."

"I don't really need to go anywhere..."

"Plan a trip," Cody said firmly. "I've always wanted to fly on an airplane. Give me a reason."

Maddie tapped her on the shoulder with the bills. "It's a deal."

—⁂—

Cody found herself praying for rain. They didn't work during storms, and as much as she wanted her new home, she wanted Maddie worse. She went to Greenville, Maddie came up to Ramp, or they met for nachos in Twined Creek. Cody was dismayed by her inability to go a whole day without seeing Maddie, but at least she was in good company.

A week later they were sitting in the roadhouse in Twined Creek, having a beer and snacking on the sandwiches Maddie had brought from Greenville. Nachos were fine in limited quantities, but she'd had her fill. The other patrons gave them puzzled looks, but she wasn't about to let that deter her from making sure Cody had a semi-decent meal.

Cody sipped at her beer, a satisfied grin on her face. "I'm happy," she said. "Just thought I'd let you know."

Maddie didn't know the area or the inhabitants well enough to be openly affectionate, so she reached under the table and patted Cody's leg until she got the hint and took her hand. "I'm assuming it's not a good idea to kiss you in public around here."

"It'd probably be fine, but I might have to get into a scuffle or two, depending on how much people have had to drink."

"We'll leave early and make out in the car." Maddie chuckled. "I don't want that pretty face rearranged."

Maddie thought about their interactions with the local populace. Two single women sitting in a roadhouse attracted a certain amount of attention, and when one of them was a recent lottery winner that attention increased. Maddie'd noticed that an occasional man would start to make his way over to them, but someone always reached out and stopped him. What they said was beyond her imagination, but it was always effective.

A few minutes later, she had her answer. Ricky came rolling in, a brassy-looking woman on his arm. Like the Sea of Galilee, the crowd parted, letting him and his lady friend walk unimpeded up to the bar.

"Your cousin makes quite an entrance," Maddie said, and Cody followed her gaze.

"Yeah. He's well known around here. *Ricky!*" She called out loudly, amazing Maddie with her uncharacteristic brashness.

He turned and offered a friendly wave to both of them. "What's shakin'?" he asked when he sauntered over.

"Not much. We're just having a drink. Can I buy you a round?"

"Don't mind if you do," he said, grinning and showing a gap that Maddie was sure used to contain a tooth. Looked like another visit to the dentist was in order.

Cody stood, pulled a twenty from her wallet and handed it to him. "We've got to scoot. See you later."

Maddie got up and followed her, and when they got in the car said, "What was that all about?"

"Nothing. I just like everyone to know who I'm related to. The roadhouse can be a very rough place, but most people know not to mess with Montgomerys."

"Then why'd we leave so fast? I barely had two sips of my beer."

Cody laughed. "Even though most people know not to mess with Montgomerys, a few knuckleheads haven't gotten the message. Ricky loves to fight, and I didn't want any shattered glass coming your way." She bowed in a rather courtly fashion. "You can thank me later."

Maddie took her hand and led her to the car. When they were seated, she reached over Cody to lower her seat. "I'll thank you now."

They spent a good half hour making out like teenagers, pawing each other through their clothes, and steaming up the windshield. "You make me crazy," Cody finally murmured, pulling away and fanning herself. "I could burst into flames."

Maddie placed delicate kisses on her flushed cheeks. "Back to Ramp? I'm game."

Cody wrapped her in a fervid hug. "God, I want to. But that's too much driving for you. Call me when you get home and we can have phone sex." She waggled her eyebrows. "I've never done that."

"I haven't either. Let's see if we can burn the wires up."

"You're on." She opened her door and let the scant breeze enter. "I have to sit here for a bit to cool off first. My hands are shaking too much to drive."

Maddie held one of her own out, and they laughed when it twitched. "Ditto." Their seats were as low as they could go, and they lay there, trying to calm themselves. "You're so pretty," Maddie said, gazing at Cody's profile. "I sit at my desk and try to picture you but I can never get it right."

She let her fingers trail along Cody's features. "The images I can bring up aren't close to how beautiful the real thing is."

Cody took her hand and kissed it, then looked at it in the dim light. "You have such pretty hands." Another kiss followed, then another, with Cody soon closing her eyes and lavishing kisses up Maddie's arm.

"That turns me on," Maddie whispered. "Everything you do turns me on. My hands were never erogenous zones until right this minute."

Cody's eyes blinked slowly. "I don't think we're doing a good job of calming down. If there was a motel anywhere near here…"

Maddie scooted up and looked to her left. "The woods?"

Letting out a soft laugh, Cody said, "Mosquitos, ticks and chiggers." She waited a beat. "It's worth it to me."

Wrapping her arms around Cody, Maddie cradled her in her arms. "I'm in with mosquitos, but ticks scare me, and I have no idea what chiggers are."

"You do not want to know," Cody said somberly. She raised her seat and settled her hair. "Phone sex isn't gonna do it. On to Greenville." She started to step out but Maddie put a restraining hand on her arm.

"Are you sure? You'll have to get up an hour earlier."

Cody smiled warmly. "Losing an hour of sleep to gain an hour making love to you? No contest."

—⁓—

The next night, Maddie called as soon as she got home from work. "I've got an idea for how to spend some quality time together without either of us having to drive home in the morning. Are you game?"

"Silly question. Name it and I'm there."

An hour later they met in the deserted parking lot of the Twined Creek Medical Center. Cody got out of her car and walked over to where Maddie had just pulled in. "Nice parking lot," she said, smirking.

Maddie jumped out of her car, and Cody let out a low wolf whistle.

"Good thing it's summer," Maddie said, doing a quick twirl to show off her simple cornflower blue print sundress. "This plan would be impossible in cold weather."

"Boy, you look good," Cody said, nearly salivating. "I'm crazy about you in a dress."

"Grab the picnic basket from the back seat and follow me." They took a few steps, heading for a grassy area behind the building. Maddie turned sharply and made a tsking sound. "Are you checking out my ass?"

"I *am*," Cody said, sounding a little slow witted. "I'm glad it was winter when we met, 'cause I would have made an even bigger fool of myself if you'd been walking around the bank in that dress."

"I don't wear dresses like this to work. This is for play."

"Whatever game you want to play, I'm ready to go."

Maddie wrapped a hand around Cody's arm. "I'm sure you'll like this one." She stopped her when they were completely out of sight from any vantage point in the parking lot. It was dusk and there wasn't a single light on in the clinic, further evidence that they'd have their privacy. Maddie reached into the basket and pulled out a blanket, then snapped it open and laid it on the ground. "I looked chiggers up today. They shouldn't be able to get through a wool blanket. Same for ticks." She sat down and took the basket from Cody. "I have sandwiches and a pretty good-looking fruit salad."

Cody dropped down to sit alongside her. "You're a very good provider. My shorts would fall off me if you weren't making sure I got fed at night."

With her eyes bugging out in alarm, Maddie grasped Cody by the shoulders and placed a long, sweet kiss on her lips. "I was so immersed in our picnic, I forgot to kiss you the second I saw you!"

"Don't let it happen again," Cody growled. "Kisses come first."

They dug into their repast, with Cody nearly inhaling the food. It seemed like she was consciously trying to slow herself down when she said, "Hey, have you planned our trip yet? We could get away for a long weekend any time you want."

"No, I haven't really given it much thought. I don't want to mess up your schedule."

A dark expression settled onto Cody's face. "I worry about you stuck here. We've got to do the things you like to balance off doing the things that I like."

Maddie squeezed her hand, smiling warmly. "I appreciate that. But I'm fine. We can wait until your house is finished."

"We really don't need to. Let's go to New York. Next weekend."

"New York?" Maddie's eyebrows popped up. "That's where you want to go?"

"Not necessarily, but I think that's where *you'd* like to go. It's the biggest city in the country, right?"

"Yeah, but I could be happy going dozens of places. I want you to pick the first place we go."

"Me? You want me to pick?"

"I do. Pick someplace you've always wanted to see. Someplace you've wondered about. Any place in the whole world."

Remarkably, it only took a few seconds. "England," she said simply.

"England? London?"

"Yeah, that one. I want to see the places Jane Austen wrote about and where *Middlemarch* took place. And London, of course, to see whatever's left from Dicken's time. Oh, the places from *Vanity Fair* too. Could we do that?"

Excitement building, Maddie nodded vigorously. "We certainly could. But that'll take a lot longer than a weekend."

"If you give me two weeks at home during deer hunting season, I'll go for as long as you think we should."

"We're not leaving that garden," Maddie teased. "I've been dreaming about those tomatoes and that sweet corn."

"Fine. We'll go in the fall, once the garden's spent. Will you plan the trip?"

"I'd run home and start now, but I've got a date with a hot woman."

Cody took the last bite of her sandwich, then lay back on the blanket and stretched out. "This is a nice date."

Maddie lay down and cuddled up alongside her. "Wanna make it nicer?" she asked, trying to put as much seduction into her voice as possible.

"I truly do," Cody said, a happy grin covering her face.

Putting her hands on Cody cheeks, Maddie held her still and kissed her tenderly. In seconds, the tender kisses gave way to bolder ones, and soon they were grinding against each other, their desire spiraling out of control. "I want you so bad," Cody whispered. "I never knew how crazy love could make you." She blinked slowly. "I can't get enough of you."

Maddie placed Cody's hand on her thigh, kissing her hotly while moving her hand up and up until it came to rest on her ass.

Cody groaned as she filled her hand with smooth, bare flesh. "You brazen thing," she murmured. "Going out in public with no panties."

"Just trying to save a few seconds."

Cody's hand hadn't stopped caressing bare skin. "You're so hot. I'm *so* lucky."

"I'm the lucky one," Maddie insisted, kissing her again and again. "You won the lottery, but I won you."

It took four more weeks, four incredibly long weeks to get the house, or more correctly, houses ready for fixtures and furnishings. Cody had created another clearing, laid another foundation, and built another, smaller log home to house guests and a home office. It would only have an efficiency kitchen, but it would be ideal for Maddie's parents, who were already begging to visit. All of that work had really set Cody's schedule back, but she seemed very, very happy with it. The little house was close to the main house, but not too close. Whoever stayed there would feel like they had their own place, and she and Maddie wouldn't have to worry about being overheard—which was vital for a private person like Cody.

The occupancy permit hadn't been issued yet, but that would come any day. When Maddie drove up on Friday night, Cody was waiting for her, freshly showered and neatly dressed. "Who inaugurated her new shower?" Maddie asked, sniffing all around her fresh-smelling neck.

"I did. I'll tell the inspector I was just testing it. It was awesome, by the way. Come on in. I've been waiting for you."

They went in hand-in-hand, unconsciously slipping into that habit every time they were together. Maddie made a fuss over every neat detail that had been added in the last five days, praising Cody's choices and her skills in assembling everything.

Standing in front of a large, double sliding glass doors, they stared at the mountain across from them, both enraptured by its beauty. "I want to see that every morning when I wake up," Cody said. "Right after I see you lying next to me, of course. You'll always be first, because you're prettier than the most beautiful landscape in the world."

"Are you ready to take the leap?" She beamed a smile. "I was hoping it'd be soon."

"I couldn't have you living in my trailer. It just wasn't nice enough for you. But this…this is nice," she said, her chest puffed out with pride. "I…" she looked down, then lifted her chin just enough to show her eyes. "I named it for you."

"You did?"

"I did." She led her back to the front door, where Cody had carved or burned or somehow removed wood from a big block to make it read "Madborne." "I played around with your name for weeks, and that's what I came up with. It reminds me of an English estate," she said, still looking a little shy. "Every good house needs a name, and I want this house to be a place you feel belongs to you."

"Oh, Cody." Maddie kissed her, holding her close for a long time. "I'd love nothing better than to live with you. It'll be a long-assed drive into Greenville, but you're worth every mile."

"I wasn't sure," she said, seeming hesitant. "I know you hate to have to get up so early."

Maddie stood there for a second, thinking of her reasons for being so reluctant to stay overnight during the week. "I think I can make some adjustments. I just didn't want to do anything to draw attention to my schedule while we were…before it was…while things weren't settled," she concluded. "I don't need to be in the closet at work, but I didn't want to put gasoline on the gossip flames before I had to."

Looking at her with a flicker of doubt, Cody said, "Do you think you can be happy up here?"

Showing all of her confidence, Maddie said, "I couldn't be happy anywhere without you. You're the key ingredient, and you're here."

"I just don't want to make things harder for you. Maybe we'll figure something out where you won't have to drive so far."

"I'm not going to mooch off my rich girlfriend, so don't even go there."

Cody kissed her neck, nuzzling her face against her for a long while. "I could keep you busy up here. Even without hunting."

"I'd need a plan, which I don't have yet. There's no way I'm going to sit around and sponge off you."

"You're not a sponger. I've never, ever thought you were interested in my money."

"I never will be interested in your money. It'd be fine with me if you gave every cent away. If you didn't have a penny, I'd know you'd still be able to keep us in food."

"But you'd have to learn to like squirrel."

Maddie kissed her on the nose. "Then you'd better not go broke."

CHAPTER TWENTY-FIVE

ON HER FIRST DAY of driving into Greenville from the new house, Maddie showed up at eight thirty, smiling at the guard, who was anxiously pacing in front. "I'm so sorry, Ripley," she said, squeezing his arm with one hand while digging in her purse for the keys. "I forgot to tell you I'd be coming in later today."

"That's all right, Miz Osborne. I was just worried something had happened to you."

"It has," she admitted. "I've moved about an hour away, and I won't be coming in so early any more. Don't expect me before eight thirty."

He gazed at her warily, like he was about to make further inquiry, but he merely nodded, and followed her inside.

Throughout the day she heard murmurings that she'd moved to Huntington, Charleston, and towns she'd never heard of, must less visited. She had absolutely nothing to hide, and would have gladly told anyone who asked that she was living on the top of the big mountain that crowned Ramp. But no one had the nerve to actually ask. People seemed to prefer conjecture to fact.

It wasn't until the next day that Geneva, ashen faced, came into her office. She closed the door and said gravely, "Lynnette's been telling people that you've"—she sucked in a breath—"moved up to the mountain to live with Cody Montgomery."

Maddie sat perfectly still for a moment. It amazed her that she still got a knot in her gut when she had to come out. But no knot would ever stop her from being proud of who she was. "Lynnette's right," she said, slightly worried that Geneva would faint. "I'd rather not talk about my personal life, but I have nothing to hide. I'm in love with and living with Cody Keaton." She smiled briefly. "She's a Keaton *and* a Montgomery." She watched a full panorama of emotions fly across Geneva's face. It couldn't have been easy hearing that your boss was not only a lesbian, in a town where being out was just not done, but also that she was living with a member of the most notorious family in the area. But Geneva handled it well, all things considered.

She got up, visibly shaken, and said quietly, "Okay, then. I'll…" And then she exited, not even able to finish her sentence.

Maddie watched her go, wondering what Geneva would do. She might try to quash the rumors, but since they were true that would be awkward. Or she could ignore them and hope they died down. No matter what, Maddie would roll with the punches. Having Cody's money to rely on was undeniably nice, but even if she hadn't had that massive cushion she was sure she would have acted the same way. People couldn't make your life miserable unless you let them, and her dignity was one thing she'd protect to the death. When you thought about it, it was really the only thing you had complete control over.

The first week of living together was a series of small, almost constant adjustments. But they were strangely fun adjustments to make. Being rabidly in love made everything seem like fun. Wednesday was warm and humid, and they stayed outside until it was time for bed. Cody wore nothing but her bug resistant shirt, since she unaccountably refused to wear insect repellent. Maddie chose the more revealing tactic of wearing only a light spray of DEET. Even though it was hot, they couldn't keep their distance from each other, and when the phone rang it took Cody about six rings to extricate herself from their entwined state. "Who's calling at bedtime?" she grumbled, letting the screen door slam behind her.

Maddie listened with half of her attention until she heard the tenor of Cody's voice change radically. "How bad is he hurt?" Cody asked. Maddie jumped to her feet and rushed to Cody's side, putting a hand on her when she saw her face contort with concern. "Yeah, I guess it was lucky he wanted such a big car. Might have saved his life." A sick feeling hit Maddie in the gut. Brett must have wrecked his big SUV. Cody was nodding, then said, "I can go down there with you." Another pause, then she added, "No, I don't mind. Tell Aunt Thelma not to worry. We'll get it sorted out." She put down the phone and let out a heavy sigh. "Brett fell asleep...or so he says...on I-95. Wrecked his car and broke his leg."

"Oh, Cody, I'm so sorry! Is he okay otherwise?" She stopped, then said. "I-95? In Virginia?"

"North Carolina," Cody said, her expression grim.

"What was he doing in North Carolina?"

"I don't know what he'll *say*, but the prescription drugs they found in his car means he was taking the Oxy Highway from one of those pain clinics in Florida."

"Oxy Highway? What in the hell are you talking about?"

Cody moved away and walked over to her favorite chair, plunking down on it gracelessly. "I didn't know he was involved in this particular thing, but a lot of people drive down to Florida to get prescriptions for narcotics. I guess his new car let him expand his reach." She let her head drop into her hands. "I might as well have given him a gun to shoot my Aunt Thelma in the heart."

Maddie sat on the arm of the chair and stroked her head. "Hey, it's not your fault."

"He couldn't have made it in his old car. I knew it was a mistake to buy him something so powerful."

"I'm not buying it." Maddie lifted Cody's chin and looked directly into her eyes. "Don't beat yourself up for your cousin's bad judgment. You're not responsible for him."

"No?" she asked, bitterness showing through. "Then why am I going to North Carolina tomorrow with my uncle?"

"I don't know," Maddie said, trying to convey her empathy. "Why are you?"

Cody sighed, her shoulders rising and falling sharply. "Why do you think?"

"I think it's so you can pay to get him out of trouble." She waited a second and added, "If you're willing to do that."

"What choice do I have?" Cody asked sharply, looking at Maddie with cold eyes.

Maddie didn't reply for a full minute. Finally, she said, "Only you can answer that question."

It took over six hours to reach the hospital near Rocky Mount, North Carolina, and Cody spent the entire ride thinking. Both of her uncles were in the front seats of Melissa's new car, with Cody riding, silently, in the back. They'd left early, before Maddie had even left for work, so they arrived not long after lunch.

It took a while to find Brett, but they eventually located him in the orthopedics section. He was terribly bruised and banged up, bad enough that Cody wouldn't have recognized him if the nurse hadn't directed them. And her uncle Shooter was so pale and shaken it made her heart hurt. Brett was an unholy mess, but he was still Shooter's boy and Cody expected you ignored an awful lot of the bad when you looked at your son beat up in the hospital.

Shooter reached for Brett, giving him a surprisingly tender hug that lasted long enough to embarrass Cody. "You're in some bad trouble, boy," Shooter said when he pulled away.

"I didn't do anything wrong, Daddy. I just fell asleep. I was too tired to be driving."

"I meant about the drugs they found in your car."

"A real doctor wrote those prescriptions," Brett said defensively. "It ain't against the law to have drugs on you if they're legal."

Cody wasn't sure what kind of legal footing Brett was on, but she knew he'd driven to Florida only to buy drugs to resell in West Virginia. That couldn't have been legal, and if it was, the system was more screwed up than she thought.

When Brett was ready to be discharged, without a second thought, Cody went to the business office to settle up his bill. She was staggered by the price, and resolved to buy medical insurance for everyone, whether they wanted it or not. She was met by her Uncle Cubby as she left the office.

"Shooter's gonna meet us by the car. It's gonna take a while for them to take Brett down in a wheelchair."

They went outside and sat down on a concrete bench in front of the main entrance. "This isn't going to go over well," Cody said solemnly, "but I'm not going to buy Brett another car."

Cubby nodded. "I can understand that. He'd probably do better on a moped."

She gave him a half smile for his attempt at humor. "I think most people will understand me not giving him a car." Taking in a breath, she added, "They might not understand not paying to get him out of whatever trouble he's in with the law."

Cubby let out a soft whistle. "That'll be tougher," he agreed. "Is your mind made up?"

"Yup." She nodded gravely. "I don't mean to be cruel, but if all of the boys know I'll get them out of any kind of trouble...I can't even guess what they'd get up to. I've got to draw the line."

"Thelma will have kittens," Cubby said.

"Surely so. But selling drugs to the addicts around us is wrong any way you look at it, Uncle Cubby. I can't be a part of it. If Brett has to go to jail again to learn to live an upstanding life, then so be it."

Quietly, Cubby said, "I don't think you learn how to be upstanding in jail."

"No, maybe not. At least it didn't help the first time he went. But my mind's made up. I won't help Brett or anyone else when they're involved in this kind of stuff. If nothing else, it'll send a message to the younger kids that there's consequences for their actions."

When Shooter and Brett emerged from the front doors, Cody took note of the obvious. Brett would never fit in Melissa's car. "I'm gonna call Maddie," she announced. "Have her get on-line and find us a van or something."

"Thanks," Brett said, his bruised and swollen face smiling up at Cody. She went back inside the hospital, fairly sure Brett's smile wasn't going to last too long.

As she expected, Maddie arranged for everything, managing to find a rental van only two hours away. Cody offered to drive it, and she finally picked Brett up at five p.m. He'd been cooling his heels in the lobby for over four hours and was grouchy and whiny when they finally got him loaded into the backseat.

As they took off, Brett said, "I've got to take a pain pill pretty soon. Will you stop and get me a soda first thing?"

"Sure. I could use a little caffeine to keep alert. It wouldn't do to have me fall asleep. Two accidents in two days would test even your luck."

Cody intentionally passed a couple of opportunities to get Brett a soda. She knew it was mean, but she wanted him to be wide awake when she told him her decision. Having him in pain wasn't her goal, but she had to admit it wasn't an unpleasant side effect. "You know," she said conversationally, "I've never gotten involved in your personal business."

"No, you have not," Brett agreed. "You're not like my sisters, always on my back about something."

"Right. Well, the reason I've never gotten involved is because it was none of my business. You know right from wrong, and you're able to make your own decisions."

"I *am*," he said pointedly, already getting his back up.

"That's not gonna change," she said quickly. "If you choose to sell drugs, that's on you. I just want to make it clear that I won't help you out if you need it. Like now," she added. "I assume North Carolina or even the DEA might come after you. If they do—you're on your own."

She caught sight of him in the rearview mirror, rolling his eyes. "You're not gonna let me rot in jail. My momma would never stand for that."

"Your momma doesn't have access to my bank account," Cody said coldly. "And I'm promising you today—they can put you away so deep they have to pump oxygen to you and I won't pay a dime to help. I can't stop you from pushing drugs, but I am *not* going to pay to help." She turned sharply at the upcoming exit, catching another glance of Brett, glaring a hole in the back of her head.

It was late, very late when she got home. But Maddie was curled up on the sofa, waiting for her. Her heart skipped a beat when she saw her, sound asleep, looking as innocent as an angel as she lay, curled up in a ball in just a T-shirt and panties. She'd never done it before, and wasn't sure she could do it now, but Cody squatted down and slid her arms behind Maddie's neck and legs. She let out a hearty grunt when she stood, but when those beautiful blue eyes blinked open and smiled at her she got a burst of strength.

"Are you carrying me to bed?"

"I am." Cody pressed a quick kiss to Maddie's cheek. "I'm also regretting I didn't stick with the one story design." Smiling, she slowly ascended the stairs, then deposited Maddie on the bed. "Safely delivered."

"I missed you. I worried about you all day."

"I was fine." Cody started to strip off her clothing. "I've got to drop the van off at the airport in Huntington tomorrow. Can you come pick me up after work?"

Maddie sat up and looked at her curiously. "Is that really what you want to talk about now?"

Cody perched on the edge of the bed. "No, not really." She put her arms around Maddie and held her close. "I decided not to help Brett if he gets arrested…which he *should*."

Maddie drew back a few inches, her gaze meeting Cody's eyes. "Are you sure? There will be big repercussions."

She was giving nothing away. Cody couldn't tell if she agreed with the decision or not. "I am. It's the right thing to do."

Now those lovely blue eyes softened and filled with what Cody read as pride. "I'm really glad."

Wow. Three little words that meant more than Cody could have predicted. Having the respect of someone you loved was worth whatever she'd have to go through with the rest of the family. Maddie's opinion mattered more. That was amazing, but absolutely true.

—⁓—

It didn't take but two days. It was almost dinnertime, and Cody was working in her garden when she heard a quiet engine strain a bit coming up the hill, then heard the engine shut off and a door close. Two minutes later Melissa appeared, nodded, and said, "You know why I'm here."

Cody was on her hands and knees. She stood and knocked the dirt from her legs before she spoke. "I think I can guess." She pointed at a cooler she'd brought with her. "Want some sweet tea?"

"No, you go ahead." Melissa stood there, looking remarkably uncomfortable. As Cody poured a glass for herself, she considered how surprised she was to have Melissa be the one to come beg for Brett. She'd always been the most mature of her cousins, the one least likely to need bailing out of trouble, or having much sympathy for those who did. But Brett was her brother, and blood blinded you to a lot of things. Plus, Aunt Thelma had no doubt been on her to plead his case to Cody.

"I'm not going to pay for Brett's legal bills," Cody said, deciding to get it over with quick.

"God damn it, Cody! At least let me ask!"

Standing there getting ready to argue made the sun baking down on them seem hotter than it had when her hands were busy. Cody nodded her head in the direction of the house, then started for it. Melissa followed along behind, not saying a word until they got to the porch. Cody could head Maddie's footsteps cross the living room, then heard them depart after a few moment's pause. She could probably see the steam coming out of Melissa's ears.

Both women sat down and after a few beats, Cody said, "I don't want you to waste a lot of energy asking, 'cause you can't change my mind."

"Listen to me," Melissa said, sounding like she was about to cry. "You don't know what it's like to have a brother like Brett."

The cup almost fell from her hands. Cody's limbs tingled, and a jolt of heat flushed her face. "I don't? My brother's lying in the ground because of drugs, and I don't know?" She stood up, on the verge of throwing her tea right into her cousin's face. Then she looked up, noticing movement. Maddie was right there on the other side of the screen door. It was a little hard to see her clearly, but Cody squinted to read her lips. "Need me?" she mouthed.

Mad as she was, she couldn't help but smile. She knew darned well Maddie hadn't been anywhere near the porch. How had she known Cody was upset? Love seemed to give them some kind of ESP. That was the only answer. She shook her head, and Maddie disappeared as quickly as she'd come.

Melissa hadn't seemed to notice Maddie's appearance. She was too busy making a mean-looking face and scowling for all she was worth. "I'm not saying it's better to lose a brother, but at least it's over." Leaning over, she let her head fall onto her open hand. "God damn it, Cody. It never ends with Brett. I know how hard it was to lose Keith, but it feels like the same damn thing's gonna happen to Brett. Only it's gonna take a hell of a lot longer." When she looked up a load of fear and pain showed in her dark eyes, shocking Cody. Melissa was a tough one, never the kind to show too much emotion. "Every time he gets into a fix it takes a little more out of my mama."

That was surely true. Losing Keith had destroyed Cody's own mother, had drained the last bits of her lifeblood right out of her. Seeing Melissa's pain let Cody pull back a bit and collect herself. She sat back down and took a long drink of her tea. "Let's say I paid for the best lawyers in West Virginia. Can you look me in the eye and tell me Brett learned his lesson from this?"

"No," Melissa said, her voice clear and sharp. "Can you look me in the eye and tell me that you'd say no to Keith if it was him?"

"No," Cody said, hearing all of her confidence drain from her voice. "I can't. I'd just hope to God I'd have the guts to." She got up and moved over to sit on the arm of her cousin's chair. It made her nervous to be so close. That just wasn't how they were. But being near Maddie always made difficult conversations go down easier, and she thought it was worth taking a chance. "It's not the money, Melissa. I'd give my whole bank account to save Brett's life if he was sick or hurt. But giving him money to get out of trouble that he deserves to be in isn't going to help him. It'll just give him permission to keep going—to keep going until he winds up like Keith."

Melissa's head snapped up and she glared at Cody for a long time. "You'll let him go to jail again."

"I don't have any power over that. If he goes to jail it's because of his own decisions. I won't feel guilty about letting him suffer the consequences." She swallowed, her body itching to move away, to escape her cousin's fiery gaze. "I wish Keith *had* been arrested. More jail might not have made a difference, but it might have taken him away from that meth lab on that day. I'd give anything for him to have another chance."

"That's not gonna cut it for my mama. You know that."

Cody nodded, then got up and went back to her own chair, already able to breathe easier. "I know that." She surely did.

Her aunts visited in order. Thelma was first, since Brett was her boy. Cody was almost sick over having her aunt cry and plead and beg for help, but she stood her ground. No money for anyone when it came to drugs. She'd pay for a bar fight or any of the dozens of other ways her cousins had come up with to spend some time in the county lockup, but not drugs. The scourge that destroyed her family would likely continue, but not with her help.

—⁓—

Aunt Lurlene was almost as pitiful as Thelma, probably because she knew her Ricky was always walking a fine line with the law. The funny part was when first Merry, then Lily showed up. Both of them clearly stated how hard it was for a mother to try to keep her children on the straight and narrow. Both said they'd promised Lurlene they'd plead for Brett. But there was an undercurrent that Cody read clear and strong, and that unspoken message was that they didn't want Brett to get a bailout this time. It was subtle, but unmistakable. They'd had enough, and they quietly agreed that the boys would never police themselves. They needed to know they were on their own

It wasn't a huge vote of confidence, but Cody felt better about the whole thing. At least she'd learned to say "no" to something. It was a start.

CHAPTER TWENTY-SIX

THE BEST PART OF THE summer flew by so quickly, Maddie wished she could slow time down to enjoy it even more. When the weather was fine, which it often was, Maddie would pull up to the house at the end of a long day to find Cody sitting on one of their comfortable chairs, acting like she'd been right there all day, idly reading her book. But Maddie knew better. Dinner was ready, sitting on the table Cody had built. Maddie had bought small metal domes that covered their plates and kept bugs off, and Cody politely never called her a wimp for her aversion to anything crawling on her food.

Their meals were simple, and mostly from Cody's garden. Tomatoes and basil covered with olive oil and the balsamic vinegar Maddie brought to their partnership, corn, beans, cole slaw, and fish or chicken cooked on the big barbecue built by Cody and her uncle Shooter.

Cody was still tinkering with the little house, doing much of the plumbing work herself, somehow managing to work hard and still look fresh and carefree by six o'clock. She was a marvel.

—·—

It was a hot night, but the house temperature stayed remarkably stable. Cody said the thickness of the logs and the way they'd placed the windows for flow-through ventilation was responsible for that. Whatever it was, Maddie was very glad to not need air conditioning. She'd hated being in her little apartment on hot nights, sealed up against the heat, the cool air making the place feel like a chilled, arid box. Now it felt like they were living among the trees, with protection from the fiercest elements, in harmony with the benign ones.

Cody was just finishing off another ear of corn when she used the spent cob to point at Maddie. "What's on your mind tonight? You look awfully happy."

"I was just thinking about how much I love being up here with you. I *do* love it, you know."

"I do. You must, since you still haven't planned our trip."

Maddie chuckled. "I'll get to it. I just couldn't leave when the garden's throwing vegetables at us. That'd be dumb."

"You could plan it for October. We'll mostly have pumpkins then."

"Yeah, but I might get those goats. There's too much going on!"

"First chickens, now goats. Are you going to turn this place into a farm?"

"No, but I think it would be cool to make my own cheese."

Cody leaned over and kissed her. "You're going to have this place cleared of trees and be riding around on a tractor if I don't put my foot down."

"Oh, no, I'm not into cultivation. Just little, cute animals."

"With names," Cody teased.

"Hey, you have to name your chickens." She elbowed Cody playfully. "I know you won't be tempted to wring Cluck-Cluck's neck now that you know her name."

"I would never harm your chickens. Even though Bluebell would probably fry up really nice."

"You'll note I never ask where the chicken you cook comes from. Just let me believe it falls from the sky."

"It does…after a fashion. Just don't ask me what the fish I catch get traded for."

"You can keep your secrets. Actually, I beg you to keep them."

—⁓—

A few nights later, Cody and Maddie were sitting outside, watching and listening to rain thrum against the roof. They'd finished dinner, and were thoroughly enjoying the symphony nature was playing for them. If someone had told Maddie she'd one day live in a tiny town in the middle of nowhere and would rather listen to rain beat on the roof than watch TV she wouldn't have been able to stop laughing long enough to tell them they were crazy. But her old TV sat in the little house, and she hadn't turned it on yet. A small satellite receiver perched on the roof of the little house, though, delivering both television and a fairly reliable internet connection.

She often sat in the office and played on the Internet while Cody stretched out on Maddie's former bed and read. But this thunderstorm was too exciting to ignore.

The phone rang and Cody went in to answer it. She was gone for longer than usual. When she returned she grumbled, "Jaden wants a bass boat and a trailer. I guess I've got to read up on them to make sure he doesn't buy the most expensive one made."

Maddie usually didn't say a word about the almost nightly requests, but this was nuts. "A boat? For the little rivers around here?"

"No, no, that'd be silly. He wants to start entering tournaments."

"Fishing tournaments?" Was she kidding?

"Yeah. There's hundreds of 'em. It's not a bad idea," she said, contemplatively. "I might…" She trailed off. "What?"

"You can't continue this," Maddie said, feeling her frustration boil over. "A boat…a trailer…and I assume he'll need a bigger truck to pull the damn thing."

"His truck's big enough." Cody chewed on her lip for a second. "Actually…he didn't buy a big one. That's probably next." She shook her head. "I hope he'll let the others use it so I don't have to buy a bunch of 'em."

"I've tried," Maddie said, consciously forcing herself to stay calm. "To keep my mouth shut, but this is getting crazy. You act like Santa Claus! Your money's gonna drip away like it's escaping from a leaking faucet. It seems like a few drips, but before you know it gallons and gallons have gone down the drain. You're got to stop, Cody. You've got to!"

"I drew the line with Brett," she said, sticking her jaw out. "And they put a lot of pressure on me."

Maddie got up and put her hands on Cody's shoulders. "I know that, and I'm proud of you for having the guts to stand up for what you thought was right."

Cody shook off the embrace and moved away. She leaned against the mantle, looking wary. "But since the sheriff didn't even bother coming out to interview him…"

"That was lucky for Brett. And I'm glad you didn't have to stand up to the whole family if it came down to that."

"You don't think I could," Cody said, glaring hotly.

"Of course I do!" It was clear she was irritated, but Maddie had to go to her and offer some degree of comfort. This time when she put her hands on Cody they were allowed to stay. "You stood up for principles with Brett. Now you have to take the next step and wean everyone off the money teat."

"I can't," she said glumly, averting her eyes. "They're not smart enough about money to be able to handle it."

Maddie had just a second where she could have stopped herself, but she'd gained too much momentum. "Neither are you," she said, cringing when hurt clouded Cody's face. "I don't mean that as an insult, but you're not a savvy enough money manager to handle this. You need help."

"I've been advised," she snapped, as though one discussion with a financial planner had been the equivalent of earning an MBA. "But I didn't like her ideas. I don't want some stupid foundation, I don't want some big bank to dole it out and I don't want to split it up. I just don't want to!" She wrenched away from Maddie's hold and stormed into the house, making the screen door shiver when she slammed it.

Maddie stood there for a few minutes, going over what she'd said. She hated to hurt Cody. Hated it as much as if she'd hurt herself. But she had to be honest with her. Cody was screwing this up and hurting her family in the long term. That wasn't what Cody wanted, but she couldn't see her way out. Maddie had to help. That's what partners did.

She found Cody sulking in front of the big, stone hearth. Sitting on the footstool at her feet, she said, "I'm sorry I hurt you, baby. I really am."

"Don't apologize if you're not really sorry."

Maddie put her hands on her knees, just to have some contact with her. "I *am* sorry for hurting you, but I meant what I said."

"That I'm too stupid to handle my own money," she snapped.

"I didn't say stupid. But I wouldn't buy a powerful rifle and take off to hunt deer. Not knowing how to hunt doesn't make me stupid. I'm just not experienced. That's how you are with money. Inexperienced."

Cody folded her arms across her knees and dropped her head onto them. "I know that," she mumbled. "But I don't like any of the options I have. I can't stand the thought of splitting up the money and watching my relatives waste millions of dollars."

Maddie stroked her leg gently, choosing not to say the obvious. Cody was going to be the one to waste millions if she continued to feed every request.

—◆—

After a particularly long day that included a drive to Huntington, Maddie pulled into their drive, got her briefcase and trudged up to the front steps. She normally perked up at seeing Cody, but since she hadn't stopped back at the office after her meetings at headquarters, she was home a half hour early and Cody was nowhere to be found. She was probably tending her garden, and had gotten so engrossed that she hadn't been listening for Maddie's car.

Maddie went upstairs and changed into shorts and a T-shirt. She was just about to go out when the phone rang and she picked it up to hear her mother's voice. "I'm not interrupting, am I?"

"No, not a bit. I just got home and my gardener's still out working. If I let her put lights in, she'd be out there all night."

"You sound a little cranky, honey. The honeymoon's not over, is it?"

"God, no." Maddie laughed. "It's just started. I'm tired...of driving mostly. I had to go to Huntington today and that tacks another two hours onto my total—on a good day. This wasn't a good day. There was all kinds of construction and it took me two and a half hours to get home."

"No luck on finding something to do closer to home?"

"No, there aren't any jobs around here. I'd get my teaching certificate, but the high school's as far as my office."

"I didn't have any any idea you wanted to teach."

"I'm not sure I do. But teaching's the only thing I can think of that I *might* like."

"That sounds like a long-shot, honey."

"It is. The school district's probably not hiring anyway. It was just an idle thought."

"I know you want your independence, but I hate to think of you making that drive during the winter."

"You and me both. If I could make a living cleaning up around here I'd be set. But I don't think anyone pays you to pick up trash." The back door opened and closed, and in a few seconds a steamy set of arms surrounded her waist and Maddie was engulfed in the scents of their garden. Cody smelled of tomatoes and topsoil and the sun and Maddie felt all of the tension of her day evaporate. "My vegetable delivery woman just came in, Mom."

"I'll let you go. I was just calling to remind you it's your nephew's birthday next week."

"I've already sent a present. But thanks for keeping track. Love you."

"I love you too. And give Cody a big kiss for me."

"I think I can come up with a spare. See you soon." She hung up and delivered two big kisses. "One was from my mom, but that was probably a little more intimate than she would have delivered in person."

"Your mom's cute, but I prefer you." Cody went into the kitchen to wash her hands. "Did I hear you say you wanted to get paid to pick up trash?"

Maddie jumped up onto the counter, dangling her bare legs. "Yeah. I'm itching to quit my job. I learned today that they want to cut back by having only a manager and a head teller, cutting out the assistant manager. If they take Geneva away, I'll have to work every Saturday."

"Quit," Cody said clearly. "There's no reason in the world to keep a job you don't like."

"I want to. I *really* want to. But I've got to do something productive." She accepted the cold beer Cody handed her. "That's what I was saying to my mom. I'd love to be able to pick up trash as my job. The clean up program was the most satisfying thing I've done since I've been here."

Cody slapped a hand down on either side of Maddie's butt, standing nose to nose with her. "Then do that. I know you. If you have something you're passionate about, you get on it. I'll give you all the money you need to start."

"Really?" She leaned forward and kissed Cody's dusty lips. "You'd like that?"

She raised an eyebrow. "Do I love where I live?"

"Yup."

"Would I love for it to be pretty?"

"Yup."

"Then get it done, baby. Get it done."

—⁓—

Over the next few weeks, Maddie investigated every type of recycling, waste removal, and landfill option known to man. But she had to squeeze her research in after work, wasting their precious hours together. Maddie was working away one night when Cody took her chair and wheeled her away from her computer. She continued to type in the air, acting like she hadn't moved.

"That's the only way I get to see you," Cody complained. "I think it's time to pull the plug."

"Which plug is that?"

"The one that has you tethered to the bank. I want you to quit so you can devote your time to figuring out a way to keep Summit County clean. Cleaner," she amended. "I don't want to hope for too much."

Maddie was itching to get back to work, but she sat there for a moment, really thinking about what Cody said. "Does it mean a lot to you to have me home more?"

Cody gazed at her with those warm, dark eyes. "It means an awful lot. I've got a ton of money and a partner who drives hours a day to go to a job she doesn't love. Then she spends the evenings on the computer. That's not what I hoped for when you moved in."

Maddie took her face in her hands and kissed it. "I'll quit tomorrow."

"That's it?" Cody asked, looking stunned.

"If you're not happy, I'm not happy."

"That's really all it takes?"

"That's it." She turned off her computer and took Cody's hand. "Let's go to bed. It's very, very late."

"It's eight thirty," Cody said, frowning.

"After a couple of hours of making love, it's going to be very, very late."

—⁓—

It was surprisingly hard to actually make the call, but Maddie got her boss on the line bright and early the next morning. "I think I've got a great idea for how to save money at my branch," she said.

"Excellent! I'm looking to cut every wasted dollar."

"Well, I don't think these dollars have been wasted, but you won't have to pay my salary any more. I'm taking a very early retirement."

―――

Two weeks later, she was free. Geneva was happy to be promoted, Lynnette was happy Maddie was leaving, and Maddie was happier than both of them put together.

She went to Huntington for her exit interview, spent a couple of hours with her boss, going over all of her observations about the state of the branch, then had lunch with Avery. He was unapologetically unhappy about her leaving, but he'd bought her a lovely pen with her initials engraved on it and a T-shirt imprinted with "Wage Slave" dramatically crossed out in bright red. They stood in the parking lot of the restaurant, sharing a tearful goodbye. It was hard to imagine they'd spend time together in the future, since their interests didn't intersect in the least, but Maddie knew she'd miss him. He'd been a good friend, lending a hand and providing hours of laughs. But he was a work friend, and her corporate days were over. It wasn't clear how she'd spend her time, but she would never have to sit in another meeting, having some suit threaten all of their jobs just because he had a little power. Cody might not have been able to enjoy her fortune, but now that she was certain Cody wouldn't resent supporting her, Maddie knew she'd adjust to the security of the Keaton fortune like a baby to the nipple.

―――

Her first morning of her new career found her up with the sun and raring to get to work. Cody was just leaving, headed for wherever she went when she took off, but she stopped long enough to offer a soft, tantalizing kiss. "I'll be home for lunch," she promised. "I think I'd like…you."

"You've got it. I can't think of a better lunch date for my first day of freedom."

After a quick breakfast, Maddie went to the little house and got to work. It was frustrating to waste hours on a lead and come up with nothing, but she'd done just that. She would have been grumpy, but Cody was going to be home for lunch soon, and she cheered herself up thinking of how she could please her lover's voracious appetite…and make her lunch too.

As she left the small house, she heard a car, dismayed to have a guest when she was planning such an elaborate lunch. To her surprise, Devin got out of the car and stood in front of the house for a moment, just looking at it.

They'd never been alone together, and she'd never gotten even a flicker of warmth from him. She would never admit to Cody that he still gave her the creeps, but when he spied her, he gave a fairly easy smile. "Cody home?"

"No. She will be soon though. I was just going to make lunch. Join us." The things you did for love.

—⁘—

Cody got home while Maddie was slicing tomatoes for a salad. "We have company," she called out.

Walking into the kitchen, Cody set a bucket down and slapped Devin on the back. "We can have trout for lunch if you want."

Maddie went over to offer a kiss, then stopped in her tracks. She didn't want to make Devin uncomfortable, but she also didn't want to have to act stilted in her own home. Cody must have sensed her indecision, for she moved towards her and offered a big hug and a chaste kiss. "Missed you."

"Me too." They broke apart and Maddie said, "I was going to make grilled cheese. Would you rather have trout?"

"No, I'm fine with whatever." Cody went to the sink to wash up. "I'm glad to see you Dev. How's everything?"

"Fine," he said. He took a sip of the beer Maddie had offered. "Well, not really." Another sip followed, then he took a big breath. "I need some help."

Cody sat next to him at the table. "Whatever I can do."

"I…uhm…" He looked furtively at Maddie, paused, and continued. "I'm not doing as good as I was when I was helping on the house."

"I'm going to start on Uncle Shooter's in a week or so. The county just has to approve the plans."

He shook his head. "I need more than building. I heard about a program the VA has in Washington." He looked into her eyes. "For PTSD. I wouldn't have to pay to get in, but I don't think I could stand to live with a bunch of people. If you could see your way clear…I'd appreciate it if you'd pay for an apartment or a space in a house for me." He shivered noticeably. "I just don't think I could go if I had to be Army twenty-four hours a day."

"I'd be happy to," Cody said. "I meant what I told you a few months ago. I'll pay for anything you think will help. Private doctors, anything."

"I know." He looked down, shifting his eyes nervously. "I think I'd do better with other guys around. Guys who know…what it's like. I just think I need a little space to myself. Too many people make me jumpy."

Cody looked up, seeing the quick smile Maddie sent her way. "I'm the same. You figure out what you need and we'll get it done."

Maddie walked over with their sandwiches.

"Thanks, Maddie," he said with a genuine smile that Maddie found strangely charming.

"My pleasure. I know the Washington area pretty well, so I could help find you an apartment. Heck, we'll drive you up. I'm always looking for an excuse to visit my parents."

"That'd be nice," he said. He chewed for a moment, then gave Cody a sly smile. "I wasn't jealous of your money, but having a…wife to make you lunch is something I'd dearly love."

Cody beamed a smile at him. "Money's nothing compared to love." She winked at her partner. "But having both is awfully sweet."

―∞―

After weeks of research, Maddie had the germ of an idea. She was fairly certain there would be little money in it, but she was guardedly optimistic she could break even. That was her only goal. She simply wanted to clean the local towns up, provide a few much-needed jobs, and break even. She was no Henry Ford, but it was a start.

The idea centered on China. A burgeoning economy with a natural resources deficit was just what she needed. The Chinese needed paper and various kinds of scrap metal, iron, steel, and aluminum, and the cargo ships they used to delivered goods to the US often went back empty. All Maddie had to do was find the materials they needed, get them into trucks or train cars, and ship them to the ports the Chinese used to deliver goods. Easy as pie.

CHAPTER TWENTY-SEVEN

A FEW DAYS AFTER they'd gotten Devin squared away in an apartment close to the big VA facility, Cody was working in the garden when she heard a rough-sounding engine laboring up her drive. She put down her hoe and went over to the house, surprised to see her uncle Cubby climb out of his truck. "I'm over here," she called out loudly.

He turned and waved, then ambled over. "No, I'm not here to beg for more tomatoes." He waited a beat. "But I wouldn't refuse any, either. I've never had a beefsteak that tasted as good as yours."

"I've found the secret," she said, happily. "I just had to move. Come take a look-see."

They walked over to the garden, with Cubby making appropriately complimentary comments about the entire set-up. "You're a damn fine gardener," he said. "Damn fine."

"Thanks. It's something I love, so it's easy." He was obviously there for a reason, but he didn't seem in any hurry to state what it was. "I'm just weeding. Mind if I keep going?"

"No, get back to it." He found a plastic five gallon bucket she used to carry vegetables, turned it over and sat on it, watching her work for a good long while.

"Things good at home?" Cody finally asked after it became clear he might sit there all day.

"After a fashion." He stood, then went over to where Cody was working, got down on his hands and knees and started pulling out weeds. He yanked at them like they were his mortal enemies, surprising Cody with the quick, vicious snap of his wrist.

"What's going on, Uncle Cubby?"

"It's Lurlene," he said, grumpily. "She's after me something fierce."

"About..."

"Hearing aid," he muttered.

"A hearing aid? She's after you about...what?"

He didn't lift his head, he just kept yanking the poor weeds out. "I don't have enough money left."

"You shouldn't worry about that. How much do you need?"

"About a thousand. Give or take."

"That doesn't seem like it'd be enough. Are you sure?"

His head dropped even more. "I've tried to make do with what you gave us, but I just can't manage." His voice was filled with...shame, anger, humiliation or some combination of the three.

Cody squatted down next to him, seeing her first guess was right. He was deeply ashamed and that hit her like a blow. "It's not a problem, Uncle Cubby. I'd be happy to buy you the best hearing aids made."

"It's not right," he said, biting off the words through gritted teeth. "It's not right to take money from a young 'un. I should be helpin' you, not the other way around."

"But I don't need any help...any money help, that is."

He looked at her, his face a mask of humiliation. "I'd never ask. But Lurlene's about to throw my ass out the house."

"What...?"

"Everybody's getting cars and houses and buying new clothes. It makes her crazy mad that everyone's getting whatever they want, but I won't ask for money to hear. She's not even talkin' to me right now. Says I can't hear anyway, so it's no use." He looked like he was about to cry, something Cody had never seen, and never wanted to see. "I tried my best to make the money you gave us last, but we had to pay for—"

Cody held up a hand, stopping him. Then she got to her feet, offered a hand, and helped him up. "I made a mistake," she said, suddenly sure of her error. "I should have divided up the money at the beginning. Maddie's been on me from day one to do something like that, but I've been as indecisive as a politician running for office."

"No, that's not the way," he said, shaking his head quickly. "I don't want to have a big pile of money. My kids would be on me all day long, begging like crazy."

She laughed at that and he smiled a little too. "Now you know how I feel. But it's time to do *some*thing." She led the way to the house. "I'm going to put another twenty-five thousand into your checking account. Buy your hearing aids and get something nice for Aunt Lurlene. She deserves it for having to shout herself hoarse for all of these years."

———

After her uncle left, Cody went to the little house and flopped down on the bed in the office. "I'm ready to make some decisions about the money."

Maddie twirled around in her chair, eyebrows raised. "Pardon me?"

"My uncle was just here, begging for something he never should have had to ask for. I've screwed this up something fierce, but I'm going to put a stop to it. Now."

———

It took a few days to find a block of time that they could all agree on, but they finally managed to schedule an afternoon meeting with Miss Norman to make some decisions. Her office was in Huntington, and Cody reflected as they drove that she shouldn't be so uncomfortable about the discussion. But she had a nagging worry that Maddie would lose respect for her if she showed just how ignorant she was.

Maddie had to have a pretty good idea of that already, but there was a chance she thought Cody had gotten up to speed thanks to the books she'd recommended. In fact, Cody hadn't been able to get through the first one. She loved to read, but reading about finance and money management wasn't something she was able to get through on her own. Things might have been different if she'd gotten the rudiments down when she was much younger, but she wasn't even sure of that. Maybe she was just slow in this area…and no one wanted her lover to know she was slow…it was just too embarrassing.

———

They sat in Miss Norman's simple office, going over how much money Cody had, how much she'd spent, and how it was currently invested. Maddie fired question after question at the woman, and Cody allowed herself to sit back and watch. But then two sets of eyes were on her and

Miss Norman said, "Tell me what you want to accomplish, and I'll tell you how to do it."

Well over two hours later, they drove home. Cody wasn't able to talk much, having to let things rest in her head before she could be very verbal about them. Luckily, Maddie seemed to understand that, and she just sat there quietly, her hand on Cody's thigh, silently offering that little sign to show she was on her side. Little tiny things like that were worth more than Cody could have ever imagined. They were what held them together... tightly.

The next night, they finished dinner, then sat out on the porch. The decision she'd made had freed up something in Cody's heart, and she felt lighter than she had in weeks. It must have shown.

"You seem content."

"Yeah, that's a good word for it."

"Are you still confident in your decision?"

"I am." She sat there for a few minutes, listening to the crickets and a few frogs that were surprisingly close. "If it was your money, would you have made the same decision?"

"No." She waited a beat, then added, "Probably not."

"How come?"

"One size doesn't fit all when it comes to financial planning."

"What would you do?"

Maddie leaned on her, rocking them back and forth for a minute. "I'd have had my parents and my brothers go with me when I claimed the prize, and I'd have said we all chipped in for the ticket. Then we'd each get a quarter and our tax bite might be lower."

"I guess I should have done that."

She felt some of her contentment seep right out of her, but Maddie put an arm around her and said, "My brothers are both good with numbers and they're pretty moderate. We'd work together to make sure everyone was taken care of. But that's just because that's the kind of information our backgrounds have given us, not because we're smarter."

"You *are* smarter," Cody grumbled.

"If you took my whole family and dropped us into the woods with traps, guns, knives, nets, fishing poles, and every kind of lure made, we'd starve to death. If we didn't shoot ourselves first. We have a certain kind of knowledge, you have another kind. It'd be nice if everyone had everything, but that doesn't happen very often, baby. We're different, but we're complementary. Together we can hunt and fish and formerly run a small branch bank. We've got it all."

Cody had to smile at that. She did have a point. And thinking of the Osbornes trying to figure out how to load a gun, much less shoot it was funny. Darned funny.

—⁓—

Once Cody had her mind made up, she liked to get on with it. That Saturday she started calling everyone at seven a.m., telling them to come over as soon as they could. It took until ten, but they finally all showed up.

"I've made some decisions about my money," she began. That got everyone's attention. She could almost see a few of her cousins hoping she was going to whip out her checkbook and write big, fat checks to each and every one of them.

"I'd been leaning towards splitting the money up between all of us. But that wouldn't solve the big problem. None of us are good money managers," she said. "We don't have the background. So, rather than having each of us struggle to manage a big hunk, I'm going to lock it all up in a trust.

"A trust?" Shooter asked. "What's that mean?"

"It's a way to have the money safe and available to us, but not as available as it is now. Here's how I'd like it to be." She looked out at her family, letting herself really see them as they were. It was all so clear now. How had she missed the obvious truth for so long. "I'd like for my mama's sisters and brothers to be in charge of the money."

"So you're splitting it five ways," Ricky complained. "I told you before that screws my branch."

"No, that's not how it'll be. Cubby, Shooter, Merry and Lily will be the trustees of *all* of the money. They'll decide who gets what. They're the adults and they know what's best." She smiled at her aunts and uncles, seeing how shocked they were. But even if they didn't know it yet, this was the right decision. Together, they'd do this right. Just like when Uncle Shooter wanted the big house, and the group had shamed him into scaling back. They'd figure out quickly that they had to be moderate to make sure every family got enough to live comfortably, but not extravagantly. She had complete confidence in that.

"I want everyone to have enough to live well, but I don't want anyone to get a huge amount and blow it. Let's face facts. Some of you would." She let that settle for a bit, pointedly not looking at Brett who had recently had a long, unpleasant interview with a pair of DEA agents.

"When you need money, you'll ask the trustees. The woman who helped come up with this plan will be a trustee too. Miss Norman will work with everyone to come up with a budget. You'll get that amount put into your checking account every month. If you need something outside of your budgeted amount, you put in a request and the trustees decide whether to approve or deny your request.

"What about you?" Melissa asked.

"Same for me."

"You're not keeping a big hunk for yourself?" Jaden asked.

"I am not."

"That's stupid," Ricky grumbled. "Now you'll be begging for money just like the rest of us."

"There won't be a need for that. You won't get enough to be able to gamble at the high stakes poker tables in Wheeling, but you'll have enough to live like middle class people do."

"And how's that?" Chase asked.

"You'll have enough to own a decent house, buy food and clothes and have a nice car and medical insurance for you and your kids. You'll also have enough for some luxuries, like the trip Maddie and I are going to take in November."

"What trip?" Shooter asked, looking very concerned.

"Your house will be finished by then," Cody said, chuckling. "We just made all of our plans to visit England."

"England?" Mandy said, clearly stunned. "What's in England?"

"It's because of her reading," her Aunt Thelma said. "She likes all of that…English stuff."

"I do," Cody said. "Actually, I'd like all of you to travel a little. We've been isolated in this hollow for a hundred and fifty years. It's time we saw what the rest of the world looks like." She met Maddie's eyes and they shared a smile that touched her heart.

"So it's more of begging for every dime," Brett groused.

"That's not true at all, but if that's how you want to look at it, go right ahead," Cody said, glaring at him.

"And if the trustees want to pay for a good attorney for me?"

"They are welcome to. Any amount over twenty-five thousand needs unanimous approval, so maybe you will be begging." Cody waited a few beats, determined to not let Brett's issues annoy her. The truth was, several of her cousins had congratulated her for not bailing Brett out. He'd have his hands full getting a unanimous vote.

"Oh," she said, remembering an important detail. "Maddie's gonna be on the investment advisory committee. She's not gonna vote about who gets money, just about how it's managed."

"Thank the good lord," Cubby said. "We don't know this investment lady. We've gotta have somebody from the family who can keep an eye on her."

Cody thought the glow of happiness she felt in her chest might just show through her skin. Uncle Cubby thought of Maddie as one of them now. That meant the world to her. And as soon as he'd said that, every other head started to nod. He was in charge again. That was as it should be. His house was a mess and he could be as lazy as a sloth, but he had a good head on his shoulders and he was kindhearted and fair. The family needed a center, someone to hold them together, and he was the right man for the job.

―――――

They spent another hour or two answering questions. By the time they'd finished, everyone seemed to understand the general outlines of the plan, and no one had voiced a serious complaint. That alone was amazing.

The day clouded over and it started to drizzle, ruining plans for a barbecue. As the last car left, Cody said, "Let's go out to lunch. Someplace nice."

"The Mountaineer? Site of our first lunch together?"

"Sounds great. You drive."

When they got in the car, Cody said, "I didn't think I needed to tell them I'm gonna take out a good chunk for your mama and daddy before I put the rest in the trust."

"Oh, Cody, that's so sweet of you."

"I should have offered before. I just didn't think of it."

"They won't want to take it, but they'll sleep better at night knowing they have a cushion to fall back on."

"I'm gonna give the girl who made me take the ticket a chunk too. That's only fair."

Maddie smiled at her. "One thing you are is fair. To a fault!"

"I take that as a compliment, even though I know you don't always mean it that way," she said, patting Maddie on the leg. She kept her hand there, always feeling her heart slow its beat when they were touching. Touching Maddie in the simplest ways centered her. Every time.

———

When they got to Main Street, Cody said, "Hey, the bank's still open. Can we stop in for a minute?"

"You heard about Geneva giving suckers to the kids again, didn't you." Maddie gave her a playful scowl. "I think you're too big to get one, but I don't mind if you try."

"Just be a good chauffeur and do as you're told."

They parked a few doors down from the main entrance. Maddie hadn't been back since her last day, and she had a few butterflies in her stomach when they entered. But Cody marched through the small lobby with her usual determination, with Maddie automatically taking her hand, waving at her shell-shocked former employees as she scampered along beside her. The vault attendant and Cody each used a key to open one of the big boxes. After taking the drawer out, Cody took it into the private room and closed the door.

She sat down and placed her hands on the grey metal. "This is just one of the four I have, but I didn't want to go to the trouble of dragging all of them in here just to make a point." She took all four keys and placed them in front of Maddie. "These are for you."

Maddie stared at the keys, then the box. "I don't know what you're talking about."

A smile was playing at the corners of Cody's mouth. "You're the one who had to go to so much trouble to get it, so it's only fair you get to keep it."

"Cody!" she shouted. "What in the hell are you doing? How much of the million do you have left here?"

"All of it," she said, smirking. "I haven't touched a cent. Everything I've spent has come out of my regular account. This has been my...hoard. But I don't need it now. I'm confident whatever I have in my account is gonna stay there."

Having a big box full of cash sitting in front of her was making Maddie's head hurt. Nothing made sense. "How can you still have all of this cash? You came to the bank every couple of days at first. What in the hell were you doing if not taking out fistfuls of dough?"

She looked down, her shy smile melting Maddie's heart. "Checking to make sure it was still here. Playing with it." She shrugged. "It was the only way I had to make myself believe it was really true."

"Oh, Cody, you're such a dear. I can just see you sitting down here counting your stacks." She laughed for a moment, then let the situation hit her again. "But I don't need or want this. *Truly.*"

Cody put her hand over Maddie's, which was visibly shaking. "You're different from me. If anything happened to me—and I hope to heck it doesn't—but if it did—you wouldn't want to stay up on the hill by yourself. With this money you could go where you wanted...find a new life. Maybe finally get to San Francisco or New York."

Tears sprang to her eyes and she knew she wouldn't be able to contain them. "I couldn't be happy without you," she sniffed. "But I'd stay right here, just to feel you in the air."

"You say that now, but you don't know how you'd feel then. I *need* for you to have your own money, Maddie. I need it."

"No, no," she stood and backed away as if the money would bite her. "I don't feel right doing this. We should put this in the trust."

"No," Cody said, gently but firmly. "You never know what can happen. Once the money's in the trust, it's not mine anymore. I assume my aunts and uncles would treat you as part of the family, but I'm not going to take that risk. You might never need it, but I couldn't sleep at night if I have to worry about you. Please, Maddie, keep it for my peace of mind."

Slowly, Maddie's head started to nod. "For your peace of mind." She leaned over and placed a soft kiss on Cody's lips. "But if I'm in charge, this is going to turn from greenbacks into treasury bills at the very least. You've gotta be crazy to keep this much cash around!"

Cody started to laugh. "I thought the bank was safe."

"Not safe enough for me! And I want interest. You can't let money sit around gathering dust. It's gotta work for you! We're gonna blow Geneva's mind, but she's gonna have a very large deposit to make with the fed on Monday."

Cody's eyes were as wide as they could go. "You're gonna do it right now?"

"I could never sleep knowing I had control of this kind of money and it was sitting in cash. Go get those other boxes, baby. We've got business to conduct!" She laughed evilly. "I hope Geneva makes Lynnette count each bill. Twice."

By the time they got to the restaurant it was closer to dinnertime than lunch. Lynnette did indeed have to work with Geneva to get the money sorted out, and that gave Maddie a small bit of satisfaction. Lynnette was likely the blabbermouth who had told everyone about Cody's cousins having wads of cash, so maybe she'd tell everyone Cody had taken it all out. Her snoopiness might turn out to be a blessing.

"I talked to the attorney Miss Norman recommended," Cody said, while they waited for their dinners.

"You did?"

"Yeah. He's gonna start drawing up the papers for the trust. But when I had him on the phone I told him to write me up a new will. Everything I have will go to you, of course. I love my uncle, but you're my favorite."

She sat there with the sweetest smile on her lovely face, and Maddie leaned across the table to place a quick kiss on Cody's lips. A few heads snapped towards them, but people would eventually stop reacting to their affectionate ways. Greenville was gonna have to learn to live with lesbians, because these lesbians weren't ever gonna hide.

EPILOGUE

ONE YEAR LATER:

"THUMPER! GET BACK HERE, boy!" The big golden retriever raced through the woods, returning to his mistresses. He'd had a quick swim, and Cody knew one of them would have to brush him thoroughly to get goodness knows what from his fur before he could come into the house.

Why anyone wanted a dog in the house was beyond her, but Maddie loved to have him right at the foot of their bed. It had taken a bit of effort, but he'd eventually stopped whining to climb in with them and seemed very happy now in the dog bed Cody'd made for him. He was lean and lithe now that he got plenty of exercise, and he'd learned to hunt better than Stripes and Blue put together.

Devin had control of the hapless hunters now, since Cody knew he'd never shoot them for tearing into a kill. They'd tried to keep all three dogs together, but Stripes and Blue's bad habits had rubbed off on Thumper, rather than the other way around. It was just as well. Blue and Stripes didn't need to ever get the notion they were pets. Thumper thought he was a furry child, and that type of thinking was contagious.

The three of them went on a long walk every morning, rain or shine. The concept of a walk for no real purpose had been a tough one for Cody to accept, but it was a nice way to spend some quiet time together. Cody had learned to use the time to casually get a feel for where deer were crossing, and other bits of knowledge she could use later in the day— depending on the season.

Maddie would never learn to hunt—they hadn't even seriously discussed it. She wasn't crazy about eating game, could really only enjoy venison loin, but she never complained when Cody went out hunting with one of her relatives.

That's what marriage was—learning how to give each other the freedom to be fulfilled while still staying deeply connected. It wasn't easy, and they'd had their share of squabbles, but Maddie was rock solid in every area that mattered. She was loyal, honest, candid, and as full of love and affection as a woman could possibly be.

Cody watched her walk a few feet in front, loving the way her butt swayed when she walked on the uneven path. Forget the forest right outside their picture window. This was the best view in the county. As if Maddie knew she was looking at her, she slowed down and extended her hand, waiting for Cody to take it. "How'd you get behind me?"

"I just stopped to admire the view." Cody put on the most innocent look she could manage.

Maddie slapped her on the butt. "If it was about five degrees warmer, I'd go to the river and jump in. Then you could ogle me without any clothing in the way. Nothing feels better than starting off the day with a dip in the water."

"My city girl is just about gone," Cody said, smiling fondly. "For a woman who claimed to have never seen a river, you sure have fallen in love with them."

"You ask my mom about my outdoor life when my parents come this weekend. She'll vouch for me."

"Oh, I believe you. They love sitting on the porch, but getting them down to the water would take a net. If your dad brings that little train set like he keeps threatening, we'll never even get them to the porch."

"I know you want that train running around the top of the house. Don't even try to lie, Cody. I saw you measuring where you were gonna put the track."

"I think Thumper would like it," she allowed, trying not to smile. "What's your schedule for today? I've got to go to the hardware store to buy lag bolts for Devin's cabin."

"I'll get them if you don't need them this morning. I'm going over to Delilah to pick up a couple of cast iron bathtubs." She grinned, obviously proud of herself. "Now that I know I can sell them to people renovating old houses I'm actually happy to help hoist the darned things into the truck. I'm getting five hundred bucks for those suckers."

"Don't go hurting your back lifting things too heavy for you. That's what the kids are for."

"I'm careful, but I like to pitch in. My employees respect me more when I do."

The kids Maddie had hired looked at her like she was a supermodel, but Cody didn't want to make her lover uncomfortable if she couldn't tell that, so she let it drop. "I'd love for you to go to the store for me. Do you know what lag bolts are?"

"No. But I can look stupid and ask questions with the best of them. The manager of the hardware section is kinda sweet on me."

"I'll go," Cody said quickly. "The last thing I need is another man swooning over you."

"Did I say it was a man?" Maddie batted her eyes. "I don't think we're the only lesbians in Summit County."

"Then I'll definitely go. I don't cotton to poachers…of any kind."

Maddie stopped and wrapped her arms around Cody's waist. They hugged for a few moments. "If I were any more devoted to you, it'd be unseemly."

"That's just how I like you. It'd be awful lonely to be as wrapped up in you as I am and think you weren't as crazy as I was."

Kissing her cheek, Maddie let her go and took her hand again. "Oh, I'm easily as crazy as you are. Don't sell me short."

"That is something I will never, ever do."

"You know what we should do?"

Oh-oh. When she got that look in her eye it meant only one thing. Cody sighed. "Okay. On three. One…two…three!" Maddie took off like a shot, Cody right behind her. Why anyone wanted to run when something wasn't chasing you would always be a puzzle to her, but Maddie loved running through the forest, and Cody loved making Maddie happy.

Cody could catch her in a sprint, but Maddie had stamina and she always chose a spot far enough from home to be able to win easily. She was a competitive little devil, and Cody had to force herself to get into the spirit. Flying through the forest, with Thumper barking and wagging his tail as he ran alongside, was a heck of a nice way to get your blood moving.

But if Maddie hadn't made it into a game, Cody would have been content to walk slowly and carefully—checking for animal tracks.

Maddie was just ahead, with Cody spying glimpses of her honey-colored hair flashing in the sun. Running might not be Cody's favorite activity, but when they reached the finish line and she caught sight of her lover, standing on their porch, cheeks flushed and eyes sparkling, it was the highlight of any day. Maddie might win these little tests, but no one could convince Cody she was a loser. Not when she got to scoop Maddie up and carry her into the house, winners all.

THE END

By Susan X Meagher

Novels

Arbor Vitae
All That Matters
Cherry Grove
Girl Meets Girl
The Lies That Bind
The Legacy
Doublecrossed
Smooth Sailing
How To Wrangle a Woman
Almost Heaven

Serial Novel
I Found My Heart In San Francisco

Awakenings: Book One
Beginnings: Book Two
Coalescence: Book Three
Disclosures: Book Four
Entwined: Book Five
Fidelity: Book Six
Getaway: Book Seven
Honesty: Book Eight
Intentions: Book Nine
Journeys: Book Ten
Karma: Book Eleven
Lifeline: Book Twelve
Monogamy: Book Thirteen

Anthologies

Undercover Tales
Outsiders

To find out more visit Susan's website at
www.susanxmeagher.com

You'll find information about all of her books, events she'll be attending and links to groups she participates in.

All of Susan's books are available in paperback and various e-book formats at www.briskpress.com

Follow Susan on Facebook.
http://www.facebook.com/susanxmeagher